'Come on, Blacklaws, admit it. We know you've been stealing. We've had a stock check and a number of items are unaccounted for,' Mr Scott said in a squeaky voice that had long since earned him the nickname 'Mouse'.

Ken took a step backward and came up against a pillar. 'I'm not admitting to anything. You can't prove it was me who stole these things,' he replied, half paralysed with fear.

Stealing . . . items unaccounted for . . . Vicky had given an involuntary gasp on hearing those words. She could not believe that he had been so stupid as to have done what he stood accused of. Surely this was a mistake, a coincidence?

'We've received information that you've been stealing. The stock check confirmed that information to be correct,' Mr Scott went on.

'I don't know what information you've got, but it's all lies, lies!' Ken replied, almost screaming.

'The missing items have all walked from this department since you joined it, that has already been proven. And there was no stealing going on in this department prior to your arrival, which has also been proven. It all adds up to one answer, and one only. You're the thief.'

Emma Blair

The Princess of Poor Street

sphere

SPHERE

First published in Great Britain by Michael Joseph Ltd 1986
Published by Sphere Books Ltd 1987
Reprinted 1988, 1989 (twice), 1990, 1991, 1992 (twice)
Reprinted by Warner Books 1993
Reprinted 1994, 1996, 1998, 1999, 2001
Reprinted by Time Warner Paperbacks in 2004
Reprinted by Sphere in 2006, 2007

ISBN 978-0-7515-0935-9

Papers used by Sphere are natural, recyclable products made from
wood grown in sustainable forests and certified in accordance with
the rules of the Forest Stewardship Council.

Printed in England by Clays Ltd, St Ives plc
Paper supplied by Hellefoss AS, Norway

Sphere
An imprint of
Little, Brown Book Group
Brettenham House
Lancaster Place
London WC2E 7EN

A Member of the Hachette Livre Group of Companies

www.littlebrown.co.uk

Contents

Part One

A Strong Wind Blowing
1934–35

'Yes, A strong wind blowing, and carrying us all
with it.'

MARY STEWART, *The Last Enchantment*

One

Later, folks were to say that there was a different sound to the knocking-off hooter that evening, a sad, mournful note quite in contrast to its usual stridency. If there was such a difference, Vicky didn't notice it; the hooter sounded just the same to her as it had always done, since her first recollected awareness of it as a tiny wee lass.

The date was Friday, 7 September 1934, and Vicky Devine was washing her hair at the kitchen sink, preparing for the party that night to celebrate her Ken's seventeenth birthday.

'You'd better hurry up, girl. Your dad will be home in a minute and you know he'll disapprove of you doing that at the sink just before tea's put on the table.' Recently turned forty, Vicky's mother remained as handsome in middle age as she'd been in her salad days. Mary Devine was still a looker, was what the neighbours said.

Vicky gave her hair a final rinse, then wrapped it in a towel. She gazed into her dad's shaving mirror hanging from a nail at the window. The face staring back was bright, full of life, with the mark of determination upon it and, aye, mischief as well.

'What's for tea?' John demanded from a chair by the fireplace where he was reading the *Wizard* comic. He was thirteen years old, two years younger than Vicky.

'Stew, cabbage and boiled tats,' Mary replied, standing at the cooker and thinking that the tats had been a bad buy.

Mary sighed to herself. George would complain about them, no doubt about it. He was a good man, one of the best. If he had a fault however, he was faddy about his food.

She made a mental note to tell off Mr Emslie the green-

3

grocer for selling her potatoes like these. It just wasn't on.

'Are you going to have bevy at this "do" tonight?' John asked wickedly, knowing he was putting his sis on the spot, for if their dad thought there would be strong drink at the party he would refuse to let her go.

Vicky whirled on her brother. Little bugger! she thought. 'Mainly soft drinks with a few screwtops of beer for the older boys.'

'Oh aye!' John replied, giving her a fly wink.

Vicky narrowed her eyes, her look plainly saying: keep this up and you'll be sorry, I promise you.

John smirked. He thoroughly enjoyed stirring it for his sis, though it was best, as he had learned from long experience, not to go too far. For Vicky, if roused sufficiently, would inevitably exact some awful revenge. Like when she had dropped his lovingly-made matchstick and glue model of the Leaning Tower of Pisa out the front window so that it smashed to smithereens on the pavement below. Two whole months it had taken him to make that model! At the time she couldn't have thought of anything that would have hurt him more.

'I hope there isn't going to be hard drink at this party?' Mary said to Vicky.

'I just said there wasn't.'

'Are you certain?'

'Cross my heart and hope to die,' Vicky lied.

Mary heard the clatter of feet on the stairs outside. That would be George and the other men up the close now. She took the pan of tats off the cooker and crossed to the sink to drain them.

John watched Vicky rubbing her hair with the towel, and wished he was going to Ken Blacklaws's party. He'd have given his eye teeth to have been invited, but he was too young to run with that set. He thought the sun shone out Ken's backside, as did an awful lot of people, Ken being a natural leader with real charisma. Why, even lads much older than Ken deferred to him, hanging on his every word, anxious for acknowledgement and approval.

John continued to watch Vicky, amazed to think that

the great Ken Blacklaws was winching his sis, and had been for six months now. Ken Blacklaws, who could've had the pick of any bird in Townhead! Och well, he told himself, she was his sister after all, he probably wasn't seeing her the way other boys did. But still, her and Ken Blacklaws, he couldn't help considering it a marvel, right enough.

Vicky was the first to see her dad's face when he came in, and the sight of it made her stop what she was doing. It was a dirty-grey colour, and there were deep lines etched under his eyes that had not been there that morning. But it was his expression that was the most startling; it was grim with a capital G.

'Dad?' she queried.

Vicky's tone made Mary turn round from the sink, where she was still draining the tats. George's eyes, hard with despair, locked onto hers.

'It's bad news, Mary,' he said quietly.

Mary went cold inside and her lips thinned. Filled with a sense of impending doom, she waited for George to explain.

'I've been laid off.'

She reeled mentally on hearing what every wife she knew lived in dread of being told. 'Short-time lay-off?' she asked hopefully.

'The factory's gone broke. Everyone has been laid off permanently as from tonight.'

As if in a dream, Mary laid the steaming pan of tats on the side of the sink, wiped her hands on her pinny, then went over to the chair facing John's and sat.

'What happened?'

Vicky was equally stunned by this completely unexpected bombshell. Ken worked at Agnew's, so he too had been laid off.

'We were all called to a meeting this afternoon and addressed by Mr Robertson, the high heid one himself. He said he was sorry but the factory had been in deep financial trouble for some while. According to him, the banks have called in various loans. I didn't understand all of it, but the upshot was the factory had to close down, and right away.'

'Just like that!' Mary whispered.

'Just like that,' George echoed.

George thought of the paint factory which had employed him all his working life. He'd gone there as a lad when old man Agnew still owned the place, and had soon learned what the word graft meant. But it had been a better job than many – better than going down the pits, for example, or than the extra-heavy physical toil that his pal Danny Blues had to contend with in the chain-making factory over in Cambuslang.

He pulled out a packet of Capstan and frowned on discovering it was empty. There was a spare packet on the mantelpiece behind one of the wally dugs: Vicky picked it up and handed it to him.

Vicky noted that her dad's hands were trembling as he lit a cigarette. She had never seen her dad's hands tremble before. She asked the question Mary couldn't bring herself to utter.

'What now, Dad?'

George sucked smoke into his lungs and felt nothing. His entire body might have been shot full of anaesthetic.

'I don't know, I just don't know,' he replied hollowly.

Mary wanted to scream at the top of her voice and smash every breakable thing in the house. 'We'd better have the tea before it spoils,' she said instead.

Vicky picked at her meal. Never a big eater at the best of times, she had completely lost what little appetite she might have had. A glance round the table confirmed that she was not the only one in this state. Her dad was gazing into space, while her mum stared fixedly at a boiled tat as though it were a crystal ball. John was the only person doing justice to what had been set before him.

George turned his attention to Mary. 'Do you know there are only three men living in Parr Street who didn't work for Agnew's?' he said softly.

Mary nodded. 'Aye, I know. It had already crossed my mind.'

Parr was a fairly short street, with Black Street running parallel to it on the one side, Glebe Street on the other – the same Glebe Street where Scotland's most famous fictional family were supposed to stay: the Broons, who were featured weekly in the *Sunday Post*, and were known, and followed, by Scots from Tallahassee to Timbuctoo. Black Street also had a minor claim to fame in that it was where the area VD clinic was sited – or perhaps, in Black Street's case, the word should be infamy.

George pushed his plate away with a muttered apology for the waste and, rising, went to sit by the fireplace. It wouldn't be long before winter came on, he thought, and the amount of money the Labour gave out wouldn't run to coal, not by a long chalk. Mary would be doing well if she could provide a half-decent meal a day on it, let alone anything else. Then he remembered the rent: a half-decent meal every two days, he corrected himself. By half-decent he meant porage and dry bread, that sort of thing.

'I won't go to the party tonight if you don't want me to, Dad,' Vicky offered.

'No, lass, you go and enjoy yourself while you can. After today parties are going to be in short supply around here for some time to come, I'm thinking,' he replied, giving her a soft smile that tore at her heart, for she loved her dad.

'We mustn't be over-gloomy, something might come up. You might land yourself another job no trouble at all,' Mary said, trying to inject a cheery note into her voice.

Another job no trouble at all! George knew that this was highly unlikely. Unemployment was rife in the city, with thousands and thousands laid off, in the same boat he now found himself in. For any vacancy that did occur there was always a long line of applicants, willing to take any pay, work any hours.

'Maybe so,' he replied, trying to appear positive for Mary's sake.

Vicky glanced from her mother's face to her father's, and saw that they were both pretending, making a bold show of it.

'I suppose this means I have to stop my comics,' John said. He was used to getting the *Wizard* and *Adventure* every week.

7

'There's a lot more besides your comics will have to be stopped,' Mary told him.

John coloured. 'I didn't mean that to sound the way it came out,' he mumbled.

Mary leaned across the table and patted his left wrist. He was a good boy, if a wee bit unthinking at times. But then that was his age. 'We know that, son.'

'I have six bob saved, from pocket money and that. You'd better have it, Mum,' John replied.

Mary's eyes shone.

'And I have two pounds seven and a kick. I did have more, but I spent it on Ken's present,' Vicky added.

Mary wished that she could have told them to keep their savings, but the lad was dead right: now was a time for everyone to muck in; from here on, every farthing would count.

George took his pay packet from his hip pocket and tossed it onto the table, where it landed in front of Mary's plate. 'I'll sign on first thing Monday morning, and as soon as I've done that I'll start making the rounds looking for work.'

Mary reached out gently to touch the buff-coloured pay packet. She did not have to open it to know how much it contained: three pounds exactly.

'What's the dole nowadays?' she asked lightly.

It was a subject Mary had always shied clear of. Her subconscious hope had been that, by not knowing about it, the evil would never befall her.

'Fifteen and threepence per week for a man,' George replied.

Mary blanched. Dear God!

'Plus eight bob for an adult dependant and two bob for each child,' George went on.

Mary did a rapid mental sum. Twenty-seven and three-pence a week, less than half of what George had been bringing home, and it had been a struggle to make ends meet on that! 'We'll get by somehow. We'll just have to,' she whispered.

George lit another cigarette. 'I stop when this lot are

finished,' he said. He had been a smoker all his adult life, but stop he would. There was nothing else for it.

Mary fought to control her tears. She would cry later when she was in bed, and George asleep. To let him see her cry would only make it the worse for him.

After helping Mary wash and dry the tea dishes, Vicky dolled herself up for the party, putting on her best dress, silk stockings and the make-up she was allowed. Normally this was something she derived great pleasure from, but not that night.

That night, it gave her no pleasure at all.

The party was due to begin at about half past seven but Vicky went early, wanting to talk to Ken before any of the others arrived.

Ken lived further down on the other side of Parr Street. When he let her in, in answer to her chap, he said that his parents had already gone out visiting, which meant they were alone.

Mr and Mrs Blacklaws had promised Ken that they would visit his Aunt Bell over in Carntyne so that he could have his party without them being present. Despite the day's happenings – Mr Blacklaws had also been employed at Agnew's – they'd kept their word, though visiting, and being away from their own home, was the last thing they wanted in the circumstances.

Once she was inside the hallway, and with the door shut, Ken encompassed Vicky in his arms and kissed her.

'Oh, Ken, what dreadful news,' she whispered when the kiss was over.

He cupped her left breast and gently squeezed. 'Aye, you can say that again,' he replied.

'And there was never any hint of what was to come?'

'None whatever.'

He kissed her again, thinking how gorgeous she was. He drank in the smell of her scent: heavy, and musk, and mouth-watering.

'I could eat you,' she whispered.

He gave a throaty laugh and adjusted his glasses. He was

very short-sighted. Without glasses, his clear vision was limited to half a dozen feet. Beyond that everything became hazy and jumbled.

Ken had long since got used to wearing glasses, having had them since a child, but he had never stopped hating them. His bad eyesight was the one defect in an otherwise excellent and muscular body.

'My parents are worried sick about what's happened. The atmosphere at home's awful. It's as if there's been a death in the family,' Vicky said.

'Let's have a half together before the mob get here,' Ken proposed and, taking her by the hand, led her through to what Mrs Blacklaws somewhat grandly referred to as the front parlour, and which most other people in the street just called the big room. Most of the furniture usually in there had been moved to other parts of the house and the carpet rolled back. To one side stood an opened-out gateleg table with a clean cloth over it. On the cloth were various soft drinks and a number of screwtops.

'I've got a bottle of whisky, but I'm keeping that planked,' Ken explained, producing the bottle from a built-in press.

He poured them both good-size halves, then went into the kitchen to get water for Vicky, for she insisted her glass be topped up with that.

'Happy birthday, Ken,' she toasted and, having taken a sip of her drink, handed him his present.

'Och, you shouldn't have,' he said, smiling in delight as he accepted the gift. He opened the small brown-paper parcel to find a box, inside of which, cradled in satiny material, was a Ronson lighter.

'It was the best in the shop,' she said proudly.

'It's really smashing, Vicky. I'll treasure it always,' he told her, giving her a peck on the cheek.

The lighter was silver-coloured, with a firm igniting action. His initials had been engraved on one side in fancy script.

'The only trouble is, you won't have a use for it now you'll be giving up smoking,' she said.

Ken frowned, not understanding. 'Why should I do that?'

'Being on the dole, you won't be able to afford to smoke. My dad's stopping after he's finished those he's got at home.'

Deliberately, in a gesture of defiance, Ken, using his brand-new lighter, lit a cigarette and blew a perfect smoke ring at the ceiling.

'I won't be signing on for long, damn right and I won't. They're not going to chuck Ken Blacklaws on the scrapheap,' he declared vehemently.

His tone, and intense belief in himself, caused the fine hairs on the back of Vicky's neck to rise and a shudder to ripple through her.

'I've got my whole future ahead of me. That future isn't going to be the Broo and the semi-starvation that goes with the Labour handout. I've always had plans, ambitions, to be somebody. I view this as a minor setback, no more. In fact, maybe it's even a blessing in disguise, for I was getting far too settled at Agnew's. It was high time I made a move to something with real prospects.'

He was unbelievable, she thought. Here he was, in the teeth of adversity, not only insisting he would soon land himself another job, but one with prospects, a proper career even! Who else but her Ken would have reacted like that?

His eyes became partially hooded and brooding. 'The world's full of nobodies, those content to be picked up and dropped at the whim of the big boys, those at the top, with power. Well, I tell you, Vicky, someday, I swear, I'll be one of the stringpullers. Completely my own master, and the master of many.'

Vicky opened her mouth and her breath came slowly streaming out. If Ken said it would happen, then it would. If he'd said he was going to fly to the moon, she'd have believed that too. With Ken, anything was possible.

As Ken threw the remainder of his whisky down his throat, there was a knock on the outside door. With that, the spell his words had cast over the room was broken. He started to leave the room, halted, came back to Vicky and kissed her once more. 'Just to keep me going.' He smiled, and lightly ran a hand over the swell of her buttocks.

'I might have known it would be you,' Ken said when he

opened the door to discover Neil Seton there. Neil lived in the next close, and the pair of them had been good pals since the infants' class at school, where they had shared a desk. Prior to that they had already known each other from playing out on the street.

Neil had a name for being brainy and had stayed on at school when Ken left to go to Agnew's. It was Neil's intention to take his Highers, and if they were good enough – which they would undoubtedly be – and he could win a grant or bursary, go to university after that.

Neil had brought a bag of screwtops with him which he took through to the front parlour and placed beside the ones already there. He tapped his inside jacket pocket. 'I've got a wee half-bottle here, but that's not for general consumption,' he said.

'Talk about great minds thinking alike!' Vicky exclaimed.

'She means I've got one planked too. Only in my case it's a full bottle,' Ken explained.

Neil gave a thin smile. No matter what he did, Ken always seemed to go one better. It had been that way as long as he could remember.

'How's your dad taking the layoff?' Ken asked, pouring himself and Neil a dram, Vicky having shaken her head when he had raised an eyebrow in her direction.

'He could be a shell-shocked soldier straight out of the last war. He's walking about the house in a complete daze, hearing nothing and seeing nothing,' Neil replied.

Ken shook his head in sympathy.

'As he's well over fifty, he hasn't a snowball in hell's chance of finding something else, and he knows it. It's the end of the line for him,' Neil went on.

'Does that mean you'll have to leave school?' Vicky asked.

'What would be the point of that? I'd just be adding to the unemployed. No, I'll be staying on.'

It suddenly struck Vicky that there was a selfish streak in Neil, something she'd never noticed before. From his stubborn expression she guessed he would have refused to leave school even if a job had been handed him on a plate.

'Black Friday, that's what today will become known as in Parr Street,' Ken mused.

Neil swallowed some of his drink. He was not all that keen on alcohol, but pretended that he was so as to be the same as the other lads who couldn't get enough of it.

'You're all alone then, Neil, no lassie with you?' Vicky teased, and watched Neil mentally squirm.

'Neil's never been a great one for the girls, have you, Neil?' Ken grinned.

'I wouldn't say that,' Neil replied softly.

'Well, you're hardly a Don Juan.'

'Like some we know have been in the past,' Vicky jibed at Ken.

'It's hardly my fault if they've thrown themselves at me,' Ken retorted and, half in fun, half serious, inflated his chest.

There was a lot of truth in that, Neil thought jealously. Maybe lassies didn't exactly throw themselves at Ken, but they did contrive to make themselves awfully available.

'Well, they'd better not throw themselves when I'm around, or they might get more than they bargained for,' Vicky said, eyes glittering.

'What would you do to them, hen, eh?' Ken prompted, lapping this up.

'I'd mollicate them,' Vicky replied, and making a hissing sound clawed the air as if she were a cat.

Neil stared at her in admiration. Gosh, but wasn't she something! Then he altered his expression before either Vicky or Ken noticed it.

Vicky turned again to Neil. 'Honestly, though, you'd better be careful. I've heard it said that men who don't have girlfriends turn funny after a while.'

Neil was appalled. 'That'll never happen to me, I assure you,' he replied quickly.

'I'd be careful just the same,' Vicky persisted.

'Och, leave the poor lad alone, Vicky. You're embarrassing him,' Ken said.

Filled with devilment, Vicky slunk over to Neil and sensuously rubbed herself against one of his arms. 'Is that right, Neil? Am I making you embarrassed?'

Neil cursed inwardly when his face flamed scarlet; that made him feel even more foolish.

'You've given him a reddie now,' Ken admonished Vicky.

'Are you shy, Neil? Is that it?' Vicky purred.

He wished that the floor would open and swallow him up. He wished he was anywhere else but there. He wished . . . Oh God, how he wished!

She thought of teasing Neil about the scattering of plooks he had on his cheeks and forehead, and decided against it. That would be going too far. In fact, she'd gone too far already. It wasn't that she didn't like Neil; she did: he had many admirable qualities, and Ken thought the world of him. It was just that, in some ways, he was such a natural victim. If you were going to pick on someone, and he was present, there would be no question: he'd be the one.

There was another knock on the front door, which let Neil off the hook. 'I'll get it for you,' he said to Ken, and fled the room.

'You're cruel, so you are.' Ken smiled at Vicky.

'Do you think he's still a virgin?' Vicky whispered back.

Ken smothered his laugh so that Neil didn't hear, for Neil was indeed a virgin, as Vicky well knew, Ken having told her.

Despite Ken's and Vicky's attempts to liven it up, the evening was a muted affair, more like a wake than a party. But, as Ken said afterwards, that was hardly surprising as there hadn't been a single person present not directly affected by the closure of Agnew's.

On Monday morning Mary called Vicky and John at the usual time to get ready for school. Vicky found it strange to see her father still at home, as in the past he'd always already left for work by the time she and John put in their appearance. It was then that it truly sank in that her dad was unemployed.

'It's a change for us all to have breakfast together during the week. Rather nice really,' Mary said, placing a plate of margarined bread beside the teapot.

Vicky stared at the empty plate in front of her father.

She knew it was his habit to have a boiled egg before going to the factory, and bacon and egg at the weekend. There was no egg that day; eggs had gone by the board, as had weekend bacon.

Mary poured out cups of tea for them all. Vicky could tell from its colour that the tea wasn't as strong as usual. There was a bowl of sugar out, but no milk. No one asked for the milk they normally had in their tea, not even John.

George ate and drank in silence. He felt guilty, as though it was his fault he was idle. It was silly, he told himself, but he continued to feel guilty all the same. Mary kept up a steady stream of chatter, which Vicky found disconcerting. In the normal course of events it was rare for her mother to waste words at this time of the morning.

'And you'll start looking directly you've signed on?' Mary said eventually to George, who nodded.

'Will the Broo give you some leads?' John asked.

George glanced over at his son. He seemed about to make a caustic reply, but didn't. 'If they have any. But I'd be most surprised if they did,' he answered.

'Not directly round here, that's for sure. Everyone laid off from Agnew's will be doing that. I'll try further afield, though where I haven't decided yet. I'll go where my feet lead me,' George said.

Mary rose from the table and went to the cooker, where she boiled more water. This she poured into the teapot to make a second brew from the already used leaves. When the tea was masked, she poured it into a vacuum flask, which she handed to George along with a paper poke containing two slices of margarined bread.

'Your dinnertime piece, as you're going to be away all day,' she explained.

George got his jacket from the hallway and put it on. 'We'll walk down the stairs together,' he said to Vicky and John, who were now ready to leave for school.

'I'll see you when you get back then,' Mary said to George, her voice artificially bright.

Going down the stairs, Vicky did something she had not done in years; she slipped her hand into her dad's, just as though she was a wee girl again and he was taking her out. He shot her a quick sideways look, but did not comment. On reaching the closemouth, she detached her hand again.

There was a group of men standing on the corner, all of whom lived in Parr Street, and who had worked at Agnew's. Nothing had been arranged but, as if it had, they were all waiting on one another. They would go to the Labour en masse. The men of Parr Street.

Vicky spotted Ken and waved. He waved in return and gave her the thumbs-up sign. He was the only one in the entire group who appeared cheerful. Although she passed directly by the men, she did not stop to talk to Ken. It would have embarrassed her to do so in front of the others, particularly as she was wearing school uniform and carrying her school-bag.

However, Ken had no such inhibitions. 'Do you think they'll accept an X where I'm supposed to put my John Hancock?' he cried after her, making out as if he couldn't write.

Vicky laughed. Idiot! she thought. She gave him another wave, but without turning round.

Ken would brook no argument. Friday night had come round again and he was insisting on taking Vicky to the flicks. He had a few quids' worth of savings put by, and was damned if he was going to eke it out in halfpennies and farthings. Besides, it would not be long before he was back in work, earning once more.

They went to the Trocadero, or the Troc as it was known, the local fleapit. He was not particularly keen on the picture that was showing, a silent called *City Lights* starring Charlie Chaplin and Virginia Merrill. The fact that it was silent, and therefore seemed dated although it was only three years old, did not deter Vicky, who adored Chaplin. As she told Ken, the wee clown never failed to make her laugh.

On arriving at the Troc, Vicky and Ken were surprised to discover the manager standing beside the ticket kiosk.

He pumped her hand while Ken paid for the tickets. Then he pumped Ken's, all the while blethering on about how good it was to see them, and how he hoped they'd enjoy the picture and that they'd come back again soon.

'What was all that in aid of?' Vicky whispered to Ken after they had made their escape.

Ken's mouth twisted cynically downwards. 'A lot of the folk who come here worked for Agnew's, and now the factory's shut I imagine that man sees nothing but trouble for his cinema. I would say he was panicking myself, for a personal welcome won't make any difference. The only thing that'll do that is for those now unemployed to find jobs again.'

Vicky giggled. 'His smile looked as though it had been set in starch.'

Ken nodded in agreement.

Going through swing doors, they plunged into the darkness of the auditorium. They stood for several seconds, waiting for their eyesight to adjust.

'I've never known it so empty on a Friday night,' Vicky whispered. At a rough count there couldn't have been more than a couple of dozen folk present, whereas usually the place was packed.

Vicky glanced round, looking for the girl with the torch to show them to their seats. There was no girl. At that moment it came home to Vicky that Agnew's closing-down was going to affect many more people than just those who had worked there.

'It seems we find our own way down,' she whispered.

When the interval arrived, a lassie appeared with a tray of ices. Another cutback, Vicky thought. There had always been two lassies before. Ken wanted to buy her an ice, but she put her foot down at that extravagance. She told him firmly that if he bought it she wouldn't eat it, so there. As the lights were up, Vicky took the opportunity to have a good gander about her. She saw a boy she knew from school, and asked Ken if he could see anyone else from Agnew's. There was no one.

'It's spooky it being so quiet on a Friday,' Vicky said.

Finally the lights dimmed and, as the plush red velvet curtains swished open, she brought her attention back to the silver screen.

On leaving the pictures, Vicky hooked an arm in Ken's. 'That was smashing, thanks.' She smiled.

'I'd have enjoyed it more if it had been a talkie,' he replied.

Vicky said talkies might be the thing, but good old Chaplin hadn't failed her. She'd had a right laugh.

They were passing an alleyway running behind a line of shops when a movement caught her eye. There it was again, and it had something furtive about it.

'Somebody's along there,' she whispered to Ken, her grip on his arm tightening. God, she prayed it wasn't a razorman, a headcase out looking for someone to carve up.

Glass tinkled, followed by a scuffling sound. 'There's several of them, and they're breaking into one of the shops, probably the tobacconist's,' Ken whispered back.

'Move away, quickly,' Vicky urged, and forced Ken to resume walking. Her heart was hammering. 'We'd better contact the police.'

Ken pulled her to a halt. 'No, we won't. We'll mind our own business.'

'But those men were burgling that shop. They're thieves.'

'Don't get involved, that's the best policy. Do you want to go to court and have them find out who you are? Help put them away and you'd likely get a visit from their friends intent on evening the score.'

Vicky thought again of razors and shuddered. It would not be the first time a woman had been marked, and the result was not a pretty sight. 'I suppose you're right,' she said reluctantly.

They started walking again, Vicky's heels click-clacking on the pavement.

'As you wouldn't let me buy you an ice cream, how about a bag of chips?' Ken suggested.

They began arguing about that, and soon the incident of the burglars was forgotten.

.

Neil Seton was in a study class sitting by a large window below which lay a large section of the playground. He was thinking about a trigonometry problem when suddenly Vicky appeared at the far end of the playground where a gate led into the street beyond. The breath caught in his throat at the sight of her. Jesus, but she was lovely!

It was seven months since he had noticed her in another part of the playground and realised that the wee lassie he'd seen over the years playing peever, skipping ropes and the other games lassies played in the street and back courts wasn't a wee lassie any more. She had been transformed into a young woman – and, in his opinion, a proper stunner. When the penny had finally dropped that the girl he was ogling was Vicky Devine, his mouth had literally fallen open in amazement. From then on he'd been stricken. Cupid's bow had twanged and the arrow of love had lodged firmly in his heart.

Neil had wangled his way into Vicky's company, and in his own tongue-tied, stammering fashion began chatting her up – though, to be honest, he'd been so oblique about it that she'd never apparently been aware of what he'd been attempting to do.

Then he had made his fatal mistake: he had spoken about her to Ken. A double mistake: first, to discuss her with Ken at all; second, not to make his feelings clear. He ground his teeth in frustration at the memory. Why hadn't he kept his big mouth shut! Hell mend him for being so stupid.

Ken had taken a fresh look at Vicky, seeing her anew as Neil had done. And swooped. There had been no beating about the outer periphery of the bush with Ken. Oh no, that wasn't Ken's way. It had been straight in there, bang! 'Hello, how are you? Fancy going out one night?' Of course she'd accepted like a shot. Ken never needed to ask twice. Out they'd gone and that had been that, the pair of them had started winching.

Jealousy flamed in Neil. Being jealous of Ken was nothing new; he had been jealous of his pal as long as he could remember. But until now he had never wished Ken ill because of it. The trouble in this instance was that Ken had bested him in something he really cared about. Vicky was not just another bird; she had bowled him over. And no bird had ever done that before. Oh sure, there had been a few he'd liked, could tolerate, so to speak. But Vicky was different. He . . . Yes, there was no other word for it. He *loved* her.

He picked a pimple and wondered how long it would be before Ken tired of Vicky and gave her the elbow, for that was what must inevitably happen; it was the fate that had befallen every single one of Ken's women in the past. They never got rid of Ken; he got rid of them. When that happened, he must try and step into Ken's place, take over where Ken had left off.

Apprehension and uncertainty gnawed his insides. How easy it was to imagine. Take over where Ken left off. But could he? He wasn't a patch on Ken physically; Ken had the sort of shoulders women swooned over, whereas he had hardly any at all. More than once, to his bitter chagrin, he'd been described as weedy. Then there was Ken's strong and vibrant personality, where his was – well, not exactly as forceful or appealing.

If he could match Ken in any field, it was brainpower; there they were equals, with, Neil liked to think, himself having the edge. It had amazed him that Ken had left school when he had and gone into Agnew's, where the position of foreman was as high as he could ever rise. He had thought Ken mad at the time, especially as there was no domestic pressure on Ken to leave school and start grafting.

Neil, on the other hand, was going places in life, oh yes! – providing he could get a grant or bursary to the university, and when the time came no one in Glasgow, or in Scotland come to that, would try harder for one. His goal was to become a lawyer, but not just any old lawyer – one who devoted his energies to helping the poor and needy, the underprivileged, of which, God knew, there was an abundance in the city. A lawyer! He conjured up an image of himself in wig and gown. What an exciting prospect that was. He intended being the best lawyer Glasgow had ever produced.

His gaze refocused on Vicky. The best lawyer Glasgow had ever produced – and Vicky as his wife.

Now there was a dream indeed.

It had been cold for some while, but the grates in the Devine household remained empty, for, although it was now November, George had not yet been able to find another job. Neither had any of the other men, including Ken, who had been laid off from Agnew's.

Vicky chittered as she drank her morning tea; it had grown not only cold but damp, which made matters even worse. Her underclothes were clammy against her skin. Usually they were aired before the fire, but with no fire this was of course impossible.

George, lacing up his boots, was sunk in black, black despair. The streets he daily walked were endless; the phrase 'Nae work here, Jim', which he'd swear he'd heard a million times, rang constantly in his ears. His belly was taut and griping with hunger, his trousers baggy at the waist because of the weight he'd lost. And he'd lost not only weight but strength as well. Since the layoff and subsequent reduction in food, his strength had slowly drained till now he had no more strength than a gawky adolescent.

'Fuck it!' he swore when a bootlace broke and, hunching back in his chair, he covered his face with his hands.

Mary stared at him in shock and consternation. It was unheard of for George to swear in front of the children. She opened her mouth to make a comment, then bit it back.

John looked at Vicky, who, thinking he was about to make some silly remark to alleviate the situation, shook her head.

'Sorry,' George muttered and, addressing himself again to his boot, fixed the broken lace with a reef knot, then tied the boot.

'So where are you going to try today then, George?' Mary asked, a hint of tremulousness in her voice.

If George had ranted or raved, it wouldn't have been so bad. The fact that he spoke calmly and rationally made it terrifying.

'I don't think I'll bother. As far as I can see, what it boils down to is a waste of boot leather. I've tried and tried, but there simply isn't any work out there to be had.'

Vicky went prickly all over. The atmosphere was charged. It seemed as if at any moment the room and all its contents might explode like some gigantic bomb.

'You have to go, George. None of us can afford to just give up,' Mary said quietly.

'It's a waste of time, woman, I'm telling you.'

'But we have to keep trying.'

'Why?'

'Because we have to.'

'But *why*?' George demanded softly.

Mary wished she was clever, could voice what she knew and felt. 'There has to be work, some place there must be. Stay at home and it'll never be yours. Nobody's going to come chapping the door offering it on a plate.'

'I haven't been looking for the past two days. I've been going to the Monkland Canal instead, sitting there on the bank, watching the water. I've found it's very soothing to watch water. It melts away the worry and heartache and, aye, the fear.'

'You never told me this.' Mary frowned. She had never known there to be a secret between them before.

'I'm telling you now.'

Vicky knew that this was a crisis, and a deep one. Her dad had lost hope. 'Dad, can I say something? Something I think might make sense in the circumstances?'

George glanced over at her. It was on the tip of his tongue to say: mind your own business, this is strictly an adult concern. Then he reminded himself that, though she was only fifteen, Vicky was grown up and, as such, entitled to speak her piece. Also, it wasn't simply an adult concern, it was a family one.

'Remember King Robert the Bruce and the spider?' Vicky asked.

George shook his head. He might have known the story once, but if he had he'd forgotten it.

'It happened when Robert the Bruce was fighting the

English for the Scottish throne. The English had beaten him repeatedly till he'd come to believe he'd never win against them. As the story goes, he was hiding in a cave from the English one day when he noticed a spider dangling on a thread of web, trying to swing from one bit of rock to another. Six times the spider tried, and failed. But it didn't give up. Then on the seventh it succeeded, and got where it wanted to go.

'Robert the Bruce was filled with admiration, for the distance the spider had been trying to cover had seemed far too great. Yet it had tried again and again and eventually succeeded. Sheer bloody-mindedness, you could say.

'Then he realised he'd fought the English six times, and failed, and swore to himself he' d make a seventh attempt as the spider had done. And like the spider he succeeded on the seventh attempt, and because of this victory he eventually became King of Scotland.'

She was a clever lassie, Mary thought. You had to give her credit.

Vicky was right, as was Mary, George told himself. He had to keep trying. It might well be that he wouldn't find another job, that he'd be idle for the rest of his life. But for the sake of his own self-respect, and because something might just come up, he had to keep on tramping the streets.

'Bloody-mindedness, eh?' he said to Vicky and smiled. Vicky smiled back.

George took a deep breath and straightened his shoulders. Rising, he went out into the hallway, where he put on his jacket, coat and cap.

'Where's my dinnertime piece then?' he asked Mary.

When the door was shut behind George, Mary crossed to Vicky and, eyes brimming with tears, swept Vicky into her embrace and hugged her tight. 'He's a good man, you know, one of the best,' she said huskily.

'I know,' Vicky agreed.

That evening Vicky went across the road to Ken's, where the pair of them had the house to themselves, as Mr and Mrs Blacklaws had gone out visiting. They talked for a wee while, then started kissing. Vicky had come expecting to be made love to. She had first slept with Ken after they had been going out together for a month, and had been doing so ever since when the chance presented itself. Vicky had had various sexual encounters before Ken, but he was the first she had allowed to go all the way. She found him irresistible.

He opened her blouse beneath her cardy, undid her bra and began caressing her. He had such beautiful hair, she thought, running her fingers through his thick chestnut mop. She gave a little grunt, half of pleasure, half of pain, when he nipped a nipple with his teeth.

'Let's go to your bedroom,' she said, her voice breathy with passion.

Taking her by the hand, he led her there, switching on the bedside light before they both collapsed onto his quilt.

'There's no chance of them coming back early, is there?' Vicky asked, as she always did before they made love when his parents were out. It would be a nightmare, and so shaming, if Mr and Mrs Blacklaws were to walk in on them.

'They're expected where they're going; they won't be home for another hour at least,' Ken assured her as he pulled off her skirt.

When he had stripped her naked, she lay back and watched him take off his own clothes. He had a gorgeous body, she thought. His waist was trim, his shoulders wide, his buttocks firm and muscly. His skin was the colour of ivory and seemed to shine as though polished.

Lying beside Vicky, Ken fastened his hot mouth onto her shoulder nearest him and proceeded to lick. Vicky squirmed with delight. Her hands became busy, touching, fondling, caressing. It was not long before they were both roused to fever pitch. He pulled himself on top of her and prepared to enter her.

She held him off, thinking he had got carried away. 'You've forgotten something, darling.' She smiled.

'I haven't. I haven't got any,' he replied.

Her slitted eyes jerked wide open. 'You must have! You're teasing me!'

'I'm not. I couldn't buy any because I'm flat broke.'

For Vicky it was like being doused with cold water. 'Then we can't do it.'

'It'll be all right. I promise. I'll jump off at Charing Cross.'

She thrust him off her and back onto the bed. 'No, I don't trust you. I know what you're like once you get going.'

'I swear I'll jump off. My word of honour.'

For a moment or two she was tempted by the beseeching look on his face. Then her resolve hardened. 'No, I'm not doing it without a french letter,' she insisted.

'Vicky?' he pleaded. She had never refused him before. But then this was the first occasion he had been without a condom.

'What if I was to get pregnant?' she argued.

'You won't. I'll jump off. Cross my heart and hope to die if I don't.'

'Even if you did, it's a known fact that isn't a hundred per cent safe. There can be leakage before you get there,' she said.

He swore with frustration.

'It would be awful to get pregnant. Apart from anything else, I just couldn't present my father with another mouth to feed when he hasn't got a job,' she went on.

'I'd take care of any baby you had.'

'How in hell would you do that? You haven't got a job either, although you boasted to me you'd get another one quick as a wink. And not only any old job but one with real prospects, a proper career!' she said scathingly.

As soon as the words were out, Vicky wished she had never uttered them. She watched his face flame with embarrassment and shame. 'I'm sorry, I shouldn't have said that,' she whispered.

It was true, that was the trouble. He had boasted that he would pull a job with real prospects out of the hat. How hollow that boast sounded now. And not only hollow, downright stupid.

She put a hand on what for him was aching flesh. 'Ken, I can . . .'

He shrugged her away. 'Forget it,' he spat.

She stared at the back he presented to her. 'I said I'm sorry.'

Bouncing off the bed, he snatched up his underpants. His embarrassment and shame had given way to fury – fury at himself for failing to accomplish what he'd said he would. What he'd *boasted* he would. Vicky knew that she had hurt him deeply. She would have given anything to be able to retract those withering words.

She was rehooking her bra when Ken flounced from the room, and left the house, slamming the outside door loudly behind him.

After half an hour, when he had not returned, she put out the lights and went home.

Ken walked and walked, up this street, down that. When it began pelting cats and dogs, he hardly noticed. Finally his fury subsided. He knew he should not have gone off and left Vicky as he had, that it was childish. But he had felt so humiliated! He suddenly realised that his right foot was wet. Stopping, he lifted the foot to have a look at the sole. 'Buggeration!' he swore when he saw the hole there – this was the only pair of shoes he owned.

He noticed then he was standing beside the alleyway where he and Vicky had seen the burglars that night shortly after he had been laid off. In that instant an idea was born to him.

Vicky lay in bed gazing up into the darkness. The wall clock in the front room had just chimed midnight, but she was not in the least bit sleepy. It was worrying her sick that Ken had walked out on her that evening. Why hadn't she kept her big yap shut! She should never have said what she had.

As for refusing to make love, she was right about that. She just could not take the risk. As things stood, it would be disastrous for her to get in the pudding club. But if only she hadn't taunted him about his boast. If ifs and ands were pots and pans, she thought grimly.

But the situation had hardly been easy for her; she also had been worked up, and then let down. And she had been the one having to force herself to say no when she really desperately wanted to say yes. If it had been difficult for him, it had been even more so for her. Why couldn't the silly sod have understood that!

What did his storming off like that mean? Would he be round tomorrow sheepishly to make up? Or did it mean he didn't want to know any more, that she had lost him? Fear gripped her at the thought of losing Ken. She could not imagine life without him. He was the man for her, no other would ever do. Her fear was a leaden lump in her breast. He would come chapping her door tomorrow, or wait for her in the street, she tried to reassure herself. Of course he would, it would be daft of him not to. Surely some hastily spoken words would not break them up? Except that Ken was fiercely proud and she had badly dented that pride. When that happened to a man, he could react very foolishly indeed. React in a way that didn't really make sense.

Oh, please God he would continue seeing her. Please God!

Mary had made a sort of soup containing cut-up chunks of tripe, in the Glasgow manner. Vicky loathed the stuff. The sight alone of that spongy so-called delicacy was enough to make her want to throw up. She stared in horror at the evil-smelling bowlful that Mary had placed in front of her for tea. Mary, knowing full well her daughter's feelings about tripe, apologised for serving it, but said it was the only thing at the butcher's shop they could afford and, when possible, the family had to have something substantial to eat to supplement their now more or less standard diet of bread, porage and tats.

'Oh lovely!' teased John, and sucked a large piece of tripe off his spoon.

Vicky shuddered to think how slimy and slithery it would have felt as it slipped down the throat.

'That's enough, boy,' George growled, which stopped John's teasing. George was not very keen on tripe either, but had nothing like his daughter's aversion to it.

Vicky was ravenously hungry. She could've, as the

Glasgow expression went, ate a scabby-heided wean. But tripe? She doubted it.

'There's nothing else. That's it,' Mary said.

Vicky's belly heaved, and heaved again. Her skin had become hot and cold at the same time, and there was a sheen of perspiration on her forehead. She moved her spoon in the bowl and attempted to lift it. Her hand refused to obey the command her cringing brain was sending it.

Rat a tat tat went the front door.

'You get that, son,' Mary said to John, who immediately got down from the table and left the room.

'It's Ken Blacklaws,' John announced on his return.

Vicky glanced up and there, behind her brother, stood a smiling Ken.

Relief surged through her. It was four days since Ken had gone off, leaving her in his house, and this was the first she had seen or heard of him since.

'Hello,' she said shyly.

'As it's Friday night, I thought we might go out. The pictures, or dancing, or whatever you fancy?'

Vicky frowned. How was that to be possible with him skint? 'What about money?' she queried.

Ken's face broke into a broad smile. 'I'm grafting again. Nothing great, and it's only casual, but it pays, which is the main thing.'

George came to his feet. 'Congratulations, Ken. That's smashing news. It's fair bucked me up to hear it,' he said, shaking Ken by the hand.

'You're the first of all those laid off by Agnew's to find something else,' Mary said.

'Aye, well, I told Vicky I'd be – and having said that, I had to live up to it,' Ken replied.

Vicky pushed aside the bowl of tripe. 'I'll need a few minutes to get my glad rags on,' she said to Ken, eyes shining with happiness. She wanted to take him into her arms and kiss him there and then, but would contain herself until they were going down the close stairs and didn't have any onlookers. Her Ken was back! He hadn't given her the chop after all! And he was in work! Excitement bubbled in her as she went through to the bedroom to change and put on some make-up.

'So what kind of a job is it then?' George asked Ken.

'Labouring, real donkey work. But, as I said, it pays — and that's all that matters.'

George nodded his agreement. In hard times like these a pay packet at the end of the week *was* all that mattered; beggars couldn't afford to be choosers.

'Whereabouts?' Mary asked.

'I'll be moving about from site to site, all over the city, I believe. The firm itself is based in the town.'

'And what's the firm called?' Mary went on, continuing her probing.

Ken had expected to be asked these questions, so he'd prepared the answers to them at home, before making his announcement.

'McGilvray's.' There were all sorts of companies by that name listed in the phone book.

'And you say it's only casual?' Mary went on.

'For the moment anyway,' Ken answered, his smile never wavering.

When Vicky was ready, she and Ken said their goodbyes and left the house. As she had planned, she stopped him halfway down the stairs and kissed him. When his tongue jabbed into her mouth, she went tingly all over and her skin broke out in goose flesh. The warm smell of him made her feel weak at the knees.

'So where's it to be? Anywhere at all that you fancy. Tonight, money's no object,' he said when the kiss was finally over.

The kiss had left Vicky panting. 'I don't mind. Where would you like to go?'

He thought for a moment. 'How about St Andrew's Halls? The dancing's usually good there.'

'Then St Andrew's Halls it'll be,' she agreed.

As they reached the street Ken said, 'As I took you away from your tea, how about some fish suppers before we go into town?'

'Are you sure you can . . . ?'

29

He placed a finger across her lips. 'I'm sure I can afford it. As I said, money's no object.'

Fish and chips! Her mouth watered at the prospect. 'Yes please then,' she said.

They went to a fish shop in Parliamentary Road, where he ordered an extra fish each for them. 'Last of the big-time spenders!' he said to a delighted Vicky.

Oh, but that fish supper was rare! The fish were succulent, the chips gorgeous. She declared she'd never tasted anything better. Adding, of course, that hunger was the best sauce.

'Better now?' Ken asked when she had consumed the last chip and crumb of batter in her poke.

Vicky nodded. She was a new woman after that.

'I love you,' he said lightly and, taking her now empty poke from her, he scrunched it up with his own and tossed them into a waste basket.

She stared at him, those words that he had uttered so lightly booming in her mind. 'I love you too.'

This was the first time he'd said he loved her, and the first she'd admitted it to him, having been waiting for him to declare himself before she did.

He crooked his arm and she hooked hers round it. 'St Andrew's Halls and the jigging,' he said, and they started for the nearest tramstop.

He loved her, Vicky thought. *He loved her!*

She loved him so much it positively hurt.

Two

'One pound dead, that's the best I can do for you, hen,' the pawnbroker said.

Vicky stared at her mother's wedding ring which Mr Levi had placed back on the counter in front of her. 'How about making it a guinea?'

'A pound dead, take it or leave it,' Mr Levi replied firmly.

Vicky nodded, knowing it was useless to argue further, and Mr Levi moved to the till. Mary had been expecting more for the ring, but had instructed her to take whatever offered.

It was three days before Christmas and Mary had decided to pop her wedding ring in order to be able to buy a chicken for their Christmas dinner. Unemployment or not, she was determined that they would have a decent traditional meal that day. Apart from the chicken, boiled so soup could also be made from it, there would be roast tats, brussels, carrots, mashed turnip and, if there was any money left over, a screwtop, or several, for George, who hadn't tasted drink since Agnew's closed down.

Mary had said she would pop her ring, but could not face going to the shop herself. George had refused point-blank to do so. Therefore the task had fallen to Vicky.

Vicky took the pound note and ticket, then watched Mr Levi place the ring in a display tray underneath the counter. When Mary had given her the ring to take to Mr Levi's, it was the first time ever she had seen it off her mother's finger. George's face had turned pasty and he had left the room. He would have given anything to have owned something of value that could have been pawned so that the ring could stay where it belonged. But he had nothing.

On leaving the shop, Vicky discovered that it had started

to snow; large flakes were swirling all around, falling out of a leaden grey sky. She shivered, thankful that she had a good thick coat to wear, bought new for her the previous winter.

'Vicky? I thought it was you,' said a woman coming up to her. It was Sylvia Binnie, her cousin, who was four years older than her.

The Binnies lived just off the Alexandra Parade but, although it was not far from Parr Street, Vicky rarely saw her cousin, or aunt and uncle. There had been a time when she had, but her mother and Aunt Lena, Mary's sister, had fallen out a number of years back and, so far anyway, had never made up.

'I was sorry to hear about Agnew's. How are things at home?' Sylvia asked.

Sylvia was a plain girl, with a squint in her right eye. Despite these drawbacks, she was never without a boyfriend, and usually a good-looking one at that. When asked how she managed this – as she was occasionally, by other women – she answered that it was a chemical thing; men were just attracted to her.

'Pretty bad. I've just been in the pawnshop popping Mum's wedding ring,' Vicky replied.

Sylvia pulled a sympathetic face. She was employed by Copland and Lye, a big shop in Sauchiehall Street, as she had been since leaving school. Her father was a cabinet maker for a firm which made quality goods that were mainly sold in London. 'The whole unemployment situation seems to be getting worse. I heard yesterday that a large factory over in Provanmill is to shut down in the New Year. Apparently they've gone bust, same as Agnew's.'

'But your dad's all right?'

Sylvia crossed two fingers. 'So far anyway.'

'And you?'

'Still selling lots of lingerie. Thousands of folk might be starving in the city, but there are still plenty with money. I've no fears for my job.'

Vicky showed her the pound note she was holding. 'For a Christmas bird and some of the trimmings. Mum's determined it won't be porage and dry bread that day,' Vicky said, voice tinged with bitterness.

'How's your dad taking being laid off?' Sylvia asked.

'Well, he's doing his best to keep his pecker up, but between you, me and the gatepost he's the lowest he's ever been in his life.'

Sylvia groped in her bag to produce two half-crowns. 'Here, take this dollar. It's not much, but it's all I can spare for the moment. Add it to the pound for your Christmas dinner.'

'I couldn't,' Vicky said, pushing her hand away.

Sylvia's hand darted down, and the five bob was dropped into Vicky's coat pocket. 'I insist. We're family after all.' She paused, then added, 'I know your mum wouldn't like getting money from me, so tell her you got twenty-five bob for the ring.'

'It's very good of you, so it is,' Vicky mumbled.

'Och, away with you. I only wish it had been earlier on in the week and I'd have been able to give you more.'

Vicky kissed her cousin on the cheek. 'I'd better be getting on then,' she said.

'Aye, all right. I'll be seeing you about.'

Sylvia stared at Vicky's retreating back. She looked so pinched and drawn, Sylvia thought. And her hair, usually a cap of shiny curls, had been dull and lifeless. Then she remembered Bess Dickson, and what Bess had told her during the dinner break.

'Vicky!'

Vicky turned to see Sylvia hurrying after her. Stopping, she waited for her to catch up.

'Look, this might not come to anything at all, but I've just had an idea. There's a china of mine at Copland and Lye's called Bess Dickson who's decided to emigrate to New Zealand with her husband. She kept it hush-hush from everyone at work, including me, till today, when she handed in her notice. She'll be leaving Copland and Lye at the end of January, a couple of days before she and her hubby are due to sail.'

Vicky could not understand why Sylvia was telling her

33

this. What did it have to do with her? 'Uh-huh?' she prompted.

'Don't you see? If Bess has handed in her notice, then she'll have to be replaced.'

The penny dropped. 'You mean, by me?'

'You're old enough to leave school and start work, so why not? There certainly wouldn't be any harm in putting yourself up for the job. And it's a fair lassie's wage. Two pounds a week isn't to be sniffed at.'

Indeed it wasn't. 'How do I go about applying?' Vicky asked eagerly.

A little later, when she finally parted from Sylvia, Vicky had all the details, and would be presenting herself at Copland and Lye's first thing the next morning. She was bursting to tell her mum and dad about this chance which had so unexpectedly come her way.

The house was detached, made of grey stone blocks, and very, very large. Six or seven bedrooms, maybe even more, Ken thought. The driveway was red-chip gravel, and empty of cars. Although it was dark out, not a single light showed at the front of the house. Ken made his way round to the rear, which was also in darkness.

He had developed a system, and now he put the next phase into action. Returning to the front, he took a package from one of his pockets and, walking up to the door, rang the bell. If he was wrong, and someone was at home, he would ask for Mr Ivory, saying he had a package for the gentleman. Of course there wouldn't be a Mr Ivory living there, so he'd apologise, say he must have the wrong address, and leave. In the unlikely event that there was a Mr Ivory on the premises, he would hand over the package, then leave. All the package contained was screwed-up tissue paper and a stone to give it weight.

He did his best to appear relaxed and casual, but apprehension was knotting his insides. He knew from experience that the apprehension would stay with him until it was all over. No one answered his ring, so he rang a second time. When there was still no answer, he strolled round to the back of the house and chapped the door he had seen there.

The door was locked, but that did not present much of a problem. It took only a handful of seconds to jemmy it open. Heart thundering, he stepped into the house to find himself in the kitchen. Using a small torch, he located a study, closed the curtains, and switched on the lights.

There was a desk, button-down-leather chesterfield, chair to match, and two of the walls were lined with books. A third wall had a number of prints on it, the fourth a painting of a man dressed in the clothes of the previous century.

Ken went to the desk and began rifling through it. His luck was in; he found thirty pounds in fivers. His hands were shaking as he slipped the money into his wallet. Thirty quid! A bloody fortune. He wondered if he should go through the whole house. There might be more money elsewhere, and there was bound to be jewellery.

He almost jumped out of his skin when there was a sudden sound behind him. He whirled in fright, ready to lash out at the person he thought must be there. Lash out, push the person aside, and make his escape. A tortoiseshell cat with a cheeky, impish face stared up at him. It licked its chops, then wagged its tail. It was clearly a friendly animal.

Ken sagged in on himself with relief. 'Jesus!' he swore softly, and took a deep breath. That made up his mind. To hell with looking through the rest of the house. He was off.

When he was well clear of the house, and leaving the neighbourhood, he saw the funny side and began to laugh. That damned cat had given him the fright of his life!

Miss Elvin was having a period and was consequently in a filthy mood. Periods gave her a great deal of pain, and blackened her outlook. Normally a pleasant female, she became quite the opposite at this time of the month.

She glowered at Sue, her secretary, who had come into her office to say there was some wretched lassie outside asking to see her. Her official title was head of personnel.

'What's the name?' she asked grumpily.

'Victoria Devine.'

'Send her in then.'

Sue did not pay any attention to Miss Elvin's ill humour; she knew the cause of it, and that it would pass in a few days' time. She had been Miss Elvin's secretary for a number of years, and they were fairly good friends.

Vicky was sitting with hands folded in her lap. She was extremely nervous, and hoping she wasn't going to stammer or fall over her words when she spoke to Miss Elvin. She was wearing a black skirt of her mum's that Mary had been up half the night altering to fit her. The cream blouse, a sober affair, was also her mum's. She had had nothing suitable in her own wardrobe.

Vicky had walked past Sylvia on her way in and given her a conspiratorial wink. They had not spoken, as Sylvia had been busy serving.

'Miss Elvin will see you now,' Sue said to Vicky and gestured at the door leading to Miss Elvin's office.

'Come in!' Miss Elvin called out when Vicky knocked tentatively.

Miss Elvin saw a tallish girl with a good figure and intelligent eyes. Beautiful? She wouldn't have gone that far, but certainly extremely pretty.

For her part, Vicky saw a woman in her early thirties, very smartly dressed in a navy-blue suit, wearing a querulous expression and a heavenly perfume that filled the office. A strong-willed woman used to getting her own way, Vicky thought as she smiled.

'Sit down, Miss Devine,' Miss Elvin said, pointing to a hard-backed wooden chair strategically placed in front of her desk.

Vicky sat as instructed. 'It's good of you to see me without an appointment, but I wanted to come straight away and forego the delay of writing when I heard there was a job going,' she said in a rush.

Miss Elvin frowned. Vicky's words had rubbed her up the wrong way. 'And how did you know that?' she asked softly, but with the ring of steel and irritation underneath the softness.

Alarm flashed in Vicky; she'd said the wrong thing. 'I eh . . . I have a friend who works here,' she replied.

36

'Who?'

'A cousin.'

Miss Elvin's annoyance increased. She gave a thin, chilling smile. 'Don't prevaricate with me, girl. I asked a straightforward question and expect a straightforward answer.'

Vicky hesitated, then made a decision. Badly as she wanted this job, she dare not name Sylvia, for it was obvious that by doing so she would get Sylvia into trouble, perhaps even get her the sack.

'I'm sorry if my cousin has done wrong in telling me there was a job going. She certainly didn't realise she was doing so.'

'And which job was that?' Miss Elvin demanded, knowing full well which one it had to be, as there had been only one job fall vacant in the last six weeks.

'In the toiletries department,' Vicky replied.

Miss Elvin took a cigarette from a mother-of-pearl box and lit it with a Ronson lighter which Vicky recognised as being identical to the lighter she had given Ken for his birthday. 'Mrs Dickson's position was filled an hour after she handed in her notice.'

Vicky's face fell.

'The new person, a Miss Ireland, starts the Monday after the Friday that Mrs Dickson leaves,' Miss Elvin added.

Vicky became aware of a strange noise, then realised it was her own laboured breathing. She was disappointed, cruelly so.

Cow! Miss Elvin thought, referring to herself. She was being totally unreasonable, and knew it.

Vicky rose. 'I'm sorry for wasting your time. Thank you again for seeing me without an appointment,' she said with all the dignity she could muster.

She fought to control her emotions. Why had the woman been so nasty with her! Surely what Sylvia had done hadn't been a breach of the firm's rules? Sylvia would have known if it had.

Sue glanced up at Vicky's face as she went past. What she saw there made her own expression turn grim.

'Can I do anything for you?' she called after her.

Vicky halted. 'Is there a toilet please?' she replied, voice quavering.

Sue personally took her down a side corridor and showed her where the toilet was. Vicky muttered her appreciation and slipped inside.

Vicky felt sick. Sick, angry and humiliated. At least she had kept Sylvia's identity secret from Miss Elvin. It would have been a tragedy if Sylvia had got the sack on her account.

She thought of her father, who had been so excited earlier on when she had left the house. Now this: not only a let-down, but a terrible one. Then the tears she had been fighting back for the past few minutes came, a flood of them that washed the make-up from her face and created pale shadows under her eyes.

Miss Elvin opened the door to the toilet and stared in surprise at the distraught Vicky. She was instantly filled with guilt, knowing that the girl's state was as a result of the interview with her. Vicky, hand over mouth, shoulders heaving, saw Miss Elvin through a rain of tears and turned away.

The goodness and sweetness that was Miss Elvin's normal nature reasserted itself. Contrition was added to guilt as, coming forward, she fumbled for the clean hanky she knew to be at the bottom of her bag. 'Use this,' she said, pressing it on Vicky.

Vicky accepted the hanky, and bubbled into it. 'I feel so ashamed,' she sobbed.

Miss Elvin swallowed hard. 'It's hardly you who should feel ashamed, but me. I was absolutely rotten to you in my office,' she confessed in a small voice, and immediately felt the better for doing so.

Miss Elvin crossed to the sink and ran some water into a tumbler that had been standing there. 'Have a drink of this.'

Vicky took a sip, then another.

'You really did need that job, didn't you?' Miss Elvin probed gently.

Vicky nodded, and wiped her nose with the hanky.

'Your father out of work, is that it?'

Still sobbing, but not crying any more, Vicky told Miss Elvin the story of Agnew's going bust, and all its employees, including her dad, being laid off. She spoke of her father tramping the streets day after unsuccessful day looking for work, and how cold it was at home with no coal for the fire, and how desperately hungry they all were.

Miss Elvin listened in silence, the shame of how she had treated Vicky deepening with every passing second. She thought of her own good job, the excellent money it paid, and how she wanted for nothing. She resolved to make it up to the girl. It meant breaking one of her own cardinal rules about queue-jumping, but there was always the exception to every rule, and she considered this to be such.

'The job in toiletries has been filled, but one of our female packers and dispatchers is pregnant and close to the time where she'll have to leave to have the baby. The pay, at thirty shillings a week, is less than on the floor, but if you did well we could promote you to a floor at a later date when a suitable vacancy there comes up,' Miss Elvin said.

'If that's an offer, I'll take it,' Vicky replied quickly.

'We have a combination of male and female packers and dispatchers. The females unpack the more delicate merchandise and repack and dispatch the same.'

'It sounds wonderful, the very dab,' Vicky enthused, hardly able to believe this sudden turn around in her fortunes. One moment she had been in the pit of despair, the next it was as if a bright golden sun had suddenly burst from behind a cloud.

'Then consider the position yours.'

Vicky clapped her hands in glee.

Miss Elvin gave a broad smile. What a relief to have made amends for her earlier shocking behaviour! 'I'll tell you what, why don't you rinse your face at the sink while I'm in the cubicle here, then we'll go back to my office and have a nice cup of coffee while I take down your details.'

'That would be smashing.'

As she rinsed her face, Vicky thought of her father. She just knew he would whoop with joy when she told him the news.

And so he did.

It was Hogmanay, the Scottish night of nights. Bairns and the English celebrated Christmas, but the working Scot grafted right through that – those in work, that is – till the arrival of Hogmanay, then they downed tools at five or six p.m., went on holiday, and had themselves a four-day-and-night binge.

Vicky was hurrying home, having been over in Lister Street sitting with Eunace, a pal of hers who was down with a dose of the flu. They had had a good old natter together, and the pair of them had thoroughly enjoyed it. Ken was coming over later with a bottle, the plan being that she and he would see the New Year in with her family, then go over and first-foot his.

She had decided to go via the back courts, it was quicker that way, so she plunged into a yellow-tinted close, the yellow light coming from the hissing gas mantle three quarters of the way up the left-hand close wall. Once out in the back court, she paused for a moment to regain her night sight and became aware of two figures standing swaying in the darkness. The splattering sound was unmistakable: they were peeing against the tenement wall. It didn't bother Vicky to come across such a thing; it was common enough. Probably a couple of chaps caught short returning from the pub, she thought, as she hurried past.

At least she tried to hurry past, but she didn't make it. A hand shot out to grab her by the shoulder.

'Why hello there, darling,' the chap who'd caught hold of her said. He had finished urinating but made no attempt to put himself away.

She peered into their faces but did not recognise either of them. They weren't locals. She attempted to wrench herself free, but the hand on her shoulder tightened, gripping her fast. The man pulled her to him. He was nineteen or twenty, Vicky judged. The other a little older.

'She's a proper cracker, isn't she, Mick?' the one holding Vicky said.

'She is that, Tommy.'

Vicky's mouth curled downwards in distaste. Tommy's breath was stale with beer and had overtones of halitosis. His eyes were hard and vicious from drink.

Mick buttoned up his trousers, but Tommy made no attempt to do the same.

'How about a wee kiss? It's Hogmanay after all, time for celebration, making new friends and all that guff,' Tommy leered.

She started to scream, but her scream was swiftly stifled by Tommy clamping a hand over her mouth. 'Och, don't take it that way,' Tommy whispered and, removing his hand, fastened his mouth onto hers.

She struggled, but he was too strong for her. Her stomach contracted as he roughly fondled first one breast then the other. A hardness nudged her crotch.

Mick came up behind to press himself against her rear. He groped her bottom while Tommy continued fondling her breasts, then the hand which had been doing that came up under her skirt.

'Leave her go,' a new voice said.

Cursing, Tommy twisted round to face the direction from which the voice had come.

It was Neil Seton, his slim frame tight with fury.

'Bugger off,' Mick said.

Neil knew they weren't carrying weapons. If they had been, those would have been out by now. 'On you go, get walking,' he hissed.

Tommy gave a scornful laugh. It was two against one, and the one was hardly the most robust of specimens. 'Away and raffle your doughnut, pal,' he said and, provocatively replacing a hand on Vicky's right breast, proceeded to knead it.

Neil saw red. How dare they do that to Vicky, these bloody animals, how dare they!

If only it had been Ken who had happened by, Vicky thought desperately. She could see him taking on Tommy

41

and Mick and beating them. But Neil! The idea was absurd.

What Vicky didn't know was that Neil was madly in love with her, and love can do many things, including making a normally cowardly man brave.

'Let's have a bit then, hen,' Tommy said and, thrusting Vicky back against the wall, reached once more under her skirt and began tugging down her knickers.

Neil spied a brick at his feet. Snatching it up, he hefted it. 'Stop that and go, or, so help me God, I'll brain you bastards.'

Tommy paused and looked at Neil afresh. There was something in Neil's tone told him Neil wasn't bluffing.

'Now sod off the pair of you!' Neil shouted and, lowering himself into a semi-crouch, moved forward several paces.

Mick also realised that Neil meant what he threatened, and it was he who broke first. A bloke could get killed being bashed over the head with a brick. 'It was only a wee bit fun, that's all, it being Hogmanay and that. We'll move along just as you want, Jim.'

Neil's lips were wolfishly drawn back to show his teeth. He brought his concentration to bear fully on Tommy, though still aware of Mick, should his capitulation turn out to be a trick.

Tommy had been drunk to start with but was sobering rapidly now. For a moment he considered rushing Neil, then decided against it. 'It was only a bit of fun, as my china says,' he mumbled. Releasing Vicky, he put himself away and started doing up his fly.

Vicky stumbled away behind Neil, where she spat on the ground, trying to get the sour, revolting taste of Tommy out of her mouth.

Side by side, Tommy and Mick slunk off into the darkness and were soon lost to sight behind some middens.

'Oh, Neil!' Vicky choked, and fell into his arms. He dropped the brick so he could hold her properly.

How lucky it was he had happened by, Neil thought. If he hadn't the consequences were just too awful to contemplate. He gently stroked Vicky's hair to try and soothe her down. She was shaking like a leaf, and no wonder after the events of the past few minutes.

'I'm all right now,' she declared eventually, and took a deep breath. 'Thank the Lord you came along,' she said, marvelling that he'd stood up to those two. She would never have guessed he had it in him.

'They were both pissed as newts, but that hardly excuses what they attempted to do,' Neil said lightly.

'You would have used that brick too, wouldn't you?'

'Oh, aye. It was you they had, Vicky, I couldn't let them hurt you.'

Vicky frowned. There was something in his voice that she didn't understand. 'I'll need a minute or two to collect myself before I go in. I don't want to tell Mum and Dad about this. It would only cause them anxiety and worry, and they've had more than enough of that of late.'

She eased herself out of his embrace. 'I've just come from visiting Eunace Walker. She's down with the flu.'

'I was doing a stint of studying myself, and went out to try and clear a headache that had come on with a breath of fresh air.'

Trust Neil Seton to be swotting during the school holidays, she thought. He was a right keenie. 'And did it?'

He regarded her blankly. 'Did it what?'

'Clear your headache?'

He had to think for a couple of seconds. 'Well, it was still there when I came upon you and them, but it's gone now. My anger must have burned it away.'

'And you certainly were angry. I've never seen you like that before.'

He gave a self-conscious smile. 'There's a first time for everything, I suppose.'

She would rinse her mouth out with hot salty water when she got home, she thought. She could still taste Tommy.

'Do you mind turning round so I can pull myself together?' she asked.

He wondered what she was on about, then it dawned she was referring to her underclothes. 'Aye, certainly,' he replied, and did as requested.

He gazed up at the tenements lowering all around. How sad they looked, and forlorn. He couldn't see, but he knew that only a few of their chimneys would be making smoke. Normally at this time of year they would all be belching.

'There will be little Black Bun and Shortie in Parr Street tonight, and it'll be a cold welcome to the New Year for those who do stay up to greet it,' he said.

Vicky tugged her knickers into place; they'd been halfway down her thighs. 'Parr Street is a poor street tonight right enough. In fact it should be cried Poor Street instead of Parr,' she replied.

What he said next just popped into his mouth and was out before he knew it. 'If this is Poor Street, then you're the Princess of it. There's not a lassie in the street to touch you, Vicky.' He paused, then added, his voice crackling with emotion, 'Not only Parr Street, but all of Townhead.'

She stared at him in astonishment. He *did* fancy her, and rotten too from the sound of it. That was something else she wouldn't have guessed about him for, before tonight, he had never let on by even an inkling.

Well, well, this was a turn-up for the book. Swotty Seton an admirer of hers!

Neil was amazed at his own forthrightness. He could only think that some of the courage he had conjured up earlier had remained.

Vicky decided to change the subject. She did not want to embarrass him, not after what he had just done for her. 'You can turn round again,' she said.

He did, and made to speak, but before he could do so she cut in. 'I must tell you my big news. I'm not going back to school, I've got a job.'

She wasn't going back to school! That meant he wouldn't be seeing her around nearly as much as he had. 'Where's the job?' he asked, shocked.

'Copland and Lye's. I'm to be a female packer and dispatcher.'

'That's great. When did you land the job?'

'I actually knew the week before last but I didn't want to tell anyone outside the family, and of course Ken, until official confirmation came in. The letter giving me a starting date arrived this morning.'

He was pleased for her, of course he was that, there was no question her family needed the money. But to lose her from school! That was a blow, and a hard one. 'I'm happy for you,' he mumbled.

She gave a low tinkling laugh. 'You certainly don't sound it!'

She was so gorgeous, he thought. He would have given his right arm for her to be his and not bloody Ken Black-laws's. Ken could have virtually any bird, after all, whereas Vicky was the only one he wanted. 'I'd better be getting along,' he said huskily.

'I'd ask you up for a drink, but we haven't any till later when Ken comes.'

'I understand. We've no drink in either.'

She touched his arm. 'Thanks again for what you did tonight, Neil. I'll never forget it.' She paused for emphasis, then added, 'I'd be obliged if you didn't mention the incident to anyone. I know it's daft, but I don't want word of it getting round. I'd prefer if it was kept strictly between you and me.'

'I'll never mention it, you have my word,' he replied softly.

'Not to a soul, not even Ken,' she insisted.

'Stum's the word, Vicky.'

She swithered about what seemed the natural thing to do next – she didn't want him getting any wrong ideas – then kissed him on the cheek, he starting as she did.

'Happy New Year when it comes,' she said.

'Happy New Year to you too when it comes.'

When she'd gone, he gently touched the spot she'd kissed, and drank in the lingering smell of her.

He was euphoric, till he remembered he would not be seeing her during schoolhours any more. Then his heart sank.

Oh, but it was a glorious, glorious day, the best she could remember for a long time.

Vicky's shoes clattered on the pavement as she hurried along Parr Street. It was the end of her first week at Copland and Lye, and her pay packet was burning a hole in her pocket. She could not wait to hand it over to her mum.

She passed a couple of youngsters playing peerie, the home-made wooden top whirling as it was struck again and again by the home-made leather-thonged whip. Her pay packet coming into the house was going to make all the difference. The coal bunker would be full once more and meat would make a reappearance on the table. Mince and tatties, how she craved a plateful of that, her favourite, not having tasted it since Agnew's went bust. Her mouth watered at the thought.

She and Ken were going out later on. He had promised to take her to pictures in the town. The next night, Saturday, they would be staying in at his house while his parents went visiting. She smiled to herself. It was nearly three weeks now since they had last had the opportunity to make love; it would be so good to do so again.

As she turned into the close, she met Mr Smith the lamplighter coming out. They exchanged words, for they knew each other well. Mr Smith had been the lamplighter for Parr Street and the streets directly round about since she had been a baby.

She found her mum, dad and brother John in the kitchen. Right away she could see something was up, for her father was grinning from ear to ear, his eyes twinkling like blue stars.

'You look pleased with yourself,' she said to him.

'First things first,' George replied, indicating the buff-coloured envelope she was holding. He did not want to spoil her moment.

Vicky handed the envelope to Mary. 'My pay packet, Mum,' she said.

Mary proudly accepted the envelope and clutched it to her bosom. She was remembering Vicky as a wean in nappies. It seemed like only yesterday, how time had flown!

'Thank you, lass,' she replied softly.

'No more tripe,' Vicky pleaded.

Everyone laughed. 'No more tripe,' Mary promised.

George produced a ten packet of Capstan and lit one with a match from a box of Swan Vestas. He drew the smoke gratefully into his lungs. How he'd missed his fags! It had been sheer purgatory going without them. Not a day had passed when he hadn't craved nicotine. But he had never given in to that craving, not even a solitary fly one. He was proud of that.

'Remember Robert the Bruce and the spider?' He smiled.

Vicky squealed with delight. She could see what was coming. 'Oh, Dad!' she exclaimed, and throwing her arms round him gave him a big smacker on the side of the mouth.

'Aye, you've guessed it. All yon endless tramping the streets finally paid off. I start Monday as a conductor on the trams,' he said.

Two of them working. The family were going to be in clover indeed.

'Only the fourth man from Agnew's to find work,' Mary said and thought sadly of those still idle.

Vicky sniffed and wiped tears from her eyes. Oh, but this was rare.

'And I've you to thank, girl. I'm sure I'd have given up that time if it hadn't been for you and your wee story,' George said to Vicky.

'Now let's have our tea. It's mince and tatties,' Mary announced.

What a day! Her cup really was flowing over, Vicky thought.

She made a right pig of herself and had two heaped platefuls. As far as she was concerned, a French chef couldn't have cooked anything that would have tasted better.

Mince and tatties. Food of the gods!

The blood pounded in Vicky's head. All she could feel was Ken's maleness splitting her down there. Jesus, it was gorgeous! Suddenly he locked deep into her. In response, she thrust herself onto him, fully impaling herself. She gasped as the most exquisite sensation blossomed within her. A sensation belonging more to heaven than earth. Ken collapsed onto her to lay a cheek in the hollow of her neck. He was panting and streaming with sweat.

'That was incredible,' she whispered, thinking it had never been better. It was so natural with them somehow, everything fitted perfectly.

When he finally tried to withdraw, she protested, and told him to stay where he was. If she could, she would have kept him – and herself, as she was, totally happy and complete – in the same place for all eternity.

Eventually nature took its course and the joining broke of its own accord. Vicky watched the muscles briefly play on his arm when he flicked his Ronson alight. She kissed a shoulder, tasting the saltiness of his sweat, and adoring it. 'We don't get a chance to do this nearly often enough,' she complained.

'We will when we get married.'

She sat up straight to stare at him. 'Say that again?'

Icing on a cake, that was what she always reminded him of, sweet icing on a cake, he thought.

'We will when we get married,' he repeated.

Those were words she had been longing to hear, that she had dreamt of hearing. 'Is that a proposal?' she asked, suddenly coy.

'Yes and no. If you want, we will get married, but not just yet. Maybe next year.'

She threw herself at him, and hugged him. 'If I want! Of course I want. I love you,' she exclaimed.

'And I love you, which is why I wish to marry you when the time's right.'

She lay back and pulled the quilt up over her nakedness, not because she was shy but because she was cooling down and becoming aware that it was chilly in his bedroom.

'Will we live round here?' She already saw herself and Ken in a wee house of their own.

'We can, to start with, till I really get on my feet. For don't forget I've got ambitions to be somebody and "somebodies" don't live in Townhead, or in tenements even.'

'A stringpuller. Your own master and master of many,'

she said, echoing his words from the night of his birthday party.

He gave a deep laugh, and kissed her on the mouth, delighted that she had remembered what he'd said, and furthermore was even able to quote him on it.

'When we get officially engaged, I'll give you a diamond ring, you have my promise on that,' he told her.

'People don't give diamond rings any more, Ken, they haven't the money.'

'Some people do, and I'll be one of them. I swear.'

She was frowning. 'I wouldn't want to have to wait longer because you were saving up for that.'

'You won't have to wait longer.'

'You really are doing well in this job, aren't you?'

'I've no complaints. Though it's still only a temporary job, mind you, something to see me through these hard times that folk are having to contend with.'

'You say you've got ambitions, but to be what?' she probed.

'I don't know yet. Some day an opportunity will present itself. I've no idea what sort of opportunity or in which direction it'll take me, but when it does come I'll grab it with both hands, and from there on in there will be no stopping me.'

She gave a teasing smile. 'You sound as though you consider yourself a man of destiny?'

'Men of destiny are those who *make* things happen, who control life and don't just let life control them. And I'm certainly one of those,' he replied.

She reached for him and squeezed very gently, causing him to breathe in sharply. 'You're not the only one who can make things happen,' she said.

And she was very quickly proved right.

A keen March wind was gusting as Vicky left Copland and Lye by the staff entrance, having just completed her day's work. She walked round to the front of the shop on the way to her nearest tramstop.

She stopped in front of a window whose display had been

changed since she'd gone in that morning. The new display was a wedding scene, the bride in a white organza and satin dress with flowing train, the groom in top hat and morning dress. There were two boy pages, each wearing a Royal Stewart kilt, and two bridesmaids, same young age as the boys, wearing frilly pink dresses.

Marriage, Vicky thought. It had hardly been out of her mind since the night Ken proposed. 'Mrs Ken Blacklaws,' she whispered, savouring the words in her mouth. 'Mrs Ken Blacklaws,' she repeated, and a shiver ran through her.

Staring at the display, she imagined herself as the bride, Ken as the groom. She saw herself walking down the aisle on her dad's arm, a smiling Ken waiting for her in front of the minister.

'Do you take this man . . . ?'

'I do . . . I do!'

'Do you take this woman . . . ?'

'I do.'

She shivered again, feeling a fluttery, scary coldness that left her all of a tingle and slightly breathless. Their wedding would be nowhere as fancy as that depicted in the display of course and, because of financial saving, might even be in the registry office. Just as long as she and Ken were married, that was all that mattered to her.

Next year: he'd said they'd get married then. Why, that was hardly any time away at all. And with Ken a foreman now – he had been promoted recently – they might be able to get married sooner rather than later, which was to say fairly early on in the year as opposed to the middle or end. Early on in the year . . . yes, she thought excitedly, she must somehow bring that about. But she must be careful. The last thing she wanted was for him to think he was being hurried into it. She must make it appear that the idea was his, not hers.

Mrs Ken Blacklaws! She wanted that so much she could taste it. Humming 'Here Comes The Bride', she left the window display and continued on to her tramstop.

•

Ken was in the St George's Cross billiard hall, a favourite haunt of his since 'going to work for McGilvray's'. Initially his days had been long and tedious, for he could only spend so much time reconnoitring possible break-ins, and then he had hit on the idea of going into various pubs for a bevy. He had soon learned that that was not such a good idea after all. A couple of pints at dinner time had quickly developed into five or six, which wasn't only costly but meant that his afternoons and evenings were lost to him, for he certainly couldn't go reconnoitring, or breaking in, when he was bevied to the gills.

So the dinnertime visits to the pubs had gone by the board, and he had taken up going to the pictures instead. But after a while he had got fed up with going to the pictures on a more or less daily basis, so eventually he had found this billiard hall where he could either just sit and watch, as he was doing now, or play the occasional game of snooker, which he preferred to billiards.

It was quite some time now since he had to start going to work every weekday in order to explain the amount of money he was 'earning'. His so-called promotion to foreman was a ruse on his part to explain further why those earnings were so high.

Ken was sitting watching a game of snooker in progress. At least he'd started out watching it, but was now deep in his own thoughts. It was a Tuesday afternoon and, that morning, to waste an hour or two, he had gone to the Motor Market, where he'd seen a motor that had fair bowled him over. It was a big Armstrong Siddeley, bluey grey in colour, and beautifully kept. It was obvious that whoever had previously owned that motor had loved it. The moment he clapped eyes on the machine he had known he wanted it, had to have it. Forget that he couldn't drive – that was a minor detail. Once he had the motor, he'd soon learn. What a booster it would be in Townhead, not only to own a car, but to own a beauty like that! He'd be cock of the walk right enough. Not that he particularly cared about Townhead. Oh sure, it had been good to him, and the folks who lived there were nice enough, but whichever way you looked at it it remained a slum, and slums had no place in *his* future.

Today was viewing day at the Motor Market; tomorrow was the auction itself, and the Armstrong Siddeley was due to come under the hammer some time early morning. He'd inquired about that. He had also inquired about what it was likely to go for. The sum mentioned had been fifty pounds. That was an excellent price for a car such as yon. The only trouble was that at present he had only eight pounds ten shillings, plus some coppers, to his name. He was just over forty nicker short.

If he had had a week, he could have come up with the difference, but to raise that amount overnight! Almost impossible. There was no one he could borrow from. The chap to whom he sold the bits and pieces he picked up would only laugh in his face if he tried. And he didn't know anyone else with access to such a sum. Dammit to hell! he raged, and worried a nail.

He was hoping to do a break-in that night. He had three possibles lined up and would choose whichever one was empty. If none was, he would have to leave it to the following night, or even the night after that. If he did pull off a job that night, it still wouldn't help; even in the richest houses, that sort of cash was never left lying around. Why, there had only ever been one house where he'd . . .

A smile slowly lit up his face. If there was an answer to his problem, that was it. The house with the cat who'd scared the living daylights out of him. Of course the odds were against that house being empty on that particular evening, but it just *might* be. And why shouldn't there be another wad of fivers in that study desk? Having already been burgled, the owner would hardly think that lightning would strike in the same place twice. At least not in such a short space of time.

He brought his attention back to the game going on in front of him, and watched Jacky Mulhearn pot an almost impossible shot.

Almost impossible, he thought, and smiled again.

'Nice one, Jacky,' he called out, and clapped his hands. It was an omen for tonight, he told himself. Had to be.

Neil Seton stared at his open maths textbook. It wasn't figures and formulae he saw but Vicky's face, surrounded by its cap of shining curls, gazing enticingly back at him. Uttering a soft groan, he snapped the book shut, then ran a trembling hand over his forehead. Vicky – she haunted him, and how he positively ached for her.

Three months left to go till he sat his Highers and tried for the Carnegie bursary. He was also to be considered, he'd been told at school, for several Corporation grants that would be awarded after the results of the exams were known.

He was certain that he would pass all the Highers he was sitting, unless he had a total mental block that is, and such things had been known to happen, but if he performed as he was capable he should pass and pass well. The big question was, would he pass well enough to get either the Carnegie bursary or one of the Corporation grants? Competition for these awards would be stiff, he was under no illusions about that. He had been warned by his teachers that there were some very bright sparks indeed sitting the Highers next time round.

Panic welled in him, which he fought to control. He had to go to university, he told himself, he just *had to*! There was no viable alternative as far as he was concerned.

He took a deep breath, and thought again of Vicky. Oh, the dreams he had! Dreams that were really nightmares, because he could not have what he saw, and imagined, in them. This was not the first occasion that thoughts of Vicky had disturbed his studying. But tonight it was even worse than usual, tonight she was like a fever in him. Her face, her tantalising flesh; there, but at the same time out of reach.

It amazed him that Ken was still going out with her. It had to be a record for Ken, who normally ditched his birds after a month or two at the most. But ditch her Ken eventually would, and when that happened he would be there waiting to pounce. Neil allowed himself a small grin.

Pounce was a rather strong word to use in connection with himself and a female. Insidiously move in and take over was far more appropriate.

He thought jealously of how flashy Ken had become of late since starting to earn such a good screw. Foreman now, he'd been told, which meant even more mazoola per week. He, on the other hand, didn't have two brass farthings to rub together. With his dad out of work, and likely to remain so, he didn't get the pocket money he once had, and so was skint as could be. Mind you, pocket money hardly rated against what Ken must be coining a week, but it would have been better than sod all.

Rising from the spot where he did his studying, he went to the kitchen, where his mum and dad were sitting in front of an empty fireplace. Like him, both were wearing several woollies to combat the cold – cold that might not be as bitter as the past three months, but bitter all the same.

His mum had fallen asleep, his dad was gazing off into space, seeing God alone knew what. His dad was withdrawing more and more into himself, which was a great worry.

'Hello, Dad.' He smiled.

There was no answer. His dad hadn't heard.

Neil shrugged, and left it. He did not want to bellow with his mum asleep. A glance at the ticking clock on the mantelpiece told him that it was just after half past seven, early yet. What to do; more studying or something else? He thought about it, and knew he was in no fit state to do any more studying.

Then he knew what he would do. There was a meeting down at the Cooperative Hall. James Maxton, chairman of the Independent Labour Party – and fieriest of the Glasgow socialists, was scheduled to speak. It would be a treat to hear Maxton, whom he'd heard several times in the past, and whose oratory never failed to rouse his socialism and humanitarian feelings to fever pitch. Maxton would be bound to pull out all the stops with an election looming on the horizon, an election that could just restore the ILP to its former glory, when it had been a force to be reckoned with in British politics, before what many considered to be its disastrous split from its parent Labour Party.

He remembered three years previously, October 1932, when the ILP and the Communists had jointly organised the first hunger march. Now yon had been a sight: thousands and thousands of hungry and despairing men marching off to London to make their protest. To be truthful, not a lot of good had come of those marches, but they'd been an awesome and inspiring sight all the same. There was another reason to go to the Cooperative Hall, one that brought a smile to his face, and made him rub his hands at the thought. The hall would be heated. While there, he'd be warm as toast.

Neil crossed to the shaving mirror hanging above the sink and peered into it. His hair badly needed cutting; he'd get Mum to do it for him, probably over the weekend. When he was wee, his hair had been very blond and a great source of pride to his mother, who'd been forever declaring it made him look like a little prince straight out of a fairy story. However, it had long since dulled to an unexceptional fair colour, the colour of dirty straw.

He gave a soft groan to see his complexion. Those bloody pimples were the bane of his life. He'd have given anything to be rid of them. Well, *nearly* everything, he qualified, being a cautious man, and knowing there was always a price that was unacceptably high. He groaned again when he spotted a cluster of blackheads in the crease of his left nostril. He'd thought he'd got rid of those for good. Now the buggers were back!

Why did he get so many plooks and blackheads, and Ken Blacklaws never a single one! Nor boils – something else he suffered from occasionally. He shuddered at the memory of the last one, a veritable monster that had sat like a small egg on his neck. The boil itself had been agony, the treatment of it sheer hell. He touched the small scar on his neck where the boil had been.

Filling the basin from the tap, he splashed water over his face to waken him up a bit after his abortive study session and to clear his skin of surface grease. He washed his face at least half a dozen times a day to try and keep the nasties away. A doctor had once advised him to do this and he had followed the advice assiduously ever since.

Vicky marched her brother down the street. It was their parents' wedding anniversary, and Vicky had decided that she and John should leave them alone together for a couple of hours. They might be her mother and father, she'd reasoned with herself, but that didn't mean they were 'past it'. On that special night they might well fancy a wee bit of romancing, and if they did she would make certain that neither she nor John were about to spoil their fun.

She tried to imagine her parents in bed doing what she and Ken did, but somehow couldn't. She knew they must, but to imagine them at it was beyond her. Why, in her entire sixteen years she had never seen her dad without his clothes on, and her mum only once, and that when she had walked in on her by mistake.

'Where are we going?' John whined. He hadn't wanted to come out, and only some quiet and fairly deadly threats by Vicky had persuaded him to do so.

'Your father has always told us we should use our minds, and you're going to start tonight. I'm taking you to hear Scotland's greatest politician. A great man right enough, though there are those who describe him as an anarchist,' she replied.

Vicky's statement that James Maxton was Scotland's greatest politician was a contentious one. There were many in the country who would have wholeheartedly agreed with her, many would have argued that such an honour belonged to the Prime Minister, Ramsay MacDonald. A third group might have plumped for Emanuel Shinwell, known to all and sundry as Manny.

'I can already use my mind. I've been using it for years now,' John retorted sharply. He hated it when Vicky pulled age on him, as she was doing now.

Vicky sniffed. 'If that's true, you've a queer way of showing it sometimes.'

'No queerer than you.'

'Don't be cheeky!' she snapped.

56

'I'm not being any more cheeky to you than you are to me,' he replied, grinning, for he knew he had her there.

Vicky thought about that, determined to have the last word. 'I was being acerbic, you were being cheeky, that's the difference,' she said airily.

John's grin vanished. What the hell did acerbic mean! He certainly wasn't going to ask her, as she well knew. He ground his teeth in frustration. She always won, even when he was right!

They arrived at the Cooperative Hall to find a crowd milling round the entrance. They were passing inside when Vicky was hailed.

'Vicky, over here!'

She glanced across to see Neil Seton frantically waving at her, and boring through the crowd in her direction. He couldn't believe his luck. Vicky without Ken: his night was made.

'So you've come to hear Maxton speak. It should be quite a treat,' he said enthusiastically on reaching her side.

'My dad raves about him, but this is the first time I'll have heard him myself,' she replied.

'Well, take my word for it, you're in for something special. He's the best orator since Cicero.'

They were into the hall itself now and standing at the top of an aisle.

'Follow me,' Neil commanded, leading the way down.

That had been said with authority, Vicky thought. It was a side of Neil's character that was new to her, and pleasing. She liked authoritative men, as Ken was.

When they sat, Neil contrived it so that he was between Vicky and John. The scent of her, strong in his nostrils, made his head spin. He and Vicky talked and talked, all about politics, and Glasgow politics in particular, till finally it was time for Maxton to appear.

Maxton came on to roars and shouts, and a standing ovation. Normally Neil would have sat entranced while Maxton spoke, but not that night. In fact he hardly took in a word of what Maxton said. All he could think of, and be aware of, was Vicky next to him. Every few minutes he used his handkerchief to dab sweat from his brow. His discomfort had nothing whatever to do with the heat in the hall.

Elation surged through Ken. He could hardly credit it: the house *was* empty. Although it was pitch dark out, not a light was showing either front or back.

He had to make dead certain though, and went into the next phase of his system. Carrying the package for Mr Ivory, he walked up the gravel path to the front door and rang the bell. When there was no reply, he rang a second time. When there was still no reply, that confirmed there was no one at home.

Nonetheless, the usual apprehension knotted his insides as he made his way round to the rear of the house and the door he'd jemmied previously, which he now jemmied afresh. It was a new lock, but no stronger than the last one, he noted to himself, as he slipped into what he knew to be the kitchen.

Heart thudding, he put the jemmy away, and pulled out his small torch. The narrow beam pierced the blackness, lighting his way to the study. Inside the study he closed the door and the heavy curtains and switched on the overhead lights.

It was just as he recalled. The button-down-leather chesterfield, chair to match, and two of the walls lined with books. The man in the painting in nineteenth-century clothes seemed like an old friend.

Moving towards the desk, he went straight to the place in one of the drawers where he'd found the wad of fivers and, sure enough – he felt like letting out a whoop of joy – there was another wad, and this one even thicker than the other. Quickly he counted this new wad of fivers to discover that, in all, there were fourteen of the large white beauties. Why, that was seventy pounds! Tons more than he needed for the Armstrong Siddeley.

Seventy pounds – half a year's wages for a working man, he thought gleefully as he stuffed the notes into his wallet. He had really fallen on his feet tonight.

Should he have a rifle through the rest of the house or leave now? he wondered. Then he remembered that he had promised Vicky an engagement ring; he would have a look upstairs to see if he could find her one.

He switched off the study's overhead lights and his small torch back on. He padded along a hallway till he came to a staircase leading to the upper floors. There was nothing of interest to him on the first level, so he went up another flight, which brought him to the bedrooms.

He closed the hall curtains, returned to what was clearly the master bedroom, and closed the curtains there. He then switched on twin bedside lights. The decor was sumptuous, with a lot of velvet and gilt and deep-pile carpet. The sheets on the bed were baby-blue silk, he noted enviously. Whoever owned this place, they certainly didn't stint themselves, Ken thought, crossing to a vanity table laden with bottles, phials, boxes and make-up accoutrements of all sorts.

The box was covered in blood-red leather and bound with silver filigree. He opened it and gasped at what was inside. There was an eight-row string of pearls, pearls that just couldn't be anything other than the genuine article. It was all real: the ruby bracelet, sapphire pendant, two ruby rings in gold settings, a number of gold chains of varying lengths, an amethyst brooch in what he thought might be a platinum setting, a silver ring with a green stone in it – which, he decided, was jade – an eternity ring encrusted with diamonds, and a diamond engagement ring that was made up of a very large central diamond surrounded by rubies.

'Jesus Christ!' he whispered. It was mind-boggling to think how much all this must be worth.

The jewels mesmerised him. How they glittered and sparkled and shone. How fabulous they were! He twisted the engagement ring between thumb and forefinger. He couldn't possibly give this to Vicky. She would know he'd have to have come by it dishonestly.

There was a sudden sound behind him, coming from the direction of the door. Ken froze.

That cat again! he thought, and smiled with relief. It

must be the tortoiseshell cat with the cheeky impish face who'd put the fear of God into him during his last visit. Still smiling, and holding the engagement ring, he turned to the door intent on whispering, hello kit-ee-kit-ee-kit-ee.

His smile vanished abruptly, and the intended words stuck in his throat. It wasn't the cat, but a stark-naked middle-aged man glaring at him out of puffy eyes.

The man hadn't been asleep on this level – Ken had already checked it out. So he must have been sleeping on one of the higher ones. Why hadn't he answered the doorbell!

Ken shot to his feet and the jewels went scattering in all directions, the red-leather box coming to rest on its side so that it gave the impression of an open, mocking mouth.

The stark-naked man was liberally covered in body hair and reminded Ken of a gorilla he'd once seen in a travelling circus menagerie. This gorilla took a deep breath, and the barrel chest seemed to go on expanding for ever. Though strong, Ken was completely outclassed here. The gorilla was quite capable of tearing his head off – and probably would, given half a chance, judging from the expression it was wearing.

'Caught you, thief!' the man hissed in a heavy foreign accent, and formed his hands into enormous fists.

'You wouldn't hit a chap wearing glasses, would you?' Ken said, his mind racing, trying to think of a way out of this, and failing to do so.

The gorilla charged.

There was a standard lamp between Ken and his adversary, and the flex from this, snaking across the floor, caught the gorilla's right foot, to send it, with a surprised yell, sprawling.

Ken reacted instantly. He leaped round the gorilla, flew to the staircase and took the stairs down four at a time. If only he could get out of the house and onto the street he'd be safe, for a naked man wouldn't follow him there, he told himself.

He shot through the kitchen and threw open the rear door so hard that it smashed into the wall on his left.

Gulping for air, he whirled round the side of the house and headed for the gravel path and the street beyond. The chips scrunched beneath his flying feet as he pumped both arms in an effort to increase speed further. He swiftly glanced behind to see the gorilla still chasing him. Then he was into the street. The gorilla would give up now, he assured himself.

But the gorilla kept coming on.

A naked man doesn't run along a public street! Ken thought in amazement, but this one did. This one didn't seem to care who saw him in his birthday suit.

Ken whizzed past a driveway as a woman came out. Seconds later she screamed, a shrill shredding sound that tore at the eardrums. He went round a corner into another street, better lit than the last. 'Shite!' he muttered, and put a hand in front of his face to try and mask it.

About a hundred yards further on, he glanced back again, just in time to see the gorilla come up short, clutching his heaving chest. The gorilla bent over double and was sick onto the pavement.

Round another corner, and yet another, went Ken, entering a main road where there was a tram just ahead of him drawing to a stop. He was almost spent himself by now, and was thankful on reaching the tram to climb aboard and sink into one of the downstairs seats.

Oh Christ, that had been close! If the gorilla hadn't tripped over that flex, it would have been all over with him. It would have been a right doing from the gorilla, followed by a spell in Barlinnie Prison.

'A fourpenny please,' Ken said to the conductor, asking for the first fare to come into his head. He had no idea where the tram was going, nor did he care – as long as it took him away from the gorilla and that house.

Reaction set in. He went chill all over and began to shake. Control yourself, his brain commanded his body, but his body wasn't paying heed, and he continued to shake. The engagement ring! He had been holding it when he'd made his dash for freedom. He wasn't still holding it, so he searched his pockets in vain. Somewhere along the line he had dropped it, probably even before he had left the house. It didn't matter about the ring, or the other jewels. He had got safely away, that was all-important. And he still had the money, the seventy pounds. He patted his wallet, revelling in how bulky the sheaf of fivers made it feel.

The next thing Ken knew he was somewhere down by the docks and, spotting a pub, he jumped off the tram and went inside. He desperately needed a drink to try and calm himself.

'A large whisky and a pint of heavy,' he instructed the bartender. His hands were still shaking when he lit a cigarette, though not as badly as they had been. The rest of his body, with the exception of his thighs, was now still.

He swallowed the dram in a single gulp, closed his eyes and shuddered. Oh, but that was good! He ordered another large one, and had a mouthful of his pint.

He was on his third large whisky, and second pint, when he became aware of the lassie staring at him from the other side of the pub.

She was a ginger-haired girl about his own age, and attractive in a gallus sort of fashion. Even at that distance he could make out that she was freckly, and that her eyes were green – the same colour green as that jade ring back in the house he'd fled from. She was with a group of men, all a lot older than her, two of whom were in suits and wearing bowler hats. The men were talking animatedly amongst themselves.

Ken glanced away, drank more beer, then looked back again. She was still staring at him, her expression deadpan. Somewhat flummoxed by the situation, and still all of a jangle from what he'd just been through, he gave her a nervous smile.

The deadpan expression slowly melted into a warm reciprocal smile, then she turned her back to Ken and began speaking with one of the bowler-hatted men.

Ken ordered another pint and fell to dreaming about the Armstrong Siddeley he was going to buy in the morning, for, with seventy quid to his name, he sure as hell wasn't going to be outbid!

A little later he went to the cludgie; and when he returned the girl and the men with her had gone.

By the time he got home to Parr Street he had forgotten all about her.

Vicky gazed at Ken in admiration. What a clever, marvellous man he was. She had nearly died when, coming out of work, he had hailed her from behind the wheel of this beautiful car. How the other girls had chattered and nudged one another, envying her, as she had climbed inside to sit beside him. Then, with a blast on the horn, and a wave from him to the goggling, giggling girls, they had been off.

Questions had immediately tumbled from her lips. Whose car was it? Since when could he drive? Did he have a licence? Where were they going?

The car was his; he'd owned it for six weeks now, he told her, and during that time he had learned to drive, taking and passing his test that very morning.

If he had owned the car for six weeks, why hadn't he mentioned it before? she demanded. And he replied with a grin that he hadn't wanted just to show it to her, but to take her for a spin in it. What did she think? Wasn't it a humdinger?

It was that indeed, she confirmed, but where had he got the money to buy such a car? Something like this must have cost a pretty penny indeed.

He replied that it hadn't cost nearly as much as she might think – quite cheap really, considering. He had paid for it out of the money he had saved since going to work at McGilvray's. And she wasn't to worry about the engagement ring, that would be the next big item on his list.

He drove her right round the central area of the town, Argyle Street, Buchanan Street, Sauchiehall Street. Up and down and round about they went, till finally he announced that he was taking her back to Parr Street and the biggest kick of all: parking the Armstrong Siddeley in front of his close and the pair of them getting out of it with all the neighbours watching on.

He explained that, so far, he had been keeping it in a

wee garage over in the Cowcaddens, but from now on it was going to be parked in front of his close, the first car the street had ever boasted.

When Parr Street hove into sight, Vicky sat up straight and bounced up her curls. How thrilling this was! She had never felt so grand, or spoiled, or cherished.

As they entered Parr Street, Ken gave a couple of toots on the horn, knowing that the noise would bring everyone to their windows out of curiosity and nosiness. Until now the only cars to turn into Parr Street had been the doctor's, those belonging to the local undertaker, and taxis when folk were getting wed.

'I love you,' Vicky whispered, and in an intimate gesture touched the swell of his left buttock.

'And I love you too,' he answered.

Mary heard the tooting and hurried through to the front room to find out what was going on. 'George! Come right away!' she called out excitedly.

George and John went ben to join her at the window. 'Well, I'll be a monkey's uncle!' George exclaimed to see it was his Vicky getting out of the car, and that it was Ken who'd been driving it.

'Do you think it's his?' Mary asked.

'Oh aye, look at the way he's behaving,' George answered.

'The jammy beggar,' John said, green with envy.

Mary shook her head in amazement. Someone from Parr Street owning a private car, and when so many of the men were out of work! Who would have credited it?

Down in the street Ken was thoroughly enjoying himself, adoring every minute of this. 'Look around,' he whispered to Vicky as he locked her door.

Vicky glanced about. There wasn't a single window in the street without a face pressed to it. She saw her parents and John, and waved. In response, Mary's hand flashed like semaphore.

Then Vicky noticed Neil in his window, and waved to him. While she was doing this, Ken was waving to his astonished parents, whom he'd also kept in the dark about the car.

Neil returned Vicky's greetings. A car! Trust Ken Blacklaws to pull a stroke like that, he thought bitterly. Vicky really was the Princess of Poor Street now, no one could dispute it. A princess whose prince had supplied her with a bright shining chariot. He stared down at Ken, hating Ken, *hating him*.

'I'll see you to your door,' Ken said to Vicky and, in sight of the watching street, kissed her.

'This is just the start of what it's going to be like,' Ken told her as they made their way to her close.

Vicky believed him. At the moment she would have believed him if he had said he was the Archangel Gabriel himself. 'And the engagement ring is the next big thing you buy?'

'On my word of honour,' he promised.

As she mounted the stairs, Vicky felt every inch the princess that Neil had termed her.

Three

Vicky was thoroughly enjoying the task she had been assigned by Mr Ferrier, her supervisor. A consignment of crystal chandeliers had arrived from Murano, Italy, and it was her job to unpack them and reassemble each one – they had been dismantled into individual pieces for greater safety during transit.

It was delicate and responsible work: enormous care had to be taken, for if any section was chipped or broken it meant that the entire chandelier was useless and would have to be scrapped at the loss of a considerable amount of money.

Vicky, brow furrowed in concentration, glanced up to find Miss Elvin gazing at her. 'It's just like doing a jigsaw,' she said, which caused Miss Elvin to smile.

'Let's go to Mr Ferrier's office. I want a word with you,' Miss Elvin replied.

What was all this about? Vicky wondered, as she laid the chain of crystal teardrops she'd been holding onto a cradle of tissue paper. Sudden panic flared in her.

'My work's all right, isn't it?' she stammered.

'Your work's very good indeed, we're all pleased with you. You don't think you'd have been trusted with those chandeliers if we hadn't been,' Miss Elvin answered.

That was a relief, Vicky thought. For a moment there she'd been worried. She had thought she was doing well, but then, you never really knew.

On entering Mr Ferrier's office, empty by arrangement between Miss Elvin and Mr Ferrier, Miss Elvin told Vicky to sit. She remained standing.

'So how are you enjoying being with Copland and Lye's?' Miss Elvin opened.

'I'm enjoying it very much. What I do is interesting, and the folk are all nice,' Vicky replied truthfully.

That was what Miss Elvin had expected to hear. She had been keeping close tabs on Vicky, and knew that Vicky was happy in Packing and Dispatch, and that she was well liked by her fellow workers. Mr Ferrier had nothing but praise for her.

'The reason I've come to have a chat with you is that – and this is in strictest confidence for the time being – Miss Cobb in the Furs department has informed me she's getting married in September to a businessman who has said she's to cease work at that time. Consequently, her position will be coming available and I've earmarked you for it.

'The Furs department, because of the large amounts of money involved per item, is one of the most important departments in the shop, and only specially selected people work in it. We consider the positions there among the plums that Copland and Lye have to offer,' Miss Elvin said.

Vicky had been holding her breath, which now came out in a whoof. 'Let me say how grateful I am, Miss Elvin, and deeply honoured.'

'Don't think I'm doing you a favour. I'm not. It's my responsibility to select the best available for that department, and in my opinion you're the one for the job. Your wages will rise accordingly, of course, and you'll also be on commission, two per cent of the retail value of all you sell, settled on a six-monthly basis.'

Commission into the bargain, better and better! Vicky thought jubilantly.

'Mr Ferrier will sorely miss you here, but he has told me he'll do nothing to stand in your way of promotion, which he and I agree you richly deserve. We only hope we can get someone as good to replace you,' Miss Elvin went on.

'So I'll continue here till September, then I'll move up to the Furs department, is that right?' Vicky queried, wanting it all spelled out clearly.

'Not quite. You'll move up at the beginning of the third week in August. Miss McKissock, who's in charge of Furs, will give you a fortnight's training prior to you being allowed to deal with the public.'

'I understand,' Vicky said. She was so excited that she wanted to shout and yell and do a little dance on the spot. She couldn't wait to tell Ken and her parents.

Miss Elvin was thinking how much she enjoyed being the bearer of good news. Her interview with Vicky had quite made her day. What wasn't enjoyable, indeed was often loathsome, was the other side of the coin, the reprimands and sackings. They had to be done however, being part and parcel of her duties.

'Pleased?' she asked.

'You know I am.'

'And I know I can count on you. You're not the sort of girl to let me down, which is one of the main reasons I'm giving you a position on Furs. Mistakes on that department can be very costly indeed.'

The Furs department! Sable, beaver lamb, red fox, mink, blue mink, chinchilla. Vicky could hardly wait.

Vicky slipped into the front passenger seat of the Armstrong Siddeley. Ken had come to pick her up from work as he had promised.

'You'll never guess what,' she said breathlessly, eyes blazing with excitement.

Ken put the car into gear, and they moved away from the kerb. 'You lost a tanner and found a pound?' he joked.

In a cascade of words she told him about her promotion, explaining that it was not just onto the floor, but into one of the best and most important positions that Copland and Lye had to offer.

'That's terrific, Vicky, I'm really pleased,' he enthused when she had finally finished.

She wriggled in her seat, unable to keep still. She had been like that since speaking with Miss Elvin earlier on.

'This calls for a celebration, something special. What do you say?' Ken demanded.

Vicky clapped her hands in glee. 'That would be great.'

'I'll tell you what. We'll go into town this Friday night

and have a drink at someplace really posh. Or, better still, we'll have a meal and a drink. How about that?'

Doubt creased Vicky's face. 'The meal's fine, but I don't know about the drink. I'm still only sixteen, don't forget.'

Ken considered that. There were pubs he could take her to where her age wouldn't be questioned, but they weren't at all the sort of places he had in mind. A little further on they had to stop at traffic lights, and Ken pulled out his wallet and extracted a five-pound note, which he handed to Vicky. 'Get yourself a really grown-up dress, a sophisticated number that'll make you look older. And while you're at it have your hair done in a more mature style. The combination will be bound to fool them when Friday comes round.'

Vicky fingered the fiver. 'You're awful good to me, Ken,' she whispered.

He reached across and patted her thigh. 'Nothing's too good for my future wife,' he replied.

Future wife. To hear him say that sent prickles coursing up and down her spine.

'I'll go up to Dresses during my dinner break tomorrow,' she said and then fell to thinking about how she could have her hair done.

It had been arranged between Vicky and Ken that he would pick her up at seven p.m. that Friday. He arrived promptly at one minute to and chapped the door. He was let in by John and ushered through to the kitchen, where he found George and Mary enjoying a dram in front of a roaring fire.

'Will you have a touch of the cratur?' George asked, indicating the bottle on the table.

'I will indeed, that's kind of you,' Ken replied.

This was a ritual in which both George and Ken were playing their parts. As drink was in evidence, it was deemed polite for George to offer his guest some – just as it was deemed polite for Ken, as a known imbiber, to accept that offer. Anything else would have been an insult.

George made it a large one, topping up the glass with lemonade at Ken's request.

'Slainthe!' toasted Ken.

'Slainthe!' George and Mary responded.

Mary took in the neat blue suit, shining white shirt and fancy tie. 'You look like you've just stepped out of a bandbox, so you do,' she said approvingly.

'You're doing well right enough. I'm proud of you,' George smiled.

Ken's suit had come from the Thirty Shilling tailors and was the first suit he had ever had made for himself. 'You're doing not badly yourself now, Mr Devine,' Ken replied.

George didn't even try to hide his pleasure and gratification to be told that. 'It's true, I can't deny it. Getting the job with the Corporation was a godsend, and now Vicky's about to be promoted, which will mean even more money coming into the house.'

'To Vicky's new job,' Ken toasted, and the three drank in unison.

Vicky entered the kitchen, having been putting the finishing touches to her make-up when Ken arrived. 'What's the verdict then?' she asked, and slowly twirled so that Ken could get an all-round view of her new dress.

This was the first Ken had seen of the dress he had paid for. When Vicky had brought it home in the car, she had kept it in its box, saying that he would see it on her and not before.

He whistled in appreciation. 'It's a knockout,' he said.

'And the hair-do?'

'If you told me you were a London model, I'd believe you,' he replied.

Vicky laughed. She liked that.

George, on the other hand, was frowning. This was a woman standing in front of him. Where was his wee lassie?

'Don't you think the overall effect is a bit old?' George queried hesitantly.

Vicky glanced at Ken: that was the whole object of the exercise.

'Older, but not too much so. I'd say it's just perfect,' Ken replied.

George was not at all sure he agreed with that. Then

again, maybe he was just being a typical anxious parent, he thought.

'Where are you off to?' Mary asked.

'Ferrari's,' Ken answered.

George gaped. 'You mean, yon restaurant at the end of Sauchiehall Street, the one facing the Empire Theatre?' he spluttered.

'The same.'

'But that's real grand, not at all for the likes of us.'

Ken's face went cold and a hard smile came to his lips. 'There's no rule says that, Mr Devine. Ferrari's is open to those who can pay its prices, which I can, and who are suitably dressed, which we are. As long as we conduct ourselves in an appropriate manner, which we will, there is no reason on earth why Vicky and I shouldn't spend an evening there.'

'Argue as you like, Ferrari's is for the nobs, those with big houses in Kelvinside, Whitecraigs, Thornton Hall and such, not workies from Parr Street,' George countered.

Ken's smile became thin and stretched, while his eyes glittered in such a way as to make Mary shiver. 'Some day I fully intend to have one of those big houses in Kelvinside or Whitecraigs or Thornton Hall, so the folks at Ferrari's better get used to seeing me around, for if I get my way this is only the start of my joining the ranks at that level.'

It was a revelation to George that Ken had such high aspirations. Nor had he previously realised just how ruthless Ken was, for in Ken's present mood that ruthlessness stuck out a mile.

'Then good luck to you, son,' George said and finished off his dram.

Mary hadn't liked at all what she had just heard, and foresaw nothing but trouble for Ken. She had been brought up to believe that everyone had their place and should know it and stay in it. This was for the general social good.

'We'd better be going,' Vicky said quietly to Ken.

They were a sombre couple as they left the house, but Ken soon had Vicky laughing. And he kept her laughing all the way into town.

·

Vicky was in Ferrari's ladies' toilet touching up her make-up, Ken was paying the bill. Soon they would be leaving.

The evening had been a huge success, Ferrari's quite out of this world. As for the meal, it had been simply the best Vicky had ever tasted. To begin she had had melon, followed by sirloin steak, sauté potatoes and diced baby carrots, while Ken had ordered veal and spaghetti to follow his prawns. For sweet she had chosen the most scrumptious chocolate cake with a cherry on top, Ken the fresh-fruit salad. They had drunk red wine – she couldn't recall the name of the wine, but it had been French – and, after the sweet, coffee and liqueur. They had both gone for Drambuie, she the one glass, Ken spoiling himself by having three.

Vicky dreaded to think what it had all cost, but Ken had said money was no object that night and insisted that she ordered whatever she fancied from the menu regardless of price. Feeling very daring, and for some reason ultra-feminine, she had taken him at his word. The sirloin steak had been one of the more expensive dishes on the card. There had been no question asked about her age, which was a huge relief. The wine waiter had not even glanced in her direction when Ken ordered the wine and Drambuie.

She sucked on her lips and put her lipstick away. Normally she would have plumped up her curls next, but couldn't because of her hair-do. She was not particularly pleased with the hair-do, but it had served its purpose. She decided to give her hair a thorough wash next morning in the hope of restoring its usual style.

As she left the toilet, Vicky became aware of a commotion in the lounge where she was to meet Ken. As she entered the lounge, she saw two men struggling together, and with horror realised that one of them was Ken. The other was middle-aged and wearing a red and white checked Arab headdress.

'Got you you thief, you thief!' the Arab screeched hysterically.

Ken's face was ashen as he fought to break free. He had been caught completely unawares when the gorilla pounced.

The shock of meeting up with the gorilla again, and in such circumstances, had made him go all weak inside, and filled him with blind panic. All he wanted was to be out of there, to flee into the night.

People in the lounge were looking on in consternation as the two men heaved to and fro.

'Call the manager,' someone shouted.

'Thief! Thief!' the Arab repeated and, getting his hands round Ken's throat, started to squeeze.

Vicky dashed forward. She did not know what this was all about, but the Arab had to stop choking Ken before he killed him, which he seemed intent on doing. She carved a passage through the tables and chairs, and came at the Arab from behind. On reaching him, she pummelled his broad back, to no avail, then scratched and gouged his left cheek – again to no avail. Ken, glasses skewwiff, had turned puce. His eyes were bulging in their sockets.

A desperate Vicky spied a marble ashtray on a nearby table, and snatching it up crowned the Arab, smashing the ashtray ferociously down on the man's headdress.

The Arab buckled at the knees, and released Ken, who, clutching his throat, staggered backwards, at the same time gulping breath after breath into lungs that felt as though they had been set afire.

Vicky dropped the ashtray and made to go to Ken, only to be grabbed by the Arab.

'Let me go, you brute!' she squealed, and clawed again at the already damaged cheek which was bleeding profusely.

The Arab struck her, sending her reeling off to one side and into a small alcove. Someone who was clearly the manager came running up to the Arab and grasped hold of his jacket, trying to restrain him. 'What's going on?'

'He is the thief who broke into and robbed my house,' the Arab answered, pointing at Ken.

Vicky frowned. What was the man yabbering on about? Thief? Robbed his house? The Arab had to be mistaken.

Ken bolted. Elbowing his way through several gawpers, none of whom made any attempt to stop him, he ran to the main door and out into the night.

As Ken went through the door, the Arab howled, broke free of the manager and gave chase. The manager followed the Arab and the pair of them, the Arab in the lead, disappeared after Ken.

A babble of conversation broke out in the lounge. Everyone, in a high state of excitement, began to remark on the events that had just taken place. Vicky was bewildered and confused. Of course it was a case of mistaken identity, had to be. Only – if he'd been innocent, why had Ken run as he had?

The alcove she was in was darkish and, glancing about, she realised that her part in the proceedings seemed to have been temporarily forgotten. But not for long. Once the Arab and the manager returned, she would be bound to be questioned.

If Ken was innocent, *why had he run?* The question throbbed in her brain.

The Arab and manager reappeared outside the glass main door and angry words were exchanged between them. Then the Arab threw a punch which sent the manager sprawling onto the pavement. Everyone in the lounge, with the exception of Vicky, surged to the door for a better view.

This was her chance to get away, she thought, hurrying to the rear of the lounge and out into the vestibule beyond. There had to be a back exit somewhere, she would make her escape that way. Luckily, she already had on her coat. There was a passage off the vestibule that seemed to be heading for the rear of the building, so she plunged into this, walking quickly. She should have stayed, she told herself, her behaviour was ridiculous. There had to be a rational explanation for what had occurred. Only, *Ken had run!*

To her disappointment, the passage eventually became a dead end, as did the second one she tried. In desperation she mounted a short flight of stairs, wondering if she could find a route to the back of the building that way. When she heard the approaching clamour of a police siren, she swallowed hard. As it came closer and closer, she had no doubt that its destination was Ferrari's. With relief she happened upon a window which, on testing, slid smoothly open. There was a drop of about a dozen feet to a narrow alley below. She hiked up her coat and new dress, and swung first one leg over the sill, then the other. Turning round, and holding the sill tightly, she slowly dropped her body down. When she was at arms' length, and could go no further, she took a deep breath and released her grip, falling the rest of the distance.

She broke a heel on landing, and counted herself fortunate that she'd broken nothing more. Breathing heavily, her heart going *thump thump thump*, she hobbled the length of the alley, squeezed past some dustbins and found herself in a dingy street. She paused to get her bearings, then headed in the direction of where Ken had parked the Armstrong Siddeley.

When she reached the spot where the car should have been, she found it gone. She bit her lip. Ken had run, and kept on running, abandoning her. At that moment the suspicions she had been nurturing during the past few minutes began to solidify. She worked out where her nearest tramstop would be and set off in the direction of it.

The Armstrong Siddeley was parked outside Ken's close when she arrived back in Parr Street, a figure huddled in the driver's seat. As she reached the front passenger door, he opened it for her and the pungent smell of whisky wafted out.

'Did you tell them who I was?' he demanded.

'No, while they were fighting amongst themselves, you obviously having given them the slip, I made myself scarce. I talked to no one,' she replied.

Ken was completely still for a second or two, then shook himself the way a dog does. 'We'd better talk,' he said cheerfully, but his cheerfulness had a false ring to it.

She got inside the car and closed the door behind her. He had managed to buy a half-bottle somewhere, she saw. She shook her head when he offered her a swig.

'Why did you run, Ken?' she asked quietly, steel below velvet.

'Wouldn't you have, if some madman had been trying to strangle you! All I could think of was to get the hell out of there, and fast.'

'He called you a thief, said you robbed his house.'

Ken gave an unconvincing laugh. 'Oh sure, Burglar Bill, that's me. I'm a dab hand at breaking and entry, didn't you know?'

'I thought it must be a case of mistaken identity.'

He seized on that. 'Had to be, what else?'

'And yet you ran when the manager appeared, leaving me in the lurch, the girl you say you love and are going to marry.'

The latter was a key speech she had prepared, one she wanted his reaction to. Her worst fears were justified when he went a deep shade of red and the guilt he had been trying to hide crept unmistakably into his eyes.

She took the half-bottle from him and had a swig after all. She had not planned to do what she did next, it just sort of happened. She slapped him across the face as hard as she was able, then choked back a sob.

'You bloody fool,' she said.

Ken hung his head in shame.

She had another swig of whisky and pulled herself together. She felt as if she were in the middle of some nightmare. 'You'd better tell me all about it.'

Deep down he had known he wouldn't be able to lie to her, that she would see through his charade. Still, he had hoped he was wrong, that somehow he could pull it off.

'Tonight scared me, I've never been so scared before,' he admitted.

'Start at the beginning,' she whispered.

He did, taking her back to the time when they had heard, and vaguely seen, the burglars when they were coming home from the pictures, and explaining how, later, when he was desperate for a job and money, he had remembered the incident and got the idea of doing a spot of burgling himself.

Vicky listened in silence, her hands clasped, fingers continually twisting upon each other. At last, he finished his tale.

Vicky was numb all over, her brain might have been turned to solid ice. She got out the car, closed the door and waited while he rolled down the window.

'Vicky I . . .'

She cut him short. 'No more, Ken, not tonight. I have to sleep on this.'

He stared up at her with an expression of wretchedness. 'How about I pick you up in the morning and we go for a run in the car down the coast?'

'No. I'll come to you when I've thought this thing through. Until then leave me alone. Please?'

'If that's how you want it.'

She left him gazing after her, crossed the street and entered her close. She found the flickering yellow gaslight comforting, as she did the familiar smell of the close. She climbed several of the well-worn grey stone stairs, then stopped and leaned against the wall as the tears came.

A burglar! Her Ken was a burglar, a thief. There was no job at McGilvray's, never had been. There wasn't even a McGilvray's – that was all part and parcel of the lie he had concocted to explain away the money he'd been stealing. Bile churned in her stomach as the tears rained down her cheeks. This was a nightmare right enough, a nightmare to end all nightmares. Only she wasn't going to wake up next morning to find it was all a dream. What she had been told that night was horrible reality.

She started up the stairs again, but managed only a couple more before she felt scalding bile and nausea flood her throat. She fled to the back court, where she was violently sick, throwing up the meal she had so enjoyed, and which was now poison to her stomach and mouth.

Vicky was still awake when dawn crept over the slate rooftops of Parr Street. There had been no sleep for her since getting into bed, not a wink. Her mind had been in turmoil, as she went over and over what Ken had told her and tried to decide what she might do about it.

Give him up? She had rejected that early on. She loved him, and would continue to do so no matter what he'd done. But she could not allow matters to continue as they were, this pretence of his that he was out grafting, when in fact he was housebreaking.

The housebreaking was going to have to stop. The trouble was, though she could make Ken promise, swear even, that he was finished, how could she be sure he would keep that promise when the money petered out and things got rough again? She worried a nail as the pale morning light gradually seeped into every nook and cranny in the room. *How to ensure he kept his word?*

Sex? She could threaten to deny him if he backslid. But that might only drive him into another female's arms, the last thing she wanted. Why, only the other day, she had seen Helen Morrison from Kennedy Street giving him the come-on – that cow wouldn't have to be asked twice to go on her back for him. No, denial of sex was a bad idea, for it would deprive her of control.

Then the answer came to her. Simplicity itself. And that way she would maintain complete control. She was smiling grimly, and with satisfaction, when sleep finally claimed her. Ken would do as she instructed. He would have no choice.

As for Helen Morrison, she could go and boil her can.

Vicky let Ken stew all day Saturday. Then, on Sunday, after dinner, she went over and knocked on his door. His father answered, and cried out that Vicky wanted him. He was there like a shot.

'Let's go for a walk,' she said.

'I'll get my jacket.'

He invited her in to wait. She replied that she would wait in the street, and he joined her there a minute later.

It was a braw May day, the wind fresh off the Clyde, and with the tang of salt to it. Smoke from several chimneys gusted hither and yon, while the sky was a duck-egg blue liberally dotted with fluffy white clouds. The blue sky made Vicky think of summer, which was not far off.

She knew where she wanted to go and led the way, he quietly following her, not even bothering to question her about their destination.

The banks of the Monkland Canal had long been a favourite haunt of Vicky's, ever since her dad had first taken her there as a wee lassie not yet at school. It was a place she escaped to when she wanted to be alone or to think, or in this instance have the sort of conversation she intended having with Ken.

When they were facing the White Horse Distillery, she stopped. 'You've been lucky so far, but that luck's running out, as Friday night proved. Keep on burgling and it's only a matter of time, probably sooner rather than later, before you end up in Barlinnie.'

Ken winced and lit a cigarette. 'Bumping into that bloke was a chance in a million,' he retorted.

'Chance in a million or not, it came within a whisker of doing for you. If I hadn't been there to intervene, you'd be in jail the day, and up before the sheriff tomorrow morning. By tomorrow afternoon you'd have been ensconced in Barlinnie, the only question being how long for. One year, two years or three.'

Ken took a deep drag on his cigarette. His face had turned a muddy colour.

'I've heard tell of what conditions are like in Barlinnie, grim in the extreme. And you'd be living, if that's the right word, amongst the worst scum in Glasgow,' she went on relentlessly.

Ken knew that Vicky was not exaggerating, Barlinnie was a right hellhole, that was common knowledge. 'I was only burgling till I found myself a job,' he said.

'You haven't been looking for one! You told me yourself on Friday night that, when you haven't been housebreaking or sizing up prospective houses to burgle, you've been spending all your time in billiard halls and picture houses,' she snapped back.

No wonder he had shied away from seeing so many of the flicks she'd suggested of late, she thought. The sod had already seen them all!

'I fully intended . . .'

'Fully intended, my Aunt Fanny! You considered yourself to be on a soft number, and had every intention of sticking with it. You may have kidded yourself on that you were eventually going to look for a job, but that's all it was, kidding yourself on.'

'Not to start with!' he protested.

'Maybe so, but that's how it became. Come on, admit it. Admit it, Ken!'

He shrugged.

'And I always gave you credit for being intelligent, for having a good brain in your head.'

'I *do* have a good brain.'

'Aye, a criminal one, it seems,' she said scathingly.

'Och, Vicky,' he whispered, and tried to take her in his arms.

'Don't attempt to soft soap me. We're going to get this mess sorted out here and now, and until we do you can keep your mitts to yourself,' she told him, wagging a finger under his nose.

She broke away from him, picked up a chuckie and threw it into the still brown water. She loved doing that, listening to the plop the chuckie made as it entered the water. She must have thrown a million chuckies into the Monkland Canal since she'd been coming there. She gave a sudden grin – maybe not a million, it just seemed that many.

'And the same man chased you stark naked down the street?' she asked.

Ken nodded.

'And he was covered all over in hair?'

'More or less. He reminded me of a gorilla I once saw in a circus menagerie.'

'*Stark* naked, nothing on at all?'

'Not a stitch.'

Vicky laughed. 'That must have been a sight!'

'I could hardly believe it at the time. I mean, nobody, but nobody, runs starkers down the street. But that Arab did.'

'Tell me again about the jewels.'

Ken had only mentioned the jewels in passing on Friday night. Now he described them in detail. Vicky's eyes grew huge as she listened. Imagine having such an engagement ring as he was talking about! she thought in wonder and envy. It was a ring fit for a queen. She threw in another chuckie, but this one went chink, not plop. It had hit something metal just below the surface.

'How much were you averaging a week as a burglar?' she asked, curious.

Ken did some mental arithmetic. 'Weeks varied tremendously, but on average I'd say between ten and fifteen quid.'

Vicky whistled. Burglary was a profitable business. 'That's all over and done with now. You've burgled your last house, understand?'

Ken had been expecting this. She was hardly likely to condone what he had been up to, after all. He would keep her sweet. 'Completely over and done with,' he agreed.

Vicky glanced sideways at him. His reply had been too glib, his agreement too easy by far. 'I'm serious,' she said.

'So am I.'

'You'd better be, because if after today I ever find out that you've burgled another house I'll personally turn you in to the police.'

He grinned. 'You wouldn't, Vicky. You love me.'

'And it's precisely because I do love you that I'll turn you in, to save you from yourself.'

His grin wavered. Jesus, did she really mean this!

'I promise you, Ken, on everything I hold holy, one more burglary and you're for the high jump. I'll hate doing it, I'll have to drag myself down to the police station, but drag myself I will, and I'll put the finger on you.'

That business on Friday night had put the wind up him, and he had decided to lay off for a while. A fortnight say, maybe even a month. By then Vicky would have accepted that thieving was how he came by his money. Oh sure, she might not like it, and bend his ear about it upon occasion, but she would have come to accept the situation.

'You'd put me in Barlinnie?'

'The way I see it, if you continue burgling, you'll

inevitably end up there anyway, so all I'll be doing is bringing matters forward. So you've a straight choice, Ken, and I guarantee I'm not bluffing. You either stop burgling or it's prison.'

He was still grinning, but his grin now had a sickly quality. She *meant* what she said, she'd convinced him.

He tossed his dog-end into the canal and lit another cigarette. There was a crazy logic about it, after all, he told himself. She would do what she threatened because she loved him, to save him from himself, as she put it. And because he knew she'd do it, he would comply with her wishes and stop burgling.

'I'll be skint again before long,' he said.

'At least you'll be free. And this time round I'll be working, so it won't be like it was when you got laid off from Agnew's.'

'You mean, you'll buy the french letters,' he jibed, bitterness in his voice.

She ignored that.

'Of course I do have an alternative. I could stop seeing you,' he said casually.

She went cold inside. She had not foreseen this possibility. She was stricken at the thought of losing him, but remained resolute nonetheless. 'That would mean you don't love me, as you've said you do. But it wouldn't make me change my mind. If I saw you continue to have money, I'd know where it had to be coming from, and I'd be down to the police station,' she said quietly.

He was beaten. She had him. 'If only there was work available,' he sighed.

'It's hard to come by, granted, but not impossible. My dad proved that. You just have to keep on looking, and never give up.' Heart hammering nineteen to the dozen, she threw another chuckie into the water. 'Are you going to keep on seeing me?' she asked.

His reply was to take one of her hands in one of his, clasp it tightly, then kiss her. 'Let's walk further on.'

Her anxiety drained away, to be replaced by a sense of achievement and contentment. She had saved him from prison and what might have ended up as a life of crime. He might not thank her now, but he would some day. She prayed to God that he would find a job – it didn't matter what, just as long as it kept him occupied and paid a reasonable amount.

'Tell me about those jewels again,' she requested.

And she listened, riveted, as he once more described them in detail.

'You're hurting me,' Vicky complained as Ken's fingers dug into her bare flesh.

They were nude, making love on the rug in front of the kitchen fender. She gave a soft whimper when a gouging nail drew blood.

Ken didn't have to be told he was hurting her, he'd been aware of the fact and enjoying it. From behind half-closed eyelids he watched her face contort in pain as he gathered a fistful of buttock and squeezed.

Vicky writhed, her heels drumming on the rug. She could not understand why he was doing this to her. It was so unlike him, and so unlike his usual lovemaking, which was tender and considerate, if selfish at times.

It was a Wednesday night, the day of George and Mary's wedding anniversary. To celebrate, George had booked tickets for the Alhambra theatre, second performance, where he and Mary now were, having taken John with them.

Vicky had also been invited, but had declined, saying, truthfully, that she had already seen the show the previous month with Ken. She would not have wanted to go anyway, for with the family safely out of the way it gave her and Ken a chance to be alone together, and to make love.

When it was over for Ken, she pushed him from her. She had not enjoyed that one little bit. In fact she'd hated it.

A quick examination on her part revealed that, luckily, the blood he'd drawn had not stained the rug they'd been lying on. A large patch of her right buttock was red and tender to the touch. She knew that by morning that area would be black and blue.

'Why?' she demanded angrily.

He shrugged, refusing to meet her eyes.

'You wanted to hurt me, I could tell.'

He lit a cigarette from a packet of five Woodbine. That's what he was reduced to, he thought bitterly, a rotten lousy packet of five.

'I suppose I was getting my own back,' he said quietly.

'For what?'

'The fact that I have to take the Armstrong Siddeley into the motor market tomorrow.'

Her furrowed brow cleared. Now she understood. He blamed her for losing the car, his pride and joy.

'So it's come to that, eh?' she commiserated.

'I'm down to my last half-dollar, I need the cash.'

'It's a pity you haven't been able to land a job before the car had to go. It would have been nice for you to hold onto it.'

'Aye, it would have been.'

'Look on the bright side. At least you're free. You might not have been if I hadn't found out about your burgling,' she said.

That was true, but it did not make his having to sell the car any easier.

'There'll be other cars, you'll see,' she went on, trying to give him a sense of perspective.

He had a sudden desire to hit her hard, clenched fist, right in the mouth. There were times, like now, when she got under his skin so much that that was what he wanted to do to her. What he didn't want was bloody sympathy, or to be told about other cars. He wanted the Armstrong Siddeley, and he wanted it here and now, in 1935, not 1945 or whatever!

Men: they all had an unreasonable streak in them, Vicky was thinking. Why, look at Ken. He was like a big wean about to have his favourite toy taken away from him, a toy he had no right to in the first place, because he'd acquired it through dishonest, and therefore as far as she was concerned invalid, means.

'I'll tell you what. Why don't we go for a sail this weekend?

We could go down the Clyde?' she suggested, trying to dispel his brooding gloom.

Then, remembering her recent talk with Ken on the banks of the Monkland Canal, she had a better idea. 'Or how about a wee cruise on the Firth and Forth Canal? You know how much I like canals, and I've heard so much about that one, yet never been on it.'

'Why not, I'll have the car money by then.'

'My treat,' she insisted.

He closed his eyes and thought of prison. It gave him the creeps to imagine himself locked away for umpteen hours of the day, *every* day. That would be purgatory right enough.

She was correct in forcing him to give up burgling, he told himself. And yet . . . Christ! but it was so awful and humiliating having to scrimp and scrape, to look after every ha'penny.

He recalled the seventy pounds he had taken out of the Arab's house on his second visit there, and the jewels that could so easily have been his if he hadn't been so damnably unlucky. A few more minutes and he'd have been clear with a pocketful of sparklers that would have set him up for years to come. He would not have got anything like their real value for them, but he would still have realised hundreds and hundreds of pounds, maybe even as much as a thousand. A thousand pounds! What he could do with that, the life of Riley wouldn't be in it.

'I said *my* treat,' Vicky repeated.

'Aye, all right, fine,' he replied.

'Well, don't sound so enthusiastic!'

'Sorry, my mind was elsewhere.'

She gently rubbed the area of her right buttock that he had squeezed in his fist and which had begun to throb. 'I appreciate how you feel about losing the car, but if it has to be it has to be,' she said.

'It's just that . . . I truly thought I was on my way, Vicky, that a new door had opened for me, a door through which lay the future I've dreamed of.'

'It was a door for fools, Ken, a door leading to prison. You must realise that.'

He didn't answer. He knew she was right, but deep down was unwilling to accept it.

He started to get dressed. 'I'll drive you to work in the morning, it's on my route to the motor market,' he told her, changing the subject.

He didn't wait for her parents to return from the Alhambra but left early, pleading tiredness.

After he had gone, Vicky applied cold compresses to her sore buttock. He had never been cruel to her before; she hoped he never would be again.

But she understood, and forgave him.

That Saturday Vicky and Ken went to Port Dundas, there they embarked upon the *Fairy Queen* for Craigmarloch, where, according to the man who'd sold them their tickets, there would be amusements for the passengers.

The *Fairy Queen* was a grand wee boat with a single stack that belched black smoke into the sky. It was a slowish journey along the Forth and Clyde Canal but, as Vicky said to Ken, there was no rush, they were out to enjoy themselves.

An awning had been erected at the rear of the boat for folk who wanted to be in the shade. It was a sunny day, and a dense knot of people had gathered there. Vicky and Ken elected to go to the boat's prow because it was less crowded.

'I bumped into Neil Seton last night, he's gey worried about his dad,' Vicky said.

'Oh aye?'

'He's taking to mooching round the house in his semmit and longjohns, refusing to get dressed.'

Ken knew old man Seton well and liked him. Often on a paynight Malkie Seton had slipped him a Saturday penny for no other reason than he was pals with Neil.

'Why's he doing that?' Ken asked.

'Depression at being idle. Neil says it's really getting through to him now.'

'I know how he feels,' Ken grumbled.

'Och, away with you. You're a young man, you'll find

work eventually. You have hope. The trouble with Mr Seton is that at his age no one's going to take him on again, and he knows it. He might have gone out looking like everyone else, but in his case he was only going through the motions,' Vicky said.

Fifty-odd and on the scrapheap. It was a terrible indictment of the society they lived in, Ken thought. 'Why isn't MacDonald doing something about it all!' he said tightly, referring to the Prime Minister.

'It's not just Glasgow, or Britain even, it's all over, so you can't blame him. Look at America, they're in just as bad a state as we are, and they're supposedly one of the richest nations on earth,' Vicky replied.

Ken glanced down the left-hand side of the boat and a vaguely familiar face caught his attention. It belonged to a ginger-haired lassie standing beside an older man, whom she appeared to be with. Now where did he know her from? It was the freckles and green eyes that reminded him: she was the lassie in the pub down by the docks the night he'd been chased by the gorilla. And the older man with her was one of the two who had been there wearing bowler hats. Now he was wearing a flat cloth cap, or doolander as they were often cried.

The girl, becoming aware that she was being stared at, turned and looked in his direction. The deadpan expression dissolved as she recognised him. He smiled, and she returned the smile.

Imagine their paths crossing again! he thought, and wondered what her name was.

A woman joined the lassie and older man – her mother, he reasoned, for there was a likeness there. That meant that the older man must be her father. Right enough, he could now see the resemblance there as well.

'So what do you think will be the outcome of the next election, which must surely be just round the corner?' Vicky demanded, and she and Ken fell to discussing and speculating upon that.

When the cruise was over – and thoroughly enjoyable it had been too – they disembarked at Port Dundas. There

Ken watched the ginger-haired lassie and her parents climb into a chauffeur-driven Riley.

Whoever she was, she was well off, Ken thought as the Riley disappeared round a corner. He and the lassie had exchanged smiles several times during the cruise and stop-over at Craigmarloch, but hadn't spoken; that wouldn't have been at all appropriate in the circumstances.

When Vicky and Ken arrived back in Parr Street they were greeted with the awful news that Malkie Seton had hung himself from the kitchen pulley. Mrs Seton was in hospital in a state of total collapse. Neil, attended by a number of neighbours, was under sedation administered by the doctor. As a mark of respect, condolence and profound sorrow, every set of curtains had been drawn, every blind lowered. The normal cries and shouts of the children at play in the street and back courts had been stilled, the children taken indoors.

Everything was quiet, as quiet as the grave.

Four

Vicky was darning her father's and brother's socks. John's were in by far the worse condition, for he was heavy on socks, and not a week went by but he went through one heel, often the entire heel, if not two. George was reading an evening paper, John his comic, the *Wizard*, and Mary was baking.

George stopped his reading to sniff the air. 'That smells rare,' he said, looking forward to a good tuck-in later on. He had regained all the weight he'd lost when idle, and even, as though in compensation or defiance, added a few extra pounds.

Mary opened the oven door and took out a steaming applecake, followed by a fruitcake, which she laid on the table. She then popped an identical couple of cakes and a tray of jam turnovers into the oven to be baked. She wiped a sweaty brow, for it was hot work baking in this June heat. The kitchen window was wide open to let in any breeze.

'Get your shoes on. I want you to take these to Mrs Seton over the street. I'm sure the poor soul would appreciate a wee tasty bite,' Mary said to John.

'Aw, Mum, I'm just settled here,' John complained.

'Do as your mother says, and less lip, boy,' George growled.

Muttering under his breath, John stood up, made to throw his comic angrily onto the chair where he'd been sitting, then thought better of it. That might earn him a clout from George.

'I'll tell you what, I'll go over. I haven't seen Neil since the funeral and would like to know how he's bearing up,' Vicky said, laying aside her darning. Malkie Seton's funeral had been ten days previously, and the entire street, with the exception of Mrs Rae, who was bedridden as a result of a stroke, had turned out for it.

'Fair enough.' John beamed, and within seconds had his nose buried once more in his comic.

While Vicky got herself ready, Mary wrapped the applecake and fruitcake in clean teacloths and told Vicky to be sure she brought the cloths back with her. Mary then carefully placed the baking in a wicker basket she used when shopping.

As Vicky went down the stairs, she thought of the funeral. It had been a long trudge up the Springburn Road to Sighthill Cemetery, nearly too long for some of the older mourners, but the old ones had stuck it out, and they all arrived together as they'd begun. There had been few flowers, for the simple reason money was too tight to buy them, and nearly all those there were had come, one way or another, from gardens and allotments.

Mrs Seton, though clearly riven with grief, had borne herself bravely throughout the proceedings. As for Neil, he had looked like a wee boy again, lost and very scared. After the coffin had been lowered and the minister had spoken, they sang 'Abide With Me' and 'There Is A Green Hill Far Away', the latter because it had been Malkie Seton's favourite hymn.

Only relatives had returned to the Seton house afterwards, the boiled-ham meal and whisky being paid for by Malkie's younger brother from Edinburgh – he'd apparently flitted through there years previously – who was in work.

Arriving at Neil's door, Vicky chapped and waited. She heard the scuffling sound of slippers on linoleum. It was Mrs Seton who answered.

'From my mum. She thought you probably hadn't got round to baking again yet,' Vicky said, proffering the basket.

Mrs Seton's eyes were watery. Vicky guessed correctly that she was still having weeping jags, and that she had had one recently.

'Oh, that's kind of Mary. Come away in, girl,' Mrs Seton replied, and led the way through to the kitchen, where she unpacked the applecake and fruitcake.

'Will you have a cup of tea while you're here?' she asked.

'I won't if you don't mind, I'm not long after a couple,' Vicky replied.

Mrs Seton put the baking on plates, then neatly folded the teacloths and placed them back in the basket.

'Folk have been so good since . . . since what happened. We couldn't have wanted for better neighbours,' Mrs Seton said.

'And you're getting by all right?'

'Oh aye. The parish are seeing to that. It's hardly a life of luxury, mind, but no worse than others in the same situation.'

'And Neil, how's he? I haven't seen him for a while.'

'It hit him hard, you know. He and his dad were very close. Would you like to speak to him? He's been studying.'

'I would, please,' Vicky replied.

Mrs Seton took Vicky through to Neil's bedroom, where they found him hunched over a mound of papers and textbooks. Other pieces of paper, some screwed up, a few ripped and torn, lay scattered around.

Vicky was alarmed at the sight of Neil. He looked absolutely dreadful. He was gaunt and hollow-eyed, and gave the impression of being feverish. His cheeks had sunken in and, beneath the unshaven wisps on his chin, he had a fresh attack of plooks, the most virulent yet.

Neil rose to greet Vicky effusively, saying she was a welcome break from the maths problem he was trying to puzzle out.

'Her mum's sent over an applecake and fruitcake for us,' Mrs Seton said to Neil.

'Smashing.'

'Malkie aye liked a freshly . . .' Mrs Seton broke off and gulped.

'I'll be in the kitchen, give me a shout when you leave, Vicky,' she said in a husky voice, and fled.

'Do you want to go after her?' Vicky asked quietly.

Neil shook his head and pushed hair away from his forehead where it had fallen in a tangle almost to his nose.

'She'd prefer to be left alone,' he replied, equally quietly, as though they were sharing a secret.

Vicky glanced at the mound of papers and textbooks. 'I'm surprised you're still able to carry on studying.'

Neil frowned. What was she havering about? 'Why shouldn't I be?'

'Because of your dad. I would have thought you'd have left the exams till next time round.'

Neil's face contorted into an almost savage grimace. 'I'll sit my Highers this session, and what's more I'm determined to get the best results I'm capable of, the *very* best, so that I'm assured of winning that bursary or one of the grants. I have to do that, for my father's sake. It's something I've promised myself, do you understand?'

Vicky had never before seen Neil so intense, and she found it just a little frightening. 'We'll all be keeping our fingers crossed that you get to the university. You know that, Neil.'

His eyes gleamed fanatically. 'I'm going to go, Vicky. Nothing will stop me. I'm going to get qualified, and you know why?'

She shook her head.

His voice became bitter. 'Because some day . . . some day there *must* be a better world than that we're living in now, a world where a man isn't driven to hang himself because of his frustration and shame and complete inability to influence his circumstances. And I want to be part of that new world, Vicky. In fact, I want – no, *intend* – to be more than merely a part of it. I intend to be a driving force, one of those responsible for shaping it.'

Vicky had been caught up by his excitement. The way he had just spoken reminded her of James Maxton; he had the same qualities of fire and total belief. She realised then that the Neil she had known had gone for ever, that his father's death had turned him into a man.

'I want to give the people back their freedom, and self-respect. And I shall accomplish this, to honour my dad's memory,' Neil added.

Emotion clogged her throat. She could imagine what

torment Neil had been through since Malkie had hung himself. Well, if this new commitment of purpose was the result, Malkie's death had not been in vain.

'Give them work, Neil, that's what they need above all else. Give them work and the rest will fall into place, including, if they're honest and hard-grafting, self-respect.'

Her words were music to his ears. 'My God, you're a woman and a half, Vicky. Why, with you behind him there's nothing a man couldn't do, nowhere he couldn't go. He could move mountains, fly to the moon . . .'

'Or create a new world?' she chipped in.

'Exactly!' Neil thundered back.

Vicky laughed. 'I don't know if that's what Ken has in mind.'

'What do you mean?' Neil asked, his face creasing into a frown.

'We've been keeping it quiet, but I've been bursting to tell someone and, because you and he are such great pals, I'm going to tell you. Ken and I are unofficially engaged to be married.'

'How unofficial?' was all Neil could think to reply. Her statement had stunned him, made him feel sick inside.

'He wants to find his feet first before buying the ring, which has hardly been helped by him losing his job. Still, it's only a temporary setback. When he finds another job, we'll make it official just as soon as we can.'

'Congratulations,' Neil said, trying to keep his voice from betraying the shock and turmoil he felt. Ken and Vicky getting married! He had never dreamed it would go this far. He had been convinced that Ken would eventually give her the bullet, leaving the field free for him to step in. Damn Ken! Damn damn *damn* him!

Vicky touched Neil on the wrist. 'I'm sure when the time comes he'll want you to be best man,' she said.

Neil gave a weak, pained smile.

It was only then that she remembered that Neil fancied her, as she had found out on Hogmanay when he'd saved her from the two would-be rapists. She had hardly thought about it since.

You're a stupid, insensitive bitch, she told herself. But she had been so enthralled by Neil's words and vision that confiding to him about her and Ken's unofficial engagement had happened naturally as part and parcel of their conversation. She could see she had hurt him, the last thing she had wanted to do, particularly now, when he was still in mourning for his father.

'I'd better get along,' she mumbled.

'Aye, and I'd better get back to studying.'

'How long till the Highers?'

'I start next week.'

She had not realised, though she should have, that they were so soon. Since going to work at Copland and Lye, she had lost all track of school timetables and events.

'Good luck.' She smiled. She considered adding a kiss to the cheek, but decided against it, just in case he misinterpreted the gesture – though it was hard to see how he could after what she had just told him. Anyway, she hated kissing plooky faces. It aye scunnered her.

When Vicky was gone, having cried her goodbyes to Mrs Seton in the kitchen, Neil returned to his bedroom and sat again before his papers and textbooks. He gazed darkly at them. Jesus! He'd have given his eye teeth for Vicky to be his. More, he'd have given an arm and a leg.

Then he had a thought. The engagement was still unofficial. Could it possibly be that Ken was playing Vicky along, never intending the engagement to become official? It would be quite like Ken to pull a rotten trick like that. Even if Ken was serious about her, it would be ages yet before they could get married – years perhaps, for who knew how long it would take Ken to find another job! And where there was time, there was hope, hope for *his* cause with her. For the fact remained: Ken was a ladies' man, and Neil couldn't believe that that particular leopard was going to change its spots. Certainly not when he was still of a fairly young age.

Neil smiled, a thin razored smile that appeared to slice his face in two, and would have been chilling to a beholder. He had not lost Vicky yet, not by a long chalk. Not by a mile.

He focused his attention on the book he had been immersed in when disturbed, and forced himself to concentrate on what was written there and, temporarily, to forget about Vicky.

George took six screwtops of beer out of a paper bag and laid them on the sideboard. 'Do you think six will be enough?' he asked Vicky.

'Oh aye, plenty, I'm sure. Mum and I won't have more than half a one each.'

'And what about me?' John demanded, trying to sound indignant and hard done by.

'You'll get a thick ear if you're not careful,' Vicky replied.

'And are you going to give it to me? You and whose army?' John snorted.

'Enough! You can have a glassful and that'll be your lot, understand?' George said.

John nodded. That was acceptable, and the best deal he was going to worm out of George. He adored having a wee taste with his parents: it made him feel so grown up.

The wall clock in the front room chimed eight times. The alarm clock standing on the mantelpiece tinged in unison.

'Ken will be here any moment,' Vicky said unnecessarily. They all knew that he had been invited for eight. The four adults were going to while away a couple of hours playing rummy and having a good old natter. Mary was the card fanatic in the family and often attended the whist drives put on at the local Labour Hall.

'How is he anyway? I've seen him round and about, but haven't spoken to him for nearly a week now,' George asked.

'Fine.'

'I take it, as you haven't said anything, that he hasn't found another job yet?'

'He's trying hard, but so far it's the same old story, nothing doing,' Vicky replied, pulling a face.

'He should never have tempted fate the way he did. He was just asking for what happened to him,' Mary said.

The story Ken had put round the street, and which George and Mary believed, was that McGilvray's had been forced, due to a short order book, to contract their labour force, and he had been one of the unfortunates laid off. Vicky was the only person other than himself to know the truth of the matter.

'How do you mean "tempted fate"?' Vicky queried, puzzled.

Mary hesitated before replying, then shrugged. 'What he said about some day owning a house out in Whitecraigs, Thornton Hall or Kelvinside, and that the nobs had better get used to seeing his face around for he fully intended joining the ranks at that level,' Mary said disapprovingly.

'I fail to see how that's "tempting fate"?' Vicky replied.

Mary glanced over at George, then went on. 'And that big car he bought which he swanked around in like nobody's business, that turned a lot of folk against him, I can tell you.'

'They were just jealous that's all.'

'Well, they weren't jealous for long, for the car's gone by the board now, as has his job,' Mary retorted, becoming fairly heated.

'You sound pleased about that,' Vicky snapped back.

'Maybe losing his job and car will teach him a lesson. We all have our God-given place and should stick to it. It doesn't do to try and be what you're not.'

'With all due respect, I've never heard such nonsense,' Vicky said.

'Vicky!' George growled in warning.

'I don't mean to be cheeky, Dad, but if everyone believed as Mum seems to then no one would ever move up in the world.'

George did not entirely agree with his wife, but he did in some respects. 'You have to admit he was getting gey big for his boots. I've nothing against Ken. On the contrary, I've always liked the lad. But he did seem to be getting real flashy Dan above himself. And as for taking you to the likes of Ferrari's, that was really sticking his nose in where it wouldn't be welcome.'

Mention of Ferrari's alarmed Vicky. Did they know something and not let on? 'Why did you bring up Ferrari's?' she asked quietly.

'Because I was astounded he had the bare-faced cheek to take you to a place such as that,' George replied, now embroiled in the argument.

They *hadn't* heard anything about the business at Ferrari's and Ken's flight from there, Vicky thought with relief. For a moment she had been scared that he had been seen by someone who knew him and word had got back to the street.

'Are you saying your own daughter isn't good enough for Ferrari's?' she riposted.

'What we are trying to say is that we don't want you getting hurt, which you will be if you attempt to swim out of your depth,' Mary answered.

'So you *are* saying I'm not good enough, and that neither is Ken?'

Mary sighed. 'You have to recognise that you're both working-class keelies. Get ideas above your station, you or him, and it'll only bring unhappiness.'

'Ken is ambitious. I see absolutely nothing wrong in that,' Vicky retorted, glowering at her mother.

'And there is nothing, as long as that ambition is within reason,' George said.

'And what do you call within reason?'

'Well, I'd certainly call thinking of living at the three places Ken mentioned outside of it.'

'Why?' Vicky demanded.

'Because only grand folk live there,' George explained.

'And who's to say Ken couldn't become grand, or me?'

Mary laughed, a high shrill laugh filled with scorn and derision. 'Neither of you have the education, for one thing. And you both talk common, for another.'

'There's nothing wrong with good plain Glasgow speech,' Vicky said, infuriated.

'Nothing at all, I agree. Unless you live in Kelvinside, Whitecraigs or Thornton Hall, in which case, because they all talk with jorries in their mouths, you'd stick out like a couple of sore thumbs. You'd be different from the rest and, by being different, alienated.'

'You listen to your dad, he knows what he's speaking about,' Mary said.

'Anyway, there's no hope of Ken living in any of those posh places, he hasn't even got a job,' John chipped in, smiling.

'You be seen and not heard!' Vicky shouted at her brother.

John's smile turned into a supercilious smirk. He did not often score against Vicky, but he considered that he had there.

'Ken will go far, you just wait and see if he doesn't,' Vicky declared defensively.

'Maybe as far as Australia, you can't go much further than that,' John instantly replied.

Vicky glared at him. If her parents had not been present she would have slapped the cheeky bugger. She would soon have wiped that infuriating smirk off his face.

'That's enough, boy,' George admonished.

'I think we should drop this now, it's gone far enough,' Mary said, taking the heavily embroidered velvet tablecover off the table in preparation for playing cards.

'I've never heard you criticise Neil Seton. He's another determined to go places,' Vicky protested.

'Neil's attending to his education, that's the difference between him and Ken,' Mary answered.

'He still talks common, like the rest of Parr Street.'

'Neil might be determined to go places, but I doubt he has delusions of grandeur, as Ken seems to have developed. I have no worries about Neil, as I do about Ken,' Mary said.

There was a knocking on the outside door.

'I'll get it,' John said, and vanished from the kitchen.

Vicky was fuming. They were being unfair about Ken. He *wasn't* flashy, nor was he a swanker.

The outside door banged shut, and Ken, followed by John, strolled into the room.

'Come away in, son, it's lovely to see you.' Mary smiled, and gestured that he take one of the good seats by the fireplace.

Hypocrite, Vicky thought.

'I brought a bottle of whisky. If we're going to stay in, we might as well do it in style,' Ken said, and produced a bottle of whisky from behind his back, which he placed on the sideboard beside the screwtops. He then sat down.

Vicky stared at the bottle in dismay. That was quite unnecessary when he was out of work, and would have used up even further the rapidly dwindling cash he had got from the sale of the Armstrong Siddeley.

Mary glanced at Vicky, a glance that spoke volumes, and made Vicky writhe inside.

'You shouldn't have,' Mary said to Ken, her rebuke ever so gentle, the type usually given, and expected, when such a generous gesture had been made.

Vicky looked again at the bottle. She could have hit Ken with the bloody thing.

Vicky sat alone, toying with the tomato, cucumber and lettuce salad she had chosen for her midday break, in Copland and Lye's canteen. She was deep in thought, worrying about Ken and the fact that he still had not found a job. She was pushing a slice of tomato round her plate when she became aware there was someone standing beside her. She glanced up to find that it was Miss Elvin.

Miss Elvin was holding a cup of coffee. 'Do you mind if I join you?'

Vicky did not really want company, which was why she had sat apart from the others, including her cousin Sylvia whom she often lunched with, but she did not feel she could say no. Miss Elvin was one of the shop's VIPs, after all.

'Please do,' she replied.

Miss Elvin sat, and spooned sugar into her cup. She had a weakness for sugar and was forever fighting a losing battle against it. 'Why so glum? Is it something to do with the work?'

'No, work's fine. I've no complaints there,' Vicky answered quickly.

'So what's the problem? There obviously is one.'

Using the edge of her fork, Vicky cut the slice of tomato

she'd been pushing round her plate into halves, then quarters, then eighths.

'It's . . . Well, it's my boyfriend. He's been laid off for the second time and, this is in confidence, we were supposed to be getting engaged and married next year.'

'And now, because of lack of money, that's all off?'

Vicky nodded.

'What rotten luck. And I suppose you're very much in love?'

'Oh yes,' Vicky breathed in reply, her eyes suddenly shining where before they had been dull and listless.

Miss Elvin sipped her coffee. She had been in love once, now a long time ago. It had not worked out, and there had been no one important since. Men in her life yes, but no one she could truly say she loved. Which was why she had remained a spinster, married to her job. 'Had you planned a church wedding?' she asked.

'I don't mind, church or registry, just as long as we get married.'

Miss Elvin approved of that. The trappings, though very nice, were only superficial. It was the ceremony, and joining, that was important. 'I hope he gets something soon then,' she said.

'Thank you.'

'What's his name?'

'Ken. Kenneth Blacklaws,' Vicky replied.

Her young man had been called Pharic. He'd been a Highlander from Inverness, working in the whisky business. He was doing very well, she believed, and had three bonny children by the woman he had chosen over her to marry. Miss Elvin drank more coffee and put all thoughts of Pharic McCrone out of her mind. It usually made her weepy to dwell on what might have been.

'I came to the canteen especially, hoping to find you here,' Miss Elvin stated.

There was that about Miss Elvin's tone which made Vicky's heart sink. 'Is it about my being promoted to Furs?' she asked.

'I'm afraid I've got some bad news.'

Vicky stared at Miss Elvin in consternation.

'Oh, you're still being promoted. Only I'm sorry to say there's going to be a delay.'

Vicky relaxed a little. Her promotion was still on. For a horrible few seconds there she'd thought it had gone out the window. 'Am I allowed to ask why there's been a delay?'

'Of course. Miss Cobb has just been up to my office to tell me that her fiancé was hurt two days ago in a climbing accident in the Cairngorms. Fairly seriously too, according to her – the man he was with was killed.'

'How awful,' Vicky said.

'So the wedding has had to be postponed, and they're now thinking about December rather than September. And if not December then January, the final date depending on the progress he makes. He broke both legs and damaged his pelvis.'

'I take it, then, that Miss Cobb will be continuing in Furs till close to the new wedding date?'

'That's what she wants to do, and has every right to do, not having yet handed in her notice.'

It was a setback, but only a temporary one, Vicky told herself. And the position, when it did fall vacant, was still hers, that was the main thing. She would just have to bide her patience a while longer than she had expected.

Her big worry, the one she had been brooding about when Miss Elvin appeared, remained Ken's spending. He could not seem to hold onto cash; if he had it, he spent it. He had almost completely gone through the money he had got for the Armstrong Siddeley; she had winkled that out of him the previous night. And when that lot went, he would be reduced to what he received from the public assistance, and which would have to be handed over to his mum anyway towards the upkeep of the house.

She had reminded him forcibly that she'd meant what she had threatened: if he returned to burglary, she would inform the police, and it would be prison for him. He reacted by growing tight-lipped, then changed the subject. But before he had been able to do the latter she had seen in his face that he believed her.

Miss Elvin had been well aware of how much Vicky had been looking forward to moving to Furs, and had not at all enjoyed being the bearer of ill tidings. She hated disappointing people once she had promised them something, and even though the cause of this disappointment had nothing to do with her she still felt somehow responsible.

Vicky stared at what had been a slice of tomato. The eighths had become squashy sixteenths. She looked up. Miss Elvin had started speaking again.

'I'll tell you what. I'll put it to the powers that be, to see if they're agreeable, that your wage is put up to the two pounds you would have got in Furs from the date you were supposed to go there. I'm sure that would be some compensation for having to wait to move until December or January.'

'That would be marvellous!' Vicky exclaimed. How kind of Miss Elvin to think of that.

'I'm not promising anything, mind, but I'll have a word in the proper place and hope to twist an arm or two.'

Shortly afterwards Miss Elvin left the canteen feeling better than when she had entered. She was pleased she had had that idea; it salved her conscience a little.

The trick would be to pull it off.

It was early Monday morning and Vicky was making for work. Clattering down the stairs she turned into the street, heading for her nearest tramstop. She was almost at the end of the street when Neil appeared, clutching to his chest a white paper bag. When they came alongside one another, she stopped, as did he.

The delicious smell emanating from the paper bag was mouth-watering and unmistakable. 'Hot rolls, nothing better first thing.' Vicky smiled.

'Not only rolls, but baps as well.' He smiled back.

'Special treat, is it?' she asked, knowing how hard up the Setons were, and how every farthing counted.

Neil nodded. 'My exams start the day. Mum said I could have whatever I fancied for my breakfast, and I chose these,' he replied.

stairs, which means his job will be falling available,' Miss Elvin said.

A job for Ken! Her disappointment vanished, to be replaced by elation. She jumped for joy.

'Of course I must interview him first, make sure he's suitable,' Miss Elvin added.

'Ken's very hard-working and conscientious. You won't find anyone better,' Vicky blurted out.

Miss Elvin smiled at Vicky's enthusiasm. 'If he's anywhere near as good a worker as you, we won't have any complaints. So you're saying he *would* be interested?'

'Definitely.'

Miss Elvin glanced at an open diary in front of her. 'Then ask him to come and see me tomorrow morning. Ten o'clock be all right for him?'

'He'll be here,' Vicky stated emphatically.

'I'll look forward to meeting him.'

Vicky left Miss Elvin's office feeling as though she were walking on air. To hell with her own disappointment about not getting her pay rise until December or January. This more than made up for it. If the job came off, and Miss Elvin had more or less indicated it was certain that it would, she and Ken would be working in the same department for the next four or five months, seeing each other every week day. And afterwards, when she moved to Furs, they would still be able to come to work together, and go home the same way.

And . . . She stopped dead in her tracks. With him employed again, they could set a date for their engagement, and eventual wedding. She was so excited! She was bursting to tell Ken about this stroke of good fortune.

That evening, when she returned from Copland and Lye, instead of going directly to her house, as she normally did, she went instead to Ken's. His mother informed her he was down in the back court.

There she found Ken helping a couple of lads from the street mend their bogey that had been broken in a crash. The bogey consisted of an old stout orange box fixed on a plank of wood. At the front and rear of the plank were single crossbars below which had been attached pram wheels. The front crossbar, for guiding purposes, was able to swivel left and right, tugged in either direction by a loop of rope that ran back to the orange box, the latter being the cockpit. The rear crossbar was immobile.

Ken, having nothing to do all day, had been feeling bored, when, looking out the kitchen window, he had spied the boys trying to mend their broken bogey. He had come down to offer assistance, because he had nearly always kept a bogey himself as a young lad, and was a dab hand at their construction and repair.

'Hello, pet,' Ken said to Vicky, waving a hammer at her in greeting.

She did not want to break the news to Ken with the two boys squatting beside him, earwigging in. 'Come over here a minute, I've got something to tell you,' she said excitedly.

'I'll be right back, lads,' Ken muttered to the boys, and tossed the hammer to the nearest one. Now what was this all about? he wondered as, rising, he followed Vicky to another part of the back court.

'I've got you a job at Copland and Lye's. You've to go for an interview at ten tomorrow morning,' she said in a rush of words.

This was so out of the blue it rendered Ken temporarily speechless.

'Well?' Vicky queried with a broad smile.

He automatically groped in a pocket for his cigarettes. All he had was a fag end, which he lit using the Ronson Vicky had given him.

'What sort of a job? And how have you managed to get it for me?' he asked at last.

She recounted her chat with Miss Elvin, saying that Miss Elvin had more or less promised him the job. All he had to do was turn up on time, looking smart, and the job was his. Now how about that?

'What does it pay?' he asked.

'The other men in the department get thirty-seven and six.'

Ken scratched his chin. That was seven and six more than Vicky was getting as a female packer and dispatcher, but half a crown less than the counter assistants were getting, which meant that Vicky would be earning more than him when she moved to Furs. Quite a bit more once her two per cent commission was taken into account.

She stared at his face. She had been expecting jubilation, not this expression of dour introspection. 'What's wrong?'

He shrugged. 'I know they say you shouldn't look a gift horse in the mouth and all that, but thirty-seven and a kick a week! It's pocket money beside what I was earning before.'

She knew he was referring to the proceeds of his burgling rather than what he'd been bringing home from Agnew's. 'It's an *honest* thirty-seven and six, Ken, that's the difference,' she retorted.

'I still won't get fat on it.'

She blew up. Of all the ungrateful sods! 'If that's how you feel, then hell mend you!' she spat, and stormed away.

She had just reached his back close when he caught up with her, stopping her by grabbing her arm. 'Here, don't take it like that. I was only passing comment.'

She turned to stare coldly at him, and did not reply.

'I'll be pleased, no grateful, to take the job if it's offered. And, presuming it is, thank you for getting it for me, Vicky, it's a life saver.' He smiled.

Her anger died as quickly as it had flared up. This was more like it.

'Packing and Dispatch needs only be a beginning for you at Copland and Lye, Ken. There's no reason why you shouldn't become a supervisor or counter assistant in time or, who's to say, even a buyer! Now they earn really good money.'

'That's how I'll look at it then,' he replied.

'You've got the brains to go up the ladder. We've just got to get you back on the first rung,' she said.

He hooked his arm in hers. 'Let's away to your house and discuss it further. Tell me all about Miss Elvin. And what do you think I should wear tomorrow?' he asked, knowing full well that she would adore talking about what he should wear and say and how he should conduct himself. But it continued to niggle him nonetheless. Grafting again was one thing, earning less than his lassie soon would be quite another. It was hardly manly, and if there was anything he prided himself on it was being that.

For her part Vicky soon forgot about his initial reluctance, ingratitude almost. Providing everything went all right tomorrow, and it surely would, then Ken would be working again, earning an honest wage. Och, but life could be lovely right enough, she thought. And it was the dark patches that made the bright ones seem even brighter.

It was Ken's first day in Packing and Dispatch, and Vicky had connived it so that it was she who showed him around. As of yet, the rest of the department, including Mr Ferrier, did not know Ken was her boy-friend but, as they had no intention of keeping it a secret, the others soon would.

The overall Ken was wearing had belonged to Alistair Gillies and was several sizes too small for him. Vicky had not been able to stop herself giggling when she'd seen him in it, thinking he looked ridiculous. He was getting a new one, he'd told her huffily when her giggling had subsided, Mr Ferrier had promised him.

Vicky indicated a squat stack of boxes. 'This is another consignment of chandeliers that has just arrived from Italy. I put the last lot together,' she said. She selected a box from several standing by the main stack, and opened it to show Ken the dismantled pieces within. The many-faceted pieces of crystal caught the light from the bulb above their head, and sparkled. Golden rays shot out in all directions.

'It's beautiful, don't you think?' she asked.

'Oh aye, but nowhere near as beautiful as you.' He smiled back.

'Patter merchant!' she accused.

'Not at all, just telling the truth.'

It was patter, but she loved it nonetheless.

'How much would a chandelier like that cost in the shop?' Ken asked.

She told him and, eyes opening in surprise, he whistled.

He glanced again at the contents of the open box, and a sudden thought made him laugh. 'Here, can you imagine one of these chandeliers hanging in a house in Parr Street?'

Vicky also laughed. 'Not on your Nellie Duff!'

Still laughing, they moved along the aisle they were in, to stop before an already opened, and partially unpacked container. Inside the container were rank upon rank of items each individually wrapped in blue tissue paper. Curious, Ken unwrapped one to reveal a large glass.

'This is heavy,' he said, amazed at its weight.

'It's a whisky glass, also crystal.'

He twisted it one way, then the other, so that it sparkled as the pieces of chandelier had done. 'You'd have to be gey rich to be able to fill this right up to the brim every time,' he said, being used to thimble glasses, or small tumblers, when drinking whisky.

'Och, you don't fill it up to the brim, daftie. Even with a mix it should never be more than a third to a half full.'

He made a mental note of that, in case he was ever – *when* he was, he corrected himself – in company where such glasses were used.

'Well, well, you live and learn,' he murmured.

Vicky then showed him other crystal articles that the shop stocked, all of which were in that particular section. There were candle holders, bowls, ornaments, vases, various types of dishes and a whole range of glassware, ranging from champagne flutes to brandy goblets.

'I'm impressed, I have to admit it,' Ken said when they reached the end of the crystal ware.

'And the crystal is only a tiny part of what's down here,' Vicky told him.

He thought back to the whisky glass. The price of that alone was more than he was being paid in a week.

'It's just like Aladdin's Cave,' Vicky added.

He glanced around, confirmed they were out of sight of the others in the department and swept Vicky into his arms. He kissed her, and as he did so his right hand strayed down to grasp her crotch.

'And what if like Aladdin I should say open sesame?' he

whispered in her ear nearest him when the kiss was over.

She wriggled free. 'Open sesame or not, that cave stays shut, at least while we're at work.'

'Spoilsport!' he hissed.

'Do you want to get us both fired on your first day here!' she chided, but only half-heartedly, for despite her protestations, she had rather enjoyed that.

'I love you,' he whispered.

'And I love you too,' she whispered in return. Then, on a sudden impulse, she took his head between her hands and kissed him deeply, her tongue darting in and out and entwining with his. 'You don't know what you do to me,' she groaned, pulling herself away from him again.

'I do, for you do the same to me.'

She shivered to hear that. 'We'd better get on. I've thousands of things to show you yet.'

He was already impressed, but became more and more so. Vicky was right, it was Aladdin's Cave, stuffed to overflowing with gorgeous and often costly items. He was left wondering how all these many and varied objects were accounted for.

It was a Tuesday night, and Ken had promised to take Vicky to the pictures. It had been arranged between them that he would pick her up at half past six, which was when he duly presented himself. He found her ready, waiting and anxious to be on their way.

He did not say anything till they reached the close mouth, and there he stopped her with a sheepish look on his face. 'I'm afraid the flicks are out tonight.'

She stared at him in consternation. She had been looking forward to this. 'Why?'

Embarrassed, he cleared his throat. 'I've only got enough money left for my tram fares to and from work for the rest of the week. Other than that I'm skint,' he confessed.

'But it's only Tuesday! How can you be skint already?'

He stuffed his fists into his trouser pockets. He felt guilty, like a wee boy caught with a hand in the sweetie jar. He mumbled incomprehensibly.

'I didn't hear that?' Vicky snapped.

He mumbled a second time.

'And I didn't hear that either!' she snapped again, more loudly than before.

'I said I played a couple of games of snooker last night, and lost,' he retorted.

Vicky took a deep breath. She could have sloshed the silly bugger. 'How *much* did you lose?' she demanded.

'Half a sheet.'

'Ten shillings! But that's most of what your mum gives you back from your wages.'

'I thought I could win,' he said angrily and, noticing an empty tin can within tempting range, he kicked it, to send it rattling right across the street onto the opposite pavement.

'You must be soft in the head to gamble when money's so hard to come by nowadays,' she admonished.

'I'll remind you it wasn't always like that with me. It's not so very long ago I was used to spending what I wanted without having to think twice about it. And when you've grown accustomed to having money to burn it's a difficult habit to break,' he replied bitterly.

He had a point there, it *must* be difficult for him, she thought. Nonetheless, he would just have to get a grip on himself and live within his means.

'Well, we're still going to the flicks, because I want to go. It'll just have to be my treat that's all,' she said.

He refused to meet her gaze. 'Aye, all right then. As you're determined to go.'

'I am.'

She crooked her arm for him to take, which he did. And they started along the street.

'I'm sorry for letting you down,' he told her after a while.

'It's not me you let down, Ken, but yourself. You've just got to stop chucking your money about as if it's going out of fashion. You might have got used to having money to burn, but that was only for a relatively short period. A period which is now over, a fact you're going to have to accept.'

Ken sighed. That was easy enough for her to say. She

hadn't been in the position he had. Fags, booze, virtually anything – if he had wanted it, he got it. That was hard to put by for ever, to go back to worrying about tuppences and thruppences.

Vicky enjoyed the main feature, as she had known she would – a love story that soon had her groping for her hanky. Ken preferred the B picture, a thriller with lots of action and rather gory in places.

When they came out again the upset of Ken's losing ten bob at snooker had been forgotten. Vicky, having enjoyed a good cry, was in a marvellous mood.

'Now you're in work once more, don't you think it's time we set a date?' she said to Ken about halfway home.

'Set a date for what?' he asked, turning to stare blankly at her.

'Us getting married.'

'I can't afford to get married, not on what I'm earning!' he exclaimed.

'We can afford to be married, if we take my wages into account.'

'No wife of mine is going out to work, it's not right for a wife to do that,' he said adamantly.

'Oh, Ken, that's the old-fashioned view. It's well accepted nowadays for the wife to work. At least till kiddies come along, and we can ensure they don't until we decide we're ready for them.'

He adjusted his glasses, a gesture he made when angry or upset. 'I am not old-fashioned,' he replied tightly, clearly miffed.

'Times are changing, Ken, and we've got to change with them to survive. We don't want to end up like the poor dinosaur, do we? Look what happened to them – they didn't move with the times, didn't adapt, and became extinct as a result.'

He turned to stare at her. Vicky never ceased to amaze him. She could come out with the damnedest things!

'I hadn't exactly seen myself as a dinosaur,' he admitted.

'So you'll set a date then?'

He considered the question. 'I can't until I know what

the housing situation is like. I'll tell you what. Next Saturday, after work, I'll pop into various factors' offices and find out,' he prevaricated.

'That's a good idea, put us on their waiting lists. But of course we can go ahead and still get married without having our own house.'

'How do you mean?'

'There's no reason the pair of us can't stay with your parents. For the time being anyway. Until a house of our own comes along. I'm sure they wouldn't mind, and would appreciate the extra cash coming in.'

He could see that Vicky had thought this through. 'It's a possibility I suppose,' he admitted reluctantly.

'So what date would you fancy?'

'Hold your horses. We have to get engaged first.'

'Then let's get engaged now, tonight,' she said.

'No, not until I have a diamond ring to put on your finger.'

'It's not necessary, Ken. I've said that to you before, and meant it.'

'It's maybe not necessary to you, but it is to me. When we get engaged, it'll be with a diamond ring and a bit of a party,' he said stubbornly.

He had a blinking fixation about this diamond ring, she told herself. And they *cost*. The daft thing was this was the wrong way round. It was usually the woman who insisted on the niceties. 'It doesn't have to be a big diamond does it?'

'Not at all, just as long as it's real.'

'And when we get the ring, you'll set the date then?' she prompted.

'I'll set the date for the wedding the day we get engaged,' he promised.

'All right. But swear to me that from here on in there will be no more stupid wasting of money on snooker and the like? What money we can save goes towards that diamond ring?'

'I swear.'

She hugged his arm. 'We can get it from the jewellery

department at work, we'll get staff discount,' she said.

He thought of the jewellery department at Copland and Lye. Outside opening hours everything was kept in a vault, every piece checked in and out. Security was as tight as a midge's bum.

She would inquire about the price of suitable rings during her tea break next morning, Vicky thought. She wanted to know just how much they needed, so she could try and work out how long it was going to take them to save up for one. She would have been happy to settle for a plain nine-carat gold wedding band, but if he had his mind set on giving her an engagement ring, then that was how it would have to be.

Vicky lay with the hot sun beating on her face and exposed arms and legs. She and Ken were having a wee day out, picnicking on the banks of Loch Lomond, and had just made love. Her nicks were off, and in her handbag, which meant she was naked underneath her skirt. She felt marvellously wanton and very, very satisfied.

The brae they were on was called Conic Hill. Below them was the loch and, out into the loch, Inchfad Island. Ken, naked to the waist, sat smoking, staring into space.

They were in a dip carved into the brae, with trees behind and around them. They had walked there from the bus stop several miles away, deliberately searching out a secluded place where they could be quite alone together and make love.

Vicky blinked open an eye, to stare at Ken. He was lost in a dwam. 'What are you thinking about?' she asked lazily.

'The overtime rota at work.'

'Why that?'

'I was considering asking Mr Ferrier to put me onto it,' he replied.

Vicky gave a low laugh and pulled herself up onto an elbow. 'Don't bother, he'll only turn you down. Overtime is reserved for the long-serving members of the department, it's a sort of perk.'

Ken grunted, as if this was news to him. But it wasn't;

he had already inquired about the overtime situation.

'Pity about that, for I was thinking if I could get on the overtime rota it would mean more money coming in, and the more money coming in the sooner I can get your diamond ring, and we can become engaged and set a date for the wedding,' he replied, and blew a perfect smoke ring at the island.

Vicky chewed her lip, then shook her head. 'It's a good idea, Ken, and certainly one I'd be all for, but Mr Ferrier just wouldn't entertain putting you on the rota when you've hardly been there five minutes.'

A swallow dived and zoomed and skimmed the placid surface of the loch. Out beyond the island a rowing boat with what appeared to be some anglers in it had appeared.

Vicky stared at Ken, wanting him to make love to her again. She watched, fascinated, as a trickle of perspiration ran down his left shoulderblade. If she'd been closer, she would have licked it off with her tongue.

'He might not give me overtime if I ask him, but what about if you do? Now there's a thought,' Ken said. This was what he'd been leading up to all along.

'You mean give me overtime?'

'No, *you* ask him to give it to *me*. He thinks the world of you, Vicky, and it was only the other morning you boasted you could twist him round your little finger when you had a mind.'

It was true. She had said that. Just as it was true that Mr Ferrier had a soft spot for her. Nothing dirty – he wasn't at all like that – but because she was such an excellent worker.

'Well?' Ken asked.

'I could explain the overtime was to help us get engaged and married. It's possible he might make an exception because of that,' Vicky replied.

Ken threw away the remains of his cigarette and crawled over the few feet separating them. He glanced round at the anglers, but they were so far off as to be no more than dots. 'Two nights a week would be ideal. See what you can do,' he said, and removed his glasses.

Smiling, he took her in his arms.

•

'All right lads, time to pack it in and go home,' Mr Ferrier called out from the door of his office.

Ken finished off the knot he was tying and snipped the string. The parcel he'd just made contained curtain material and was to go to an address in Fife. He would stencil the address on when he returned next morning.

There was an eerie atmosphere in the department when the rest of the shop was closed, a hushed stillness that made Ken feel he should be tiptoeing through it. There were four of them working late, including Mr Ferrier. The only other person in the building was Mr Broadley, the night-watchman.

Ken took off his new overall, and put on his jacket. The next few minutes would tell him what he wanted to know.

'So how did you enjoy your first dose of overtime?' Larry Elder asked. Larry was in his fifties, and had been with Copland and Lye man and boy.

'Makes it a long day,' Ken replied.

Larry grinned. 'It does indeed, but you'll soon forget that when you get your wages on Friday, eh?'

'Wait till you've been married a couple of years, you'll be thankful of the break away from the wife,' Iain Coats called out, and all those within hearing burst out laughing. Iain was married to a big fat woman who, according to him, was an awful nag. He'd have worked late every night given the chance.

Ken glanced over to where Vicky's overall was hanging. He hadn't been wrong in thinking that she would get Ferrier to put him on the overtime rota, God bless her cotton socks! But it could still be all for nothing.

Ken, Iain Coats, Larry Elder and Maurice Webster collected together, chatting amongst themselves, till Mr Ferrier joined them. The supervisor led them in the direction of the staff exit.

At the exit they found Mr Broadley waiting. 'It's pelting down outside,' he said.

Iain Coats swore.

'Is it just a shower, do you think?' Mr Ferrier asked.

'If it's a shower, it's a gey long one, it started more than an hour ago,' Mr Broadley replied.

'No use waiting then. Goodnight, Mr Broadley.'

'Goodnight, Mr Ferrier. Goodnight all,' Mr Broadley said.

The rest of the goodbyes were said, and Ken stepped out into the teeming rain. There was no check, he thought jubilantly. *There was no check!*

During normal working hours there were spot checks at the staff door on all those leaving, and during the hours of work there were always so many folk to-ing and fro-ing that it was rare to be alone and unobserved for even the shortest length of time. And sometimes when you thought you weren't being observed, you actually were. In short, it wasn't impossible, but highly dangerous, to attempt to steal.

But on overtime, as he had now proved, stealing would not only be possible but downright bloody easy. A real dawdle. As long as he kept it small, pocket-sized, there should not be any trouble.

Ken decided that he would do a second night without taking anything, just to make sure that the non-check at the staff door hadn't been an aberration on Broadley's part because it was raining. But he doubted that it had been an aberration. Ferrier was such a thorough person that he would probably, almost certainly, have reminded Broadley.

He had briefly toyed with the idea of sending himself parcels through the firm, and stealing that way. But he had quickly abandoned the plan when he'd learned of the in-built tally system with the post office. If he had sent himself parcels, his name would have continually popped up on the postal payments sheets, and it would have been bound eventually to have been seen by someone. If that happened, two and two would swiftly have been put together.

From now on he could stop the penny pinching. Jesus, the argument he'd had with Vicky to get her to agree to that picnic at Loch Lomond – you'd have thought it was going to cost pounds, rather than a couple of bob, the way she'd carried on. And she mustn't find out about his stealing during overtime shifts. She'd stop him if she did, which was the last thing he wanted.

He cursed as some water ran down his neck. What an awful night! he thought. Then, smiling, he corrected himself. It might be belting cats and dogs, but as far as he was concerned it was a lovely night. A really smashing one.

Vicky, Neil and Ken were having a rip-roaring celebration. A letter had arrived at Neil's house that morning, informing him he'd won a Corporation grant. It was definite; he'd be going to Glasgow University in the autumn to start reading Law.

They were in the Argyle Arms, the nearest pub to Parr Street. Quinn, the landlord, was a ferret-faced Irishman reputed to have connections with the IRA.

Ken lurched to his feet, and stood swaying. 'Another round, eh?' he slurred.

Vicky was thoroughly enjoying herself but considered that they had had enough to drink. 'I think we've had sufficient,' she said.

'Sufficient, is it!' Ken replied, imitating Vicky's tone, and winking at Neil. 'Sufficient my bumbaleeree,' he added.

Neil hiccupped. His head was swimming and he was beginning to feel queasy. But he didn't want this to end. Or, to put it another way, he didn't want to lose Vicky's company. 'I'll have another pint,' he said.

'Stout lad,' Ken beamed, and staggered across to the bar.

It *was* a celebration after all, Vicky reminded herself. She just hoped Ken wasn't going to be sick. Mr Quinn would take a dim view of that, and he had been good to let her in, knowing she was under age.

Reaching over, she placed a hand on one of Neil's. 'All of Townhead is fair bursting with pride at what you've achieved, I hope you know that,' she told him.

'I had to go to uni, for my dad's sake,' he replied.

'He would have thought the world of you, Neil. Winning a Corporation grant is a huge achievement.'

Neil lowered his eyes, thinking about his dad, remember-

118

ing. 'I only wish he could have hung on, to share today with me, to know that I'd be going to university.'

Vicky squeezed his hand. 'They say that God moves in mysterious ways. Perhaps he took your dad to give you that added motivation to win a grant,' she murmured.

Neil glanced up at her in surprise. He had never thought of it that way before.

'You know something, Neil, you're a fine young man who's going to make some lassie a grand husband one day,' Vicky said.

'Pimples and all?' he replied ruefully.

'Och, you'll grow out of those. A couple of years from now you'll have forgotten you ever had them.'

He prayed that she was right about that. Dear, lovely, darling Vicky. He worshipped the ground she walked on.

Ken returned with a trayful of pints *and* whiskies. 'May as well be hung for a sheep as a lamb,' he said, getting a dig in at Vicky. He laid the tray down, slopping beer from the pints onto the tray and table.

Vicky was about to make a caustic retort when suddenly, as a result of the pints she'd already consumed, she had the overwhelming urge to be elsewhere. She hurriedly excused herself, and left the two men, weaving her way through tables and chairs, heading for the ladies' toilet at the far end of the pub.

'Here, these are *large* whiskies!' Neil exclaimed.

'And why not? It isn't every day you win a grant to the university,' Ken replied.

'But the *expense*, Ken!'

Ken glanced after Vicky, saw her disappear through the toilet door, then turned again to Neil. 'Money's no object with me, my old son,' he said.

Neil frowned. 'What do you mean?'

Normally Ken wouldn't have let Neil into his secret, he wouldn't have let anyone into it. But the alcohol had loosened his tongue, making him want to boast. He beckoned Neil closer. 'I'll tell you something if you promise not to mention it to another soul, particularly Vicky – she'd have a canary if she found out,' he whispered.

'I promise,' Neil replied, puzzled.

'Word of honour?'

'Cross my heart and hope to die if I don't.'

That was good enough for Ken. It was the vow they'd aye taken as children; to break it meant the breaker would die a horrible death, eaten slowly alive by thousands of man-eating spiders, or some such.

He produced his wallet and from it took a wad of notes. 'What do you think of that lot?' he demanded.

Neil gaped. He could see that there were only a few single notes in the wad; the rest were all fivers. 'What did you do, rob a bank?' he replied.

'Closer than you think,' Ken answered and, sniggering and smirking, he told Neil about the stuff he was taking from Copland and Lye's and flogging elsewhere.

'Careful you don't get caught,' was all Neil could think of to say when Ken had finished.

Ken tapped his nose. 'Not me, I'm far too fly.'

Ken nicking stuff! He wouldn't have believed it if he hadn't heard it from the horse's mouth, Neil thought in wonder.

Everything had become hazy for Ken, he was in a rosy land, floating along on a comfy white cloud.

'Vicky wouldn't understand, not at all,' he said, and belched.

Neil thought of Vicky's touching his hand only a few moments since, and her talk about his making some lassie a grand husband. If only that lassie could be her.

'You and Vicky have been going a while now, I must say. Knowing you, I'm surprised it's lasted so long. I thought you would have moved on to pastures new,' Neil said.

'The grass isn't always greener, Neil. I'll tell you this, I've had some good fucks in my time, some really tremendous ones. But Vicky? She's the best of them all,' Ken slurred.

Cold anger erupted in Neil. How dare Ken discuss Vicky in that way! It just wasn't done, not when you supposedly had feelings for the girl.

'You get inside her and, well, it's even better than drink,' Ken said, and laughed.

Neil's face had gone stony. He wanted to punch Ken, to lay the bastard out flat.

'You did me a great turn when you put me onto her, I'll never forget that,' Ken went on.

Ken ran fingers through his hair, leaving it sticking up in places. Whew! but he was pissed. When he peered at Neil through his glasses, he saw two Neils.

'She's got a gorgeous body, tits like melons, thighs you could cry over. And her arse, Christ! I could die for that arse.'

Neil's fists were so tightly clenched they were milk white right up to their wrists. It made him sick to hear Ken talk about Vicky as though she was just so much flesh. Why, she might have been a whore the way he was going on.

'But then you don't know a lot about women, do you, Neil?' Ken leered.

Neil shook his head.

'No doubt you'll learn at university, there'll be lots of willing crumpet there. Crumpet that laps up the intellectual type. Why, there'll probably be so many open legs on offer you won't know which pair to stick it up first.'

'I doubt if I'll ever be promiscuous,' Neil answered, voice trembling.

'Don't knock it until you've tried it, son,' Ken said, and laughed raucously, thinking that awfully funny.

'So are you going to go ahead and get engaged then?' Neil asked.

'Oh aye, no buts about it,' Ken replied.

He didn't deserve her, he *didn't*! Neil thought in despair, and self-pity, and outrage.

At the far end of the pub Vicky reappeared. Ken saw her, and peeled one of the single notes off his wad. 'Listen, I'd better not buy any more bevy or she might get suspicious. You buy the next couple of rounds, tell her it was a wee something you'd put by for a rainy day, or extra-special occasion,' he said, and thrust the pound note into Neil's hand.

Neil didn't argue. A couple more rounds meant even longer in Vicky's company.

Vicky heard the commotion and made in the direction it was coming from. She found Mr Scott, the general manager of the shop, Miss Elvin and Mr Ferrier grouped round an ashen-faced Ken. Other members of Packing and Dispatch were forming an outer ring, which she quickly joined.

Mr Scott, a small tubby man with a florid complexion, stabbed an accusing finger at Ken. 'Come on, Blacklaws, admit it. We know you've been stealing. We've had a stock check and a number of items are unaccounted for,' he said in a squeaky voice that had long since earned him the nickname 'Mouse'.

Ken took a step backward and came up against a pillar. 'I'm not admitting to anything. You can't prove it was me who stole these things,' he replied, half paralysed with fear.

Stealing . . . items unaccounted for . . . Vicky had given an involuntary gasp on hearing those words. She could not believe that he had been so stupid as to have done what he stood accused of. Surely this was a mistake, a coincidence?

'We've received information that you've been stealing. The stock check confirmed that information to be correct,' Mr Scott went on.

Mr Ferrier glanced sympathetically at Vicky. It was he who had received the phone call and taken its message to Mr Scott. Poor lass, he thought to himself.

'I don't know what information you got, but it's all lies, lies!' Ken replied, almost screaming.

'The missing items have all walked from this department since you joined it, that has already been proven. And there was no stealing going on in this department prior to your arrival, which has also been proven. It all adds up to one answer, and one only. You're the thief,' Mr Scott said.

'Admit it, Ken, it's the best way,' Mr Ferrier urged.

'I'm telling you, I'm innocent,' Ken gabbled desperately.

Vicky was looking directly at Ken, but he steadfastly refused to meet her gaze. It was that which told her that this was no mistake, no coincidence – that he was guilty.

'Mr Ferrier, ring the police,' Mr Scott instructed.

The police! Vicky thought in alarm. Once they became involved, the business of the burglaries was bound to come out, for Ken was sure to have left fingerprints in at least several of the houses he had broken into. And then there was that Arab, the one they had run into the night at Ferrari's. He'd clearly been a VIP, a diplomat even. If Ken was connected with that burglary, the authorities would throw the book at him. Why, he could be facing ten to fifteen years in prison.

She staggered where she stood. Ten to fifteen years – a lifetime! She couldn't let that happen to him, there had to be some way out of this.

That same way was obvious. To save him, she would take the blame on herself. They would not go hard on her. Why, the shop might not even prosecute, she being a girl and such a hard worker. She'd lose her job of course, but that was a small price to pay to keep Ken out of prison for such a horrendous length of time.

Ken was about to lunge past Mr Scott and attempt to make a run for it when Vicky spoke. 'He *is* innocent, Mr Scott, I'm the person you want,' she said.

Mr Ferrier, almost at his office door, stopped to turn and stare at Vicky, as did everyone present.

'You!' Mr Scott queried in amazement.

'I've no idea where your information came from, but it's incorrect. Maybe they've got mixed up between Ken and me because we're a lot together, but I'm the one who's been stealing from the department,' she went on.

'I don't believe that!' Miss Elvin exclaimed.

'It's true. Just as it's true that I've only been stealing since Ken started work here. It was all to help with our engagement and wedding, you see.'

That was the moment when Ken knew he should have confessed, said that Vicky was only trying to protect him. But he kept his mouth shut.

'Miss Devine, and you Miss Elvin, I think we'd better

proceed with this matter in Mr Ferrier's office,' Mr Scott said, quite thrown by this turn of events.

Vicky started for Mr Ferrier's office, with Miss Elvin and Mr Scott following behind.

'Do you want me to come also?' Ken croaked, but his voice was so quiet that nobody heard.

Once they were inside his office, Mr Ferrier shut the door, thinking to himself that he had never been so mistaken about someone's character. He would never have dreamed in a million years that Vicky was a thief.

Vicky stood with head bowed, hands clasped in front of her.

'Well, I don't know what to make of this at all,' Mr Scott said. He was well acquainted with Miss Elvin's report, and Mr Ferrier's report, on Vicky, and that she was scheduled to be promoted to Furs.

'I suppose the question is, do we prosecute?' Mr Scott asked Miss Elvin.

Miss Elvin was suddenly furious with Vicky as it sank in on her how badly Vicky had let her down. She had broken one of her own cardinal rules about queue jumping to give Vicky the job in Packing and Dispatch, and it was on her *personal* recommendation that Vicky had been accepted for Furs. And it was she who had got Blacklaws his job, entirely on account of Vicky. Why, she had bent over backwards at every turn for Vicky, and this was the result. Vicky had more or less spat in her face. How dare the little baggage, *how dare she!*

'I think dismissal would be punishment enough. Give her the sack, and let that be that,' Mr Ferrier said.

'Oh no! She's a thief, and therefore has to be tried by the law as such. That's only right and proper,' Miss Elvin hissed vehemently, determined on revenge.

Vicky's hopes, which had momentarily risen when Mr Ferrier had spoken, now plummeted.

'I don't know, she is a girl after all, and a young one too,' Mr Scott prevaricated, rubbing a hand over his pink and shining chin.

'Her sex and age have nothing to do with it. That she's a thief and has stolen from this shop are what's important.

You must give her over to the police, and prosecute,' Miss Elvin insisted.

Still Mr Scott hesitated. He had a daughter at home the same age as Vicky.

'Fail to prosecute and you'll only encourage others to try it on,' Miss Elvin said.

Mr Scott sighed. She was right of course. If he didn't prosecute, he would be failing in his duty. Crossing to Mr Ferrier's desk, he picked up the telephone. 'Put me through to the police,' he told the operator when she answered.

Miss Elvin flashed Vicky a venomous look of triumph. That'll teach you to make a fool of me, the look clearly said.

Vicky thought of her mum and dad – this was going to cut the feet right out from underneath the pair of them.

That night Neil turned into his close to discover that the gas light had gone out. And the one on the first landing too, he saw, glancing up at the half-landing, which was also in total darkness. He groped his way forward.

He had just reached the bottom stair, and was about to ascend, when he was suddenly grasped tightly by the arm.

'Hello, Neil, I'd like a word,' Ken's voice, hard and grating, said out of the darkness.

Fear clutched Neil's insides. Ken was here when he shouldn't have been, and he *knew*!

Neil tried to wrench himself free, but failed to do so. Ken literally dragged him into the dunny, a secluded section of the back close just before it opens out onto the back court, and a great favourite of courting couples because of that seclusion.

Neil gasped as Ken thrust him hard against a paint-flaking wall. 'Information received was what they said at Copland and Lye. Information fucking received,' Ken spat into Neil's face.

'I don't know what you're talking about,' Neil whimpered.

'Only one person in this world knew I was nicking from

the shop, and that was you. You're the only one I let on to,' Ken said.

'I'm still not with you, Ken?'

Ken hit Neil with the flat of a hand, knocking Neil's head first one way, then the other.

'Why?' he demanded.

Neil's fear dissolved, and his feelings all boiled up to come gushing out. 'Because I love Vicky and want her, and because she can't really mean anything to you. How can she when you talk about her as you did that time in the Argyle Arms? Why she could have been a slut and a whore the way you were going on.'

Ken took that in, then laughed, a low-pitched rasping sound that had a wild, skin-tingling quality about it.

'Oh, you stupid bastard, Neil, you stupid stupid bastard. Instead of getting me the jail, you've got her it instead,' he replied.

'Eh?'

'There's a lot more to this than you're aware of, so when I was accused Vicky stepped in and said it was her, that she'd been doing the stealing, so as to protect me.'

Neil closed his eyes. 'Oh my God!' he whispered.

'She'll be up before the sheriff and sentenced, tomorrow,' Ken added.

'Oh, my God,' Neil repeated.

Ken thought of Vicky in a jail cell with no knowing what sort of scum, and the fury that had been in him since he had realised that it had to be Neil who'd been in touch with Copland and Lye now erupted, filling him with awesome violence. He released Neil, then hit him as hard as he could. And hit him again.

Neil tried to defend himself, even to fight back, but, weakened by guilt, he was no match for the raging Ken, who, in a flurry of blows, overwhelmed him. Sobbing, Neil sank to the stone floor, thinking that, by doing so, Ken, considering he'd had enough, would surely stop.

But Ken didn't stop, he merely changed to using his feet rather than his fists. Neil's sobbing changed to a shrill scream as Ken's lashing foot caught him full in the genitals.

Pain such as he would not have believed possible, and which made what had gone before pale into insignificance, scalded through him.

He tried to turn over, but even as he did Ken let go with the other foot which, in turning, he went straight into. This also took him in the genitals, throwing him backwards to go banging into the wall behind.

Neil's fluttering hands tried to protect his crotch, to no avail. When the toe of Ken's shoe seemed to flatten his testicles, the shriek he gave was blood-curdling to hear.

When the red haze finally lifted from Ken, it was to find that he had kicked Neil unconscious. He was panting from exertion and wringing with sweat. He steadied himself against the closest wall while he regained breath.

Then he heard the sound of inquiring voices, and footsteps, on the stairs above, neighbours coming to investigate. Stumbling out into the back court, he ran to his own back close and disappeared inside.

Part Two

The Fallen God
1935–37

'. . . We make Gods of men and they leave us.'
OSCAR WILDE, *Lady Windermere's Fan*

Five

Vicky stared numbly out into the black night. She was still stunned by the sentence the sheriff had given her earlier. She had been hoping that the sentence would be suspended or, failing that, if she did go down, that she would get three months, six at the maximum. Sheriff Dunlop had had other ideas. The sentence had been three years, to be reviewed in two years' time, on her eighteenth birthday.

Vicky had managed to hold back the tears until she was out of the courtroom; then they'd come, in torrents. She had been escorted to the same cell in which she had previously been held while waiting to go before the sheriff, and there a hatchet-faced policewoman had told her that she would be taken to a borstal later that day. It had been nine p.m., and her tears had long since dried, when they finally came for her.

There were two of them, Detective Inspector Copelaw, a tall, prematurely bald man, and wpc Lundie. They had walked her out to the police car, where she had been instructed to sit in the rear with the wpc. The detective inspector drove.

Three years! The figure hammered in Vicky's brain and, although it was only mildly cold, she shivered all over.

Her mum and dad had been in court, as had Ken and Miss Elvin. Miss Elvin had gloated as Vicky was marched away; her mum and dad had been just as stunned as she was. Ken had been so shaken that he had had to sit down. He had watched her, his eyes never leaving hers, till she disappeared through the side entrance leading to the cells.

Vicky eventually roused herself when she smelled the unmistakable tang of the sea. 'Where are you taking me?' she asked in a dull, dispirited voice.

WPC Lundie glanced at her superior, who nodded. 'It's down the coast this side of Port Glasgow. It's a borstal institution called Duncliffe,' she replied.

Vicky ran a hand through her hair. She felt manky after her night in jail, and wondered if she would be able to get a bath and hair wash where she was going. 'Is it going to be awfully hard there?' she asked.

WPC Lundie's lips thinned. 'It won't be a Sunday school picnic, you can bank on that.'

Three years *without* Ken! How would she survive? Vicky thought in desperation and abject misery. She groaned and turned away from the WPC, burying her face in leather upholstery and imagining that the leather was Ken's cheek against her own.

Eventually the police car, having come cross country via Houston, joined the coast road and, as it did so, the moon broke through the heavy cloud layer above. Vicky listened to the muttering of the sea and soft sighing of the wind. Her mind was filled with images of Ken and the pair of them together.

'We're almost there,' Detective Inspector Copelaw said a little later.

Vicky sat upright in her seat. The brooding, forbidding pile she saw ahead appeared to be a small castle. Only two lights showed, like a pair of yellow eyes staring unblinkingly out into the night. Malevolent eyes, on watch.

Copelaw stopped the car in front of a set of heavy iron gates and gave a short sharp toot of the horn. A figure materialised out of the darkness; there was the rattle of a key being inserted into a lock and the gates swung open. As Copelaw took the car past the figure, Vicky saw that it was an old man stooped from either age or rheumatism, or perhaps both.

Detective Inspector Copelaw brought the car to a halt before some steps leading up to a door. 'All out,' he said.

Vicky found herself in a large courtyard, but just how large it was she could not quite make out. The old man appeared beside the car and politely asked them to follow him.

Inside the building he guided them by means of a torch, explaining as they went – for neither the detective inspector nor the WPC had previously been at Duncliffe during the hours of darkness – that this was how he made his rounds. The Head did not approve of wasting electricity. The old man wove his way through a maze of corridors. Eventually he paused at an oaken door and knocked respectfully.

'Come in, Strachan,' a female voice called out.

Vicky's initial impression of the room was of austerity. There was a bed in one of the corners, a desk, chair, a bookcase crammed with books, a standard lamp, desk lamp, and a rug on the stone floor. The walls were whitewashed brick. The ceiling had been plastered, and also white-washed.

The female sitting at the desk bordered on middle age; she was slim, with a finely chiselled face and hair cut in a pageboy style. Her eyes were the palest blue Vicky had ever seen.

Strachan knuckled his forehead. 'I've brought along the new arrival and her escort, as you told me to, Miss Ganch.'

'Wait in the corridor. This will only take a few moments,' Miss Ganch replied, voice crisp with authority. It was a voice used to being obeyed instantly, without question.

Strachan hurriedly left the room, quietly closing the door behind him. Miss Ganch waited till he was gone before extracting a printed form, with attached copy, from an already opened drawer in her desk.

'Name?' she demanded, looking directly at Vicky.

'Victoria Devine.'

'Victoria Devine, *miss*.'

Vicky swallowed hard. There was something about Miss Ganch that terrified her. 'Victoria Devine, miss,' she repeated.

Miss Ganch wrote Vicky's name onto the form and copy, then pushed them across her desk, glancing up at Detective Inspector Copelaw as she did so. Copelaw came to the desk and countersigned the form. He tore off the original, folded it and placed it in an inside pocket.

'Goodnight, safe return journey to Glasgow,' Miss Ganch said, dismissing the police.

Their business concluded, Copelaw and WPC Lundie left, and Vicky found herself alone with Miss Ganch, who was studying her in the most disconcerting manner.

'How old, girl?' Miss Ganch asked, after what must have been a full minute had slowly passed.

'Sixteen, miss.'

'Hmmh!' Miss Ganch murmured thoughtfully. She again reached into the open desk drawer and took out a second printed form and attached copy, which she spread in front of her, smoothing it flat with her hand.

'I am Miss Ganch. You are to be in my section. That means that from now on you belong to me. Understand?'

Belong! Vicky did not like the sound of that at all. 'Yes, miss,' she replied.

'This room, my room, is at the head of the dormitory where my girls sleep, where you will be sleeping from now on. Understand?'

'Yes, miss.'

'Have you eaten?'

'I had a corned-beef sandwich at around five o'clock, but nothing since.'

'Pity, for I'm afraid the kitchens here are closed. However, I do have a tin of digestives. You can have some of those.' Miss Ganch opened another desk drawer to produce the tin. She rose and, coming round to Vicky, handed it to her. Her stern features suddenly relaxed into a smile. 'Help yourself while I go and get your bits and pieces. I couldn't have them ready waiting for you as I didn't know what size you were. Thirty-six bra, I'd say?'

'Yes, miss.'

'I'm usually spot on about that,' Miss Ganch said, and walked from the room, leaving the door open behind her.

Vicky slumped where she stood. Miss Ganch might have been smiling latterly, but she did not trust that smile, not one little bit. Miss Ganch reminded her of a garden snake her brother John had briefly kept when a wee lad. The woman gave her the horrors just as that snake had done.

Mum, Dad and John – she hoped they were bearing up. They would all be worried sick about her, as would Ken. Three years! Her spirits sank again. But it probably would not be that long, she argued with herself. Her sentence was to be reviewed on her eighteenth birthday. If she kept her nose clean, which she had every intention of doing, she would surely be released then. That realisation brightened her a little.

She was surprised to find herself not only hungry but ravenously so. The digestives were delicious. She wolfed down half a dozen and had just started on yet another when Miss Ganch, still smiling, returned. She laid the pile of clothes she was carrying on her desk and placed the form she had previously put on the desk beside them.

'That form contains a list of what you've been issued. Check each item off by ticking it. If you agree you've got everything, sign the form in the first space provided. The second space is to agree the list I will now draw up of those clothes you're handing in and will be given back to you on your eventual release. Understand?'

'Yes, Miss Ganch.'

Miss Ganch took the tin of digestives from Vicky and replaced it in her desk. Sitting again, she made a pyramid with her hands, watching Vicky over the top of it while Vicky checked what she had been issued against the list.

'It's all here,' Vicky acknowledged and signed the form and copy.

'Now strip, and get into one of the nightdresses provided. I'll itemise what you take off once you've done so.'

There was a hiatus while Vicky glanced round, but the glance only confirmed what she already knew from her earlier scrutiny of the room: there was no screen, or anything else, to hide behind while she changed.

'Strip *here*, miss?'

'To the buff, everything,' Miss Ganch spelled out.

Vicky took off her jacket, then the maroon cardy that was a great favourite of hers and which her mum had knitted. Heart thumping, she started to unbutton her blouse. Miss Ganch did not even pretend to be doing something else.

Leaning back in her chair, she watched unashamedly. When Vicky reached her bra and knickers, she felt that she could not go on. It was so humiliating!

'Well?' Miss Ganch prompted, and the word was a threat, promising Vicky that something awful would happen to her if she didn't continue.

Vicky undid her bra and her breasts fell free. When it came to her knickers, she turned sideways on to Miss Ganch. As she pulled her knickers down and off, her face, neck and breasts flamed with embarrassment. She hurriedly put on the grey flannelette nightdress she'd been issued, thankful that the degradation was over.

Coming forward in her chair, Miss Ganch took the form Vicky had signed and separated it from its copy. She itemised what Vicky had taken off/first on one sheet, then on the other.

After Vicky had signed in the second space, agreeing that the itemised list was correct, Miss Ganch handed her the copy. 'Yours. Hang on to it.'

Miss Ganch reached into the drawer containing the tin of digestives and brought out a thin pair of cotton gloves, which she slipped on. 'This next bit is usually done by the nurse, but as she's off duty, and it has to be done as part of the admittance procedure, I'm afraid it's up to me. Please bend over my desk and lift your nightdress up over your buttocks.'

Vicky was aghast. 'What are you going to do to me?'

'I have to examine your rear passage for haemorrhoids – piles, that is – and also to make sure you're not trying to smuggle in anything you shouldn't that way. I also have to examine your vagina for signs of disease, and the smuggling reason as well.'

Vicky gagged.

'It's standard procedure. Every girl arriving at Duncliffe has to undergo it.' Rising, Miss Ganch came round to stand beside Vicky. 'Bend over and lift your nightdress.'

Slowly, Vicky bent over the desk and, even more slowly, rucked up her nightdress to expose her buttocks. She closed her eyes, and shuddered inwardly when Miss Ganch's hands

136

spread her buttocks. She choked back a sob when a probing finger entered her anus.

The finger stayed a lot longer than necessary, Vicky thought. And what a strange sensation it was, extremely uncomfortable and painful. She gave a sigh of relief when the finger was finally removed. Then she remembered that her vagina was also to be examined.

'Put your bottom against my desk, spread your legs, lift the front of your nightdress and lean backwards,' Miss Ganch said matter-of-factly.

When she was in that position, Vicky thought to herself that, if it had been degrading to be naked before Miss Ganch, how much more so it was to be as she now was. She shrank against the desk when her sex lips were prised apart. Feeling completely defiled, she wanted to wail in anguish. From behind what had been shut eyelids, she peeked out to see that Miss Ganch was on her knees peering up and into her. She groaned when a finger forced its way into her dryness. Please God, let this be over! she screamed inside her head.

Miss Ganch stood and removed her gloves, which she tossed onto the desk. 'Sorry about that,' she said.

Vicky didn't think she sounded sorry at all. The bitch had enjoyed it. She looked into Miss Ganch's eyes and saw an amused glitter there, and the glitter itself, a reflected sheen, again reminded her of John's garden snake.

Vicky had already dropped the front of her nightdress and now tugged it down as far as it would go, wishing it reached all the way to the floor instead of merely to her knees.

'Pick up your new issue clothes and follow me.'

When Vicky had the clothes cradled in her arms, she turned to discover Miss Ganch holding a torch similar to the one Strachan had used. Out in the corridor she went in the opposite direction to that from which Vicky had been brought and almost immediately they were into a dormitory.

The light from Miss Ganch's torch revealed the room to be narrow and fairly long. There were heavy curtains at the windows, all drawn. One of the sleepers, a girl on the left-hand side, was snoring loudly and rhythmically. It reminded Vicky of her dad. They came to the sole bed in the dormitory not occupied. 'Put your issue in there and be quiet about it,' Miss Ganch whispered, pointing to an empty wooden locker standing beside the bed.

Vicky worked by the light of the torch, bundling everything in as neatly as she was able.

'Into bed and asleep. Reveille's at five.'

Vicky climbed into the hard bed; it was so unyielding that she might have been lying on solid rock. The sheets were the roughest she'd ever come across. Miss Ganch, without uttering further, vanished from the dormitory and Vicky was plunged into Stygian darkness. Her skin was still crawling from what she had been through, the feeling of having been defiled still strong within her.

What terrible place was this? Would all the people in charge be like Miss Ganch? She prayed not. Oh Ken! she howled silently. Why had he been so stupid to steal from Copland and Lye! Why why *why*!!!

If it hadn't been for Miss Elvin, Mr Scott would not have prosecuted. But she could understand Miss Elvin reacting as she had; Miss Elvin had been made to look a right mug after all.

Gradually her heaving, jangled emotions quietened. She found solace in the snoring coming from the opposite line of beds. She pretended she was at home, listening to her dad. Finally, exhausted after the day's events, and thinking of Ken, she fell asleep to dream of him.

The shrill blast of the whistle pierced Vicky's brain, causing her to come awake with an exclamation and sit up straight in bed. The lights were on, and Miss Ganch was standing in the centre of the dormitory. She had a riding crop in one hand, the whistle in the other. She blew a second blast, at the end of which Vicky was the only one still in bed. All the other girls had been galvanised into action.

'Hurry! Hurry! Hurry!' Miss Ganch bellowed, and striding to the nearest window ripped its curtains wide open.

It was freezing at that time of the morning, and Vicky

saw that it was still dark out. She gaped to see that all around her girls were whipping off their nightdresses to reveal themselves nude and dressing in a flurry where they stood.

'Sweater and slacks, you'd better be quick about it,' the girl from the bed on Vicky's left whispered to her.

'Hurry! Hurry! Hurry!' Miss Ganch screamed, and ripped open more curtains.

By the time Vicky reached her plimsolls, nearly everyone else was ready and that included having made their beds and straightening their lockers. As each girl finished, she came to attention at the foot of her bed.

Vicky was acutely aware of Miss Ganch, again standing in the centre of the dormitory, glaring at her. She was the last to finish. Then she too came to the foot of her bed and took up a position of attention.

'You're allowed one day's grace, Devine, and one only. Starting tomorrow you'll be expected to have learned what's what. Understand?'

'Yes, Miss Ganch,' Vicky replied.

The riding crop shot out to point at a dark-haired girl whom Vicky judged to be fourteen or fifteen. 'You, McCrimmond, you were last. Prepare to receive punishment.'

McCrimmond gulped. Turning round, she bent over the end of her bed, presenting her bottom. Miss Ganch crossed to McCrimmond and the riding crop whistled through the air. The blow, when it landed, was a sharp crack. Vicky winced, thinking how painful it must have been.

'McCrimmond leads. Now go! Go! Go!' Miss Ganch shouted.

McCrimmond ran off through the dormitory door at the speed of a startled gazelle, the rest of the girls in pursuit. Vicky found herself in the middle of the pack as they jostled along corridors and down several flights of stairs. Eventually they left the building by a different entrance from the one she'd arrived at the previous night.

Dawn was breaking and she could spot several other packs of girls, heading in various directions. They descended steep stone steps onto a beach of golden sand. The sea was rough, crashing ashore to go hissing out again. The wind was gusting, sometimes drenching the runners in spume, other times whirling and eddying about them.

Vicky gritted her teeth. Already her lungs and legs were sore and she was having to struggle for breath. She was not used to sustained running – running for a tramcar had been her limit up until now. She dropped to the back of the pack, a glance over her shoulder confirming that Miss Ganch was bringing up the rear.

Miss Ganch suddenly darted forward to slash with the riding crop. A plump girl, who had been last in the pack, yelped, and spurted forward. After another two girls had been struck across the backside, Vicky got the message: to be last meant a stroke from Miss Ganch's riding crop.

They came to a clump of dunes dotted with marram grass, which they struggled up and over. Beyond the dunes was more beach, and then a formation of rock. At its highest the rock was about sixty feet off the ground, and it had to be climbed. Vicky was coughing and choking as she went up hand over hand.

Coming down the other side, she realised with alarm that she was now last and Miss Ganch was directly behind her. When the riding crop wasn't used on her bottom, she remembered what Miss Ganch had said in the dormitory: this was to be a day of grace for her *and her only one*. The run became a nightmare, but Vicky forced herself to complete it, knowing that she was going to have to do so the next day. She dreaded to think what the punishment for not doing so was.

The finishing point was the castle courtyard, and there the pack halted. Vicky collapsed to the ground, where she lay, chest afire, feeling as though she was about to die. Other packs arrived in the courtyard, six in all, a full complement being a hundred and twenty girls.

The sensation of impending death passed as Vicky's breath returned. She got back onto her feet, thinking that they would all be going off to breakfast now. She was wrong.

One of the women in charge barked out that they were to get in their lines, and the girls formed six lines, each line a section. Then began thirty minutes of gruelling physical jerks. The conclusion of the physical jerks found Vicky devastated. She swayed on the spot, a limp rag that had been squeezed and squeezed again.

'Dismissed!' the woman who'd conducted the physical jerks shouted, and instantly the lines broke up.

It *had* to be breakfast now, Vicky thought, for, despite her condition, she was ravenous. Again she was wrong. Her section returned to the dormitory, where they collected towels from their lockers. From there they trudged to an adjacent shower room, where they started stripping off.

Vicky caught sight of Miss Ganch watching her, and knew she was expected to follow suit. She stripped naked and joined the others in the showers. The water made her gasp – it was ice cold! The steam she'd seen rising didn't come from the water but the bodies it was battering against. Within seconds she was so cold that her teeth were chittering. She lathered herself with the poor soap provided; it had the feel and texture of candle wax. The water ceased abruptly and, thankfully, the showering ordeal was over.

Vicky scampered across to her towel and began briskly rubbing herself dry. Some of the girls were talking, and even laughing amongst themselves – so silence was not obligatory.

The last girl dressed got a swipe across the buttocks from Miss Ganch's riding crop, then they were marched off down the corridor, arms swinging, military fashion.

This time it *was* breakfast. The dining hall was domed and had a wooden floor. Trestles had been laid out in six lines, each line for a section. The meal was served from a seventh line of trestles at the top of the hall, set square on to the others. Off to one side, and quite apart, was a circular table. Vicky guessed correctly that this was where Miss Ganch and the others in charge sat.

Whatever else she thought of Duncliffe, she could not accuse them of being stingy with their food, or 'scoff' as she heard it referred to by several of the girls. There was juice, cereal, boiled and fried eggs, bacon, sausages, kidneys, toast, plain bread, jam, marmalade, tea and cocoa. And you could help yourself to as much as you wished. Vicky devoured her heaped plate, then sat back, over her tea, to study the faces around her. It was her first proper chance to do so.

Some of the girls looked downright nasty, and she made a mental note to keep away from them. Others appeared pleasant enough, and she wondered what they'd done to end up in Duncliffe. Several were beauties, real crackers, a handful plain in the extreme, with one poor lassie so ugly that she made Vicky thank God that she hadn't been born like that. The remainder were middling, not too good-looking, not too plain.

Most of the girls chatted as they ate but, although a few curious glances were cast in Vicky's direction, no one started up a conversation with her. Nor did she with them, thinking that the wisest course for the moment.

When she went up for another cup of tea, Miss Ganch came over to her. 'Directly after breakfast you've to go to the Head's office. She wants to meet and assign you.'

Assign? 'Yes, Miss Ganch.'

Miss Ganch then gave Vicky directions on how to find the Head's office, after which she returned to her table.

Vicky was halfway through her second cup of tea when a bell rang. Immediately everyone rose and began filing from the hall.

Miss Ganch's directions had been explicit. Consequently Vicky had no trouble in finding the Head's office, which was in a small turret on the seaward side of the castle. The brass plate on the door said HEAD OFFICER. Vicky knocked and waited.

'Enter!' a voice cried out from within.

Vicky judged the woman behind the desk to be in her late fifties, possibly just turned sixty. She wore black-framed spectacles, and her pepper and salt hair was tied severely back in a bun. She had a wedding band on, but no engagement or eternity ring.

'I'm Mrs Meehan, you call me Head. Understand?'

'Yes, Head,' Vicky replied.

The Head picked up a manilla folder, opened it and carefully scrutinised the contents.

'Stealing eh?' she said, glancing up at Vicky.

'Yes, Head.'

The Head laid the folder, still opened, down in front of her. She studied Vicky, her eyes bright and penetrating. 'Steal anything, anything at all, while at Duncliffe and you'll rue it. Understand?' she said softly.

Soft, but deadly, and meaning every word, Vicky thought. 'Yes, Head.'

'Do *anything* you shouldn't while at Duncliffe, and you'll rue it. Tough nuts don't stay tough here for very long, we have tried and tested ways of dealing with them. Understand, Devine?'

'Yes, Head.'

'I hope you do, for your sake.'

Vicky shivered and went prickly all over.

The Head gazed at the top sheet in the opened folder. 'Three-year sentence, to be reviewed on your eighteenth birthday. You're going to be with us quite a while then.'

'Yes, Head.'

'Plenty of time to learn a useful skill, something to earn your living by when you're released. We have a number of courses on offer. Book-keeping for example.'

The Head paused and a small, cynical smile twisted the corners of her mouth upwards. 'But perhaps not that for a thief. Too tempting, eh?'

Giving no reply, Vicky lowered her eyes. How galling to be considered a thief, but that was what she'd branded herself, and what she now had to live with.

'We also train girls to be tailoresses, a popular course that, hairdressers, cooks, shorthand typists . . .' The Head broke off, her brow creasing in thought. 'Yes, shorthand and typing, we have a vacancy there. How would that suit you?'

'Just fine, Head,' Vicky replied. She would really have preferred to learn hairdressing, but considered it best to agree to the Head's suggestion.

The Head nodded her approval: Vicky learned quickly. 'Mrs Gardener is in charge of that course. I'll take you along and personally introduce you. Besides, there's something I want you to see on the way.' She closed the folder.

The Head walked with a limp, and Vicky saw that one leg was shorter than the other. She wondered if the woman had been born like that or if it was the result of accident or disease.

The Head did not speak again until they had reached a black-painted door. Here she stopped and selected a key from a bunch dangling from a chain at her belt. 'This is the Black Room. Offenders who've spent time in it are rarely keen to repeat the experience.' She unlocked the door, which swung silently open, and a shaft of light knifed into the small room. The stench of defecation hit Vicky, causing her to take an involuntary step backwards. The smell was so strong that it threatened to make her gag.

The room was square, with no windows. There was no lightbulb, or gas mantle, or any other form of illumination. When the door was shut, and it had been especially fitted to exclude all light from the corridor, there was total darkness inside. The only form of ventilation was a grille set into the skirting board, just big enough to ensure there was some airflow.

A girl sat on an army-style cot staring at them. Her eyes were wide, her mouth trembling. Beside the cot was a brimming chamber pot.

'Hello, Kathy, how are you today?' the Head asked.

Kathy slid from the cot onto her knees, her hands coming together in supplication. 'Please, Head, let me out. I'll be a good girl, I swear. On my life I swear.'

'No more brawling?'

'No more, Head.'

There was a pause. Seconds ticked past. 'Maybe another twenty-four hours, just to make absolutely sure the lesson has been driven home.'

Tears burst from Kathy's eyes. 'Please, Head, please?' she whimpered.

'Tomorrow,' the Head decided and, slamming the door shut, locked it once more.

From inside the room came the muffled sound of crying.

'As I told you, we have tried and tested ways of dealing with troublemakers. Be warned,' the Head said and started off down the corridor. Vicky, appalled and thoroughly frightened by what she had just seen, hurried after her.

Vicky was out on her feet when she left the dining hall at the finish of tea, a meal as splendid and generous as the two preceding it. All she wanted to do was topple into bed and dream of Ken.

She thought about what a revelation the day had been, the most enjoyable part being the shorthand/typing class under Mrs Gardener, who was a gem of a person and a natural teacher. After shorthand typing it had been dinner, and then outside again, where she had learned that there was far more to Duncliffe than the castle building.

Miss Ganch had explained to her that it was the Head's policy for Duncliffe to be as self-sufficient as possible. Vicky was shown fields where potatoes and all manner of vegetables, root and otherwise, were grown, and fields where cattle and sheep were grazing. The girls did everything themselves – with the exception of slaughtering, which was done at a Port Glasgow abattoir – right down to making the jam and conserves from the soft fruit from the many berry bushes. They were allotted chores and, because some chores were harder than others, the sections took them in turn. Miss Ganch's section was currently in charge of the livestock, which included, apart from the cows and sheep, horses, pigs, ducks and chickens. Vicky's task had been to assist in mucking out the cow byre, and, pitchfork in hand, she'd been engaged in this all afternoon.

On entering the dormitory, Vicky was instantly aware of an atmosphere. She came up short when she saw a lassie rifling her locker – one of those whom at breakfast time she'd classed as a beauty. In a quandary as to what to do, she went slowly forward. 'Excuse me, that's my locker you're going through,' she said on reaching the end of her bed.

The lassie turned to face Vicky. She was clutching the second of the sweaters Vicky had been issued, the as yet unworn one, which she now held up against herself. 'You're the first newcomer into this dormitory for ages who's my size. One of my sweaters is threadbare, so I'm swopping it for yours. Hope you don't mind.' The girl smiled sweetly.

Vicky was flabbergasted. What barefaced cheek! 'I do mind,' she snapped.

The lassie raised an eyebrow, then twirled the sweater round her shoulders, tying it at its front by its sleeves. 'Tough tittie,' she replied.

Vicky was no pushover. Being brought up in Townhead, she had learned to fight for what was hers. In other circumstances she would have forced the matter, but all she could think of was the Black Room and Kathy, who had been incarcerated there for brawling. 'I'll complain to Miss Ganch,' she said.

The lassie threw back her head and laughed. A loud, gutsy, pealing laugh. 'You do that, dearie,' she said, and swaggered past Vicky out of the dormitory.

Fists clenched, Vicky watched her go.

'Don't even think about it. It wouldn't be worth it,' a voice said behind Vicky.

The speaker was the same girl who had spoken to Vicky that morning, advising her what to wear, and whom Vicky had subsequently spotted as being another member of Mrs Gardener's shorthand and typing class. The girl now came over and sat on Vicky's bed, while a muted hum of conversation began round the dormitory, the dorm having fallen silent during the confrontation.

'Her name's Muriel Mitchell, and that's her way of telling you she rules the roost round here,' the girl explained in a whisper.

Vicky sat across the bed from the girl. 'How do you mean?' she asked, also whispering.

'She has, shall we say, special privileges. If Muriel tells you to jump, it's best you do just that.'

Vicky frowned. 'I don't understand. How does she get away with it?'

'She's Miss Ganch's friend. *Special* friend, get my meaning?'

Vicky had to think about that, then the penny dropped. 'Are you saying they actually . . . together?'

The girl nodded.

Vicky remembered Miss Ganch's examination of her the previous night, and how much Miss Ganch had enjoyed it. At the time she had thought it pure sadism on Miss Ganch's part, causing her hurt and humiliation; now she knew there had been more to the woman's enjoyment than she'd imagined. Her skin crawled at the memory of that probing, exploring finger.

'By the by, I'm Tina Mathieson,' the girl said and extended a hand.

They shook. 'And I'm Vicky Devine, pleased to meet you.'

'How do you feel?'

'A total wreck.'

Tina smiled grimly, recalling her own first day at Duncliffe. 'It's hard going to begin with, but if you're healthy you'll soon get used to it, feel the better for it even,' she said.

Tina was considerably shorter than Vicky, and plumpish, with auburny hair. There was a warmness about her, and something more, something engaging, the combination of which Vicky took to right away. Vicky wondered what crime Tina had committed to be sent to Duncliffe; she looked as if butter wouldn't melt in her mouth.

'What about the others, are they friendly enough?' Vicky asked.

'Most of them, once they get to know you. But there are a few like Muriel about the place whom it's best, whenever possible, to keep well clear of.'

'And what's the situation with mail and visitors?'

Tina gave a sudden grin. 'There's a boyfriend then?'

'Yes. His name's Ken.'

Tina's grin turned to a sigh. 'Mine was called Robin, a real handsome lad, and a collier from Bellshill. But he's mine no more, he met someone else,' she said wistfully.

'Ken will wait for me, we're in love,' Vicky told Tina, and gave a little nod of the head as if to underscore that both points were so.

How many times had she heard that said! Tina thought cynically. Still, some chaps did wait, that couldn't be denied. She hoped Vicky's would be one of those who did.

'Visiting day is the last Sunday in every month, but as you're new you have to wait till the second visiting day comes round, and then it's only one visitor at a time. You're allowed to send a single letter out before that, but not to receive any. After your first visitor you can send one out every week, and receive as many as arrive. Incoming mail is handed round by Miss Ganch after tea on Saturdays, and only then,' Tina explained.

'I see,' said Vicky, working out how long it would be before she was due her first visitor. She groaned inwardly with the realisation that it was six and a half weeks away. And no mail before then either!

'What about days off, any of those?'

'Sunday, after obligatory church service, is your own to do with as you like. Saturday is different still; you don't attend your course on that day, but spend the entire working day, after the morning run and PT, doing chores.'

'Is there a run and PT on Sundays?'

Tina smiled and nodded.

'Well, when I leave here, I'm certainly going to be fit,' Vicky commented ruefully.

Muriel Mitchell, wearing Vicky's sweater, came back into the dormitory.

'If she's Miss Ganch's special friend, why didn't she just ask Miss Ganch for a new sweater?' Vicky asked in a whisper.

'She can't have been very bothered or she'd have had a new one long before now. She was probably only using the sweater business to show you she's top of the pecking order in this section,' Tina whispered back.

They talked for a while longer, Tina telling Vicky all the things she should know, and Vicky grateful for the information. She was also grateful for the tips Tina gave her, tips to make life at Duncliffe a little easier. But Vicky was most grateful of all for the fact that she had found a friend and ally.

Lights out in the evening was at eight forty-five. Vicky was already tucked up reading a book that Saturday night when

Miss Ganch strode into the dormitory to stand by the light switch.

'One . . . two . . . three . . .' Miss Ganch began counting.

There was a great scurrying as those not already in bed hastily dived into them. To have still been out on Miss Ganch's reaching the count of ten meant a trip to the bottom of the bed, bending over it and receiving a slash from the riding crop.

'Ten,' said Miss Ganch and the lights flicked off. The curtains were already drawn, McCrimmond having done this after tea. It was a task allotted to a different girl every week.

Vicky settled down. As Tina had said, she was beginning to get used to the strenuous life at Duncliffe. She still ached all over from the hitherto unaccustomed exercise and manual graft, but the aches were beginning to fade and should soon be gone altogether. She was amazed at her appetite; she would never have believed she would eat as much as she was now doing. She was putting it away at every meal as if she were a starving Irish navvy. She was certainly looking a lot better in the short time she'd been at Duncliffe. Thanks to the sea air, her city pallor was quickly replaced by a rosiness in the cheeks and general freshness of the skin.

It was about half an hour later, and Vicky was on the point of dozing off, having been thinking about Ken and remembering various times they'd had together, when she dimly heard the soft pitter-patter of feet. Someone off to the toilet, she thought.

'Vicky, are you still awake?' Tina whispered a few moments later.

'Yes.'

Vicky stiffened in alarm when her bedclothes were pulled aside and a body got in beside her.

'It's only me.'

'What are you doing in my bed?'

Tina chuckled softly. 'Don't worry, I'm not one of *them*. It's just easier to talk and be together this way.'

'We're not supposed to talk after lights out, you know that,' Vicky said, thinking of the Black Room.

'It's Saturday night, "pash" night, we can chat for hours if we want to, as long as we keep it fairly quiet, that is. And do other things too, like having a drink. Do you fancy one?'

'Wait a minute, what's this "pash" night?' Vicky asked.

'Pash, short for passion. That was Muriel leaving the dormitory. She's away, as she goes every Saturday night after lights out, to Miss Ganch's room. There the pair of them have a fine old time, culminating in sex. Now do you want that drink or not?'

'Yes, please. What have you got?'

Tina gave a soft chuckle. 'Ever heard of Fowler's Wee Heavy Ale? It'll blast your head off. Well, I've managed to get hold of three, that's one each and one to share.'

Tina had brought the small bottles into Vicky's bed with her and an opener. She de-capped two, and gave Vicky one. 'As I said, it's right powerful stuff that, so don't gulp, just sip,' Tina instructed.

Vicky pulled a face. The Wee Heavy was bitter, and Tina wasn't joking, it was strong. It was a bit like drinking runny bitter treacle.

'Hardly my first choice for a Saturday night boozing session but all I could get. And lucky to do so,' Tina whispered.

'How did you get it?'

'We all have our secrets in Duncliffe, Vicky, and where I lay my mitts on the occasional bevy is one of mine. As they say, ask no questions, get no lies . . .'

'Shut your mouth, and you'll catch no flies!' Vicky chipped in, finishing off the well-known children's doggerel.

They both laughed softly and had another sip of Wee Heavy.

Vicky could hear now that they weren't the only people to be having an after-lights-out natter. Quite a few of the girls were paying a 'visit' to their pals.

'Tell me something, do you know if Muriel has always preferred women to men?' Vicky asked.

'Don't be soft, she's as normal as you or I. She does it for the perks.'

'And what are those?'

'The biggest I would say is that she does hellish little in the way of hard work. She's forever being allowed to skive off, and spends most of the time sitting on her backside smoking like a lum, ciggies that Miss Ganch provides.'

'And what else?'

'While she's in Miss Ganch's room on "pash" night, Miss Ganch spoils her rotten. Miss Ganch keeps beautiful clothes there that she's allowed to dress up in, silk négligé and stockings, embroidered housecoat, velvet slippers, that sort of thing. Then there's sherry, wine and chocs, boxes of those, Muriel can stuff herself to the gills with them if she wants to.'

Vicky cocked an ear. 'Is that music?' She could just hear faint strains.

'Oh aye. Miss Ganch has a gramophone she brings out for the occasion. They play records and dance together.'

'And does Miss Ganch get all dressed up as well?'

'To the nines, Muriel says. And over and above the clothes and other goodies I've mentioned, Muriel also gets to use Miss Ganch's perfume and powder, both of which are the very best money can buy, according to Muriel.'

Vicky had another sip of Wee Heavy; she could already feel the effect and she'd hardly dented the contents of the bottle yet. 'What I can't understand is why the Head puts up with such goings on. I mean, she must surely know about Miss Ganch?'

'She knows all right. She knows everything that goes on in Duncliffe. I've wondered about that myself, and I can only suppose she tolerates it because she must have trouble getting staff to come and work here. It's a foul job really, living out in the wilds, cut off from family and social life. Who would want that? Very few. And Miss Ganch is good at the job, you have to give her that. Our section is one of the best, and most efficiently run, at Duncliffe.'

'Thanks to that riding crop,' Vicky said.

'Have you had a taste of it yet?'

Vicky shook her head. 'I've been lucky so far.'

'Well, it's only a matter of time before you do. The only person who doesn't get hit is Muriel, another of her perks.'

'Is it awful sore?'

Tina gave a thin smile at the memory of the countless times she'd been at the receiving end of that detested riding crop. 'It hurts like buggeration. I thought, to begin with, that you'd get used to it after a while. But you don't.'

'Have you been here long then?'

'Eleven months. I've got another thirteen to serve.'

'Can I ask what you did, or isn't that polite?' Vicky queried.

'I stabbed a lassie for trying to get off with that ex-boyfriend of mine I was telling you about,' Tina replied sombrely.

'Stabbed her?'

'I didn't mean to. It just sort of happened in the heat of the moment. But the polis picked me up, and the next thing I knew I was at Duncliffe. I've always thought the sentence harsh as I was a first-time offender. I'd never been in trouble before, not even as a wean for ring-bang-scoosh.'

'I'm a first offender also, and I too thought I might be shown leniency, and wasn't,' Vicky said.

'And what did you do?'

'I stole from the big shop where I was working, and eventually got caught,' Vicky replied, giving Tina the official version of events. Then she changed her mind, deciding that she would tell her new friend the truth.

Tina listened wide-eyed to Vicky's tale of how it had been Ken who'd been nicking from Copland and Lye, and of the burglaries he'd committed previous to that, and how Vicky had sacrificed herself in order to save him from a heavy sentence – only to be landed with a sentence far heftier than anything she had envisaged.

'That's dead romantic, so it is,' Tina whispered when Vicky finally stopped speaking.

'I'm going to write and ask him to be my first visitor. I can't wait to see him again,' Vicky said.

'Is he handsome?'

'A Greek god, with specs that can make him look ever so distinguished.'

'He sounds just rare.' Tina was envious and jealous of Vicky, but in the nicest way, wishing that she had a Ken of her own.

'Oh, he is, he is,' Vicky answered.

Tina spent an hour in Vicky's bed before returning to her own. Vicky considered it the best hour she had had so far at Duncliffe. She fell asleep thinking about the letter she would write Ken on Sunday, the one letter she was permitted to send prior to her first visitor, inviting him to be that visitor.

It was a bitter November morning, with the temperature below freezing and a cruel biting wind blowing in off the sea. Vicky stood chafing her hands, waiting impatiently for the bus that would be bringing Ken and the other visitors to Duncliffe, a chartered bus organised by the Head which picked visitors up from an assembly point in Port Glasgow, and returned them there afterwards.

The previous night had been a bad one for Vicky. She had had little sleep; it had mostly been spent tossing and turning in a fever of impatience for the coming morning – and Ken. Now the morning was here, and any minute now she would be in his arms again, have his lips on hers. The prospect made her all of a quiver.

She glanced across the courtyard to where Tina was standing chatting to a knot of girls. Tina wasn't expecting anyone, but had come outside to have a gander at Ken. Tina saw her, and waved. Then gestured into the distance. When Vicky looked in the direction Tina was pointing she saw that the bus was at long last in sight.

The double decker meandered along the coast road. The damn driver couldn't have gone more slowly! Vicky thought, and mentally raged at the man. Eventually the bus stopped before the heavy iron gates at the entrance to Duncliffe. Strachan unlocked the gates – taking his time about it too! – and ponderously swung them open. The bus crawled forward to halt in the courtyard, and its passengers started getting off. The next one would be Ken, Vicky told herself and, when it wasn't, the next, and the next. She could not help the squeal that burst from her when he finally did appear.

'Ken!' she cried, and ran to him, arms flung wide.

It was the moment she had waited for, the anticipated moment which had borne her through pain, exhaustion and downright despair. He hugged her tight, then in front of everyone kissed her deeply, tongue in mouth.

When they broke off they both had to gasp for air. 'You look terrific! You're positively gleaming with health,' he said.

There was something different about him, something she couldn't quite put her finger on. And then she had it.

'You've grown a moustache!' she exclaimed.

'Do you like it? Everyone says it suits me.'

'It makes you seem older.'

'And even *more* handsome?'

'Don't be so vain!' she scolded, and they both laughed.

She hooked an arm in one of his. She intended being alone with him, and had already decided where they would go. She took him across the courtyard, then round to the steep stone steps that brought them onto the beach. From there she headed for the dunes.

'This is the first chance I've had to thank you for what you did,' he said.

She glanced into his face, then away again, staring out to sea where whitecaps were dancing, preparing to come surging ashore. 'You were stupid to steal from the shop. You should have known you'd be caught.'

It was on the tip of his tongue to say that he wouldn't have been if Neil hadn't informed on him, but he bit that back. Well, he'd had his revenge on Neil, and sweet revenge it had been too. The bastard hadn't walked for a week after the kicking he'd given him. And Neil had kept stum about the identity of his assailant, so no one in Parr Street knew. That had been a wise move on Neil's part, for to say anything would have meant divulging that he'd informed on a pal and was directly responsible for Vicky ending up in Duncliffe.

'I'm only sorry you're the one who's having to pay for that stupidity,' Ken said contritely.

They reached the dunes, and there they sat facing the sea. 'How are my folks, and John?' she asked.

'They're all fine, and send their love. I'm sure they were disappointed that you wanted me to come today and not either of them, but I'm equally certain they understood.'

'Are they awfully ashamed of me?'

Ken lit a cigarette. 'I don't have to answer that. You know how they must feel,' he mumbled in reply.

Her parents must be mortified, Vicky thought for the hundredth time. Her poor mum would find it difficult keeping her head held up in the street.

'The neighbours have all been right decent about it. It's just simply never referred to,' Ken said.

She made a fist and chewed one of her knuckles. 'I had to do what I did. If they'd found out about your burgling, and they were bound to, they would have sent you away for anything up to ten years,' she whispered.

His throat was suddenly dry at the thought of that. And he felt uneasy to be with Vicky, because she had been his saviour. 'Ferrier at Copland and Lye sends his regards, the old goat,' Ken said, thinking, Jesus! it's cold out here: I'd much prefer to be indoors.

'I liked him. He was a nice man who must believe I let him down.'

'No, he doesn't. He knows it was me who was stealing, and not you.' Ken blew a stream of smoke seawards.

Vicky looked sharply at Ken. '*How* does he know?'

Ken shrugged. 'I've no idea, but he does. He told me, in a round-about way, that I could forget about any advancement at Copland and Lye. I'll stay put in the job I'm in.'

Panic welled within her. 'You haven't been stealing more things have you?' she demanded shrilly.

'Of course not. That wouldn't just be stupid, it would be suicidal. Anyway, I couldn't even if I wanted to. Since your confession, there's been no more overtime for me, and Ferrier watches me like a bloody hawk.'

Vicky swore, using a word she'd never have spoken before coming to Duncliffe. Ken glanced at her in surprise. 'Is it rough here?'

She wanted to tell him exactly how rough it was, to pour out her heart to him, which was what she'd intended. Only now, somehow, that didn't seem right. Why hadn't he inquired straight off how she was! Now that he had come to ask, it had been almost as an afterthought, as if he didn't really care.

'Rough enough,' she answered vaguely.

'So it's not bad then?'

She didn't reply.

'I must say it seems all right, big castle and all that. How's the food?'

'Very good, and plenty of it.'

'Bit like a holiday, eh? Like going camping with the Girl Guides.'

She could've sloshed him. How could he be so dense and unfeeling! She might appear healthy enough, but couldn't he sense some of what she'd been through! Now she was confused. She had been looking forward so much to his visit, and it wasn't turning out at all as she'd hoped. He could have at least restated that he loved her: there had been no mention of that either.

'It's gey chilly down here. Couldn't we go inside?' He shivered.

Vicky led the way to the castle building, her expression as chilly as the weather he was complaining about.

Vicky sat on a wide inside window ledge staring out to sea. It had started to rain about an hour since and was now teeming down. It would have been a dismal journey home to Glasgow for Ken, she thought, and remembered how they'd parted at the bus, she trying to hide her anger and dismay, he saying that he'd enjoyed himself – enjoyed! what sort of word was that to use – and that he'd come again after her parents had both been. Right up until the last moment, she had waited for him to utter the magic phrase. But it hadn't been forthcoming.

She sighed, and her brooding mind took on a new course. She was being daft, she told herself. She'd been expecting too much of the visit, so of course it had been an anti-climax. As for his offhand manner, couldn't that be a result of the terrible guilt he felt? Guilt at her being in an institution of correction when it should have been him? That had to be it, and it was her fault for not realising sooner what the problem was. She had been selfish, completely self-centred, wallowing in self-pity. After all, think how hard it must have been for him to come and face her, to see her in a borstal as a direct result of his actions and dishonesty.

Vicky cheered up. It all made sense now; she understood why he'd acted as he had. Squirming from the ledge, she strode in the direction of her dormitory. There was time for her to write a letter to him before tea. Time to write, and apologise. For it was entirely because of her lack of insight and understanding that the visit had been a failure.

It was June 1936, a month that had come in as a scorcher and remained one. Vicky and Tina had recently been delegated responsibility for one of the chicken coops, of which there were three, and that afternoon found Vicky feeding their charges, with Tina inside the coop collecting eggs. The chickens were clucking noisily as Vicky moved amongst them scattering corn left and right. The big rooster called Sandy, comb blood-red and standing up straight, was strutting to and fro as if he personally had arranged these proceedings.

Vicky was halfway through what she was doing when she suddenly caught sight of Miss Ganch at the side of the coop gazing over at the castle. She followed her gaze and realised that it wasn't the building itself Miss Ganch was staring at but a car just leaving the courtyard.

The car stopped at the iron gates, waiting for Strachan to open them. As it went through the open gates, Miss Ganch raised an arm, and gave a small salute.

Vicky remembered then that Muriel Mitchell was due to

leave Duncliffe that day, it must be her being taken to Glasgow for her official release. The car sped off and vanished from view, leaving Miss Ganch with arm still upraised. She turned abruptly, exclaiming in surprise to find Vicky there. Her eyes were moist, her face drawn and haggard. Vicky glanced away and continued feeding the chickens. Miss Ganch hurried off.

Vicky finished feeding the chickens, then went into the coop to help Tina. Tina had already gathered two baskets of eggs and said that plenty more remained to be picked up. Vicky said that she would make a pile of those while Tina took the filled baskets to the kitchens and returned with empty ones.

Vicky was at the far end of the coop, by the door there, when she became aware of a strange noise outside which she couldn't place. She opened the door and stepped out into a secluded part of the chicken run.

Miss Ganch, slumped against a wall, was dry-heaving into a handkerchief. Her cheeks and chin were awash with tears. Here, temporarily, was no longer a formidable woman, but a very sad and lonely one, Vicky thought. A woman who had just lost, so it would appear, someone she cared a great deal about.

'I'm sorry,' Vicky commiserated quietly.

'She was so beautiful,' Miss Ganch choked.

'Yes, she was.'

Miss Ganch tried to say something further but was too overcome to do so. A huge spasm wracked her body and she threw up.

Vicky went back into the coop, closing the door gently behind her.

Ken had a swallow of his pint and glared balefully round the pub. Saturday night and he was on his tod again, the fourth Saturday night on the trot. All the mates were winching, leaving him spare. He wondered whether he should bother with another pint or head back to Parr Street. It was no fun drinking alone, being miserable, when everyone else was having so much fun.

It was ten months since Vicky had been committed to Duncliffe, ten long lonely months. Even if she did get out on her eighteenth birthday, and she was convinced she would, that was still an eternity away. He had played the white man so far, dead true and all that, never straying, not even the once. But it hadn't been easy. Where he had looked forward in the past to Friday and Saturday nights, he now dreaded them.

He drank more heavy and watched a lassie and her bloke leave. Probably off to the jigging, he thought. It was getting a bit late for them to be aiming for the flicks. He spied a lad he'd been to school with – what was the bugger's name again? – and gave him a nod. If the chap had been alone, he'd have strolled over, but Ronnie – aye, that was the name, Ronnie – was with a bint. And a pretty bint too. He stared jealously at the bint – not in Vicky's class, nowhere near, but at that moment looking very attractive indeed.

Dougie Steele from the Parli Road came into the pub, and Ken's spirits briefly brightened, only to plummet again when he saw Dougie was 'with'. Dougie saw Ken, gave him a wink of greeting, and steered his bird in the opposite direction to Ken. He was much enamoured by this wee bird whom he'd only met the night before, so why take chances? Best to keep clear of any possible competition while he got on with his chatting up, consolidating his position.

Ken finished his pint. He was off home, he decided. If he hurried, he could still buy a half-bottle to share with his dad. Out in the street he paused to rift and, as he did so, changed his mind. To hell with home and a half-bottle; he was going dancing.

He walked into Sauchiehall Street and paid his entrance money at the first dance hall he came to. Inside it was jam-packed, but it would have been unusual for a town dance hall not to be at the weekend. He began eyeing up the available talent.

She was standing by a pillar with another lassie, and this time he recognised her straight off. It was the ginger-haired girl from the *Fairy Queen*, the one who'd been in the pub down at the docks before that. The one he'd thought attractive in a gallus sort of way. He made his way across.

'Well, hello there,' he said to her, and smiled.

The green eyes came round to fasten onto him and he was surveyed from behind a deadpan expression.

'Hello there,' she replied.

'Taken any boat trips lately?' he asked.

The hint of a frown creased her freckly forehead. She glanced at her pal, then back again at Ken. 'Do I know you?'

'We've never spoken up until now, but seem to have the habit of bumping into one another. Remember the trip on the Forth and Clyde Canal to Craigmarloch and back?'

The green eyes twinkled with memory. 'You had a female with you then,' she replied.

'That's long finished,' he lied.

'And the time before that was . . .'

'In a boozer down by the docks. You were with your father and some other men,' he finished for her.

He was even more handsome than she recalled, she thought.

'It's funny, but I always felt we'd cross paths again,' he said.

'Excuse me, I must powder my nose,' the lassie's pal said diplomatically, seeing how things were going, and moved off.

'My name's Lyn Fyfer,' the ginger-haired lassie told Ken.

He stuck out a hand, and they shook. 'I'm Ken Blacklaws. Are you for up?'

'I'd love to dance, thanks,' she replied and, taking him by the arm, led him onto the floor.

A thrill ran through him as they came together. She was gorgeously soft and smelled delicious. As for her green eyes, he could have stared into them till the cows came home.

'I take it you're on your own?' she inquired as they started to waltz.

He nodded. 'And what about you? Are you here with that china of yours?' he replied, making sure she was there with a female friend and not a male one.

Lyn also nodded.

A few minutes later the music stopped and everyone applauded. 'Will you stay up?' he asked her.

She looked him directly in the face and saw that he was as enamoured as she was. 'I will.'

They both knew then that it was a click.

'All right, what's up? Your face has been tripping you ever since we met,' Lyn asked Ken, who had been in a mood when they'd rendezvoused quarter of an hour previously, a mood that had since worsened. They were sitting in an Argyle Street pub where they had come for a mid-week drink.

Ken scowled into his pint. 'It'll just have to be a single bevy the night, I'm afraid. I can't afford more than that.'

So that was the source of his ill humour, *embarrassment*, Lyn thought with relief. She had been worried sick he was going to say he wanted to stop seeing her, that would have been a catastrophe as far as she was concerned. For, in the three months they had been going out together, she had taken a big shine to Ken Blacklaws. A very big shine.

'It's not a problem. I've money,' she told him.

'Och, I couldn't take money off you, it wouldn't be right,' he said, for it was considered extremely bad form for a Glasgow man to accept money from a bird he was only winching, and neither engaged or married to. It was a matter of pride.

'I'm not short, I assure you. And we've just arrived. I don't want to be rushing off again right away,' she argued.

He hadn't wanted to come out that night, not when he was verging on being skint. But the arrangement had already been made, and he had no way of contacting her to break it and make a new one.

The frustration and resentment he had been trying to keep a lid on for so long now boiled over. 'It's that effing job of mine. The pay's diabolical and for some reason the bastarding supervisor hates my guts. The bugger's made it known to me that I'll never get promotion, thereby blocking me from earning a larger pay packet.'

'So why not leave?'

'You think I'm not trying to! But you know what the work situation's like, jobs aren't exactly ten a penny.'

It was news to Lyn that he felt this way about his present job. He had never talked about it before other than to tell her what he did when she'd inquired.

'You say your pay's diabolical. I know one isn't supposed to ask this question, that it's rude, but how much is it exactly?'

'Thirty-seven and six a week,' he mumbled in reply.

That was diabolical right enough, not a man's wages at all, she thought. 'And I suppose you give some of that to your mum for your keep?'

'Twenty-five bob of it.'

She took a cigarette from her packet and offered the packet to him. He couldn't disguise his eagerness to light up, a dead giveaway that he'd been gasping.

Ken exhaled smoke and gave a bitter laugh. 'It's not all that long ago that I was boasting to someone about how ambitious I was, how I intended getting on, that nothing would stop me. I said I'd be one of those who achieved power, a stringpuller who made others dance to his tune. I said I would completely be my own master, and the master of many. Somebody really important. What hollow words they sound now that I'm stuck with no prospects, in the Packing and Dispatch department of Copland and Lye.'

'Something's bound to come along,' she sympathised.

'Oh aye, sure, and pigs will sprout wings and fly,' he retorted and had a savage pull at his pint.

The idea came to her then of how she could help him, and herself into the bargain. For if he earned more money, he would be able to see her more often – and he'd be obliged to her.

'Are you strong?' she asked.

He blinked. What had that to do with it? 'Fairly,' he replied.

'And are you a grafter, not afraid of getting stuck in?'

'I am,' he said softly, wondering what this was leading up to.

Lyn glanced at her watch, had a think, and nodded.

'Finish that pint and let's go. We should just catch him.'

'Catch who?'

'You'll find out,' she said mysteriously and swallowed what remained of her whisky and lemonade.

Lyn rose from the table as the last drop of heavy vanished down Ken's throat. She led the way out into the street to where her car was parked. It was a brand new Austin 7, with a deep-blue body, black mudguards, running boards and roof. The wheel spokes, originally black, were now the same colour as the body – she had painted these herself. The overall effect was, in her own words, 'to make the car look really eye-catching'.

Ken was much taken with the Austin; its distinctive colouring appealed to him. Of course it wasn't a patch on the Armstrong Siddeley he'd so briefly owned, but it was a wee smasher nonetheless.

They got in and started off. Before long they had left Argyle Street and turned down into Finnieston. The river came into view, dark and brooding at this time of night. For a short while it was lost to sight, then it reappeared as they entered Queen's Dock. The rest of the river had been quiet, ominously so, but not here. Queen's Dock outer basin was abustle with activity; a large ship was being unloaded.

Lyn parked the car just beyond the perimeter of the pool of light that flooded the ship and the warehouse into which the ship's cargo was being unloaded.

'The *Star of India*. It was three days late berthing because of bad weather. As its entire cargo consisted of fruit, it's being unloaded as quickly as possible to get the fruit into the market and shops before it spoils,' Lyn explained.

'How come you know so much about it?'

'Ever heard of the Honourable Society of Dock Workers?' He shook his head.

'Well, it's one of the four unions that control the docks in Glasgow, and my father is its president. It's his men who are unloading that ship tonight, and I happen to know he negotiated a special rate for the job which will give each and every one of them a fiver for his night's work,' she said.

Ken whistled. Five pounds for a night's work! Earned

honestly, that was very good going indeed. In fact it was spectacular.

He had known that her father was connected with the docks, but had presumed – remembering that flashy chauffeur-driven Riley at Port Dundas – that Mr Fyfer was on the management side.

'I can't promise you power to be able to make others dance to your tune, or even to be your own master, but the basic rate is one pound ten a day, which adds up to nine pounds, before stoppages, for a six-day week. On top of that you'll have overtime and special jobs such as the *Star of India* there, hoisting your take-home pay to between twelve and fifteen pounds a week, some weeks even more.'

He stared in astonishment at the outline of her face in the darkness. 'Are you offering me a job as a dockie?'

'If you're agreeable, let's go over and see my dad. I'll put it to him,' she replied.

If he was *agreeable*! He reached out and drew her close. 'I think you're smashing,' he whispered.

'You're a bit of all right yourself,' she told him, also in a whisper.

He kissed her, their tongues flickering together. She broke away when he squeezed her right breast and was swiftly out the car. Laughing, she strode towards the warehouse where she knew her father would be.

Ken, straightening the tie he was suddenly glad to be wearing, hurried after her.

Vicky and Tina were leaving tea together when Miss Ganch came up to them and addressed Vicky. 'Follow me, Devine,' she snapped, and walked quickly away.

Vicky's stomach contracted with fear. Had she done something wrong, been remiss in one of her duties? She glanced at Tina, shrugged to say she hadn't a clue what this was all about, and ran to catch up on Miss Ganch.

Miss Ganch, expression stern to the point of being fierce, made for her room. Once inside, she stood with hands on hips, and gazed about. 'This place is filthy. I want it cleaned from top to bottom, *thoroughly*. Understand?'

'Yes, miss.'

'Then hop to it,' Miss Ganch said, and sat at her desk.

Vicky muttered a quiet excuse and left the room to get the cleaning things from the corridor cupboard. She lugged them back to the room and, with Miss Ganch apparently immersed in paperwork, started in.

Miss Ganch was right: the room was manky and couldn't have been touched for months. Before long the sweat was lashing off her as she swept and scrubbed, dusted and polished.

'I'm finished, Miss Ganch,' she proclaimed at last, having been at it for several hours.

Miss Ganch laid down the pen she had been using and regarded Vicky thoughtfully. Vicky was again reminded of John's garden snake.

'There's no need for me to check. I've been watching you and know you've done a good job.'

'Thank you,' Vicky said, and made to gather the cleaning things together, to return them to the cupboard.

'Wait. There's no need to do that just yet,' Miss Ganch told Vicky, and smiled.

Vicky immediately halted what she was doing. It had only been a suggestion, but from Miss Ganch that amounted to a command.

Miss Ganch rose and crossed to her bed. Kneeling, she pulled out a sliding drawer that had been concealed beneath it. There were a number of bottles and sweetie boxes in the drawer, and various types of glasses. 'How about a sherry as a reward?'

Oh God! Vicky thought and quailed inside. 'I'm under age, miss.'

'Then we'll just have to keep this to ourselves, our little secret between you and me.' She poured out two hefty sherries.

Vicky accepted hers, mumbling her thanks.

'You've settled in well at Duncliffe, we're all pleased with you,' Miss Ganch said, regarding Vicky over the rim of her glass.

'I'm trying to do my best, Miss Ganch,' Vicky replied,

thinking she didn't know much about sherry, but this tasted like an expensive one.

'How do you find that?'

'Lovely, miss.'

Miss Ganch snapped her fingers. 'Tell you what, you must try one of the new chocolates I've bought. They're Swiss.' She opened a box from the underbed drawer, and proffered it to Vicky. Vicky chose a chocolate in the shape of a unicorn. It melted in her mouth – it was simply exquisite.

'Very nice, miss,' she said, not wanting to show too much enthusiasm.

'Have you ever mentioned to the others about the day Muriel left?' Miss Ganch asked softly.

'No, miss.'

'Are you certain? Not even to Tina Mathieson? You and she appear to be great chums.'

'Not even to Tina, miss, I swear. That was a moment of private grief for you. I wouldn't blab about something so intimate and personal.' Vicky lied, for she had told Tina. But it had stopped there; neither had thought it politic for the story of what she had witnessed to go further.

'In which case you've earned a further reward, and I know just the very dab. Come with me.'

Miss Ganch, with Vicky tagging along behind, left the room and crossed to a door on the other side of the corridor, which she unlocked with a brass key. Vicky knew what lay beyond, but had never seen inside. It was Miss Ganch's private bathroom. The woman went in and beckoned Vicky to join her. In trepidation, Vicky did so.

Miss Ganch closed the door. 'How about a hot bath? And you can use any of my crystals and powders that take your fancy.'

A hot bath! It had been nothing but ice-cold showers since she had come to Duncliffe. Vicky could not think of anything she desired more – with the exception of Ken, that was.

Miss Ganch put the plug in the huge white enamelled tub and twisted a tap. Steaming water gushed forth to splatter on the bottom of the bath. Her eyes glinted. 'Take your time, enjoy yourself. Just don't fall asleep, that tub's big enough to drown in.' She left Vicky, reshutting the door as she went.

Vicky slumped her body with relief. She had had the horrible suspicion that Miss Ganch might want to stay with her while she had the bath – or, worse still, join her. There was a snib on the door, which she snecked. She felt a great deal better for that.

There was a jar of pink crystals and another of blue. She chose the pink, which had a flowery smell to them, and tipped in a fair amount. The flowery smell filled the bathroom. She found towels in a cupboard, half a dozen in all, each one thick and soft as down. When the bath was ready she undressed. Slowly she slipped into the water, groaning with the sheer pleasure of the experience. She sank up to her neck and closed her eyes.

After a while she poured in a little of the oil standing on the side of the bath. Its odour was musk and mingled fragrantly with that of the crystals. She had forgotten how stupefyingly luxurious a hot bath could be; aches and pains that had become part and parcel of her everyday living gradually seeped from her body as it relaxed, unwound and was revitalised.

Eventually, reluctantly, she climbed out of the bath and towelled herself dry, after which she liberally doused herself with talcum powder. She ran a comb through her hair which she'd washed when in the bath. It had not felt so clean since she'd last washed it at home – why, it actually squeaked when she rubbed it with the towel!

She had been reluctant to get out of the bath; she was even more so to leave the bathroom itself. But finally she did so, sighing as she shut the door on that place of heavenly delight.

She found Tina in the dormitory waiting for her. 'Well?'

Before Vicky could reply, Tina's nose twitched and she took a deep sniff. 'Is that powder or perfume?'

'Both,' Vicky answered, and went on to relate what had happened.

Tina, chewing a thumbnail, listened in silence. 'You

know what this means, don't you? Ganch wants you as a replacement to Muriel,' she said when Vicky was finally finished.

'I'd already arrived at the same conclusion myself.'

'So?'

Vicky shook her head, appalled at the idea. 'I'm in love with Ken. Why, I couldn't go to bed with another man, no matter how attractive, far less a woman.'

'It might not be that bad, and consider how easy life would become for you.'

'I find the thought of it quite repulsive. Even if there wasn't Ken, I couldn't go through with it. That sort of thing revolts me. Doesn't it you?'

Tina shrugged. 'Before I came here I'd have said yes. But now? I'm more broadminded than I used to be, and certainly less dogmatic. If Ganch propositioned me, I'd certainly give it serious consideration on account of the perks involved.'

'You really would!' Vicky exclaimed, amazed.

'What she did to you wouldn't be that hard to endure. Surely you've learned to take yourself off inside your head by now? Detach yourself, float away in the mind. I soon learned that was the only way to survive bloody Duncliffe at times.'

Vicky knew exactly what Tina was talking about; it was a trick she also employed when it all got too much. 'But you'd have to live with yourself afterwards, and that's the bit I wouldn't be able to stomach.'

'Maybe it won't go any further. If she sees you're not keen, she might settle for one of the other girls, one who'd jump at the chance as Muriel did.'

'Aye maybe,' Vicky said, fervently hoping that would be the case.

Vicky awoke with a start to find a hand clamped over her mouth. Miss Ganch, torch in other hand, was staring down at her. Terrified, she swallowed hard and waited for the hand to be removed.

After a few moments it was, and Miss Ganch crooked a beckoning finger. She then padded off down the dormitory, pausing at the entrance, waiting for Vicky to catch up.

It had come at last, the summons Vicky had been dreading. Why else would Miss Ganch wake her in the middle of the night, and with such secrecy? Shaking, she followed her to her room, where Miss Ganch shut the door and switched off the torch. 'I was sitting here all alone and thought I'd like to talk to somebody. Hope you don't mind?' Miss Ganch declared, giving a thin slash of a smile.

'No, miss,' Vicky replied, wondering what else she could possibly have said!

Miss Ganch dropped her gaze to stare – hungrily, it seemed to the apprehensive Vicky – at Vicky's body. 'Why, you're shivering, my dear, but it is midnight, and this is December.'

Going to her wardrobe, a fairly new acquisition, she took out a beautiful cream quilted robe, which she brought to Vicky. 'Slip this on, it'll soon warm you up.'

Miss Ganch helped Vicky with the robe, tying it at the waist for her, and smoothing the material down at the shoulders where it had become momentarily bunched. Vicky wanted desperately to scream for help, but knew that would have been futile. She might have brought people running, but what then?

'Would you care for a drink? I'm on whisky myself.'

'Perhaps a small one,' Vicky replied, forcing a smile.

Miss Ganch poured the whiskies, and handed Vicky hers, which was anything but small. 'When we're alone together, you can call me Jo,' she said.

She didn't look at all like a Jo, Vicky thought. Jo was a nice name; hers should have been something horrid, such as Gertrude or Senga. Vicky had always considered Senga a particularly horrid name, associating it with a girl she had once known who'd been a proper nasty piece of work.

'Yes, Jo,' Vicky replied unenthusiastically.

'How did you enjoy your hot bath the other day?'

'It was tremendous.'

'Those crystals make all the difference, don't you think? So relaxing.'

'Yes, Jo.'

Miss Ganch drank some whisky, then slowly licked her lips in an overtly sensuous and vulgar manner. Laying her glass aside, she picked up the riding crop and began running a hand up and down it, stroking it as if it was a male sexual organ.

Vicky stared, fascinated and repulsed at the same time.

'There are lots of little treats I could put your way if I had a mind to,' Miss Ganch purred.

Vicky wondered if she should say straight out that she wasn't interested, that she didn't want to know. She held back, hoping that she would be able to refuse in a more oblique fashion.

'Treats that could make your stay at Duncliffe far less harsh than it's been up until now,' Miss Ganch continued, hand still moving up and down the riding crop.

Vicky gazed into those palest of blue eyes, which had taken on a hypnotic quality. They made her think of the sea in summer, still and enticing.

'All you have to do to earn my gratitude is show a wee bit of affection,' Miss Ganch murmured, voice now low and husky.

There was a charisma about the woman that Vicky had not before been aware of, and which was now reaching out to envelop her. Nor had she realised that Miss Ganch had such lovely skin, skin that would be smooth and silken to touch.

Miss Ganch's bosoms started to rise and fall. Staring at Vicky, she imagined her naked; the vision was so exciting that it made her belly twist inside. She glided over to her. The breath caught in Vicky's throat when Miss Ganch kissed it. Then a hand delved inside her robe first to touch, then caress, a thigh.

That broke the spell. For the past few moments she had been the rabbit mesmerised by the snake, the prey transfixed by the predator, all set to be devoured.

'No, please,' she pleaded, and pushed down on the hand, trying to thrust it away.

But Miss Ganch was not to be so easily put off, and in the tussle that followed Vicky lost her balance, and went tumbling to the floor, Miss Ganch falling on top of her. With a quick and strong yank, Miss Ganch tore open Vicky's robe and nightdress so that her breasts were exposed.

Vicky knew she was no match physically for Miss Ganch; the bitch was just far too strong for her. There was only one thing she could think of that would possibly stop this. Her nails sank into Miss Ganch's cheeks and ripped downwards, gouging furrows in the flesh as they went.

Vicky's legs were leaden. She was sickeningly tired, not having slept a wink after fleeing Miss Ganch's room. She had lain in bed waiting for the wrath she had been certain was about to descend. So far, it hadn't.

At reveille Miss Ganch had behaved as normal, blasting on the whistle, flinging the curtains open, causing the section to go like the clappers to avoid being last dressed.

Her cheeks did not look as bad as Vicky had feared they would; the gouge marks were obvious, and would later be a matter of intense discussion and speculation amongst the section, but they were not the horrendous wounds that had grown in Vicky's imagination during the early hours of the morning.

Vicky's feet pounded sand. The section was halfway through the morning run, and she was third from last. So far Miss Ganch had said nothing to her, and Vicky had avoided her gaze when it swept her way.

'Jenny Connors, move your arse!' Miss Ganch suddenly shouted, and the riding crop cracked home on the named girl's backside.

Vicky winced. From the sound of it, that had been a particularly vicious swipe – even harder than the sort Miss Ganch normally ladled out.

The castle courtyard, and end of the run, was in sight when Vicky stumbled and measured her length on the ground. Winded, she lay there, unable to move until she had caught her breath. Those girls who had been behind her flashed past, leaving her last. She was gulping in air and attempting to struggle onto her knees when Miss Ganch came up to her. She was for it now, she thought. She had given Miss Ganch the opportunity she must have been praying for.

Out of the corner of her eye Vicky saw the riding crop begin to descend and gritted her teeth in anticipation of the blow. The first of many, she was convinced.

Wonder of wonders, the blow turned out to be a mere tap, a tickle on the rump.

'Come along, Devine, come along,' Miss Ganch said sweetly.

Vicky couldn't believe it; there was to be no thrashing after all. Had she been forgiven? It seemed so. Hardly able to credit her luck, she staggered back to her feet and finished the run.

Vicky was in Mrs Gardener's class, busy on a shorthand exercise, when the crunch came. A girl arrived to tell Mrs Gardener that the Head wanted to see Vicky straight away in her office.

It had to be about what she'd done to Miss Ganch, Vicky thought grimly as she left the class. There had been no reprieve after all; it had no doubt amused Miss Ganch to let her think that there had.

'Enter!' the Head called out when she knocked the office door.

The Head was seated behind her desk, with Miss Ganch standing to one side. There was no expression on Miss Ganch's face but her eyes were as cold as charity.

The Head adjusted her spectacles, a gesture that reminded Vicky of Ken, then leaned forward and fixed Vicky with a baleful glare. 'I warned you the day after you arrived at Duncliffe that if you stole anything while here you'd rue it,' she said softly.

'But I haven't stolen anything!' Vicky exclaimed, thrown by the accusation. It wasn't at all what she had expected to have to defend herself against.

'You attempted to,' the Head went on.

Vicky glanced at Miss Ganch, then back at the Head. 'I swear on my word of honour that I did no such thing.'

Miss Ganch snickered. 'Word of honour, indeed!'

'Are you attempting to deny that, while Miss Ganch was out of her room late last night, you entered it and were about to steal a bottle of her perfume when she returned and caught you in the act?' the Head elaborated.

'I never touched her perfume last night. I was in her room, but at her invitation,' Vicky replied.

The Head's gaze slid sideways. 'Miss Ganch?' she prompted.

'I was having trouble getting to sleep and decided to have a bath. I was about to get into the bath when I realised I'd left my book behind. I put on my dressing gown and returned to my room, where I surprised Devine in the act of leaving it. She was holding a bottle of my perfume which she was clearly in the process of stealing.

'When I challenged Devine about this, she pleaded with me not to report her, but I said I had to, the offence was far too serious for me not to do so. When she saw I meant that, she flew into a berserk rage and attacked me, the results of which are all too evident. That is a true account of what happened,' Miss Ganch said.

'It's not true at all. It's a complete lie, coming from a dirty lesbian who tried to seduce me last night!' Vicky burst out.

'So you admit you did attack Miss Ganch?' the Head said.

'I didn't attack her. I was defending myself. She was sexually assaulting me, and digging my nails into her cheeks was the only way I could think of to make her stop, and get off me.'

'Lesbian, sexual assault! What utter nonsense and total fabrication,' Miss Ganch hissed.

'You were trying to bribe me. You said that, if I slept with you, you'd make life at Duncliffe easier for me, that you'd give me lots of little treats, as you put it,' Vicky retorted.

'The girl's not only a thief but an accomplished liar as well it seems,' Miss Ganch said to the Head.

'I'm not the liar. *You* are!' Vicky yelled.

'Then it's her word against mine as to what happened,' Miss Ganch said, continuing to look at the Head.

Seconds ticked by. The Head exhaled, long and slowly, then rose. 'Follow me, Devine,' she said, and went to the door, where she paused, waiting for Miss Ganch to open it.

Vicky knew what was going to happen to her, what her punishment would be. She had known it when the girl arrived in Miss Gardener's class to say she was to report to the Head.

The Head went first, Vicky behind her, and Miss Ganch behind Vicky. They walked like that, in a straight line, one behind the other, till they arrived at the black-painted door which was the entrance to the Black Room. The Head unlocked the door and it swung open.

The room was as Vicky remembered it: square, with no windows. There was no lightbulb, nor gas mantle, nor any other form of illumination. There was the same army-style cot, but in a different position. On the cot, at one end, were two neatly folded blankets and a pillow. At the other end of the cot, and underneath it, was the chamber pot, now empty and clean. The smell of disinfectant impregnated the air.

'Go in,' the Head commanded.

Vicky, heart hammering, the small of her back prickly with goosebumps, stepped inside.

The Head stared at Vicky, then turned to Miss Ganch. 'How long for?'

Miss Ganch pondered that. Then a malicious, evil smile twitched the corners of her mouth upwards. 'Till my face is completely healed,' she pronounced.

The black door was then closed, leaving Vicky in total and profound darkness. She knotted a hand into a fist and stuffed the fist into her mouth. It wasn't fair, it just wasn't fair! Damn Ganch, damn the bloody cow to hell! With that, Vicky crawled onto the cot and wept.

Day and night ceased to have meaning for her. There was only darkness, punctuated at intervals by the brief coming of light and the food that went with the light. Seconds of precious blinding light. One second, two, three, four, five, six . . . Bang! The door was shut again, and she was plunged once more into darkness.

Then, out of the void, and smiling, Ken came. He had a surprise for her, he said, handing her the most enormous bunch of red roses. No, not the flowers, he laughed, and from behind his back produced a small box of the type one gets from a jeweller's shop.

She opened the box and gasped. It was an engagement ring boasting a solitary diamond, but what a diamond. It was the size of a pullet's egg! He'd promised her a diamond ring, he said, and he wasn't a man to fall down on his promise. No, sir!

She told him the ring was gorgeous, and hugged him close. He replied that that wasn't all; he had something else to show her.

The next thing she knew they were in a house in Parr Street – *their* house, he proclaimed, just waiting for them when they were married. Literally dancing with joy, she went from room to room, saying that the bed would go there, her dressing table over there, and here would be the sofa, while there would stand the table and chairs they would have to buy.

Then, out of that same void from where Ken had emerged, slithered Miss Ganch, human above the waist, a snake below, hissing that she would destroy Ken and the house, and all Vicky's dreams. As she cackled horribly, Miss Ganch's tail whipped through the air to encoil Ken and, with him firmly trapped, she began to squeeze, intending to squeeze him to death.

But Ken, screaming to Vicky that she wasn't to fear, that she could always depend on him, made a titanic effort and burst free of his entrapment. Somehow he gathered the writhing and screeching snaky Miss Ganch above his head and bore her to the window. He tossed her out the window, where, hissing and cackling horribly, and screeching all at once, she fell from view. Quick as a wink Vicky was in his arms. There she was safe and secure, and with him would be so for ever.

After that Ken came often, and with each visit stayed longer and longer.

The door opened and light flooded the Black Room. This time it did not bang shut again almost immediately. Vicky forced herself to concentrate. She saw a hazy figure, then another. She blinked. The light was hurting her eyes.

'Enjoyed yourself?' Miss Ganch asked, and gave a low, cruel laugh.

Vicky sat up on the cot and tried to focus. But everything remained blurred. Why was Ganch here? Was this to be a taunting session? She tried to make out who the other figure was, but couldn't.

'Punishment's over. My face is healed,' Miss Ganch stated.

It could be another lie, with the door to be slammed shut on her when she attempted to leave, Vicky warned herself.

'Nothing to say, Devine?'

Vicky did not reply. Was that other figure Tina? She thought it might be.

'Take her to the showers. She stinks like a pig, a pig who's been wallowing in shit,' Miss Ganch said and walked away.

It *was* Tina who was now beside her, embracing her. 'I can't see very well,' she whispered.

'That'll soon clear.'

'Do I really smell that bad? I've grown used to it, I suppose.'

Tina glanced down at the brimming chamber pot, which had only been slopped out twice since Vicky's incarceration. 'You smell worse,' she replied.

Vicky laughed tremulously. Good old Tina! 'How long?' she asked.

'You may be interested to know you hold the record. You've been in here for twenty-four days,' Tina answered.

'It seemed like twenty-four years.'

What a state Vicky was in, Tina thought. She was nothing but skin and bone. She had a sickly, haunted pallor, with dark bags under her eyes. What the poor darling must have been through, she shuddered to think!

She helped Vicky to her feet, then put an arm round her. 'You'll feel a lot better after you've had that shower,' she said sympathetically.

Vicky found that she was terribly weak, and was thankful for Tina's support. Initially anyway, she wouldn't have got far without it.

'We all knew you were in the Black Room, but not what for,' Tina said as they made their way, Vicky staggering, down the corridor.

In a few terse sentences Vicky told Tina what had happened in Miss Ganch's room that fateful night, and the false charges brought against her the following day.

'I thought your disappearance into the Black Room and those rip marks on Ganch's face had to be somehow connected,' Tina remarked.

Vicky halted by a partially open window and gulped in some chill January air. Oh, but it was good! A gust of wind swirled round them, and that was even better.

They resumed their journey to the showers, where Tina left Vicky while she dashed off for a towel. Vicky slowly stripped, the first time she had had her clothes off since going into the Black Room. The buffeting water was ice cold as always, but she welcomed it as it dashed away the stench of the Black Room. Using soap, Vicky scraped and scoured her skin till it tingled and glowed.

When she was done, Tina wrapped a towel round her, and they sat. Vicky, her sight rapidly improving, though her eyes remained sore, saw that Tina, without being told, had brought her a fresh set of underwear and clothes.

'I wouldn't have survived that hole if it hadn't been for Ken's visits,' Vicky said, her voice strangely hollow.

Tina stared at Vicky in astonishment. 'What visits?'

'He came to see me a great deal. We'd talk and laugh and do things together. It was his love that kept me sane, in an insane sort of way.'

'You mean you *imagined* he came to see you?'

Vicky gave a wry smile. 'In that room reality and

imagination become mixed. There were times when, try as I might, I wasn't able to tell whether I was awake or asleep. The two states, like reality and imagination, had become indistinguishable.'

'You're saying he seemed real to you when you imagined him there?'

'As real to me as you are now,' Vicky replied, and smiled, her smile both wan and ethereal, for she had not yet fully returned to the world.

'Love, his for me and mine for him, that was my saviour,' Vicky added after a while.

Tina then got Vicky dried and dressed and took her off to the dining hall for tea.

After tea, it being a Sunday evening, Vicky and Tina went for a stroll, and Tina brought Vicky up to date on all the gossip.

Hannah McCrimmond was Miss Ganch's new special friend, who went along to Miss Ganch's room on 'pash' night. And, for no reason the section could figure out, Miss Ganch had changed the route of the morning run to what was generally thought by the section to be an easier one . . .

Tina was still waffling on when they returned to the dormitory, where another bit of fuss was made of Vicky by those who had not yet spoken to her since she had come out of the Black Room. Holding the Black Room record as she now did, she was something of a heroine.

'Oh, by the by, there's some mail under your pillow that came when you were locked away. I put it there waiting your release,' Tina said.

Vicky's eagerly groping hands quickly found the letters. The writing on the envelopes told her that two were from her mum, the third from Ken. She tore that open first.

Her body froze as sharply as it had under the shower. Then she felt numb in mind and body alike.

'What is it?' Tina asked.

Vicky attempted to reply, and found she couldn't. She salivated and tried again. The words came out in a dry crackle. 'It's all off between Ken and me. He's found someone else. He's going to marry her. The date's been set for next month.'

'Oh shit!' Tina swore softly.

Vicky knew she had to get out of there, she had to be alone. 'I'm going for another walk . . .'

'Let me come with you?' Tina interrupted, suddenly scared stiff by Vicky's expression.

'No. I want to be by myself.'

'All right, but you won't do anything silly will you? Swear to me you won't.'

Vicky rubbed her forehead. She could not think. Then it dawned on her what Tina meant. 'I won't do anything silly,' she promised, her voice so low that it was barely audible.

Tina did not believe her. 'You can go on your own, but I'm tagging along behind to keep an eye on you.'

It didn't matter to Vicky what Tina did; it didn't matter to her what anyone did. In fact nothing at all mattered to her any more. In a stunned daze, totally unaware of what was going on around her, she left the dormitory.

But Ken loved her. *Loved her!*

Covering her ears with her hands, she ran, shrieking at the top of her lungs, along the beach.

Shortly after lights-out someone slipped into bed beside her. She stiffened, but only slightly.

'Don't take this the wrong way. I just thought . . . well, I thought you might appreciate a cuddle,' Tina whispered.

'Oh, Tina!' Vicky choked in reply.

Tina took her friend in her arms and rocked her as she would a baby.

They were clinging together when Vicky, riven with grief and pain but finding comfort and succour in Tina's embrace, eventually drifted into a fitful sleep.

Vicky stared at the infamous Duke Street jail for women offenders. It was made of grey sandstone punctuated by small barred windows. It was the bleakest, and grimmest building she had ever seen. It was 25 March 1937, the day after her eighteenth birthday, and the day after her sentence had been reviewed.

Miss Ganch had had her final revenge. She had submitted an adverse report on her, a report that had made the review board decide that she had to serve her sentence in full. As she was now too old for borstal, it meant that she had to serve the remaining seventeen months of her sentence in an adult prison – the dreadful place now in front of her.

Lines from an old Glasgow street song crowded into her mind, a song she recalled singing often as a wee lassie:

> There is a happy land
> Down in Duke Street Jail
> There all the prisoners stand
> Tied tae a nail
> Ham and eggs you never see
> Dirty water for your tea
> There you live in misery
> > *God save the King!*

Prodded from behind, she stepped through an opened door set in one of the huge pair of iron-studded wooden gates.

The door crashed shut behind her.

Part Three

A Night Full of Mystery
1940–41

'The night is full of mystery,
whose understanding is
In trying no more to understand.'

WILLIAM MONTGOMERIE, *Estuary*

Six

A lump clogging her throat, Vicky gazed down Parr Street, thinking that it was far smaller than she remembered – smaller, meaner and dirtier. It was the first time she had been back since that awful day four and a half years ago when she had been arrested at Copland and Lye. High above the Parr Street roofs floated a barrage balloon, one of the many tethered thereabouts. They had been there since shortly after the declaration of war four months previously.

A man walked by, giving her a curious glance as he passed. His name was Waddell and he lived in number 22. He had not recognised her.

Picking up her suitcase, she headed for her close. On reaching it she paused to look over and up at what had been Ken's window. She wondered how he was and where he was living. Another house in Parr Street perhaps? If he was, she would take digs elsewhere.

The smell rekindled a thousand memories. The Glasgow tenement close has a unique smell – though, as with fingerprints, no two are exactly the same.

She stopped outside the family door and put down her case. What if she wasn't welcome? What if the family didn't want her any more? There was only one way to find out. She chapped.

Mary answered the knock. 'Aye, can I help you?'

Vicky didn't reply, but waited.

Mary gave a sudden exclamation, took a step backward and clutched at her throat.

'Vicky? Is it really you?'

'It's me right enough, Mum.' Vicky was so overcome with emotion that she could hardly get out the words.

'I wouldn't have known you. You're so . . . changed,' Mary said.

'It's the suntan and Yankee clothes that do it.' Vicky smiled. Through misty eyes Vicky noted that Mary had aged a great deal. Her mum had grown old and, like the street, somehow smaller.

With a sob Mary threw herself at Vicky and clutched her daughter to her bosom. 'Oh, lass, it's so good to see you,' she whispered, tears cascading down her face.

'And it's good to see you, Mum.'

They finally, reluctantly, broke apart and Mary, tears continuing to flow freely, wiped her nose with a hanky she had luckily had in her pinny pocket. 'Let's away in then,' she said, and attempted to lift Vicky's case.

'Don't you dare. It's far too heavy for you,' Vicky admonished, and took the case from her.

Vicky's heart seemed to turn over as she entered the house she'd been born into, and brought up in. If going into the close had rekindled a thousand memories, going into the house rekindled a million.

'I'll put the kettle on,' Mary said and began filling it at the sink.

There were a few new bits and bobs in the kitchen, but not many. On the whole the room was as it was when Vicky had left. Lovingly she caressed one of the wally dugs sitting atop the fireplace mantelpiece. These had been treasured possessions of her mum's as long as her mother and father had bided in Parr Street.

'So where have you been and what have you been up to, and why did you do a vanishing act when you got out of Duke Street?' Mary demanded.

Vicky laughed. 'One question at a time, eh?'

'As you asked in your letter just before you got out of Duke Street, we never came to meet you on your release. We waited here for you, at home. But you never came.'

Vicky sat in a chair by the fireplace. A fire had been laid but not lit. It was ready for her dad when he returned from work. It was a well-stacked fire, which would give a cheery,

184

welcoming blaze when it got going. Her dad hated a green fire.

'When I wrote that letter, I still thought I might be able to come back here, but when I was actually faced with it, I just couldn't. That was why I didn't want you there: I might have felt obliged.'

'Was it because of Ken Blacklaws?'

Vicky nodded.

'Aye, we thought it must have been that. But nonetheless, you might have had the decency to tell us where you'd gone, and what you were doing. You must have known how worried and anxious we were, and have been ever since.'

As Vicky had been expecting, there was anger in Mary's voice.

'I should have at least written, I can't deny that, but . . . Every time I sat down to do so, something stopped me and I couldn't write a damn thing. I think, at the back of my mind, and purely because of Ken, I wanted to sever all connections with my past – with Glasgow, Scotland, and even Britain as a whole,' Vicky said quietly.

Mary stared at her daughter, beginning to understand just how deeply she had felt for Ken. *Had?* she wondered.

'As you're here the day, do I take it you're now over him?' Mary asked.

'I think I am. In fact I'm certain of it,' Vicky replied with as much conviction as she could.

'Is there anyone else now?'

Vicky gave a tight smile. 'No.'

Mary set out two of her best cups and saucers, the service she used for special occasions. 'So what did you do after Duke Street?' she queried.

'I landed a position with the Ellison Line as assistant to the purser,' Vicky answered.

'You went to sea! Help ma bob, I'd never have thought of that,' Mary exclaimed.

'The *Atlantic Star*, that was the ship I was on. We did the South American run,' Vicky explained.

Without saying anything, Mary got out the tea caddy.

Then she demanded, 'So now you finally have returned to Glasgow, is it for good, or what?'

'For good, and I'd like to stay here again, if you'll have me, and depending,' Vicky replied.

'Of course we'll have you lass. But what do you mean "depending"?'

'Do Ken and his wife live in the street? I couldn't bear staying here if they did.'

Mary could well understand that. 'They don't. Ken moved away when he got married. I couldn't say where, but certainly not locally. His folks have moved as well. They flitted to Largs shortly after the marriage. Mr Blacklaws found a job there, so they packed up and went off down the coast.'

'In that case I'll have my old bed back again,' Vicky said.

The kettle was now singing, so Mary turned off the gas and made the tea, putting the pot in a nice cosy she'd knitted herself.

'When war was declared, I thought I'd stay on at sea, at least for a while, but then our sister ship, the *Atlantic Sun*, was torpedoed off the Azores, and that was that. Because the war had made it too dangerous, the company decided to stop employing female personnel. All of us were to be paid off when the ship reached a home port. In the circumstances, it seemed to me right and proper to come home to Glasgow,' Vicky said.

Mary poured the tea and handed Vicky a cup. 'Were there many killed on this *Atlantic Sun*?'

'All on board,' Vicky answered softly.

Mary sighed. She had been Vicky's age when the Great War was fought – the war to end all wars, as it had been called at the time. What terrible destruction had been wrought then, and now it was starting all over again.

'Talking of ships being sunk, do you remember Ian Holt? Him that lived in Glebe Street and whose father worked at Agnew's?'

Ian had been very swarthy, Vicky recalled. But his disposition had belied his looks. He'd had a right sunny personality. 'I remember him well.'

'He joined the navy eighteen months or so ago, and was

on the *Royal Oak* when it was sunk in Scapa Flow last October. He was one of the eight hundred and ten that were lost,' Mary said.

Ian had kissed her once, long before she had met Ken. Vicky offered up a silent prayer for his soul.

'And what about my dad, how's he?'

'Just fine, never better. He was made a driver last year, which he much prefers to conductoring. And it pays more too.'

'And John?'

Mary's face clouded over. 'He got a grand job as an apprentice monumental sculptor with J. & G. Mossman in Cathedral Street after he left school, but as soon as war was declared the silly bugger broke his apprenticeship and went for a soldier. He's with the HLI.'

John a soldier! Who'd have believed it? Vicky still thought of him as the wee lad he'd been last time she'd seen him, the day of her arrest. For John had never been allowed by George and Mary to visit her at Duncliffe. With something of a shock she recalled that there was only two years between her and John, which made him eighteen now. It was just that he had always *seemed* so young beside herself.

'He's over in France with his regiment,' Mary added, a catch in her voice.

Vicky pondered that. 'Has he seen action yet?'

'Not so far, but he's bound to before long. You know the reputation of the HLI. If there's fighting, the Glasgow boys will eventually be in the thick of it. During the last war their casualties were horrendous.'

Vicky sipped her tea. It was fairly weak tea and tasted best without milk. Her mum had always made it like that.

'When will Dad get in?'

'In about an hour. Is he going to be chuffed!'

Vicky gave a smile as weak as the tea. 'Do you think it'll come round to him having to go?'

Mary's eyes filled with fear, fear that had already caused her endless sleepless nights of late. 'He's not all that far off fifty, which of course is in his favour. I suppose it all depends on how this thing works out. If the war's a short one, then he should be all right. But if it drags on, and casualties mount, then it might well be he'd have to go into uniform.'

Vicky and Mary continued to talk, catching up with one another, till there was the sound of a key turning in the front-door lock.

Mary had already lit the fire, which now glowed brightly, giving out an intense heat. Just the fire for a man to come home to after a hard day's work in bitter January. Vicky stood up, smoothed down her dress and folded her hands in front of her.

'Hello, Dad, how's yourself?' she said when George walked into the kitchen.

George came to an abrupt halt to stare at her in astonishment. 'You're back then, girl,' he said slowly.

'Aye, Dad, I'm back.'

'For good too,' Mary added, beaming.

He took off his hat and laid it aside. Then he went over to Vicky and embraced her.

He'd grown old too, Vicky thought. But not as much as her mother had. 'You're a driver now, I'm told. Congratulations,' she said.

He held her at arm's length, studying her, drinking her in. Tears crept into his eyes. Vicky could not remember ever having seen her father weep before. Glasgow men just didn't.

'Here's me greeting like some big wean,' George said and crossed to the fire, ostensibly to warm his hands but really to give himself a few moments to pull himself together.

'That was quite a shock,' he said huskily.

'She chapped the door right out of the blue, no word of warning or anything,' Mary said.

'I wanted to surprise you both.' Vicky smiled.

'Well, you certainly succeeded with me,' George said, keeping his back to her while he struggled to regain his composure. How he'd dreamed about this! There had been dark times when he had almost come to believe that he would never clap eyes on his daughter again, that she had gone out of their lives for ever.

'She's been at sea, as a purser,' Mary said to George.

'*Assistant* to the purser,' Vicky corrected.

George rubbed his hands and sat. 'You can tell me your story, young lady, while your mother gets the meal.'

Mary frowned. 'I should have thought, but forgot in the excitement. I haven't got enough in to include Vicky. I'll have to hurry round to the shops.'

'Tell you what, I'd love a fish supper, fish supper with black pudding. How about us getting three of those, my treat?' Vicky proposed.

'Are you sure?' Mary queried, thinking that she would prefer to cook something herself for Vicky, something special for her homecoming.

'As far as I'm concerned, a fish and black pudding supper would be perfect. Followed by some French cakes. You wouldn't have any of those, have you?'

Mary laughed. Vicky had always had a soft spot for French cakes. As a young lassie, given half the chance, she would have eaten them by the barrowload. 'The City Bakeries will still be open. I'll pop in and get a box.'

As her mother was getting ready, Vicky delved into her case to produce a bottle of bourbon, which she gave to George. 'That's Yankee whisky, I thought you might like to try it.'

'You two have a dram while I nip out and get the doings,' Mary said. When she left the house a few minutes later, she had a ten-shilling note of Vicky's in her purse, Vicky insisted it was to be her treat.

'You'll be going after a job then?' George said when Mary was gone.

Vicky watched her father pour the bourbon into thimble glasses, filling the glasses to the brim in Glasgow style.

'Aye, I'll sign on the Labour this Monday.'

'What sort of job will you go for, or will you settle for anything?'

'I'm an experienced shorthand typist and secretary. I'll go after a position as either of those.'

He'd forgotten that she had been taught shorthand typing at Duncliffe. 'You'll find there's a deal more work available in Glasgow than there used to be, and no doubt the war will create even more,' he said.

'So you don't think I'll have much trouble in finding something?'

He shook his head. 'Not in the least. As I say, it's changed days here.'

George swallowed the remainder of his bourbon and poured himself another. The taste was strange, alien to him. Not really to his liking, he decided. He wished she had brought a bottle of ordinary whisky – preferably Red Hackle, that was his favourite.

'How do you think the street will react to me?' she asked.

'Curious more than anything, would be my guess. Other than that, I would imagine their attitude to you will be as it's always been. After all, you're hardly the first jailbird we've had round here, you know. Townhead is fairly hoaching with them. Though, I must admit, you're the only female one that springs to mind,' he replied.

Vicky winced to hear herself described as such. But it was true: she was an ex-jailbird. She had not intended to tell her parents the truth of the matter, but now she decided she would. Why should she keep faith with Ken when he hadn't with her!

She knew that her father was deliberately being light-hearted about her having been in borstal and prison, but at the time, and probably even yet, he had been mortified by her supposed stealing – and undoubtedly, though he had never said it, had considered that she'd brought dis-honour on the family, dishonour and black disgrace. And the lightheartedness, the attempt to make it easy for her? Because her dad still loved her dearly. Despite everything, neither he nor her mum had stopped loving her.

Later, when Mary had returned, and the meal had been consumed, she requested that they all sit round the fire. When they were settled she proceeded to tell them what had really happened at Copland and Lye, and why she had done as she had. When she was finished, it was just as well for Ken Blacklaws that he had moved away from Parr Street.

For, if he hadn't, and George had been able to lay hands on him, George would probably have murdered him.

'Vicky! Vicky Devine!'

Vicky was hurrying along Parliamentary Road, having just been to sign on at the Labour. Halting, she turned in the direction of the voice that was hailing her.

He came charging across the Parli Road, nearly running slap bang into a coalman's horse and cart.

He stumbled at the kerb, almost sprawling his length on the pavement, which made her laugh. My God, he hadn't changed! Then she had a closer look at his face and saw she was wrong: he had.

'Hello Neil,' she said.

Neil Seton smiled hesitantly. When he'd spied her across the road, his calling out had been spontaneous. 'I heard you were back, the street's buzzing with it,' he told her.

They stood gazing at one another, sizing each other up.

'Your plooks and blackheads have disappeared. I promised you they would eventually,' she said.

'You did that, I remember. They've been gone a couple of years now. It was just like magic. One week they were there, virulent as ever, the next gone, never to return.'

He paused, then tapped his head. 'Touch wood,' he added.

It wasn't only that his skin was now clear as a bell: his face itself had altered somehow, sort of filled out, she thought. The effect was to make him quite handsome. And his hands – she'd noticed those when he'd tapped his head, those too were different. They had become long, slim and elegant; the type of hands she would have imagined belonging to a concert pianist.

'You look absolutely terrific,' he said. He was on edge, apprehensive inside, waiting for the tirade.

'You don't look so bad yourself, a big improvement on what you were.'

Neil blushed.

'Does it embarrass you, me saying that?'

'Not really, I know I was very much the ugly duckling

191

when younger. Mind you, it was those damn spots that were to blame, they were the bane of my life.'

Vicky resumed walking, and Neil fell in beside her.

'You're back to stay I hear?' he said.

'That's right.'

'I'm pleased about that. You were sorely missed.'

'Was I?'

'Oh aye, very much so.'

'If you include yourself in that, how is it you never came to visit me? I appreciate Duncliffe was a fair bit away, but not Duke Street.'

Neil glanced sideways at her. Still no signs of anger, no tirade. Had Ken kept his mouth shut after all?

'I always meant to visit you, but somehow never did,' he replied weakly, lying.

'I suppose your studies and new grand friends at university kept you busy,' she jibed.

He cleared his throat. He didn't want to pursue this. What he did want was to find out whether or not she *knew*. 'Did Ken ever mention me when you were at Duncliffe?' he asked, trying to make the question sound casual.

Vicky had to think about that. 'Not that I remember. Why?'

Relief surged through him. She *didn't* know. 'Nothing important, just wondering,' he replied vaguely.

He had become something of a dish, Vicky thought. It was he who had mentioned the ugly duckling, but hadn't the ugly duckling turned into a swan!

'Are you still studying?'

'I finish in June, five years' hard labour!' he replied with a laugh, which died when he saw her expression.

'Sorry, that was hardly the right thing to say in the circumstances . . . eh . . .' He shut up.

'And then what? Will it be straight into the forces?' she asked, initially put out by his tactlessness, then finding it rather funny, but not showing that she had. She recalled that Neil had aye had a talent for sticking his foot in it, a talent that he apparently retained.

Neil's lips set into a thin, stubborn line. 'This bloody war is a proper nuisance. My next step should be to work in a junior capacity for a law firm, but whether that will come about or not I don't know. After I leave uni, my call-up papers could come at any time,' he said bitterly.

'The war is going to interrupt a lot of lives, Neil. Yours will only be one of many. And it's going to do more than interrupt some, it's going to terminate them,' she admonished.

'Aye, you're right,' he conceded, but his lips remained thin and stubborn.

They walked a little way in silence. 'Speaking of Ken, do you still see him since he moved?' Vicky asked.

Neil thought back to that hellish night when Ken had given him such a terrible kicking in the rear-close dunny. He had thought that he would never walk again, and for a whole week his testicles had been swollen to the size of golfballs. If it hadn't been for the neighbours investigating his screams, the bastard might well have gone on to kill him. They had never spoken after that night, the night of the day Vicky had been arrested.

'No,' he replied tightly.

'What, did you fall out then?'

'I went to university and he got married. You know how these things are,' Neil prevaricated, and shrugged.

'And what about you? Have you married?' Vicky asked, thinking that, looking as he now did, the lassies at the university must be falling over themselves to get their claws into him.

Neil shook his head.

'Winching surely?'

'Oh aye, but no one special. They come and go, whole strings of them,' he said airily.

She wasn't sure whether that was true or not. It certainly *could* be.

'You were at sea, I'm told,' he went on, changing the subject away from himself.

'That got round quick enough!'

'Aye well, you know what it's like,' he replied, giving her a lopsided grin.

She talked about the *Atlantic Star*, about some of the people she had met and known and the exotic ports she'd visited, and recounted various anecdotes, till they arrived outside her close in Parr Street.

'It's been great seeing you again, Neil,' she said, offering her hand to be shaken.

He ignored the hand. 'There's a dance on at the uni this Saturday night. They're usually quite wild and fun. Do you fancy going?' he asked, trying to be nonchalant about the invitation yet sincere at the same time.

That caught Vicky on the hop. 'Are you certain you want to take me? You being a budding lawyer and me with my shady past?'

He hadn't thought of it that way. All he'd thought was that he'd be taking out Vicky, the same Vicky he had fallen for years ago, and for whom his feelings had never changed.

'I'll knock your door at seven sharp,' he said and, without waiting for a reply, he wheeled about and strode off across the street to vanish into his close.

Well well well! Vicky thought. And she fell to wondering what it would be suitable to wear for a university dance.

THE HONOURABLE SOCIETY OF DOCK WORKERS, the brass plate proclaimed. Vicky had found the address she had been seeking. She climbed the broad stone steps and went inside. Returning to the Labour Exchange that morning, she had been told that they had fixed her up with six interviews, three for that day, three for the next.

The place could do with a good cleaning, she thought, eyeing the grimy walls and ceiling. She doubted that it had seen a fresh lick of paint in twenty years or more.

'Can I help you?' a friendly-faced lassie asked, emerging from a doorway.

Vicky explained who she was and why she was there. The lassie took her through to an ante-room, told her to have a seat, and left.

Five minutes later a different girl poked her head round the door. 'Will you come with me please, Miss Devine. Mr Fyfer will see you now.' The girl smiled.

Vicky went back out into the carpeted corridor, which they started along. 'Is Mr Fyfer your personnel manager?' Vicky asked.

'We don't have a personnel manager. All personnel matters are handled personally by Mr Fyfer, the union president,' the girl replied.

She was to be interviewed by the union's president! Vicky was impressed.

The girl misinterpreted Vicky's expression. 'Don't worry, he'll not eat you, he's awful nice.'

They left the corridor to go up a twisting, carpeted stairway. The building might be a bit run down, seedy almost, but it had an atmosphere which Vicky decided she liked. She could tell that the folk who worked here were happy to do so.

Vicky judged Mr Fyfer to be in his late fifties. He had an honest, couthy face which she took to straight away. He was of middle height, and powerfully built, and he radiated energy. His office was in a right clutter. There were papers, diagrams, maps and all sorts strewn everywhere.

'Pleased to meet you, Miss Devine,' he said in a strong working-class accent, and ushered her to a seat that had already been placed in front of his desk.

He made a gesture that encompassed his office. 'Excuse the mess, but I can't function properly when everything's neat and tidy. Find it too constraining,' he apologised.

Mr Fyfer sat behind his desk and contemplated Vicky from underneath shaggy eyebrows. 'The Labour Exchange sent me a letter that said you'd been to sea. That could be useful to you and us if you came to work here.'

'The same thing crossed my mind as well,' Vicky replied, quite relaxed in Mr Fyfer's company.

'You've come ashore because of the war, is that it?'

'The company decided to discontinue employing women after we lost a ship,' Vicky explained, and went on to give Mr Fyfer all the details of her engagement with the Ellison Line.

Before the Ellison Line, she said, she had been at college, learning shorthand and typing, and before that unemployed since leaving school. She passed over her reference from the captain of the *Atlantic Star*, and her shorthand typing diploma, which Mrs Gardener had arranged, as Mrs Gardener did with all the girls at Duncliffe who passed the course, to be in the name of a well-known and established college.

After that Mr Fyfer asked her to take dictation, a short letter of six paragraphs only, which he rattled off at speed. When he had completed his dictation, he asked her to read back what she had taken down.

She clearly passed that test, so he took her to the typing pool, where she was introduced to three girls, then given a typewriter and told to type the letter. On finishing, she removed the letter and copy and gave them to Mr Fyfer, who studied them closely.

They returned to the corridor outside the typing-pool room, and there Mr Fyfer extended a hand. 'Thank you for coming in, Miss Devine,' he said.

Vicky shook the proffered hand. He wasn't going to say one way or the other, but that was normal practice.

'Can you find your own way? Or shall I have someone take you?' he asked.

She guessed correctly that the question was a trick, and another test. He was trying to find out if she had any initiative.

'I can find my own way no bother, thank you.' She smiled.

He gave the slightest nod of approval and left her. Going back to his office, she presumed. She quickly located the twisting stairway and went down to the ground floor. Her interviews for that day now completed, as she headed for the front door she began thinking about her first interview of the next morning, at William McPhail & Co.'s Violet Grove foundry in Grovepark Street.

Hearing voices, one of them raised in anger, she came up short in sudden shock as it dawned on her whose the angry voice was. No – it couldn't be, she was imagining things! she told herself. Hesitantly, heart thudding in her chest, she slowly walked in the direction of the noise. At a corner she stopped, took a deep breath and looked round it.

The two men were about a dozen feet down the passageway, and both were in working clothes. The one in half profile facing away from her, and now shouting loudly, was Ken Blacklaws.

'No ifs and buts. You'll do as your shop steward tells you, and that's the finish of it!' Ken ranted.

Some girls appeared at the far end of the passageway to stare anxiously at the two men.

The angry exchange continued, the other man having begun to shout as well. Vicky stood transfixed, her emotions churning within her. She was hot and cold at the same time, and there was a strange whistling in her ears. Ken! *Her* Ken!

Then she reminded herself that he wasn't her Ken any more, but another woman's, his wife's. She forced her legs to uproot themselves and move. Once past the passageway she broke into a run. In the street she collapsed against some iron railings. The inside of her head was whirling, and it seemed to her that at any moment she could faint clean away. She could still hear his voice, bellowing from inside the building.

The man at the Labour gazed at the sheet of yellow paper he was holding. He was thin and very pale, and made Vicky think of a fish that was more dead than alive.

'Congratulations. Of the six jobs you went up for, four have offered you a position,' he said without smiling.

'Which four?' Vicky asked.

The man told her. The Honourable Society of Dock Workers was third on the list.

'And I'm at liberty to choose between them?' Vicky thought this was a far cry from the days when she had first gone looking for a job.

'Of course. The usual thing is to go for the firm paying the highest wages,' the man said, not even a hint of smile or expression on his face.

'And which firm is that?' Vicky queried. Dreading to hear the answer, whatever it was.

'The union. The Honourable Society of Dock Workers. They'll pay a full pound more than the others.'

Vicky closed her eyes. There it was on a silver platter: the chance to see Ken again. But did she want to see him? She just did not know.

What she did know by now was the reason he had been at the union headquarters. From inquiries she had learned that he was now a dockie, having left Copland and Lye some time back. So he would have been at union headquarters on union business – a dispute of some sort that he'd been involved in, from what she had overheard.

Just because she had seen him there once didn't mean he went often, she argued with herself. It was entirely possible that, working there, she would never run into him again.

Then there was the money to consider. An extra pound a week was not to be turned down casually. Why the hell should she lose out because of sentiment? Because of an affair she had once had with a union member?

The truth was, she further argued with herself, she would be plain daft to turn this job down. For, of the six jobs she had been up for, this was the job that, because of the people involved – forgetting Ken – and the atmosphere, had attracted her most.

Then a niggle of anger asserted itself. She had lost so much already on account of Ken flaming Blacklaws, why should she lose this opportunity also! So what if she did bump into him occasionally! For a big city, Glasgow could be an awfully small one. No doubt she would have bumped into him from time to time in the normal course of events anyway. Sod him. An extra quid a week was an extra quid, after all!

Vicky's eyes snapped open. 'I'll take the job. When do I begin?' she said.

Later, having thought over her argument with herself, Vicky knew that it was not fully convincing. Partially so, but not fully.

She really did not know whether or not she wanted to see Ken again.

She did.

Then again she didn't.

She was due to start work at the Honourable Society of Dock Workers that coming Monday morning.

The sweat was running off Vicky, a combination of the exertion of dancing and the heat of the hall. Neil, sweating also, suggested they sit down and have a drink. He found an empty bench and parked her there. He left her staring round when he went off for the drinks.

Vicky was thoroughly enjoying herself: the band was good, and Neil had turned out to be a fine dancer. She smiled at him when he returned carrying two pint glasses. Nor was she the only female who had smiled at him that night: he was popular with the girls, as she had thought he would be.

'I hope you like scrumpy,' he said, handing her a pint.

She knew scrumpy to be extremely strong cider, but this was the first time she had ever had any. She took a swallow, decided she liked its slightly sour taste, and took a deeper swallow.

'Don't down it too quickly. That stuff bites back,' Neil warned her.

'Sometimes I enjoy being bitten,' she replied, eyes glinting with amusement.

He stared at her in open admiration. Jesus, but she was gorgeous! — if anything, even more so than she'd been when younger. But there was now a sad, haunting quality about her that hadn't been there before. It made him ache inside when he noticed it.

He tore his gaze away from her and glanced out over the dance floor, which was filled with hundreds of heaving bodies.

'The middle class at play, God bless their cotton socks,' he said.

'Aren't you one of them now?' she teased, keeping a straight face.

'No, I am not! I'm working-class through and through, and proud of it,' he retorted softly.

'That pleases me,' she told him. And it did.

He knotted a hand into a fist. 'There's so much wrong with Glasgow, and it just seems to get worse. Take the housing, for example. A lot of it isn't fit to keep pigs in, far less human beings. Parr Street is bad, but nothing compared to many of the tenements I've been in, as I'm sure you have. Some day they will all have to be swept away and decent housing constructed in their place.

'And employment, that's another thing. Oh sure, it's all right at the moment, as there's a war on. But what about after, when peace comes again? I'll bet you a pound to sixpence it'll be back to how we were before: a hundred men after one job, and ready to kill one another to get it.

'I'm telling you, Vicky, the ILP may be a spent force, but they had the right ideas. Their brand of socialism is what Glasgow needs, is crying out for. The old order must be dismantled and swept away for all time,' Neil said vehemently.

He took a quick gulp of cider, then hurried on. 'It breaks my heart to see what's become of this city. Even in our lifetime the decay has been enormous. It's horrible; it's like watching someone you love die slowly, and in great agony, of some terrible disease.'

Neil gestured at the dance floor and dancers. 'That's why that lot annoy me so much. Most of them were born with silver spoons in their mouths, and haven't the foggiest what poverty's like, the sheer degradation and humiliation of it. All they can think about is their silly selves, and their careers, and getting on and making money. Probably the latter more than anything.

'They're here tonight, surrounded by squalor, and I doubt if one in a hundred, even that, is aware of it. They . . . they disgust me. They disgust me and make me want to throw up.'

'You're a revolutionary, that's what you are!' Vicky declared when he finished.

'If I am, so what? There are times when revolutionaries are needed!'

'I'm not criticising, Neil, not in the least. As you say, the world needs men like James Maxton and Neil Seton. To voice its conscience, if nothing else.'

He laid down his glass. 'Let's go back up. If I keep on like this, I'll just get angry, and possibly boring, and ruin your evening.'

'I don't find politics boring, Neil. They fascinate me, and always have. I'd prefer to keep on talking if you don't mind.'

So they talked politics. Maxton, Brockway, Cripps, Churchill, Harry Pollitt, Baldwin, Morrison, Bevan, Attlee were only some of the names that were mentioned – and argued over, for Vicky didn't believe in everything Neil did. Though, she had to admit, they did see eye to eye on an awful lot of things.

They had the last dance together, the traditional slow waltz, then went home.

They stopped outside Vicky's close, with rain drizzling down, and Neil was suddenly nervous. He hoped it didn't show.

'Thanks for a marvellous evening,' Vicky said.

'How about us going to the pictures one night next week? Something local,' he asked hesitantly.

'Shouldn't you be studying?'

'Don't worry. I won't fall behind on that, not with my finals looming on the horizon.'

She decided that she would like to go out with him again. He had been excellent company, stimulating too. 'All right then.'

They made the arrangements. He would chap her door just after six on Wednesday night.

He took her hand. 'Can I kiss you?' he asked softly.

She pulled him inside the close and along to the dunny. There she offered up her lips.

Bliss! he thought as his lips touched hers. Absolute bliss!

On the Tuesday morning, Vicky's second day with the Honourable Society of Dock Workers, she was emerging from the ladies' toilet, when Ken Blacklaws walked by. He gave her a smile in passing. It was almost as big a shock for her as it was for him, but the difference was that she had known that the possibility of their meeting existed; he hadn't.

He was about to enter a doorway when he suddenly stood stock still. He whirled round to gape at her.

She had been watching him, waiting for his reaction. Now she crossed the corridor and went into the typing pool.

She sat down, put her hands on her typewriter, then hurriedly stuffed them into her lap, for they were quite visibly shaking. For a moment there she almost hadn't recognised him because of the elegant suit he was wearing. But why was he wearing a suit, and looking every inch an executive rather than the dockie she knew him to be?

Vicky rubbed her forehead. It hadn't been a daydream, had it? No, of course not, she assured herself. It had been him all right, in the flesh.

'Tea's up!' Madge Gallacher, one of the other three typists in the pool, said, and plonked a cuppa on Vicky's desk. As it was morning tea there was a plain biscuit on the saucer; in the afternoon it was a digestive. Vicky was halfway through her tea when the door opened and Ken entered. His gaze went straight to her and their eyes locked.

It was a titanic struggle for Ken, but somehow he managed to look away from Vicky. 'I've signed my letters, so this lot is now ready for the post,' he said to Madge, and laid a sheaf of envelopes in front of her.

His letters! *His* post! Vicky thought in alarm.

'You'd better meet our new typist,' Madge replied, and drew Ken over to where Vicky was sitting.

'This is Vicky Devine. Vicky, this is Mr Blacklaws,' Madge said.

What would he say? Vicky wondered. She would take her cue from him. She rose, but didn't utter. Ken licked his lips in apprehension. The eyes boring into his were far more mature than he remembered. And they seemed so accusing!

'How do you do, Miss Devine,' he croaked.

So that was how it was to be. They were going to pretend that they hadn't known each other previously. 'Pleased to meet you, Mr Blacklaws,' she replied in a neutral tone.

They shook hands; she was thankful that hers had stopped shaking. He had put on a bit of weight round the belly, and his hair had started to thin, she noted. He had kept his moustache, which was now thicker. And the horn-rimmed glasses were new.

They made the customary small talk for the circumstances, then he excused himself, saying he had to get on.

When he was gone, she picked up her cup and drained what remained in it. She was quite stunned by the happenings of the past few minutes.

'What does Mr Blacklaws do here?' she asked.

'He's the union's vice-president, and son-in-law to Mr Fyfer,' Doreen, the girl whose desk was nearest to Vicky's, replied.

Oh my God, what had she done! Vicky thought. How could she have been so incredibly stupid to land herself in such a situation! But how was she to have known what the set-up was? No one she'd spoken to about Ken had said he had anything to do with the union, so how could she have possibly known!

She went icy to think she might have to meet his wife. No, she just couldn't bear such a thing. She had made a horrendous mistake in accepting this job, and was now going to have to correct that mistake in the only way possible. She would give in her notice this Friday.

She started to copy-type a loading agreement but made such a hash of it that she had to abandon that effort and begin again. In the end she had six tries at the agreement before she managed a passable result.

Somewhere in the middle of this her hands resumed shaking.

She emerged from work to find it snowing heavily. Bowing her head against the flickering white wall, she hurried on her way. She had not gone far when she was suddenly grabbed by the arm. She gave an exclamation of fright, thinking she was being either attacked or molested. But it was Ken.

'We have to talk,' he said urgently.

She stared at him and didn't reply.

'There's a nice wee pub close by, we could go there,' he went on.

'Why should I?'

'Why shouldn't you? I was the one who let you down, after all.'

Oh you did indeed, you bastard, she thought, but didn't say so. Then she thought, why not! Wasn't that what she had wanted all along, and the real reason she had taken the job? Deep down she had wanted to see and speak to him again. It was the first time she had actually admitted that to herself.

'Lead on, MacDuff,' she replied.

They walked side by side, in silence.

She found the pub a disappointment. There was nothing particularly nice about it at all. It was no more than a very ordinary Glasgow boozer. She strongly suspected that this wasn't the pub he normally frequented in the area, but one where they were unlikely to be spotted together.

He brought the drinks over from the bar, a large whisky and lemonade each, and sat facing her.

'You've put on the beef, and I see the hair isn't what it was,' Vicky said, and smiled.

Her directness took Ken aback. Automatically he reached up and touched his hair. He was extremely sensitive and self-conscious about the fact that it was thinning. 'My hair's not that bad!'

Vicky arched an eyebrow.

'But I will admit to putting on a few pounds round the middle,' he said reluctantly.

She had him on the defensive, which had been her intention. It was a trick she had learned from Tina Mathieson.

'Did you know I worked for the union?'

She shook her head, for she hadn't. She had seen him in the building, but had not been aware that he actually worked in it. She would never have accepted the job if she had.

'So how did you come to be with us?' he probed.

'Through the Labour Exchange. I had an interview with Mr Fyfer, was offered the position, and that was that,' she replied.

Ken relaxed a little. It wasn't as he had feared. He had thought that she had deliberately come to work for the union in order to make trouble for him.

'Don't worry. Now that I know you work there as well, I'm going to give in my notice. I'll find another job,' she said.

That was a relief. Or was it? 'Probably for the best,' he muttered.

Remembering how she had clawed Miss Ganch's face, she had an intense desire to do the same to him, to inflict physical pain on him in revenge for the mind-bending mental anguish he had once inflicted on her. She saw him glancing surreptitiously at her left hand.

'No, I'm not married,' she said.

The hint of a blush stained his cheeks. 'I just wondered, that's all. I've often wondered . . .' He trailed off in confusion.

'How about you? Children?'

'A wee boy, five months old.'

'So your wife wasn't pregnant when you married her?'

That verbal stiletto thrust made Ken wince. 'No, she wasn't. Vicky . . .' He searched for words. Jesus, but this wasn't easy! It was because of him that she had gone to borstal and jail and, while she was there, he had ditched her.

'You were away for an awful long time. I suppose you might say I just couldn't last it out,' he said, the words stumbling from his mouth.

'You could have found yourself a fuck without having to marry her, surely?' Vicky retorted, being intentionally crude, and smiled again.

What remained of his blush vanished, and his face went stark white. 'It wasn't like that,' he mumbled.

'Oh? What was it like then?'

Vicky was not making this easy for him, but then he could hardly have expected she would. 'It wasn't merely sex, there was more to it than that.'

'You fell in love with her. Out of love with me, and in with her. Is that it?'

'Yes,' he lied, for he had never been in love with Lyn. He had married her for the career advantages that it brought him. Love had had nothing whatever to do with it.

Vicky fought back her bitterness and anger. 'What's your wee boy's name?'

'Kenny, after me.'

'Original,' she said scathingly.

'Aye, well. It wasn't my choice. It was Lyn's.'

Lyn, so that was his wife's name, now she knew. He had never mentioned it in the letter he had sent to Duncliffe, the letter breaking it off between them.

She downed her whisky. She'd needed that. And she'd have a repeat. She took her purse from her handbag and extracted a ten-shilling note, which she placed in front of Ken, 'Get another round in, will you.'

'That's all right, I'll do it,' he replied, pushing the ten-bob note back at her.

Her eyes snapped fury – fury caused not only by the dispute over who paid for the drinks. 'I said I'll pay for this round. Now will you please go up and get it in, or do you want me to go up to the bar myself?'

He saw her insistence on paying as an insult to him. For, as a man who was neither her fiancé nor her husband, it was his place to pay, his male place. Vicky saw it as a gesture of independence. He picked up the note and glasses, and left her.

When he returned with their refills, she sent him back again to the bar with hers to have more lemonade added to it. There was enough really; she was just cracking the whip a little.

'Are you staying in Parr Street with your folks?' he asked when he came back the second time.

'Aye, I am.'

'As you'll know, I moved out when I got married, and right pleased I was to leave the dump.'

Dump! How dare he! 'There might be a lot wrong with Parr Street, but there are some good folk live there don't forget,' she retorted.

'I wouldn't deny it, but then neither can you deny it's a slum. A place to get the hell out of when you've got the chance.'

'I suppose you live in a Bearsden mansion since you became vice-president of the union!' she replied sarcastically.

'Not yet, but one day, one day,' he mused.

'Still as ambitious as ever, eh?'

He couldn't help boasting, for he was proud of the fact: 'I've got letters after my name now. I'm an ACIBS.'

'Oh aye, and what's that, when it's at home?'

'It means I'm an Associate of the Cambridge Institute of Business Studies,' he explained.

Vicky was impressed, but didn't let him see that.

'It's a correspondence course that usually takes three years to complete. I did it in under two.'

Even if he had left school early, he had never lacked grey matter, she thought.

'I'm now studying for my Fellowship. Another eighteen months, maybe less, and I'll have that under my belt as well.'

'My, you have been busy,' she acknowledged in a voice that was ever so slightly mocking.

Vicky glanced down at her glass. She wanted to know more about the wife, was dying to know more. 'Where did you meet . . . Lyn, is it?' she asked, trying to make her question sound casual, as if the answer was of no consequence to her.

He told Vicky that they had met in a dance hall, which was true, if only part of the truth. He then went on to give Vicky a potted history of his life since that last letter he had sent to Duncliffe.

He had certainly fallen on his feet marrying this Lyn Fyfer, Vicky thought. It was on the tip of her tongue to ask him where he would be if she hadn't taken the blame for his thieving, but she restrained herself.

'And what about you? What became of you after Duke Street?' Ken inquired.

'So you knew I was sent there to complete my sentence.'

'I heard. But what happened? You always thought you'd get out, be set free, when you reached eighteen.'

How could she tell him about Ganch and 'pash' night? And particularly her incarceration in the Black Room, which she still had nightmares about? Or how could she tell him that for a long time after her release from the Black Room, and the time when he had broken it off between them, Tina had feared for her sanity? How could she tell a man who had spurned her these things? A man who had been the direct cause of her suffering?

'I got myself into a spot of bother, and having to complete my full sentence was the result,' she replied evasively.

'Bad luck.'

She closed her eyes and remembered Duke Street. Duncliffe had been awful. Duke Street, in a different way, ten times worse. She had had to endure things there that now made her shudder just to think of them. But one point in Duke Street's favour was that it didn't have a Black Room. She doubted whether she would have mentally survived another dose of that horror.

Ken glanced at his watch. 'I'll have to make a move. Can I give you a lift? I've got a car parked a few streets away.'

'I'll take the tram,' she replied, and pulled her coat back on.

Outside the pub he stopped to say goodnight, but she walked straight past him into the flurrying snow.

The tram rattled along, swaying and shoogling as it went. Vicky sat hunched against the cold, thinking about her conversation with Ken.

Then it came to her. Fallen on his feet marrying Lyn Fyfer, her Aunt Fanny! He had fallen on his feet all right, but not by chance. He had met this Lyn, seen the opportunity there was for him with her, and grabbed it.

Dockie to vice-president of the union: it all fell neatly into place. His next step would be the presidency itself. And how did she know this? Because she knew Ken Blacklaws, knew him for the opportunist he had always been. Did he love his wife as he claimed? Maybe he did, maybe he had even talked himself into believing he did. With Ken, that was entirely possible. So, the fact was he'd thrown her over for his ambition, not for another woman. The woman had been, and presumably continued to be, a means to an end.

Vicky took some consolation out of this knowledge. But only some.

Ken sat holding a large whisky, watching Lyn nurse wee Kenny as he suckled noisily and greedily at the breast. How contented she was since having had the child, how positively cowlike. Cowlike, passive and obsessed with the wean, obsessed to the point of ignoring all else.

He and she still had a sex life together – just. When he did get it, it was only after interminable pleading and cajoling, for she had lost all interest in lovemaking. Shortly after she had fallen pregnant, her voracious sexual appetite had, almost overnight, died right away.

He had hoped it would pass as she progressed in pregnancy. Then he had hoped it would pass with the birth of the baby. But here they were, five months after the birth, and still no signs of any sexual reawakening.

It wasn't only the sex – though Christ! that was bad enough – it was her whole attitude. Prior to her pregnancy, when she had been fun to be with, they had gone places together, done all sorts as a couple. Now she had hardly any time for him. The wean had become her entire world.

Ken lurched from his chair and crossed to the window. Pulling the curtain aside, he peered out. The snow had stopped, leaving the night crisp and clear. From his vantage point – the house was on a hill – he could see a good two-mile stretch of the docks. Over to the right was Merklands Quay, and he could just make out the floodlit stack of a cargo boat that his lads were in the process of unloading. They were doing it in conjunction with members of the Glasgow Wharf Workers' Association, one of the three rival unions.

When he had spoken to Jack Fyfer about amalgamating all four unions, Jack had said that the idea had merit but, unfortunately, was impracticable, as the other unions would never agree to it, not in a month of Sundays.

Make them agree! he'd said. When Jack had asked how, he'd replied: by any means it took. Jack had torn a strip off him then. There was enough violence in the world, he had admonished – this before the advent of war, though it had been brewing – without their adding to it.

Well, Ken didn't believe in such high-falutin moral principles. He *did* believe in taking what you wanted, by whatever methods were needed.

Jack pretended to be hard, but underneath it he was saft as shite. If only the old bugger would pop his clogs, he could step into the presidency and then . . . Oh, and then it would be a different kettle of fish altogether. He wouldn't just be president of a union; before long he would be master of the river and, as such, King of Clydeside. But Jack remained healthy and, by the union rules, Jack was president for life. Frustration welled in Ken, he wanted that presidency so much he could almost taste it. But while the old man lived, all he could do was drum his heels in impatience.

Vicky: his thoughts turned to her. And he began to cast his mind back, to remember.

He had started thinking about Vicky, and now he could not stop. Switching on the bedside light, he glanced at the alarm clock: three fourteen a.m., and sleep as far away as it had been when he had first come to bed. Beside him Lyn groaned, muttered something he couldn't make out and pulled the bedclothes up over her face. He switched off the light again.

He had so many memories of himself and Vicky, of the happy, magic times they had had together. And how marvellous she had been at lovemaking, far better than Lyn.

Even at her best, Lyn had never been a patch on Vicky. He thought back to the pub, to the exciting smell of Vicky. Her smell had always excited him. That cap of curls – he'd wanted to trickle his fingers through it, as he'd used to, and nibble an ear. She had always laughed when he did that.

He recalled the texture of her body skin, smooth as velvet, covered in soft, fine down. The skin itself had a sheen. He had adored stroking her all over; while he stroked, she'd lie with her eyes closed, sighing occasionally, loving every moment of the prolonged single caress.

A scene flashed into his mind: he and Vicky on a brae overlooking Loch Lomond. He remembered something he had done to her, and broke out in a cold sweat at the memory. That was something he'd never done to Lyn; she'd always forbidden it when he'd tried, saying it was disgusting.

Reaching under the bedclothes, he placed a tentative hand on Lyn's thigh. When she didn't object, he reached down, took hold of her nightdress, and rucked it up. Lyn grunted and made a sort of twisting motion. She tried to push his hand away.

'You'll enjoy it,' he whispered.

'Not tonight, perhaps tomorrow night,' she replied, annoyed.

'What's wrong with tonight?'

'I don't feel like it, that's why,' she said, and repeated the twisting motion.

'But *I do*!'

'Well, that's hard cheese,' she answered, her tone now one of irritation as well as annoyance.

'But it'll only take a minute, and I know you'll enjoy it,' he wheedled.

She sat up to glare at him in the darkness. 'Can't you take a telling, Ken? I said no, and I mean no. Now, will you leave it!'

With that she threw herself flat again, and within seconds was once more asleep. Ken knew she was asleep, for she had started snoring. She never did that when she was pretending.

Getting out of bed, he went to the toilet.

The next morning Vicky had hardly got her coat off when Ken breezed into the typing pool. He made a crack to Madge, making her laugh, then turned to Vicky.

'Right, Miss Devine. I'll give you a try out and see if you can do your stuff. Come to my office when you're ready. I have some dictation to give,' he said, and breezed out again.

'I certainly know what I could do with him given half the chance,' Madge commented to Joan, the fourth girl in the typing pool, and winked salaciously.

'You and me both,' Joan agreed.

It was clear that Ken had not lost his sex appeal, Vicky thought. He was still knocking the birds for six, just as he'd always done.

'What about you, Vicky, do you fancy him?' Doreen queried.

If only you lot knew! Vicky thought, and laughed inwardly. 'Doesn't do anything whatever for me, I'm afraid.'

'What sort do you like then?' Madge asked.

'*Unmarried* ones,' Vicky jibed, and left the room to the sound of laughter.

When she entered Ken's office, she could see right away how nervous he was. He had completely hidden that while in the typing pool.

'I really do have some dictation, but I wanted a word with you as well,' he said.

There was a chair set for her in front of his desk. She sat down and laid her notepad and pencil on the desk. 'I'm listening.'

'I've been thinking about you handing in your notice, and it seems so bloody unfair somehow. You've landed a tremendous job here, for old man Fyfer is terrific to his staff. He's a real joy to work for, the ideal employer . . . You get more holidays than other jobs, and a shorter working day, and it's double time if you have to work overtime or come in on a Saturday . . . Then again, there's the pay. He always pays more than anyone else, and usually by a fair whack at that.

'So, I was wondering, is it possible we could be friends?

We did mean a great deal to one another when we were together, and it seems to me that it would be criminal if all that went by the board.'

'Are you saying you don't want me to give in my notice?'

'I'm saying it would be a rotten shame on you if you did, for you'd lose financially as well as an ideal job,' he replied quickly.

He stared at her expectantly, but she didn't answer.

'If it would be any help, an inducement, so to speak, I could arrange it so that you get paid even more than you are now. Whatever your wage is, I could add another pound a week to it, and the other girls needn't know if you didn't want them to.'

That would mean two pounds a week more than she'd get anywhere else; it was certainly tempting, Vicky thought. But did she want to be in a position where she was seeing Ken day in and day out?

Ken hung his head. 'If you did stay on, it would make me feel a little less guilty about what happened. I can tell you, you've no idea *how* guilty I have felt about it.'

She was being plain stupid even to consider staying, Vicky thought. She should give in her fortnight's notice on Friday as she'd said she would.

'The last thing I want is for you to be done down yet again because of me, so please stay?' Ken pleaded.

'What about your wife. Does she ever visit here?' Vicky asked.

'She used to pop in occasionally, but hasn't since the baby was born. With the baby keeping her so busy at home, I expect it'll be quite some while before she does so again.'

Vicky studied the fingernails of her left hand. She had had beautiful fingernails when younger, but they had never been the same since Duncliffe and Duke Street.

'Does Lyn know about us?' she asked softly.

'She can hardly think I came to her unsullied and untouched! But no names have been mentioned, ever,' Ken answered, making a bit of a joke out of it.

'And there would be no problem about the pay increase?'

'None at all, I promise you.'

She had heard his promises before, she thought grimly. She should turn him down out of hand, get the hell out as soon as possible. And yet . . . she'd lose at least a pound a week if she left, gain another if she stayed. And did it really bother her seeing Ken on a daily work-week basis? After the initial shock and panic, it wasn't that unnerving.

'So what's the verdict? Can we be friends and let bygones be bygones?' he urged hopefully.

'I'll think about it,' she prevaricated, and took up her notepad and pencil again.

The matter was closed for now, that was clear. Best not to try and push it any further, Ken decided. He switched his mind over to business and, after a short pensive pause, began to dictate.

Seven

Vicky and Neil were in her back-close dunny, having just returned from a local café. Neil had been able to snatch only an hour away from studying as his finals were now less than seven weeks off. They were kissing and cuddling to the accompaniment of a fearsome domestic row in a house close by. Smash, bang, wallop, scream! It wouldn't be long before the police arrived.

One of his hands slid onto her bottom, another sought a breast.

She pushed him away. 'If we don't stop now, you'll be in no fit state to go back to your books,' she said, laughter in her voice.

'Oh, Vicky, I enjoy nothing more than being with you. When I'm not with you, I can't wait to see you again.'

'I enjoy being with you too,' she replied.

He caught her nearest hand, raised it to his mouth and kissed it.

'Gallant,' she murmured.

'These Froggies and Eyeties aren't the only ones who can be that. We Scotsmen can be as gallant as the best of them.'

Neil was very caring, she suddenly thought. Caring, sensitive and considerate. Fine and admirable qualities all, and ones she much appreciated.

'I was hoping to take you to the pics on Saturday night, but I doubt I can: money's just too tight at the moment.'

She could have paid, but he would have been offended if she'd offered. 'It must be right rough for you and your mum at times.'

'Aye, it can be that, but up until now, thanks to my grant and a few other wee things, we've managed to get by, if only just.'

She had an idea that neatly solved the problem. 'Listen, my dad got hold of a slide lantern recently. Why don't you come to our house for tea on Saturday, and we can watch some slides afterwards, have our own picture show, like?'

'That would be great, Vicky.'

She would lay in a bottle of whisky for the occasion, she thought. Neil was not much of a drinker, but her dad never said no to a dram, and she and her mother appreciated a tipple as well.

'Till then,' she said, and kissed him lightly on the lips. They made their way to the front close, where the gas mantle was sputtering out soft yellow light, and there they had another quick kiss before Vicky ran up the stairs and he went across the road to his own close, and home.

Vicky found her parents in the kitchen. Mary was just finishing off the ironing, while George was mending a pair of his shoes with some good stout leather he'd managed to come by.

'So how was Neil?' Mary inquired.

'Looking washed out from all that studying he's doing, but it has to be done,' Vicky answered.

'Brainy lad Neil, always was,' George muttered.

'I've invited him to tea this Saturday, and I thought we might have the slides after,' Vicky said.

'Oh, so that's the way of it, is it? Getting his feet under the table now!' George exclaimed, tongue in cheek.

'No harm in that. Vicky could do an awful lot worse than Neil Seton,' Mary said primly.

George hefted his hammer. '*Is* it serious, lass?'

Vicky shrugged. 'I'm not sure.'

'Then it isn't?' Mary prompted.

'I didn't say that! I said, I'm not sure.'

George hammered in a nail, then another four in rapid succession. 'What about work? Any likely candidates for your affections there?' he asked.

'Why do you ask that?' Vicky replied sharply, alarmed.

George glanced up at her, wondering at the sudden rise in pitch of her voice. 'No reason other than you never speak of the place, or those who work there with you.'

Vicky had not told her parents about Ken being vice-president of the union and had no intention of doing so. She judged it better that way, for George held a bitter grudge against Ken because of all that she had gone through on account of him.

As for her continuing on at the union, the subject of giving in her notice had never been raised again between her and Ken since that meeting in his office three months back when he'd pleaded with her to stay. She had seen out the first week, then the next, and after that the matter had drifted. She had got the extra pound a week Ken had promised; he had kept his word there.

'I didn't realise I never spoke about work. Must be because everything there is fairly routine and boring,' she lied.

Her ironing finished, Mary put the iron by the sink to cool and wiped her sweaty hands on her pinny. 'Where's John's letter? I think I'll have a read of it again.'

The letter had arrived by the second post the previous day, the first word they had had of John for weeks.

'It's on the mantelpiece behind one of the wally dugs. Why don't you read it out loud? You wouldn't mind that, would you, Vicky?' George answered.

'No, in fact I'd like it,' Vicky said.

Mary found the letter and took it from its envelope. She read slowly, haltingly, her voice crackling with emotion.

John did not actually say that he had been in action, but it was clear from some of the things he mentioned that he must have been. He and a pal called Ginger had found a cache of French brandy, and John described how their squad had had a right old hooley on that before having to move on, taking a bottle each of what remained with them. The weather was not too bad where they were, and most nights they managed to sleep under a roof, which certainly made life a great deal easier than it might have been. The rations were dull but, so far anyway, in plentiful supply. From time to time they managed to buy, and in some cases 'liberate', local grub that augmented, and made an awful lot tastier, the aforesaid rations. He was in good heart, and missing them all. He couldn't wait to be back in Sauchiehall Street on a Saturday night – that, and to have a pint of real Scots heavy.

Mary finished the letter and dashed away a tear. George, face set hard yet somehow soft underneath, returned to his shoe mending.

'I'll put the kettle on,' Vicky said quietly.

Vicky and Neil were walking in Alexandra Park, the pair of them licking raspberry-topped ice creams in cones bought from a barrow run by a very worried-looking Tally, or Italian. The man had a right to look worried, for if Italy entered the war on the German side, as seemed likely, he'd be for internment.

They paused in front of the bandstand to stare at the empty stage area. Vicky could remember George and Mary bringing her here as a wee girl to listen to concerts and watch variety shows.

'Vicky?'

She turned to him, a smile on her face.

'Will you marry me?'

The smile wavered and slowly vanished. This was no horse-play; she could tell from his expression that he meant it.

She resumed walking, and he fell in beside her. When they came to a litter bin she tossed her cone into it; she had suddenly lost her notion for ice cream.

'You're not replying?' he asked anxiously.

'Neil, your finals are imminent. This isn't the time to propose to somebody.'

'I'm not proposing to just somebody. I'm proposing to the woman I love, and with whom I've been in love for the past six years,' he retorted.

She stopped to stare at him. 'You have?'

He nodded.

'I didn't know that,' she said, and resumed walking again. She had been aware that he fancied her ever since the Hogmanay night when he'd saved her from rape and called her the Princess of Poor Street. But to fancy someone was one thing; love was quite another.

'I didn't press my suit in those days because you were going out with Ken. I'd never have stood a chance against him with all those pimples and blackheads I had then. But it's different now, and we do get on so well together.'

That was true enough. And, as Mary had said, she could do a lot worse than marry Neil Seton.

'I'll be a good and faithful husband to you, Vicky, I promise that.'

Her mind was churning. She had thought that he was falling in love with her, not realising that he'd been in love with her all this while.

'What about the war?' she asked.

His face clouded over. 'I have to admit that's the one big drawback. Once I'm qualified they could pull me in at any time, but I doubt very much if I'll be seeing any of the fighting. With my training, they're bound to put me behind a desk – and who's to say that desk might not be in Glasgow or not far away?' he replied.

She was twenty-one now, and not getting any younger, she thought. Common sense told her to accept. Then again, she shouldn't be rash and rush into anything. Of course it had occurred to her to marry Neil but – because of the war, she supposed – she'd seen any possible marriage as some distance in the future, not here and now.

Oh dammit! She didn't know what to do. He had quite caught her on the hop. 'Look, I have to think about this. Will you give me a breathing space?'

His mouth drooped. 'That means you're going to say no.'

'It does nothing of the sort. Your proposal has come straight out of the blue. I just wasn't expecting it, that's all.'

They walked a little way in silence. 'All right, a breathing space,' he agreed grudgingly.

She slipped a hand into one of his. 'You're lovely,' she told him.

'You're not so bad yourself.'

She put his arm round her waist, and hers round his. They started talking about the National Government that

Winston Churchill had formed the previous month. Neither of them ever tired of discussing politics.

It was just before her lunch break the next day when the telephone call came.

'Vicky, it's your dad,' Madge told her.

Her stomach muscles instantly contracted: something had happened – it had to have done for George to ring her at work.

'What is it?' she asked him in a tight whisper.

'I was just about to leave for my shift when an army padre chapped the door. The 51st Highland Division took an awful pasting heading for Dunkirk apparently. The HLI were in a big fight at a place called St Valery. John and a lot of his mates were killed there.'

Her wee brother dead! She had gone cold and numb all over. 'Oh, Dad!' she whispered.

'Do you think you could come home? Your mother needs you.'

There was a choking sound. Vicky could not be sure, but she thought her father was crying. 'I'll be there as soon as I can,' she said, and hung up.

Madge, Doreen and Joan were banging away at their typewriters, engrossed in what they were doing. None of them had overheard her telephone conversation.

She could not just leave without asking permission. Mr Fyfer was out, but Ken was in. She would have to ask him.

He was in his office poring over a contract when she entered. He glanced up, readjusting his glasses as he did so. 'What can I do for you, Vicky?'

She swallowed back the hot bile that had seeped into her mouth. Everything seemed to have taken on a grainy quality, and why did Ken sound so far away, as if he were in another room?

'My brother John was killed trying to get to Dunkirk for the evacuation,' she said, and fainted.

When she came to she was sitting on a chair with Ken peering anxiously at her. 'Here, swallow some of this,' he said, and placed a glass to her lips.

The undiluted whisky made her cough.

'And again,' he said when her coughing had subsided, and held the glass once more to her lips.

The pungent alcohol helped revive her; it also started to reheat her cold body.

'I'm so sorry about John, Vicky. Really I am.'

Tears crept into her eyes. 'An army padre came to tell my parents. I've got to get back to them right away.'

'Aye, of course. But just take a minute to get yourself together again. Then I'll drive you to Parr Street.'

'That's kind of you, Ken.'

'Nonsense, it's the least I can do.'

'During the entire evacuation my mum went to church every day to pray. Not only for John, but for all our boys.'

'The papers say it was a miracle as many were saved as there were,' Ken commented softly.

She struggled to her feet, but it was too soon and her legs buckled under her. Ken caught her, holding her close to him.

'Oh, Ken!' she wailed, grief overwhelming her. She sobbed into his shoulder while he muttered words of comfort and stroked her hair.

It was as if the years had rolled back and Duncliffe and Duke Street had never been. She was in Ken's arms again; the feeling was the same, only more intense, as when she had stood at the head of Parr Street the previous January staring down it. She was home, back where she belonged.

Finally – and how she hated doing it – she broke from his embrace. 'I'll go to the cloakroom and wash my face and put my coat on.'

As she left his office, she was forced to admit to herself what she had been trying to deny and hide from this long long while. She was still head over heels in love with Ken Blacklaws.

Mary was the churchgoer, but it was Vicky who had organised the service, Mary being far too distraught to do so. All of Parr Street were present, and many from round about, for the family was a popular one, and John had been well liked. The Reverend Alan Chatto, who had baptised John, as he had Vicky, led the prayers for John's soul.

Vicky glanced over at Neil. She wasn't going to marry him. How could she, feeling the way she did about Ken? She had told Neil that, because of John's death, which she was using as an excuse, she would wait until after his finals to give him her decision. After all, she didn't want to upset him before his finals – she thought she owed him that much.

She raised her gaze to the gallery. Above Neil, and to her right, was Ken. There was a woman on either side of him, but she knew that neither of these was his wife, for she had seen him arriving alone.

Ken stared impassively back at Vicky, wondering how and when he was going to make his move for her. That day in his office when she had fainted after hearing about John's death had told him all he wanted to know. He was going to seduce Vicky again, and make her his mistress. He was determined about that, as determined as he had ever been about anything.

It was after the next hymn that George, quite by chance, caught sight of Ken. For a moment he did not recognise the face, then it clicked. Anger spurted in George: to think that his Vicky had gone to borstal and prison because of that bastard, and while she was there, saving his skin from long-term imprisonment, the bastard had gone and ditched her to marry another! This wasn't the time or place, but some day, George promised himself, he would see that fancy dan Ken Blacklaws again, and when he did he would have it out with him. And he wasn't thinking just about an exchange of words either.

George looked to the pulpit and bowed his head when the Reverend Chatto started to intone.

'Our Father, which art in Heaven . . .'

Vicky returned to work on the Monday following the service. The next afternoon Ken came into the typing pool.

'Vicky, I have to go to John Brown's and I'll need someone to take shorthand for me while I'm there. Be ready to leave in half an hour, will you?'

It was a fairly common occurrence for the girls of the typing pool to accompany Mr Fyfer, Ken and other union executives to meetings at the docks and elsewhere, so none of them thought this instruction odd in any way.

Ken drove the Riley himself. The union had a chauffeur, but Ken preferred to do his own driving. He always used the chauffeur, however, if he was attending an official function, for appearances' sake.

'How are your mum and dad?' he asked when they were under way.

'As well as can be expected in the circumstances. Mum in particular took it very badly, you know.'

'Yes, that was obvious in the church.'

She touched his left arm. 'Thank you for going to the service. I appreciated that.'

They headed for Clydebank, where the world-famous John Brown Shipbuilding yard was situated. 'By the way, I've got a surprise for you,' Ken said.

Vicky was instantly intrigued. 'What sort of surprise?'

'A nice one,' he teased.

'Does that mean you're not going to tell me what it is?'

He chuckled. 'It wouldn't be a surprise if I did now, would it?'

'Beast!' she murmured, wondering what on earth the surprise could be. As it turned out, she would never have guessed in a million years.

At John Brown's they went into the management offices, where Ken and a chap by the name of Dougie Glennie had a drink together. Vicky was offered one but refused, saying it was far too early in the day for her.

'Right then, where is she?' Ken asked when his drink was finished, standing as he did.

'Over at drydock four, that's the one by the east gate. Do you want me to take you there?' Dougie Glennie answered.

Ken shook his head. 'I know where the east gate is. We won't get lost.'

Ken and Vicky took their leave of Dougie. Outside the offices the yard was abustle with activity, the din tremendous. As she walked beside Ken, Vicky watched in fascination as a gang of riveters went about their work.

'Who's this woman you're meeting?' she asked.

'An old friend of yours. I've never met her before in my life.'

'A friend of mine! Is that the surprise?'

'That's it.'

Her mind raced. What friend could it possibly be? A school chum? Somebody she'd known at Copland and Lye? No, unless it was her cousin Sylvia.

Vicky recognised the ship the moment it came into view. It was the *Atlantic Star*, of which she had so many fond memories.

Ken laughed. 'I told you she was an old friend!'

'You remembered the name even though I only ever mentioned it to you once.'

'I did, and when I learned she was here for a refit I thought you'd like to come along and say hello.'

Men were swarming over the superstructure, which was not quite as she recalled it. She then realised that part of it had been removed. 'Why is she here?'

'Total refit. She's being turned into a troop ship, including having a number of guns fitted. Want to go aboard?'

'Can we!' Vicky exclaimed in delight.

'Everything's possible, when you know the right people. I'd already phoned Dougie Glennie before we came, and he's fixed it.' Ken smiled.

A gangplank which appeared a lot more rickety than it actually was brought them onto what had been the main passenger deck. Vicky pointed out to Ken where the swimming pool and the aft sun bar had been, both of which had now gone.

When they had had a good tour round the outside, Vicky marvelling at all the changes that had taken place, they went inside. She showed Ken what had been the ballroom, dining rooms and lounges, now all completely transformed. The purser's office remained as it had been, however, so Ken was able to see where she had worked.

'How about your cabin? Why don't you show me that?' he asked.

They plunged deep into the bowels of the ship to where the crew's quarters had been located, to discover that that area was still relatively untouched.

The cabin was tiny, eight feet by six, and without a porthole. 'It's nothing now, but I had it fine and cosy when I was here,' Vicky said wistfully.

It was funny, she thought, she had been in this cabin countless times thinking about Ken, remembering how it had been between them. And now here he was. Here they both were.

'Vicky,' he murmured, his voice husky, and swept her into his arms. They kissed, and kissed again. Then he nibbled her ear, which made her laugh, as he had known it would.

She read in his eyes what he wanted, and it was what she wanted too. But not like this, and not yet.

They kissed a third time, and this time it was she who kissed him, taking his head in her hands and pulling him to her.

'Did you plan this?' she asked.

'I planned to bring you to the ship when I found out it was here, I told you that,' he replied, playing dumb.

'That's not what I mean.'

He grinned. 'I must admit it did cross my mind, but how was I to know the cabin would still be here, and intact, with no workmen nearby?'

'I wouldn't put it past you to have arranged that.'

'I'm innocent, judge, I swear!' he exclaimed, and placed his open palms against her breasts.

Her insides went all soft while her nipples hardened into studs because it was Ken who was touching them – Ken, who had touched them and caressed them and loved them so often in the past.

'I can't, not for another fortnight,' she told him.

'Why a fortnight?' he queried, frowning.

With a sigh she turned away from him and took a moment to catch her breath. 'Because that's when Neil Seton's finals are.'

Ken's frown deepened. 'What has Neil and his finals got to do with it?'

'Neil has asked me to marry him, and I've told him I'll give him my decision directly after he's sat his exams. I'll be saying no, but it wouldn't be fair on him for me to get involved with you until I've done so.'

Ken sat on the bed and lit a cigarette. 'I'd forgotten he loved you. When I think about him, which is rarely nowadays, I only ever remember the other thing.'

'You knew that he loved me?'

'Oh aye. He told me the last time we spoke to one another, the night of the day you were arrested. I was chiselling him about what he'd done when he came out with it.'

'Done what?' Vicky queried.

'That's the "other thing' I just referred to. I don't suppose he's mentioned the telephone call he made to Copland and Lye?'

Vicky shook her head.

'He loved you and wanted me out the way. I stupidly, being drunk out my skull at the time, told him about my nicking while working overtime. He then rang Copland and Lye and put the finger on me. Only it backfired when you claimed it was you doing the nicking. So you've Neil to thank for your three years in borstal and jail!'

Vicky was dumbfounded. 'He's never breathed a word of any of this.'

'I'd be amazed if he had. I presume he's not aware that you and I work alongside each other?'

'No, I've never said. Not to him, or anyone.'

'So why should he mention it, then? As long as he believes I'm not about, how are you to find out otherwise?'

Now Vicky knew why Neil had never visited her in either Duncliffe or Duke Street. He had been afraid to in case she knew about his phone call.

She recalled how, when she had first met up again with Neil on her return to Parr Street, he had asked if Ken had spoken about him while she was at Duncliffe, and how relieved he had been when she'd replied in the negative.

Ken took a drag on his cigarette. 'Still feel you have to wait a fortnight?' He smiled.

She was sorely tempted. Then a pneumatic drill began clamouring nearby and blew temptation away.

'Forgetting Neil, when I make love to you again after all this while, I'd like it to be somewhere nice, where we can be romantic together. We certainly can't be that here, now can we?'

She was right, Ken thought. It would be a lot better in what she called somewhere nice. 'So you agree to us becoming lovers again?'

'I agree,' she whispered.

He threw what remained of his cigarette onto the floor and ground it underfoot. 'And the fortnight?'

'We've waited so long. What's another fortnight here or there? And in truth I'd be far happier if we did hold off till I can tell Neil. No matter what he's done, it would be on my conscience if we didn't.'

'All right, you're the boss,' Ken said, and stood.

Vicky unsnecked the door.

The evening after the last of Neil's exams Vicky arranged for him to come to her house. She also arranged for George and Mary to go out visiting.

'How do you think you did?' she asked, ushering him into the kitchen.

'Pretty well, but just how well I'll have to wait and see,' he replied, and tried to take her in his arms. But she wriggled free and went over to the sink, to put distance between them.

'What's wrong? Have I suddenly developed bad breath or something?' he joked.

'You'll never guess who I ran into the other day?' she said.

He raised an eyebrow, but did not reply.

'Ken Blacklaws.'

His face sort of crumpled in on itself and his body drooped. 'And?' he croaked, knowing what he was going to hear next and praying to God he was wrong.

'He told me what you did,' she stated, voice now chill.

Neil jerked like a gaffed fish. 'Fuck!' he swore softly.

'Neil, I can't possibly marry you now. You must be able to see that.'

She had been going to explain that, much as she liked him and his company, she just didn't love him. The telephone-call business made her refusal easier.

'No, I don't,' he mumbled, wishing he could think clearly, argue his case. But his brain had gone numb, refusing to function as he wished it to. Like sand running through his fingers, he could feel her slipping away from him.

'Have you any idea what I went through because of you? Three years of hell, Neil, three years of unmitigated bloody hell.'

He cringed. 'I never meant you to be arrested, that was all a horrible mistake,' he mumbled.

'I know. You wanted Ken to be arrested. Well, if he had been, I'd never have forgiven you for that either.'

'How can you say that about a man who had no respect for you? Who ditched you when you were inside?'

'I'm not going to defend Ken. What he did is between him and me. Now I think you'd better go, Neil. Goodnight and goodbye,' she said and turned away from him.

He launched himself at her, but she shrugged him off. 'I said goodbye, Neil,' she repeated, her voice a steel whiplash.

'Vicky?' he pleaded in a whisper.

Her lips thinned and set hard. She folded her arms in a gesture of finality.

When Neil was gone, Vicky burst out crying. She had hated doing that. Would she have married Neil if Ken hadn't happened along again, and despite the fact she didn't love him? She didn't know. She just did not know.

Vicky told Ken the next day that she had broken it off with Neil and he immediately asked her, winking as he did so, if she would work overtime that night. She replied that of course she would.

He came to the typing pool when everyone else in the building had left.

'I want to show you something,' he said, taking her by the hand.

Arriving at Jack Fyfer's office, they went inside. In one wall was a door which Vicky had always presumed belonged to a cupboard or suchlike. She could not have been more wrong. Ken opened the door and switched on a light. Vicky gasped. In front of her eyes was a beautifully fitted-out small apartment, including single bed.

'What's all this?' she asked.

Ken's eyes twinkled. 'How about "somewhere nice"?'

Vicky laughed and clapped her hands in glee. It was very nice. The fixtures, fittings and furniture were all of the highest quality and must have cost a mint.

Ken crossed to the window and closed the curtains, then he switched on the gas fire that replaced the original coal one.

'It's not such a mystery as it might seem. When Jack first became union president, he bought a grand house out in the village of Balfron, which is quite some distance from Glasgow.

'To begin with, Jack didn't find the drive home at night difficult, for he was leaving here at a fairly reasonable time. But then he started having to work late a great deal, and sometimes past midnight, and that was when the problems arose.

'It was a good hour and a half's drive home, and then the same back here again in the morning, which meant he was getting next to no sleep at all, and suffering from it.

'In the end it was Wendy, my mother-in-law, who suggested he have this room, which was a file room then, gutted out and done up so that if he felt it was too late for him to go home he could stay here.'

'And does he still? 'Vicky queried.

'Aye, occasionally, but nothing like he used to. With the staff now being far larger than it was, and having a full-time vice president to help, his workload has been reduced considerably to what it once was,' Ken explained.

'But won't he know we've been in here?'

'We'll tidy up before we go, which should do the trick. My father-in-law is many things, but not one of your more observant men round the house, or apartment in this case. So what do you think? Perfect eh?'

'Couldn't be more so.' She smiled, and shivered in anticipation.

Ken poured them both drinks and, when she was sipping hers, switched off the light. The glow from the fire became their sole illumination.

They kissed lightly, butterfly kisses, and touched one another, she as eager to touch him as he her. She didn't say it, but she had had no one since the last time she and Ken had made love together. Nor had that been from lack of offers. She had had plenty of those while aboard the *Atlantic Star*, from crew and passengers alike. But she had remained celibate because she had not desired anyone that way – until Ken had come back into her life again, that was.

He slowly stripped her till she was standing naked before him. He nuzzled her left nipple, then the right. She stripped him, occasionally pausing to stroke and caress his skin as she did so. She laughed when he bent and gently bit her ear.

They sank to the floor and stretched out in front of the gas fire, its warmth washing over their bodies. It had been a long long time, she thought languidly as he moved within her. But it had been worth the wait.

Oh yes.

Neil, shoulders hunched, hands thrust deeply into his trouser pockets, walked through the night. All around him tenements loomed, foreboding and somehow sinister. He inadvertently kicked a can to send it clattering noisily along the pavement. A black moggie, which had been half asleep in a close mouth, jumped in fright.

He felt wretched, filled with despair. He wanted to shout and scream and knock down walls. He wanted Vicky, how he wanted her.

But he wasn't going to have her, not now, not ever. She had found out from sodding Ken Blacklaws about that damned telephone call, and that had been the end of her and him. If only he'd never made that telephone call! If only it had been Ken who had been put away, as he'd intended, and not Vicky! If only . . . If only . . . *If only!*

He'd have to get away from Parr Street, he decided. He wouldn't be able to bear bumping into Vicky from time to time. That would be sheer torture.

Suddenly he knew what he was going to do. It was inevitable anyway, so why not sooner rather than later?

Early the following Sunday evening Vicky turned into Parr Street having just returned from Springboig, where she had gone to try and re-establish contact with Tina Mathieson, something she had been meaning to do for a while.

She had found the address Tina had given her in Duncliffe all right, but the Mathiesons no longer lived there. According to a neighbour, they had flitted to Coventry eighteen months since, Mr Mathieson having landed himself a good job down there. Tina had gone with her family, the neighbour had been certain about that.

Vicky was lost in reverie, thinking about Tina, when Neil's mother materialised before her. Mrs Seton was in a state. She looked terrible. Her eyes were red and puffed from crying, and her face had a greyish pallor. She wagged an accusing finger. 'It's all your fault he's done what he has, Vicky Devine. You broke his heart, smashed it to smithereens, when you refused to marry him,' she said in a strident tone.

Remembering Mr Seton, Vicky was gripped by fear. Neil hadn't done anything stupid, had he?

'What's happened?'

'He's joined the army, volunteered. He left for Stirling yesterday morning,' Mrs Seton replied, sobbing.

Well, it wasn't what she'd dreaded there for a moment or two, Vicky thought with relief. 'He'd have had to go anyway,' she said.

'But not just yet, not yet a while!' Mrs Seton retorted, the beginnings of fresh tears glistening in her eyes.

'I'm sorry,' Vicky whispered.

'And so you should be.'

Neil clearly hadn't told his mother about the telephone call to Copland and Lye. Neither would she.

'He'll be killed. I know it. I know it! And I'll be left all alone in the world, no one to care for me, no one to think about me even,' she went on.

Vicky was not sure what Mrs Seton was grieving about most: Neil going into the forces or herself being left alone. She listened patiently while Mrs Seton ranted on. But finally, patience exhausted, she repeated that she was sorry about Neil but would have to away home now or her tea would be ruined.

Neil joined the army! That was a surprise, she thought, as she hurried down the street. Secretly she was pleased, though. It would have been uncomfortable having him about. She just hoped that he would be safe, for, despite what he'd done, she did not wish him any harm.

At least she had one thing to be thankful for: Ken wouldn't be going into the forces. He might work full time for the union, but that was strictly unofficial. Officially he was still a dockie, and as such in a reserved occupation. There would be no call-up for him.

She wondered which regiment Neil had joined. He should look very handsome in his uniform – he had the sort of male body that suited a uniform. He would probably be given desk work, some basic training and then desk work for the duration.

Summer gave way to autumn, and autumn to winter. During that time the Battle of Britain had been fought and won. But elsewhere the war was not going well for Britain and her Allies. At the end of September the Japanese had entered Indo-China, while a week previously, on 7 October, the Germans had entered Rumania. The outlook was bleak, but the national spirit remained strong.

The cold October winds were rattling the windowpanes when Ken visited Jack Fyfer in his office and told him what he had in mind.

Jack couldn't believe his ears. 'Strike! How can you talk about a strike when there's a war on and we've all got our backs to the wall!' he roared. Jack was a patriot through and through.

'It's precisely because there's a war on that we've got them by the short and curlies. Now is the time, when we can't be refused, to use our muscle to screw up our members' wages.'

Jack glowered at his son-in-law. 'None of the other unions would wear such a preposterous – and I may say, in my opinion, treasonable – notion. We'd be on our own.'

'I'm counting on that.' Ken smiled.

An infuriating smile, Jack thought. Old man or not, if Ken hadn't been married to his Lyn, he'd have wiped the smile off the bugger's face. 'How so?' he queried.

'When we win a large pay increase that'll mean our members are earning considerably more than the members of the other three dock unions. So what'll happen then? I'll tell you: an awful lot of members from the other unions are going to terminate their membership and apply to join us, which will boost our numbers at the expense of the other three.'

Jack shook his head. 'The other three would never allow that to happen.'

Ken and Jack fell to a furious row about the whys, wherefores and consequences of calling a strike; and, because of their diametrically opposed views, both men completely lost their tempers.

Jack Fyfer's stomach was killing him. He had already had three lots of antacid mixture but his indigestion remained as fierce as ever. He blamed Ken for the attack: what a ding-dong battle they'd had! He had felt totally drained afterwards, and a short while later the burning sensation had begun.

Jack let himself into the union building by the main entrance, carefully locking the doors behind him. Groping his way to the nearest light switch, he flicked it on.

He had just come from an after-work business meeting, and it was just as well he had had that meeting, for otherwise he would have gone home without his anniversary present for Wendy, who'd have been none too pleased. The row with Ken had driven the present clean from his mind.

However, he would retrieve it now from his desk, be driven home to Balfron, and that would be that. He wondered what Wendy had bought him. She had the knack of always getting something he really appreciated. It had been a watercolour last year, a rare volume of Robert Burns the year before that.

When he came in sight of his office, he stopped short. The door was open, the light blazing. He walked silently forward. Naked as the day she was born, and satiated with lovemaking, Vicky was lying in front of the gas fire. Her eyes were closed and there was a soft, satisfied smile on her lips. Ken had left her a few seconds previously to go to the toilet down the corridor.

She sensed, rather than heard, what she presumed was Ken's return. 'Hmmh!' she murmured, and jiggled her hips.

Jack stared at Vicky in shock and amazement. In his own little apartment, how dare she! How dare whoever she was!

Still smiling, Vicky opened her eyes. The smile turned sickly when she saw who was staring down at her. She sprang to her feet and threw herself at the place where her clothes lay neatly folded. Snatching up her blouse and skirt, she held them in front of her.

Ken, also stark naked, came striding into the apartment, to halt abruptly when he caught sight of Jack. His face drained to a milky-white.

'You!' Jack breathed.

'I . . . I . . .' Ken began, then trailed off, unable to think of a single thing to say in his defence.

Vicky dropped her gaze. How humiliating this must be for Jack, as Ken's father-in-law. She could well imagine what he thought of her.

Ken's usual glibness had completely deserted him. He might have been a naughty, tongue-tied schoolboy up before the headmaster.

'Tomorrow morning, eight o'clock sharp, the pair of you come and see me,' Jack said huskily, and walked stiff-legged from the apartment. He was to be halfway home before realising he'd forgotten Wendy's present for the second time that day.

Vicky took a deep breath, then another. 'I could use a very large drink.'

When Ken poured for them both his hands were shaking so much that he got more on the carpet than he did in their glasses.

Next morning, as instructed, they presented themselves in Jack's office dead on the stroke of eight. It had not been a good night for Vicky, but it had been an even worse one for Ken, who had seen the one big chance in his life disappearing down the plughole.

Jack fixed Vicky with a baleful look. 'You'll understand I can't possibly allow you to remain working here, Miss Devine. You're fired,' he stated.

Vicky bit the inside of her lip. It was what she had expected.

As had been agreed between Vicky and Ken, he didn't even attempt to speak up for her – that would have been stupid.

'Collect your bits and pieces and be out of this building as soon as you can. What wages and holiday pay you are due will be sent to you in the post. Now leave,' Jack said to Vicky.

She did as bid, without looking at Ken. They had already arranged to meet briefly that evening when he left work.

Jack pulled out his pipe and slowly packed it from an old, well-worn leather pouch. If it hadn't been for Lyn and wee Kenny, he would have sacked Ken as well, and been pleased about it, for he thought Ken far too ruthlessly ambitious.

'I won't have my daughter cheated on. Is that clear?' he said.

Ken nodded.

'You'll never see that Devine woman again or communicate with her in any way.' He paused and raised an eyebrow.

Ken nodded a second time.

'For, if you do, I'll tell Lyn what I saw last night: and, knowing my daughter, you'd then find yourself out on the street and cited for divorce.'

Jack used a finger to tamp down the tobacco in the

pipebowl. 'And if she throws you out, which I can assure you she will, you're finished with the union. Don't think you'd get a job as a dockie either. I'd make it my business to have you blacked along the entire length of Clydeside.'

Ken was sweating now. There was sweat running down his neck, under his arms and down the cleft of his buttocks.

'It was an aberration, Jack. It won't happen again, I promise you,' Ken pleaded. He didn't really give a damn about losing Lyn, or even the child come to that; but to lose his eventual ascendency to the union presidency – that was something else entirely.

'Not only will it not happen with Miss Devine, but it won't happen with any other female either. I'm going to watch you very closely, Ken, and from time to time, which you'll never know about, I'm going to call in some professional help to watch also.'

Having played his trump card, Jack lit his pipe and sat back in his chair to stare coldly at Ken. He was not bluffing about the professional help, and Ken knew it. He would instruct a company of private investigators within the week.

'Have you mentioned last night to Wendy?' Ken asked.

'No, it would only have distressed her.'

'So this matter is strictly between you and me and Miss Devine?'

'That's right.'

He was off the hook, but he had lost Vicky, for it was impossible for him to continue seeing and sleeping with her now. The price was quite unacceptable.

Jack was thinking, with grim satisfaction, that he now had a hold over Ken, an unspoken hold that would always be there in future dealings between the two of them. From now on he should have no trouble in remaining the dominant one in their relationship – and that domination had been under threat of late.

'Can I go now?' Ken asked meekly.

Jack made a chopping sideways motion with his right hand. Ken was dismissed.

•

Vicky glanced at her watch. It was just past knocking-off time. Ken should be appearing any minute.

Leaving the union building that morning, she had gone straight to the Labour Exchange to sign on and inquire about other work. The man who had interviewed her had not been at all happy to hear that she had been dismissed, and without a reference. He asked her the reason for her dismissal and, because she couldn't think of anything else that sounded plausible, she said that she had slapped one of the union executives for groping her. He had softened a little towards her then and promised that, even though she didn't have a reference, he would find her something. There was a war on, after all: workers were in demand.

After the Labour she had gone home and given Mary the same story. Mary had been furious, saying that she had done the right thing in slapping the dirty sod; if it had been her, she would have done more than slap him.

Vicky looked at her watch again. It was ten past now. Where was Ken? At half past it started to sleet. The sleet had a wind behind it that cut to the bone. Vicky shivered and continued to wait. Quarter to came and went. When a nearby church bell bonged the hour, she knew that he wasn't going to show.

He would get in touch, write to her, she told herself, as she headed for her nearest tramstop.

The entire advance was pinned down by murderous machine-gun fire that had already, in a very short time, inflicted a great many casualties. Under the command of General Wavell, they were attempting to take Sidi Barrani, a small town on the Egyptian coast roughly halfway between Alexandria and Tobruk. It was Wavell's intention that the capture of Sidi Barrani would start the annihilation of the Italian forces in Cyrenaica.

Corporal Neil Seton lay in a shallow depression in the sand while bullets whistled overhead and all around. To his left and right were the rest of his section, crumpled and sprawled where they had fallen. Most of them had to be dead, he thought, for they had been almost on top of the concealed machine gun before it had opened fire. Without medical attention, and in this unbelievable blasting heat, those who weren't soon would be.

Neil rasped a hand over an unshaven cheek. He was filled with fear and a terrible desperation. The spaghetti munchers would get him before nightfall: he knew that as sure as the Clyde flowed down to the sea. Fear, desperation and anger – anger that blossomed and grew.

The closing of Agnew's and his falling for Vicky Devine: the two disastrous watersheds in his life.

The closing of Agnew's, his father Malkie committing suicide, and the grinding poverty that followed. Poverty which at times had made him go off on his own and weep with frustration.

And Vicky – never a moment's peace since he'd fallen in love with her. To get to the point where he'd almost had her as his wife – and then Blacklaws, bloody Ken Blacklaws, had reappeared to blow the whole thing sky high by telling her about that accursed telephone call.

It was all so bloody unfair! What had he done to deserve such curses? He had suffered and been denied all down the line. From plooks and blackheads to a woman he was destined never to have.

His anger turned to fury. The only thing that had ever gone right for him was his going to university, but even his career had been snatched from him right at the very last, thanks to this war and Adolf bastarding Hitler.

Neil sobbed. Oh Vicky, I love you, I hate you, I love you.

Well, if he was going to die, he would do so in style. God owed him that, at least.

Private John Sullivan, shot through the pelvis and now lying doggo about twenty feet away, gaped when he saw Neil slowly come to his feet, heft his rifle and fixed bayonet into position, then move forward all by himself.

Tears ran down Neil's face as he went. He was only half there; the other half was back in Parr Street with the lassie he loved, his princess. He started to sing in a voice that was cracked and raw. 'I belong to Glasgow . . .'

·

Vicky came awake to discover that she was feeling nauseous again. This had been happening regularly since she had started work at the munitions factory. Mercifully it was Sunday, which meant a long lie-in. She twisted onto her back. Mary would bring her a cup of tea and the newspaper shortly. George was always up before his daughter on a Sunday, and read the paper first. She got it when he was finished.

She realised then that her breasts were sore. She felt a sort of tight, tugging sensation which, now she was aware of it, was really quite painful. She cupped her breasts and winced; the undersides were tender in the extreme. Now what had caused that? Was it another result of her breathing in daily doses of sulphur?

Perhaps it was best to look for another job. Her health had been acting up ever since she had started work at the factory. Why, she had even missed a period, her last, something that had never happened to her before. She had thought that her health would settle down after she had been at the factory a while, but it didn't appear to be doing so. Missed period, morning nausea, sore breasts, whatever next?

Suddenly she went very still inside and ran through those symptoms again. Could it be that she was pregnant and that what she'd seen as ill health had nothing whatever to do with the sulphur?

'Jesus!' she whispered, shocked.

Don't panic, she told herself. Could it be?

She thought of Ken. Why hadn't she heard from him! It was seven weeks since Jack Fyfer had sacked her. Surely he could at least have written – even if it was only to say that he couldn't see her for a while? She could not believe that he had abandoned her. After all, she hadn't asked him to leave his wife or precious union. She was resigned to being his mistress, and had told him so. She would give him more time to get in touch with her, but if he didn't she would contact him, she decided. There had to be a logical explanation for his silence.

Mary came bustling into the bedroom. 'You'll never guess

239

what!' she exclaimed, waving the newspaper in front of Vicky.

'Not until you tell me,' Vicky replied with a grin.

'There's a photograph of Neil Seton on the front page. He's won the Victoria Cross,' Mary announced.

'You mean our Neil, from across the road?' Vicky queried, dumbfounded at this news.

'The very same. He won it fighting the Eyeties in Egypt. There's a full account here of what happened.'

Neil had singlehandedly attacked a machine-gun post, bayoneting seven men to reach the post and shooting dead the two Italians manning it. Then, without waiting for help, he had made his way along a trench for several hundred yards, attacked a dugout and forced thirty-seven enemy soldiers to surrender.

In doing what he had, Neil had turned the tide of the battle in favour of the British by allowing them to break through what until then had been an impenetrable wall of bullets. The British had gone on to take their objective: the town of Sidi Barrani.

'Well, I'll be blowed. Our Neil. Who'd have thought he had it in him?' Vicky said, laying down the paper.

Then she remembered the Hogmanay night when he had faced up to the lads who'd had a mind to rape her. Maybe it wasn't so surprising after all.

'And apparently he came through it without even so much as a scratch,' Mary said in amazement.

He had bayoneted seven, shot two dead and gone on to capture thirty-seven others. Some desk job! Vicky thought.

There was a public phone box at the factory which Vicky was now making for, it being her morning tea break. She was going to ring Ken to tell him she was pregnant. She had missed a second period, her breasts had got larger and she had had to let out all her skirts. Thankfully the morning nausea had stopped.

Her heart was pounding as she lifted the receiver and put her money in. Nine weeks since she had last spoken to him – not that long really, but it seemed an eternity. She pressed

Button A when connected. Doing her best to disguise her voice so that the telephonist wouldn't know it was her, she asked to be put through to Mr Blacklaws. When the telephonist inquired who was speaking, she replied that it was confidential union business.

'Hello. Ken Blacklaws speaking.'

'Ken, it's Vicky. I . . .'

There was a click and the line went dead.

She took the receiver away from her ear and stared at it. She hadn't been accidentally disconnected by the telephonist – that had happened to her several times when she'd worked at the union, so she knew what it sounded like. No. The click was the giveaway. Ken had hung up on her. *Hung up on her!*

'Oh, you bastard!' she whispered as hot scalding tears crowded into her eyes.

She had been wrong. He had abandoned her.

Eight

Gibson Street had seen better and more prosperous days. These tenements had never housed working folk; it was not that sort of area. Shabby, down at heel, Vicky thought; that was how she would have described it. This wasn't a part of Glasgow she knew well, being as it was on the west side. Students lived here and arty-crafty types, and at least one struck-off doctor, the one she was going to see.

She had been told that Dr Sampson was the best abortionist in the city – a proper doctor, not some back-street wifey with a bottle of gin and a knitting needle. The last thing she'd wanted was one of those. He was pricey but, as far as she was concerned, it was worth it. She would have paid double what he asked to know that the person who aborted her had been properly trained. She had been recommended Sampson by a lassie whom she worked alongside at the factory. Elsie herself had used him, and swore by him.

Vicky crossed the street and entered the close of number 17. Today was only the examination. He would inform her when she was to return for the abortion itself.

Vicky, dog tired, was dozing in front of the fire when Mary, who had gone out to get three fish suppers for their tea, came bursting into the kitchen. George, sitting slumped across from Vicky, was also dozing.

'I've just heard. Neil Seton's in London being decorated by the King. He's coming home to Glasgow on leave. His mother says he's taking the night train and will be here the morn's morn,' Mary exclaimed excitedly.

Vicky yawned. Of late, thanks to her pregnancy, she couldn't get enough sleep. She would have slept morning, noon and night, given the chance. 'Decorated by the King himself. That's quite an honour,' she acknowledged.

George had also been wakened by his wife's return. 'And so the lad should be. He's a hero, after all,' he said.

'Mrs Seton says he was brought back so that the newspapers could photograph the King presenting him with his medal. He's to be in Glasgow for a month. That's the length of his leave,' Mary went on.

'I shall shake him by the hand when I see him. What he did was glorious, sheer glorious,' George said.

All the way through tea Neil was the main topic of conversation.

Vicky bumped into Neil two days later. Returning home from work, she was passing the Argyle Arms when he came out. 'Hello, hero.' She smiled.

Neil blushed to hear her call him that. He thought that she looked sensational. She seemed to be glowing with inner well-being.

'Have you lost your tongue? Or does a vc not talk to the likes of me, common as muck?' she teased.

'Don't be daft. You just caught me by surprise, that's all,' he stammered in reply.

She frowned. There was something wrong with his uniform. Then she realised what was bothering her. When she had read about him in the paper he had been described as a corporal; now he was wearing an officer's uniform.

'Congratulations on your promotion. What are you now?' she asked.

'A captain. General Wavell promoted me at Sidi Barrani to replace the man who'd been my captain, and who was killed in the battle.'

She had been right about him in uniform: he looked dead handsome. Really scrumptious.

Neil glanced at the door of the pub, then back at Vicky. 'How about a drink before you go home? To celebrate my promotion, if you need an excuse.'

She didn't see how she could refuse. 'All right,' she agreed, and with him smiling they went inside.

The idea came to her while he was up at the bar. She was going to Sampson's that Tuesday at eleven o'clock, and he had strongly advised that she have someone with her to take her home again. He had said that she would be weak and shaken after the operation. She had seen the sense in that, but her problem had been who to ask. Certainly neither George nor Mary; they didn't know she was pregnant, nor did she want them to find out.

There were pals in the street she could have approached but they would all be working, and she could hardly expect them to take a day off. Besides, pals or not, she wasn't exactly sure that she could trust them to keep their mouths shut afterwards.

Neil was the perfect solution. He was on leave, so there was no bother about time off, and being a man he wouldn't have the same compulsion to gossip as a woman would have. The only question was: would he do it?

When he returned she asked him about his visit to Buckingham Palace and what it was like meeting the King and Queen. She hung on his every word as he described the palace, the ceremony and what had been said by himself and the royals, both of whom he had found absolutely charming. She fired some questions at him. What had the Queen been wearing? Did she have much make-up on? Was the King really as shy as everyone said?

When they finished talking about that, Neil said he wanted to hear about her. The laughter vanished from his face when she told him she had had an affair with a man at her previous work, that she was pregnant by him and was going to have an abortion. She didn't say that the man was Ken Blacklaws.

Neil sat silent, plainly shocked, when she came to the end of her story.

'So, will you help me on Tuesday?' she asked.

Neil took a deep swallow of his pint, then another. 'What does the father say about you having an abortion?' he queried in a strained voice.

'He doesn't know. We'd already broken up before I found out I was pregnant.'

'Was it . . . you and he . . . was it serious?'

Vicky gave a grim, bitter smile. 'You don't break up when it's that,' she answered ambiguously, and Neil presumed that it was she who had done the breaking.

An abortion! Neil was appalled at the thought. It wasn't – well, it just wasn't right. 'It's murder, Vicky, you must know that,' he said softly.

Her smile widened. 'How can you talk about murder? You, who killed at least two men out in Egypt?' she mocked.

'That was different. They were the enemy, and we were at war. If I hadn't killed them, they'd have killed me.'

'What you did was still murder. The only difference between us is that your murdering was legal, whereas mine won't be.'

He swallowed more of his black and tan, and as he did so it dawned on him that Vicky's pregnancy explained the glow of inner well-being he'd noticed earlier. It was the radiance of expectant motherhood.

'You could have the baby,' he muttered.

'And bring further terrible disgrace down on my family? No, Neil, I couldn't do that to them. I just couldn't.

'And then there's me. I'd be branded a slut, a tart, easy game. You know what Glasgow's like. When it comes to that sort of thing, it's either black or white; there are no shades of grey. You're either a "respectable" lassie – in my case still respectable even though I've been to borstal and prison – or else a FALLEN WOMAN, and when they say those words they do so in capital letters. I don't think I could bear the sniggers, the sideways glances, the whispering behind my back. The laugh of course is that many of those who would be doing the sniggering, whispering and suchlike are at it themselves. They've just been lucky not to get caught out.

'Then there's the child to consider. He or she would be a bastard, literally. Remember Rossie Mair who went to school with us, and the hell he went through because he was a bastard? I can assure you I've no intention of allowing any child of mine to go through such purgatory.'

Neil minded Rossie well. He had aye liked Rossie, and would have chummed up with him if it hadn't been for his being a bastard, and therefore supposedly tainted. A particular incident was for ever etched in his memory. Poor Rossie being hounded round the playground by a great gang of lads all chanting, 'Rossie Mair's a bastard! Rossie Mair's a bastard! Rossie Mair's a bastard!' It had been horrible.

'How about flitting away from Glasgow to have it?' he suggested.

'And go where? I don't know anyone anywhere else. But, say I did move to another city to stay, how would I live? Who would look after the baby when I went to work?' She shook her head. 'No, I've thought this through, an abortion is the only way,' she whispered.

'It's such a hard decision,' he said.

'Don't you think I don't know that!'

'You want the baby then?'

'Of course I do, idiot. But it's impossible, a fact I've had to face up to.'

'And the father, there's no chance of the pair of you getting back together, and getting married? If only for the baby's sake.'

Her grim, bitter smile returned. 'I couldn't marry him even if I wanted to. You see, he already has a wife.'

Vicky finished her whisky and lemonade, and shuddered. She wasn't sure whether it was the drink that made her do that, or the conversation.

'So, will you help me on Tuesday?' she asked for a second time.

The chance was there, begging to be taken. He would be a fool to let it slip by, he told himself. She could only say no.

'You tell me there's no alternative to your having an abortion. Well, I'm going to give you one. I asked you once to marry me; now I'm asking you again.'

That stunned her.

'I love you, Vicky, and have done for years. You'd make me the happiest man in the world if you'd marry me.'

She found her voice. 'You'd still have me even though I'm carrying someone else's child?'

'Yes. And if I survive the war, I'll bring that child up as my own flesh and blood. You have my word of honour on that.' Neil took a deep breath. 'Let me put it this way. If I can save you from committing murder, and thereby allow you to have the child you want, I'd feel I'd gone some way to making up for the telephone call to Copland and Lye. And as I've just said, I do love you very very much.'

She thought of Ken. He was lost to her for ever now, no doubt about it. A whip had been cracked, and he'd jumped. She'd worked that out after he had hung up on her. If he did love her, as he had often sworn he did, he loved his ambition more.

'Get another drink in please,' she said huskily, and pushed her now empty glass at Neil, who, without uttering, rose and went to the bar.

It was a funny old world at times, she thought. Handsome, brave, a professional career ahead of him – if, as he said, he survived the war. What more could she ask for? The relief that surged through her was overwhelming in its intensity. She didn't have to go to Sampson's on Tuesday after all. Her baby was going to live. Closing her eyes, she thanked God for his mercy and compassion. Neil was a good man. She would never let him down, she swore to herself.

He returned to their table with fresh drinks and sat down to stare at her, awaiting her verdict.

'We'll have to get a special licence,' she said.

It was Neil's idea that they elope to Gretna Green – a suggestion he put forward for two reasons. First, it was more romantic to be married there than in a dreich Glasgow registry office; and second, it ensured that there wouldn't be any newspaper fuss, which, because of his vc, there might have been in Glasgow. He thought that journalists and photographers and, who knew, maybe even city dignitaries – he'd had lunch with the Lord Provost on his first day home – might have spoiled it for them, and Vicky agreed.

The only person Vicky let into the secret beforehand was

her supervisor at work. When Vicky and Neil left Parr Street for the station, they left behind notes, one for George and Mary, another for Mrs Seton.

When they reached Gretna they had a bite to eat, both being famished, then went in search of the smithy where the marriages took place and the blacksmith who performed the ceremony. They soon found both, only to be greatly disappointed when the blacksmith informed them that they had to live in the village for an establishing period before he could marry them.

'Neil here is on active duty and has to return to Egypt in a very short while. Delay means we'll be losing that time as a married couple,' Vicky argued.

Mr Yoole, the blacksmith, scratched his chin and wondered where he'd seen Neil's face before. It seemed gey familiar.

'There's a war on, you know. Couldn't you make an exception?' Vicky persisted.

Then Mr Yoole had it. It was Vicky's mentioning Egypt that placed Neil for him.

'Aren't you the chap who got awarded the vc?' he asked.

Neil nodded. 'That's me.'

Mr Yoole carefully wiped his huge mitts on a none too clean cloth, then stuck out his right hand. 'It's a real pleasure to meet you, son, an honour.'

Mr Yoole scratched his chin again and regarded Vicky and Neil thoughtfully. The lassie was right, there *was* a war on, and in wartime all sorts of rules and regulations got bent a little. And as she had pointed out, Neil had only so much leave.

'Och, tae hell with it. Have you got the ring?' he queried.

Neil's face lit up. 'Right here,' he replied and hastily produced the gold band.

They were wed over the anvil by Mr Yoole, with Mrs Yoole and a Mr Sawyers acting as witnesses.

'You may kiss the bride,' Mr Yoole told Neil when it was all over, and they were man and wife.

Neil took Vicky into his arms. As their lips met, the three other people present broke into applause.

'Have you booked a room yet?' Mr Sawyers asked when they had finished kissing.

Neil shook his head.

'Well, as it so happens, I'm the landlord of the pub over by. I'd be delighted to look after you while you're here.' He beamed. It was of course no accident that he had been called in to act as a witness for them – he was a witness whenever possible. It was excellent for business.

Neil took care of the financial arrangements, then he and Vicky, hand in hand, strolled over to the pub behind Mr Sawyers, who was leading the way. Mr Sawyers carried the two small cases they had brought with them.

'It was a brainwave for us to come here. Thank you for thinking of it,' Vicky said.

He squeezed her hand. He couldn't believe he was in Gretna Green with Vicky, and that she was his wife. It was a dream come true.

They had a drink while their room was made ready, then were taken up by Mrs Sawyers.

The room was delightful, a proper little love nest, Vicky thought. It had a view towards the English border.

'Would you like me to run you a bath? The water's piping hot,' Mrs Sawyers asked Vicky.

'That would be smashing.'

Mrs Sawyers gave an understanding smile. 'There are lots of young couples have their meals sent up. You only have to say.'

Vicky glanced at Neil, who nodded. 'We'll have tea in our room then,' she answered.

Mrs Sawyers explained where the bathroom and toilet were, then went off to run Vicky's bath.

Neil kissed Vicky again, a deep kiss that went on and on. 'I could eat you,' he whispered when the kiss was finally over, and she had laid a cheek against his breast.

A little later Mrs Sawyers returned to announce that the bath was ready. When she and Neil were once more alone, Vicky closed the curtains, laid out her dressing gown and best nightdress, and began to strip. Neil watched in fascination, unable to take his eyes off her. As she stood naked before him, his throat went dry and his heart began thumping.

She put on her dressing gown and gathered up the nightdress and a toilet bag. 'I won't be long. Why don't you get into bed and wait for me there?' she said. As she left the room, she blew him a kiss.

The bath was Victorian and massive. She put a little aromatic oil into the steaming water, a trick she'd learned while on the *Atlantic Star*, then clambered in.

When she emerged she felt dreamy and hazy – exactly how a girl should feel on going to bed with her new husband for the first time, she thought. She dabbed some powder under her arms, then placed a spot of perfume in several strategic places. When she had put on her nightdress and dressing gown, and run a comb through her thick cap of curls, she was ready.

He was in bed waiting for her, as she had suggested. She made sure to lock the door before joining him. Within seconds her nightdress was off again, tossed to the floor.

'Oh, my angel,' he whispered.

Half an hour later he was still touching and stroking – that was all.

'What's wrong?' she asked softly.

'I don't know,' came back the tight reply.

'You must be too tense. Try and relax a bit,' she said. She was pretty certain by now that she was his first woman for, if his caresses were gentle, they were also totally inexperienced. She did her best to help him, to no avail. A little later she decided it best that they halt, for they were getting absolutely nowhere.

'First night nerves. Don't worry about it. It's a common occurrence, I'm told,' she said lightly, and kissed him on the tip of the nose.

'I feel such a fool,' he muttered wretchedly.

'It'll be all right, it's just a case of us being at ease and getting used to one another.'

'Must be nerves,' he agreed.

'Listen. Instead of us having tea here, why don't we go downstairs and have it, and spend the time until it's served in the bar?' She knew that, as residents, they could use the pub's bar whenever they wanted.

'All right, fine.'

He needed his mind taken off his failure, she thought. And, although Neil had never been a heavy drinker, she would see to it that he had a good few between now and bedtime.

A good few, but not too many.

Before they left the bedroom, she had jollied him up to the point where he was guffawing at an outrageously funny story of hers which she had initially heard from the captain of the *Atlantic Star*.

'Oh Christ!' exclaimed Neil and threw himself away from Vicky. It was the fifth day of their honeymoon – and still the marriage remained unconsummated.

Outside bed everything had been wonderful. They had tramped the nearby countryside, borrowed bicycles and ridden into England and back, hired rods and fished – or at least attempted to fish, neither of them ever having used a rod before. That morning, following a heavy fall of snow the previous night, they had even built a snowman and had a snowball fight. Everything was as it should have been, with the exception of Neil's inability to make love.

He was sitting on the edge of the bed, shoulders bowed, head in hands. His posture was one of wretched despair. Vicky was at a loss. She had done everything she could think of to arouse him, even goading him into a fight to see if that would work.

'Is it me, Neil?' she asked softly, a frown creasing her forehead.

'No. I find you desperately attractive. I want you. I've never wanted any other girl but you. It's just that . . . nothing happens.'

'I am your first, aren't I?'

'Yes,' came the strangled reply.

On the one hand Vicky was not surprised to have that confirmed; it wasn't unusual for men to remain virgins until the marriage bed. Many might boast among themselves to the contrary, but that was the truth of the matter. On the other hand she had presumed from the way the girls at the university had given him the glad eye that he was bound to have had a tumble or two.

Was it because he loved her so much that his mind was stopping him? Having put her on a pedestal, was he now finding the realities of the physical side of love a debasement of her? In other words, even though he knew she had slept with Ken in the past, was he subconsciously resisting a physical relationship between them because it would defile the 'pure' image he had of her? Or was he just downright impotent? If so, she had read or heard somewhere that doctors could treat such a condition.

'I'm sorry, I'm so sorry,' he said in a cracked voice.

She went over to him and put an arm round his bowed shoulders. 'There's nothing to be sorry about. We'll sort this thing out together,' she told him.

'Shall we go back to Glasgow tomorrow?'

'Let's stay the week. Despite what you might think, I'm thoroughly enjoying myself here.'

When eventually he fell asleep, she remained wide awake, staring into the darkness.

The train rattled along, heading for Glasgow. Neil was gazing out a window, his expression bleak. Vicky was pretending to read a book.

The previous night she had managed to winkle some very private and personal details out of Neil – details which had further increased her concern for him.

She looked up from her book and over at him. Apart from themselves, the carriage was empty.

'Neil, I think you should go and see Mr Rose, the GP. Perhaps there's something he can do.'

He turned to stare at her with tortured eyes.

She went on. 'Rather than let this problem drag on, it seems only common sense to me that you go for professional advice, and right away. It could well be that by consulting him now you can have the problem sorted out before you have to return to Egypt.'

He continued to stare at her in silence.

'Would you like me to come with you or to go on your own?'

He considered that. 'I'd prefer to go on my own,' he mumbled.

'I'll make the appointment directly we get home,' she said firmly.

Was it only prolonged nerves or was it this purity theory she had dreamed up? She hoped that Mr Rose, as damned fine a GP as there had ever been, would find out.

Then she had another thought. When making the appointment for Neil, she would go in and see Mr Rose herself. She would prime him fully about why Neil was coming to consult him.

Vicky clattered up the stairs, returning from her shift at the factory. Neil had been to see a consultant at the Royal Infirmary that afternoon, his third visit to the man. He had been promised the results of the many tests that had been made during his previous visits.

She fumbled with her key in the doorlock, then was inside the house. She knew that Neil would be alone. They had arranged for Mrs Seton to go off to the early house at the pictures. He was sitting gazing into the fire, which he had nearly allowed to go out. That told her that the news was bad.

She took off her coat and laid it aside. She went over and squatted beside him, clasping one of his chill hands between hers. He looked at her for the first time; there were tears in his eyes.

'Well?' she prompted softly.

'The consultant says I have deep-seated prostatic damage caused years ago by a fractured pelvis. He pointed out the now healed fracture on one of the X-rays.'

'What does that mean?'

'It means that I'm impotent for life. It's impossible for them to cure or correct the damage,' he whispered.

She was appalled. 'Is he absolutely certain nothing can be done?'

'Absolutely.'

It was a nightmare, the worst news they could have had. So much for her stupid theory.

'When did you have a fractured pelvis?' she queried.

'I never knew I did have until the consultant told me, but then I never went to the doctor at the time, not having the money to be able to do so. I just stayed in bed till the worst of the pain was over, and then got back on my feet again,' he said, and made a sort of whimpering sound filled with such anguish that it wrenched Vicky's heart.

'When was this?'

'Remember the day you were arrested?'

'How could I ever forget it?'

'That night Ken was waiting for me in the close. He got me into the back dunny, where he told me what had happened – that you'd been arrested instead of him, and that it had to be me who'd telephoned Copland and Lye because I was the only one who knew he'd been stealing while working overtime. It must have been during that kicking that my pelvis was fractured, which in turn caused the damage to the prostate gland.'

Vicky's mouth was open, a hand covering it. Ken had done this to Neil! Ken had robbed Neil of his virility and ability to have children. And she was carrying Ken's child!

Anger crept into Neil's face. 'God damn that man. God damn him to hell! May he fry, screaming, in everlasting hellfire!' Neil choked.

She held him tight while he completely broke down.

She got the day off work to see Neil leave for Egypt. They went to the Central Station by taxi. The journey was mostly silent, with Neil sunk deep in gloom. There had been a lot of silence between them since his final visit to the Royal Infirmary. He refused point-blank to discuss anything to do with his impotence or its effect on their lives. The subject had become taboo.

On reaching the station, he paid the cabbie and they went inside. They were walking towards the arrival and departure board when he suddenly stopped and grasped Vicky by the arm.

'I'll perfectly understand it if you go off and leave me. I can't really expect you to continue on as my wife, not with me the way I am,' he said quietly.

'Don't talk nonsense. Lovemaking isn't all of marriage. It's only a small percentage of it,' she replied, equally quietly.

'I wish that was true.'

'It is. And it's not as though we'll have to do without a family. As for me, there are things I can teach you to do that will more than keep me happy that way, I assure you.'

He gazed at her, desperately wishing to believe that she would be there when and if he came home again, that their marriage could have a semblance of normality about it.

'You're still in a state of shock, Neil, and very very depressed. But I promise you, given time and thought on the matter, you'll come to see it isn't the total disaster you now imagine.'

'Whatever happens, I love you, and always will,' he stated simply.

'I know,' she whispered.

When the train left, she waved frantically till it had turned the bend and he was lost to sight. He was gone at last, for which she was thankful; the strain of the past few weeks had been awful.

She had said that she would wait for him, and she would. She had sworn to herself that she would never let him down, and she would keep that oath. The one thing he must never find out was that Ken was the father of her as yet unborn child.

Never ever.

Ken Blacklaws was in number 3 hold of the TSS *Lydia*, which was tied up in Plantation Quay having its cargo of copra, steel and powdered egg unloaded.

The *Lydia* had hit a ferocious gale en route to Glasgow, and during the gale had shipped a considerable amount of water in number 3 and 4 holds. This had only come to light when the dockies doing the unloading had discovered that a good third, the remainder, of the copra in number 3 hold and the same amount of powdered egg in number 4 hold were ruined. The water hadn't been detected by the ship's crew because the copra and egg had absorbed it. As a result, unloading was going to take longer than had been anticipated and would run well over normal knocking-off time.

The men would have to work through until the unloading had been completed, for it was imperative that the ship be away on the morning tide. It was scheduled for a run down to Southampton, where it would be quickly reloaded for a link-up with an Atlantic convoy.

Ken and Jack Fyfer had come aboard to inspect the remaining ruined cargo personally, and Jack had just gone off to hammer out an overtime deal for their members with a representative of the ship's owners. Ken had remained behind to listen to a complaint from a chap called Hyslop about a different matter entirely.

When Ken had taken down all the details of Hyslop's complaint in the notebook he always carried with him and told Hyslop he'd be in touch, he left Hyslop to climb back onto the deck, which was deserted. Ken guessed correctly that the men who had been working there had taken the opportunity to nip off for a fly smoke and cup of char.

He lit a cigarette and yawned. It had been a long hard day. He promised himself a hot bath when he got home and a few stiff whiskies.

Then he thought of Lyn and frowned. Sexually it was still bad between them. What might laughingly be called their sex life was almost non-existent, with no signs of improvement on the way. Wee Kenny remained her be-all and end-all. How he missed those sessions he'd had with Vicky in Jack's small apartment! He ached with longing and desire every time he thought of them.

Blast Jack Fyfer, and blast that private investigator who followed him from time to time. He had never actually been able to spot the man, but every so often he got a strange tingly sensation at the back of his neck which told him the man was about, spying on him.

There had been that strawberry blonde he had met only the other week. She was a real cracker, and available – she had made that clear enough. But he hadn't dared.

As for Jack, the old man was really getting on his nerves. There was no steamrollering Jack any more. Whenever he tried, Jack would stop and give an infuriating smile, and the sword of Damocles would sway above his head. Drawing viciously, he went to the ship's rail and leant on it. Down below, standing on the quayside, were Jack and the owner's representative, the pair of them engrossed in conversation.

'Sod you, you old bastard!' he thought darkly, glowering at Jack.

Apart from Jack and the owner's representative, the quayside was deserted – that smoke and cup of char again.

He glanced over to where one of the ship's derricks had been halted in mid-action. It had been transferring a crate of powdered egg from a hold to the quayside when the operator had stopped it at the moment the lads had downed tools.

Ken was turning away from the rail and about to make for the gangplank when in a flash the idea exploded in his brain. Very slowly he turned back to stare at the motionless crate of powdered egg that was dangling roughly forty feet in the air, *directly* over Jack and the owner's representative. A crate weighing – what? – two to three tons.

Ken went very still inside, cold sweat breaking on his forehead. Accidents happened round the docks every day of the week. Why not one that would be ever so convenient, and advantageous, to him?

He walked along beside the rail till he was adjacent with the derrick. The operator's cab was empty. There wasn't another soul to be seen.

He strolled over to the cab and glanced inside. The controls were of a type well known to him. He had often operated similar derricks when he had worked as a dockie himself. His eyes zeroed in on the emergency-release button.

All he had to do was press that – and ensure that no one saw him doing so, of course.

The inside of his left thigh was fluttering as he returned to the rail. The two men below had not moved an inch. He wiped cold sweat from his brow and noted that his palms had begun to leak. Did he have the guts to press that button? To kill for what he so desperately wanted?

He returned to the operator's cab, transfixed by the red button. If he was going to do it, he had to do it *now*, he told himself. Another handful of seconds and it could be too late.

A final glance round confirmed that he was still quite alone on deck, and unobserved. Leaning into the cab, he thumbed the red button.

There was a snap, followed by a crash. Even as the crash came, he was throwing himself down a companionway, hurtling back to the ship's lower levels.

When the alarm was raised, he made sure that he was seen to be well below decks. When he clambered up on deck again, he was in the company of Hyslop and five others.

'I wonder what's happened?' he said to Hyslop as they emerged into the March sunshine.

Ken stood outside what had been Jack's office, and which was now his, and stared at the door. A smile of satisfaction curled his mouth upwards as he grasped the handle and opened the door. The smile widened as he went inside. It was his first official day as union president.

At last, at long last, he was president of the Honourable Society of Dock Workers! By God, it was a glorious feeling.

The inquest into Jack's 'accident' had been held at the coroner's court. There had been no eyewitnesses, nor had any malfunction been found in the derrick when it was examined by experts. But it was known that such derricks did act up from time to time, and were far from being a hundred per cent reliable. No foul play had been suspected. The verdict was death by misadventure.

The remark had been made afterwards that it was a

dangerous life working on the docks: Jack and the owner's representative weren't the first to die there, and certainly wouldn't be the last.

Ken crossed to the drinks cabinet, took out a bottle of best Highland malt and poured himself a generous tot. He then selected one of Jack's Havana cigars, clipped the end with Jack's silver clipper and lit it. Malt in hand, trailing cigar smoke, he sat behind Jack's desk. Puffing on the cigar, he pushed back the chair and placed his feet on the desktop.

Power, that's what he had now, and what he'd always craved. Power. The next step was to enlarge that power.

Vicky gave a little exclamation of fright when she was grasped by the shoulder. She had just come off the tram, having been in town. Her mind had been elsewhere.

'Hello, Vicky.' Ken smiled.

She stared at him for several seconds, then wrenched herself from his grasp and walked away. He ran after her.

'I hung up on you, Vicky, because I panicked. I'd have lost my job at the union if Jack had found out that I'd even so much as spoken to you again.'

'And how would he have known you'd done that?'

'The telephonist might have been listening in on Jack's orders. I couldn't take the chance,' he explained.

'I hardly think she would have done that.'

'You don't understand. If he could go to the extent of having a private investigator follow me about, then he was well capable of ordering the telephonist to listen in on my telephone conversations.'

Vicky stopped and faced Ken. 'He had a private investigator follow you about?'

'He did. I was forbidden to communicate with you in any way. To have done so would have meant me out on my ear.'

'Surely you could have written? He'd never have found that out.'

Ken shrugged. 'I couldn't take the chance.'

She stared at Ken, then nodded, very slowly. 'I understand,' she said. And she did, perfectly.

Then Vicky realised that they were talking in the past tense. 'What do you mean "would have meant you out on your ear"? Doesn't it still?'

'Jack's dead. There was an accident on Plantation Quay and he was killed. I'm president of the union now.'

'I'm sorry to hear about Mr Fyfer. He was always kindness itself to me, until he caught us together, that is. So now you're the big boss, number one in command.'

'That's it.' He grinned.

'And without having Mr Fyfer to worry about, you've decided to look me up to ask me to become your mistress again?' she said sourly.

'If it was, what would your answer be?'

'To tell you to take a running jump! My God, Ken Blacklaws, you do have some brass nerve. So you think all you have to do is snap your fingers and I'll come bounding back like some well-trained mutt. Well, I've got news for you, I'm bloody not!' she hissed and strode off, fuming.

He ran after her again, caught up with her and forced her to stop.

'Will you take your hands off me, or so help me I'll shout for a policeman!'

'Vicky, I didn't come here to ask you to be my mistress. I came to ask you to be my wife.'

She thought she hadn't heard correctly. 'Say that again?'

'I want you to be my wife.'

'And what about the wife you already have?'

'I'll get rid of her. She can go and live with her mother in Balfron. You can move in as soon as she's moved out.'

'And you'll divorce her?'

'I swear it. And as soon as I'm free, you and I will marry.'

She gave a low laugh. Oh God, but this was funny. You had to laugh – it was either that or cry. For despite all that he'd done to her, she still loved Ken desperately.

'I'm afraid I can't move in with you or marry you,' she said, voice crackling with emotion.

'Of course you can. But I do understand if you need time to think about it.'

'Time won't alter matters. I can't and that's that.' She

held up her left hand so that he could see the gold band there.

He stared at the ring in amazement. It had never entered his head that she would go off and marry someone else, not so soon anyway.

She had said that she would wait for Neil. She had sworn to herself that she would never let him down, and she would keep that oath. But, sweet heaven, when she had said and sworn those things, she had never envisaged that this would happen, that Ken would re-materialise so quickly into her life and propose to her.

'And I'll give you another reason,' she said and opened her raglan coat, which effectively hid her pregnancy when buttoned. She pointed to her small but very clearly visible bump.

Ken swallowed hard, his normally agile brain now leaden with disappointment. 'Do you love whoever it is you've married?'

'Yes,' she lied instantly.

'Well, that's that then – between you and me, that is.'

She nodded her agreement and rebuttoned her coat.

There was nothing left for him to say. He didn't want to ask her any of the details of her marriage, he just didn't want to know.

'Congratulations and good luck then,' he said, giving a lopsided smile, and stuck out his hand. Vicky wanted to wish him good luck also, but couldn't. Her throat was clogged.

Tears were stinging her eyes as she made to turn a corner. She glanced back to where she had left him standing, but he was already gone. She made it to her close before collapsing against an inside-close wall. She sobbed as tears washed her cheeks. What a mess, what an awful bloody mess! It just wasn't fair. *It just wasn't!*

The doctor had told her to scream as loudly as she wished – they were used to that. She had taken him at his word, shrieking at the top of her lungs as unbelievable pain after pain seemed to be ripping her apart.

'And again, Mrs Seton, push!' the doctor's voice commanded.

Gritting her teeth, she pushed and pushed and . . .

'Aaaaaahhhhhh!'

Then it was all over. The tiny feet, legs and buttocks slipped from her body. The baby was born.

There was the sound of a smack and a lusty cry rent the air.

A few moments later the doctor said, 'It's a wee girl, and she's absolutely perfect.'

One of the nurses placed the baby, wrapped in a length of soft sheeting, into her arms.

Martha – that was what she would call her daughter, she decided. It was a name she'd aye liked. Totally exhausted, she fell asleep, and they took Martha from her.

Part Four

You're My Wee Gallus Bloke Nae Mair
1946–56

'Oh you're my wee gallus bloke nae mair,
you're my wee gallus bloke nae mair.
With your bell blue strides,
and your bunnet tae the side,
you're my wee gallus bloke nae mair.'

Glasgow street song (Trad.)

Nine

What a marvellous feeling to have so much time to myself, Vicky thought with glowing satisfaction, for this was Martha's first day at school.

She had expected the worst – tears, tantrums, the lot – but had been pleasantly surprised when Martha had gone into the classroom meek as a lamb. When she took her home that afternoon, she would make the wee mite some Melting Moments, which she adored.

Vicky was en route now to Neil's office in Renfrew Street. The pair of them were going out for lunch together, and to celebrate Martha's starting school Neil had promised that they would have a bottle of good wine as a special treat. A leisurely lunch, perhaps a bit of window shopping afterwards. Life was certainly going to be very different now that she didn't have Martha, seemingly forever demanding, tied round her neck all day long. Not that she didn't love the lassie; she loved her to distraction and so did Neil. It was just that for a while now she had craved some time off for herself, a breathing space. A little respite from Mummy . . . Mummy . . . Mummy . . .

Mary had told her that it was quite natural; she had felt positively claustrophobic when she had had Vicky and John at home together prior to their attending school – the same school Martha was now going to.

Neil worked in a junior capacity at a firm of solicitors named MacDonald, Lindsay and Hogg. They were very grand solicitors with sumptuous offices, not at all the sort of people Neil wanted to work for – but when he had been demobbed there was such a deluge of men applying for positions that he had grabbed the first offered him. The fact he was a vc had got him the job, and in particular because his vc had been won in Egypt. Michael Lindsay's son had been a desert rat who had been killed at El Alamein, the turning point of the war.

Neil's plan was to stay at the firm for a few years, then open up his own office in the Townhead area. He still wanted to help the poor and deprived. Wealth and possessions held no attraction for him.

Vicky was thinking about Neil and their forthcoming lunch – she was calling it lunch only because Neil had said she should if she spoke to anyone about it while at MacDonald, Lindsay and Hogg; to have called it dinner would have been a social clanger in those august surroundings – when a vaguely familiar face rushed by. Several strides further on it struck her who the face belonged to.

She whirled round. 'Tina! Tina!' she cried, and ran back to where Tina had stopped.

Recognition came to Tina Mathieson, and the pair of them fell into one another's arms.

'Vicky Devine, Christ but it's good to see you. You're a sight for sore eyes, right enough,' Tina enthused.

Vicky held up her left hand and tapped the gold band there. 'Not Devine any more, Seton. I'm married, with a wee girl. And you?'

Tina shook her head. 'No such luck. I'm beginning to think I'm going to end up an old maid.'

Tina was still as plump as she had been at Duncliffe, maybe even more so. Her auburn hair had faded somewhat, and had streaks of grey in it, and there were a number of lines round her eyes, several of them quite deep. One thing that hadn't changed was the warmth she exuded, and which Vicky remembered so fondly. Vicky could have shouted with delight at having run into her great pal again.

'I went to the address you'd given me, but you and your family had flitted to Coventry,' Vicky said.

Tina grasped her by the arm. 'Listen, I honestly can't stop. I'm ten minutes late with something that's desperately important. Let's name a time and place and we'll meet up for a good old chinwag,' she suggested.

'How about this Friday? Come to tea and meet the family?'

'It's a date.'

Tina opened her handbag and started rummaging amongst its contents. 'Give me your address and I'll write it down.'

'No need to do that,' Vicky answered and snapped open her own handbag. She presented Tina with one of Neil's business cards, of which she always carried a supply.

'Posh,' Tina said, visibly impressed.

'Half past six?'

'I'll be there, with knobs on.'

They kissed each other on the cheek, then Tina hurried off down the street, walking so fast that she was on the verge of breaking into a run.

'Oh, this is rare!' Vicky said to herself. She couldn't wait to tell Neil.

Vicky was waiting impatiently for Tina to arrive. The table was set, the meal in the oven. Martha was wearing her party dress with a ribbon in her hair. Neil had on his new cardigan, knitted by Vicky herself, and a pair of new cavalry twills. Vicky had wanted him to put on his business suit and tie, but he had said blow that. It was his home – theirs, since Mrs Seton had passed on two years previously – and he wanted to feel relaxed in it, so if this Tina didn't like it she could lump it.

Vicky had been miffed by his refusal but had soon got over it. She had only wanted to show him off. She supposed she could do that just as well in cardy and cavalry twills.

'I hope she's not going to be late. I'm hungry,' Neil said.

'Could you eat a scabby-heided wean?' Martha asked, repeating the old Glasgow saying (a scabby-heided wean being a baby with scabs on its head).

'Not quite, but I might if I had to wait for ages and ages.' Neil smiled. How he doted on that child; she was sweetness itself.

'Have you noticed her squinting the way she does?' Neil asked Vicky.

'Who?'

'Martha. Sometimes when she's looking at things she sort of squints. Do you think she needs glasses?'

'I've never seen her squinting,' Vicky replied hotly.

'All right, keep your hair on. I'm not implying criticism. It's just that if she does need glasses we should see to it sooner rather than later.'

Vicky hadn't noticed Martha squinting, or if she had she hadn't taken it in. 'It wouldn't do any harm for the optician to have a look at her, just to be on the safe side,' she conceded.

'I don't want glasses. They'll call me speccy at school,' Martha complained, alarmed at the prospect.

'If you have to have them, then you'll have to have them, and that'll be that. But just because you might squint occasionally doesn't mean you do,' Vicky said, placating her daughter.

'If I get specs, will I get false teeth as well? A boy in my class says his mummy and daddy both have specs and false teeth.' Martha asked anxiously.

Vicky and Neil laughed. It was amazing what the wee one could come out with at times.

'No false teeth, I promise you,' Vicky replied.

The doorbell rang. 'That'll be her,' Vicky said and rushed from the room.

Neil stood and straightened himself down. He took Martha by the hand as Vicky's voice erupted excitedly in the hallway. Another female voice spoke, as excited as Vicky's. He wasn't sure whether or not he was looking forward to meeting Tina. One thing was certain: he could not have objected to her coming over even if he'd wanted to; Vicky would have gone daft if he'd tried. All he had heard from her since she had bumped into Tina last Monday was: Tina this, Tina that and Tina the next blinking thing.

Vicky and Tina, each with an arm round the other's waist, entered the kitchen.

Vicky's eyes were shining. 'Tina, I want you to meet my husband Neil.'

Tina saw a handsome man – a smasher, she would have described him as. Vicky had done well for herself.

Neil extended his hand and they shook. 'I'm pleased to meet you,' he said.

'And this is Martha, our daughter,' Vicky went on.

Tina squatted and gazed at Martha. 'You're going to be a beauty when you grow up.' She smiled.

Martha was instantly won over. 'Hello,' she murmured and glanced at the floor.

'You're not bashful are you?' Tina teased.

Martha grasped hold of Vicky's skirt and hid her face in it.

'I've got something for you,' Tina said and from a paper poke produced several bars of chocolate.

'You shouldn't have. That must be your ration for the entire month!' Vicky exclaimed.

'The pleasure's mine to give it. And anyway, sweeties are the last thing I need,' Tina replied, and prodded her side, which wobbled.

'I've got something else for us,' Tina went on, and delved into the paper poke to pull out a small bottle. 'Fowler's Wee Heavy, do you remember? I've got six of them here.'

Vicky clapped her hands in glee. 'Remember! That was my first Saturday night in –' She came up short. Duncliffe and Duke Street were never mentioned in front of Martha. 'I remember all right, but we'll talk about these days later, when Martha's gone to bed.'

Tina got the message. 'Clear as crystal.'

Neil decided he liked Tina. There was something very winning about her.

'But now I want to hear about you and what you've been up to?' Vicky demanded.

Tina and Neil sat, Neil with Martha on his knee, while Vicky went about putting out the meal.

'Well, when I left that place down the coast, I went home and soon got a start. Time went by, with nothing much happening at all. Then one day my da announced he'd got a better job with a Coventry firm. So how did we all feel about flitting down to England?

'I must admit, I wasn't all that keen to begin with. Then I thought, why not? A clean break might be just the very thing, and so down to England we all went.

'We settled in right nicely, and got on well enough with

our neighbours. Though I must say at the beginning we had trouble with the accent, for they don't half talk funny . . .'

'I wonder what they thought about your accent?' Vicky interjected with a smile.

'Me? What accent?' Tina replied, straight-faced, and they all laughed, for she was broadest Glasgow.

Tina went on. 'Then the war happened, and my da got his papers. He went into the army and fought in D-day. He was wounded in the subsequent advance through France – nothing all that serious, but serious enough to have him sent back to Blighty. He never saw active duty again after that.

'Meanwhile, fairly early on in the war, as you'll know, Coventry took an awful plastering from the Luftwaffe, and Ma and I had our house blown up around our ears. We were extremely lucky to walk away from that. As for the city, the devastation was dreadful. Whole areas flattened flat as a pancake.'

'I saw it on the newsreel and thought about you at the time,' Vicky said, laying out plates of steaming vegetable stew. Many foods, clothes, sweets and even bread were rationed. Meat was at a premium.

They sat round the table and Neil opened three bottles of Fowler's Wee Heavy. He had a half-bottle of whisky for the occasion, which he would bring out when the Wee Heavys were finished.

Vicky continued. 'After Ma and I were bombed out, we managed to find a new place in Burton Green, a small village on the outskirts of Coventry, and while there I worked as a land-girl.

'When Da came out the army he found that his old works had gone, a casualty of the bombing, and so we decided to return to Glasgow, which we'd all missed like billy-o. When we got here we went round various factors and ended up in a really nice tenement in St Vincent Crescent, which is behind and down from Argyle Street. We're very happy there.'

'I know St Vincent Crescent. It's overlooking the river,' Neil said.

'Aye, that's right. We're on the top landing, so from our front window you can watch the ships coming and going, it can be a terrific sight.'

'And what about work, what are you doing?' Vicky asked.

'Have you heard of Tom Allen, the MP for Glasgow Kelvinhaugh, and Sandy Millar, the MP for Glasgow Bridgeton?'

'Of course, they're both well kent. Particularly Tom Allen. I've never heard him myself, but they say he's a tremendous speaker,' Vicky answered.

'Well, they share me as their Glasgow secretary, and I have an office in the Kelvinhaugh constituency's Labour Hall. I also help out with typing and clerical work for the Labour Halls in both constituencies. So Tom and Sandy each pay a third of my wages, the Labour Halls a sixth each.'

Vicky was fascinated. 'And do you like it?'

'It's fantastic. What I do is varied and exciting, and not only that but important. Up until I joined them, I wasn't much of a political animal, but I am now. I fairly live and breathe Labour politics.'

'Wasn't Tom Allen one of the original Red Clydesiders?' Vicky asked.

'He was indeed, and was locked up on several occasions because of it, once in a dungeon in Edinburgh Castle, would you believe. He and James Maxton, despite their political differences, were thick as thieves.' James Maxton had died the previous month, on 23 July, to be precise.

'A union man before he became an MP, and brilliant at it,' Neil added.

'I'd do anything for him. He's that sort of person.' Tina smiled.

They chatted on about Tina till the end of the meal, when it was time for Martha to go to bed. Neil volunteered to take Martha through and get her ready, and while he was doing this Vicky and Tina washed, dried and put away the dishes.

Neil poured whiskies as Vicky was giving Martha a goodnight kiss and tucking her in. When Vicky returned to the kitchen they settled round the fireplace.

'Now I've given you all my guff, I want to hear about you,' Tina prompted.

'First of all I want to know why you never tried to get in touch with me?' Vicky asked. She had inquired of Mary about that when she had returned from sea, and Mary had said Tina had neither written nor chapped the door in her absence.

'The answer to that is dead simple. You were due to be released in March '36. At the end of March I went to look for your address and couldn't find it. I'd lost the bloody thing. So all I could do was wait for you to contact me, which you didn't. Or at least, according to you, not until after we'd flitted to Coventry. So why did *you* wait so long?'

Vicky gave a pained smile. 'I wasn't released in March of '36, Ganch's report on me was a bad one and I was made to serve my full sentence. I served the remainder in Duke Street prison.

'Oh, that bitch, that dirty rotten lesbian bitch!' Tina swore, eyes blazing anger.

'It was her final revenge for me refusing her and gouging her face as I did,' Vicky said softly.

This was all new to Neil. Vicky had never spoken to him about Duncliffe. 'Refused her what?' he asked.

Vicky told the story, all of it, including the horrors of the Black Room. When she was finished, a silence fell between them.

'Jesus H!' Neil said after a while.

Vicky wiped away a tear that had seeped onto her left cheek. She then went on to tell Tina about her fleeing Glasgow after being released from Duke Street, and the time she had spent aboard the *Atlantic Star* as assistant to the purser.

Tina left only in order to catch the last tram. On the outside landing she and Vicky hugged one another tight.

'Telephone me at the Labour Hall in a couple of days' time. We'll arrange to meet again,' Tina said, having already given Vicky her home address, work address and work telephone number.

'I'd like that,' Vicky whispered.

They squeezed one another again, then Tina took her leave. Neil walked her to the tramstop.

When Neil returned, he found Vicky in bed, staring at the ceiling.

'I knew Duncliffe couldn't have been a bed of roses, but I never dreamed it was as diabolical as that. The Japs had a torture similar to your Black Room. It sent more than one poor bugger completely round the twist,' he said, starting to get stripped.

A shudder ran through Vicky.

'There are nights when you cry out in your sleep, a cry that never fails to waken me and cover me from head to toe in cold goosebumps. Is that you having nightmares about the Black Room?' he asked softly.

'It happens every so often. I'm back there in the blackness, the entire world crushing in on me. Other times I'm reliving the hallucinations I had, some pleasant, some unspeakably horrible. But the most awful of all is the one where I suddenly come to believe that I'm locked away for ever, that I'm never ever going to be let out. That must be the cry that wakens you.'

He was in his pyjamas now and joined her in bed. He gently stroked her forehead, trying to ease away the pain that was showing there.

'I'll have nightmares about the Black Room till my dying day. I'll never forget that place, or the morning runs, or Miss Ganch's riding crop, or dozens of other things. They're all there, for ever branded into my memory, till whenever that memory ceases to function,' she said in a whisper.

He moved his fingertips to her temples, massaging them in circular motions. 'I enjoyed meeting your friend. I hope she comes here often.'

'Good, and I hope she will too.'

'You won't ever tell her about me, will you? I don't want anyone else to know,' he said, referring to his impotence.

273

'I won't. You have my word on that.'

'Thank you,' he whispered, and kissed her neck.

He gathered her to him, and his hands began to move. She closed her eyes and remained passive. That was how he liked her to be.

A little later she gasped. He had learned well what she had taught him. He had become so skilful that it was almost as good as the real thing.

Almost.

The next Friday night Neil babysat while Vicky and Tina went to a picture house in the town. After that the two women continued seeing one another regularly. Sometimes Tina came to the house, other times they went to a café or the flicks. Occasionally Mary and George would mind Martha and Neil would go with them. On a night in early October Tina suggested the dance.

'It's a dance I'm organising at the Kelvinhaugh Labour Hall where I work. I've got a good band lined up, and at the end Tom Allen will be speaking.'

'Tom Allen! That sounds marvellous,' Vicky exclaimed.

'I'll arrange it so that you meet him if you like.'

'That would be rare,' Vicky enthused.

'I'll pay for the tickets now,' Neil said, as keen as Vicky to hear and meet the great man.

Vicky and Neil were thoroughly enjoying themselves. They had been on the floor quite a lot of the time, but at the present were taking a break in order to catch their wind.

They watched Tina swirl by in the arms of a man she had been dancing with most of the night. Tina had confided to them earlier that she thought the man was going to ask if he could lumber her home.

Vicky nudged Neil. 'Over there,' she said and nodded.

It was Tom Allen. They both recognised him from pictures in the newspapers. He was powerfully built and short in stature. His face was rough-hewn, filled with strength and resolve. Even at that distance Vicky could sense his natural charisma. She judged him to be in his late fifties.

The band played several more numbers, then laid down their instruments and left the rostrum. An excited hum of anticipation filled the hall. Tina ran up the rostrum's side stairs and Tom Allen followed her. On reaching the centre of the rostrum she held her hands aloft for silence, and then thanked everyone for coming along.

'And now, the moment you've all been waiting for. Mr Tom Allen, your MP!' she announced and led off the applause, which became a roar of clapping, whistling and stamping feet.

Tom Allen gave his audience a friendly smile and waited till the applause began to die. Then he started to speak. He wove a spell of words that Vicky found sheer magic. His theme was the chronic housing conditions found not only in Kelvinhaugh but in many parts of working-class Glasgow.

He spoke of stairhead toilets that were nothing short of abominations, of overcrowding that forced entire families of five and six to share the same inset bed in a single end, leaking roofs, running walls, rats, mice and other vermin, and of the ill health and disease that were the direct result of such a hellish environment. The old slums must be bulldozed, he argued, razed to the ground, and clean, modern units built in their stead, houses that would allow their occupants to live in dignity as human beings, and not like pigs in a sty.

When Allen finished, the applause was rapturous, and even louder than before. This time Vicky was one of those stamping her feet. He came down from the rostrum to be instantly mobbed by admirers. His back was thumped again and again as he shook hand after hand.

'Fabulous,' Vicky said to Neil, who nodded his agreement.

The band returned to the rostrum. 'Take your partners for the last waltz please!' their leader cried out, and the band struck up.

A few minutes later Tina somehow managed to disentangle Tom Allen and bring him over to where Vicky and Neil were standing.

'Tom, I'd like you to meet Mr and Mrs Seton,' Tina said.

Allen shook hands with Vicky first. 'A pleasure to meet you. Are you newly moved into the area?'

'We live in Townhead. We're here because we're friendly with Tina, and because we wanted to hear you speak. If I may say, that was one of the best speeches I've ever heard,' Vicky replied.

Tom Allen could see that she meant what she said, that it wasn't flannel. 'Thank you.' He smiled.

He shook Neil by the hand, then turned his attention back to Vicky. 'A pity you aren't local. We're always on the lookout for helpers. We only ask a couple of hours a week, but what a contribution it makes to the cause. Isn't that so, Tina?'

'They're invaluable,' Tina agreed.

'Would those couple of hours be during the day or in the evening?' Vicky queried.

'Whenever they're most convenient to the person involved,' Tom Allen replied.

Neil read Vicky's thoughts in her face; he approved of them. When she glanced at him, he nodded.

'I'd like to help, even though I'm not local. I can manage during the day while my little girl's at school.'

Tom Allen beamed.

'That's fantastic. You can be with me in my office,' Tina said to Vicky. Then to Tom Allen: 'She's a shorthand typist, same as me. We trained together.'

'Better still,' Allen replied, his beam widening.

'I'm looking forward to it,' Vicky said.

Allen patted her on a shoulder. 'Welcome aboard, Mrs Seton.'

'Oh, please, you must call me Vicky. And this is Neil.'

'All right, Vicky and Neil it is, and I'm Tom. But tell me, Neil, what do you do?'

'I'm a solicitor with MacDonald, Lindsay and Hogg.'

'Indeed! A much respected firm, and expensive. I know a dozen people needing legal advice, but none of them can afford to pay for it, far less the prices MacDonald, Lindsay and Hogg charge.'

'They're certainly not cheap, there's no argument about

that. But these people you're talking about, tell me about them. I'm interested.'

'They're poor people, Neil, unable to work because of old age, sickness, that sort of thing.'

Neil cleared his throat. 'I'd be happy to give them free advice. In fact, assisting folk like that has always been my aim, and why I became a solicitor in the first place. How about if I held a surgery once a week? Right here in the Labour Hall, say. Or, if the people were unable to get here on account of infirmity or sickness, I could go to them.'

'I think that's a splendid idea!' Vicky exclaimed.

'If you give me the names and addresses of these people, I'll arrange everything,' Tina said to Tom.

'And this wouldn't be just a one-off thing. You'd do it for some while to come?' Tom asked Neil hopefully.

'I don't see why not,' Neil replied.

Tom Allen grasped Neil by the hand a second time, and vigorously pumped the hand up and down. 'You're a gentleman, lad, a real gentleman. I'm in your debt.'

Neil flushed with pleasure. How marvellous to be held in such high esteem by a man of Tom Allen's eminence!

'He's not only a solicitor, but a damn good one too,' Vicky said proudly.

Neil flushed again, this time with embarrassment.

'I'm going to really enjoy doing this,' Neil said after Tom Allen had moved on.

Vicky kissed him on the cheek.

Tina caught sight of the chap she had danced with so much. He was hovering, trying to catch her eye, which he had now succeeded in doing. It was clear what the chap wanted, so she quickly excused herself. Her lumber was on.

On the tram returning to Townhead Vicky snuggled up to Neil. Right then she felt closer to him than she had ever felt. She still didn't love him, and didn't imagine that she ever would. But she had a great deal of affection for him, and he was an excellent husband.

'Happy?' he asked.

'Hmmh!' she mumbled.

'I'm glad we went tonight. Look what came of it.'

'Do you think the city will ever get those new houses Tom was talking about?'

His eyes glittered. 'Some day. You wait and see. Some day it has to come. And I'll tell you this, if there's any way I can help bring it about, I will.'

She glanced round, confirmed they were alone on the top deck and kissed him full on the mouth. 'You can be smashing at times.'

'You can be smashing at times yourself,' he replied.

They went back to snuggling, she thinking how tremendous it was going to be helping Tina a couple of hours a week, he dreaming about the new houses that would replace the old, squalid tenements.

The electric atmosphere in the room was generated by the burly man sitting opposite Ken Blacklaws: Gordon Tucker, known the length and breadth of Clydeside as The Rock.

The room was The Rock's office, the office of the president of the Glasgow Wharf Workers' Association, which would merge with the Clyde Dockworkers' Union when The Rock and Ken signed the papers now in front of them.

The Clyde Dockworkers' Union had come into being two years previously on the merger of Ken's old union, the Honourable Society of Dock Workers, with the West of Scotland Union of Dockers. Ken was its president. When Ken had stepped into Jack Fyfer's shoes there had been four dockworkers' unions. When these papers were signed and witnessed, there would be only two.

Ken was flanked by two lawyers, one on either side, as was The Rock. Behind The Rock stood the four men who comprised his union executive. Unknown to The Rock, two of these men were in Ken's pocket, thanks to indiscretions on their part and Ken's subsequent blackmail of them.

Ken had set up both of them. He had explicit photographs of Ross Moir having sex with a prostitute which would go to Ross's wife should Ross not do as he was told. And Ross loved his wife.

As for Keith Kirkland, Ken held a gambling note of Keith's to the value of £26,500. Keith was not aware that the roulette table had been rigged, the croupier under orders to take him to the cleaners. The gambling club had been paid handsomely by Ken for their troubles, on top of which he had bought the note from them.

Ken's plan had been to get a hold on all four of the union executive and make them force The Rock into agreeing to a merger. Under this combined assault, in accordance with the union's rulebook, The Rock would have had to give way, or resign, which would have had the same result.

This had been the state of affairs, with Ken trying to devise a way of compromising Russell Hadwin, one of the two executives not yet under his control, when the situation took on a new dimension.

The Rock was a widower who lived alone, his wife having died of cancer halfway through the war. Ken got word that his only son, Donny, who had emigrated to New Zealand twelve years earlier, was bringing himself and his family home to Glasgow for a visit. The Rock was ecstatic. Though he had never met them, Elizabeth and Jane, his five-year-old granddaughters, were the apple of his eye. Already besotted by the twins, he had really gone ga-ga over them in the flesh.

Realising how he could exploit the Tucker twins, Ken had abandoned his original intention in favour of short, sharp and devastatingly effective action – action that would give him the Glasgow Wharf Workers' Association on a plate within days rather than long-drawn-out months. The quick thrust of the poniard as opposed to the battering of the claymore: far more efficient and time-saving.

Donny Tucker and family had been enjoying a marvellous holiday – until the previous afternoon, when the professional criminals Ken had imported from London struck.

Donny had been knocked senseless to the ground, Yootha his wife thrust aside and the two five-year-olds bundled into the rear of a car. The car, containing kidnappers and kidnapped, roared away.

The Rock had ranted and raved, almost frothing at the

mouth, but wisely had done what Ken had said and refrained from contacting the police. Ken had told him that, if he did, his granddaughters would never be seen alive again.

Between the conception of the kidnap and its execution, Ken had ordered the necessary papers for the merger to be drawn up, the same papers now before him and The Rock. When they were signed and witnessed, Elizabeth and Jane would be released. All Ken had to do was make a phone call.

Ken looked directly into The Rock's eyes, which were blazing with hate and loathing. 'Shall we get on with it then, Mr Tucker?' He smiled.

The Rock lifted the pen beside his set of papers, paused for the briefest of seconds, then hastily began scribbling his signature. He signed paper after paper, and each paper as it was signed was witnessed by his two lawyers, passed to Ken, who countersigned, and then his signature was witnessed by his two lawyers.

In less than a minute it was over. The Glasgow Wharf Workers' Association had merged with the Clyde Dock-workers' Union; the new union was to retain the name of the latter.

The Rock threw his pen back onto the table and lurched to his feet. 'You'd better keep your side of the bargain,' he said huskily, referring to the release of his grandchildren.

'There's no advantage to me not to,' Ken replied levelly.

'The phone call . . .'

'. . . will be made directly you're gone,' Ken interrupted swiftly. No one in the room, other than himself and The Rock, knew about the abduction.

The Rock's chest heaved. He glanced one last time round the office that contained so many memories. He knew he would never enter it again.

'Enjoy your retirement,' said Ken.

The Rock turned and strode from the room, his lawyers hastening after him.

Ken stared at the four members of what had been the Glasgow Wharf Workers' Association executive. 'I've decided that Moir and Kirkland will be part of the new organisation. I'm afraid I can't accommodate you other two. I'm sorry.'

Russell Hadwin went white. Bob Leckie, the fourth member, slumped where he stood.

'You'd better go and clear out your desks.'

Hadwin and Leckie did not even bother arguing; they knew enough of Ken to be sure that he wouldn't change his mind.

Hadwin and Leckie trooped out of the office, leaving Moir and Kirkland.

'I want to be alone,' Ken told them. They fled, Kirkland closing the door behind him.

Ken grinned, then walked round the desk to sit in what had been The Rock's chair. Tilting the chair back, he put his feet on the desk and clasped his hands behind his head.

Only the Union of Longshoremen remained. Once he had engineered its merger with the Clyde Dockworkers', he would control all of Clydeside. Oh, what a beautiful thought that was! A Clydeside monopoly, no competition; it would virtually be a licence to coin money.

But his ambition didn't stop there, no sir. Once he controlled Clydeside, he intended picking off the other Scottish dock unions till in the end there was one huge union: a national union, the Scottish Union of Dockworkers, with him at its head. After Glasgow he would start in on Leith, then Dundee, followed by Aberdeen. When those major ports had fallen to him, the tiddlers that were left would go down like ninepins.

President of a national union: the thought of the power he would have made his mouth water. Power and money, and everything they could bring. Beautiful women, expensive cars, a mansion, virtually anything he desired could be his. He'd just have to snap his fingers and it would be there. He'd just have to utter and people would jump and scurry around like frightened rabbits, the way Moir and Kirkland had done a minute earlier.

The Scottish Union of Dockworkers *would* come into existence, and he would be its president. Nothing, but nothing, was going to stop that happening. He would bring it about by whatever means were necessary, fair or foul.

Swinging his feet from the desk, he leaned forward and flicked the intercom switch which connected him to the woman who'd been The Rock's private secretary. He didn't know her name.

'Yes, sir?'

'I want a letter sent off to every member of staff, with the exception of Mr Moir and Mr Kirkland, giving them a fortnight's notice as from this Friday. When you've done that, have this building put up for sale.'

There was a stunned silence.

'Have you got that?'

'Yes, sir. Fortnight's notice and the building up for sale,' the woman quavered in reply.

'Right,' said Ken, and flicked the intercom switch down again.

Then he picked up the telephone and made the call ordering the release of Elizabeth and Jane. He had no fear of The Rock going to the police once they were released, for he had told The Rock that, if he did, sooner or later, in Scotland or New Zealand, the twins were dead.

'Congratulations!' Vicky squealed, and fell upon Tina, hugging her tight. Tina had come over to Parr Street to tell Vicky and Neil that she had become engaged to Sammy Walker, the chap she had met at the dance in the Kelvinhaugh Labour Hall. Sammy was an electrician.

'Let me have another look,' Vicky said, releasing Tina and grabbing hold of her friend's left hand.

'I've got a wee drop of whisky in, this calls for a toast,' Neil said and crossed to the sideboard to fetch the bottle and glasses.

'It's a smashing ring!' Vicky enthused. In fact it was a very ordinary engagement ring, similar to thousands of others to be found on the left hands of working-class women in the city. Not too big, not too small, not too expensive, but not too cheap either. In other words, just right for a working man's pocket.

'The wedding's next month. You're both invited of

282

course. And, Vicky, I was wondering if you'd be matron of honour?'

'I'd love to be.'

'And you, Neil. Would you be an usher?'

'I'd be honoured.'

'That's settled then,' Tina said, accepting the glass Neil handed her.

'To a long and happy married life!' Neil toasted.

'Aye, lang may your lum reek,' Vicky added.

'Only four months you've been going out together. It didn't take the pair of you long to make up your minds,' Vicky said. Tina had met Sammy the previous October; it was now late February, 1947.

'It was a click right-off. I think we both knew within a few weeks that we were right for each other. But I didn't say, not even to you. Just in case.'

'I understand. It's always best not to tempt fate,' Vicky replied. She was really chuffed at Tina's news.

'Sammy's decided we'll go doon ra watter for our honeymoon, either Rothesay or Millport,' Tina said, meaning down the River Clyde.

'It'll be gey cold there in March, but I don't suppose that will be bothering you two any,' Vicky teased.

It was Neil who glanced away. His embarrassment was combined with a bitter resentment about his own condition. Hardly a day went by when he didn't curse his impotence, and Ken Blacklaws for making him that way.

Tina gave a lecherous leer. 'I don't suppose it will.' She giggled.

'What about a house for the pair of you?' Vicky asked.

'I'd like to get one in St Vincent Terrace because I like it so much there. Sammy's going to call on the factor my da rents his house from.'

Neil went over and poked the fire. Wind was howling outside. He paused to listen to the sound of a broken chimney top birling away good-o.

'There's just one problem about the honeymoon. I'm going to need someone to fill in for me at work, and I thought you might do it? Helping me as you have on a

283

Wednesday these past months makes you the obvious choice,' Tina said.

Vicky glanced at Neil. 'It's up to you, pet,' he told her.

'I'd like fine to do it but I'll have to speak to my mum first. It would mean her taking Martha to school and looking after her from when school came out till I got home.' Vicky sipped her whisky and thought about that. She went on, 'Tell you what, you stay here and I'll nip over the road and have a word with Mum now.'

'Terrific!' Tina smiled.

Ten minutes later Vicky was back to say that Mary had agreed. Vicky would do Tina's job while Tina was on honeymoon.

Vicky poured out a cuppa for herself, weak tea without milk or sugar. Many Glasgow folk drank their tea that way, a result of the rationing. It was Friday afternoon, and in a couple of hours she would have finished her first week in Tina's job – a week she had thoroughly enjoyed. It had been marvellous to return to full-time work. She found this job extremely interesting and rewarding. When she was at it, the hours just flew by.

Only the previous night Neil had remarked at the difference in her. She had a whole new zest and zing, a sparkle that had been missing over the past few years. There was no doubt that her relationship with Martha had improved now that her life had expanded from the narrow confines of house-house and wean-wean – as indeed had her relationship with Neil. The outside interest and stimulation made a world of difference.

She decided that in the near future, some time after Tina's return from honeymoon, she would have a long chat with Mary about the possibility of her looking after Martha on a long-term basis so that she could have a full-time job of her own. Neil wouldn't object, she was sure of that. In fact, pound to a penny he would be all for it. Thankfully, he wasn't one of those husbands who thought it wrong for a woman to have aspirations other than slaving at the kitchen sink all day. Humming happily, she resumed typing, her fingers flying over the keys.

Vicky had just returned to the kitchen from putting Martha to bed and reading *Goldilocks and the Three Bears* yet again – Martha absolutely adored the story of Goldilocks and would have listened to it twenty-four hours a day given the chance – when there was a knock on the outside door.

Neil glanced up from the law book he'd been engrossed in. 'I wonder who that is?' he said, frowning.

'Probably Mary,' Vicky replied over her shoulder, making for the door.

'It's me. I've come visiting,' smiled Tom Allen and held up a large brown-paper poke which chinked.

'This is an unexpected pleasure. Come away in,' said Vicky, wishing she had something nicer on than the old dress she slopped around the house in, and ushered Tom Allen through.

Neil jumped to his feet when he saw who their caller was.

'I hope I'm not interrupting?' Tom inquired politely.

'Not in the least,' Neil reassured him.

Tom handed Vicky the poke. 'Some screwtops. I thought we might wet our thrapples while we talked.'

The two men sat on either side of the fire and Vicky opened several of the screwtops and poured them all beer.

'Well, Tom, what brings you to Townhead?' Neil queried when the three of them had a glass in their hands and Vicky had sat down.

'You do. I want to have a chat with you.'

There was an undercurrent in his tone that caused Neil to glance quickly at Vicky. 'Is there some sort of legal problem you want me to help out with?' he asked.

'No. Although your helping my constituents in that department has got to do with why I'm here tonight. Did you know you're building something of a reputation for yourself in Glasgow Kelvinhaugh? You're very highly spoken of, and spoken about more and more.'

A tinge of redness crept into Neil's face. 'That's kind of you to say so,' he mumbled.

'And I personally like you a great deal. Which is what made me think of what Mr Attlee said to me only recently in the House of Commons.'

'And what was that?' Neil asked, intrigued.

'The Prime Minister believes that the Labour Party has now reached a point in its existence where, if it wishes to survive as a major party, it has to broaden its base of appeal.

'You see, the plain fact is that, with mechanisation, automation and the great technological advances that have taken place during the last decade, the structure of society in Britain is rapidly changing. To put it bluntly, the working class is already contracting, whereas the middle class is expanding, the latter at the expense of the working class. To avoid losing these votes to the Liberals, the Labour Party must alter its image.

'The old-fashioned street corner ranters and ravers, such as I am, are yesterday's Labour Party. The men of tomorrow will have working-class roots but will have moved on in life, as you have done Neil. Lawyers, journalists, teachers, doctors and dons, those are the sort of people who'll be leading the party before long. That is Mr Attlee's belief, and mine also.'

Neil nodded. 'I couldn't agree more. The party must broaden or eventually wither, no doubt about it. But an awful lot of folk are refusing to admit that the signs exist, far less accept them.'

'You've hit the nail on the head, particularly where Glasgow and other big industrial cities are concerned. Their thinking has become entrenched, and because of this not nearly enough new blood is brought along or even actively encouraged to be party members.

'That's why I've come to see you this evening. How do you feel about speaking on the same platform as me a week on Friday?'

Neil sat back in his chair, aghast at Tom Allen's suggestion. 'But I've never spoken publicly in my life!' he croaked.

'That doesn't mean you can't do it. I think you can, and believe you should. From the number of political conversations I've had with you I'm convinced you have a tremendous amount to contribute. And you're a professional man, born and bred working class but now in one of Glasgow's top firms of solicitors – exactly the sort of person I've just been going on about.'

Neil swallowed what remained of his beer and looked to Vicky for a refill. 'It's just so . . . unexpected, that's all. I've never even considered speaking in public.'

'Vicky, what's your opinion?' Tom asked her, for he had come to respect her judgement while she'd been filling in for Tina.

Vicky gave Neil his refill, then topped up Tom Allen's glass. 'I agree with you that Neil has a tremendous amount to contribute, and think he should do so. As for his never having spoken in public before, I'm certain he'll enjoy it once he's up there and spouting. There's nothing he likes more than spouting his views,' she told Tom.

Neil barked out a laugh. 'Enjoy! Are you mad, woman! I'd be scared stiff, absolutely petrified.'

'To begin with maybe, but you'd soon get used to it,' she countered.

'And if I didn't?'

'Then never speak in public again. No harm will have been done.'

'Except an acute case of embarrassment.'

She shrugged. 'Embarrassment won't kill you. Some of the conditions in this city do, and those are the conditions you feel strongly about.'

A gleam came into Neil's eyes. She was dead right of course. This was a golden opportunity to speak out about many of the things that so concerned him, various conditions in the city which were appalling in the extreme and crying out for something to be done about them. And on a national level he could add his voice to those already clamouring for the government to push ahead with its nationalisation plans. The coal industry had been taken into public ownership on the first of January that year, but what about electricity, gas and the railways? There must be no backsliding when it came to those.

'You're not the man I imagine you to be if you back down,' Tom Allen said bluntly and even a little brutally.

'You really do believe I can pull it off?' Neil asked Vicky. She nodded. 'I do.'

Neil made up his mind. 'Right then, I'll spout a week on Friday,' he said, and they all laughed.

Tom Allen came over and shook him by the hand.

'So what's the verdict?' Neil demanded eagerly, having just read to Vicky for the first time the speech he'd been writing.

She was disappointed, but didn't want him to know. 'It was all right.' She smiled.

His face fell. 'Only all right?'

'It was very good.'

He gazed deep into her eyes, then glanced away. Crossing to the kitchen table, he threw down his speech onto it.

'No, it wasn't, it was lousy,' he said miserably.

'It was nothing of the sort. It had many fine points. It was, however – how can I put it? Somewhat constipated and pedestrian.'

He flung himself into a chair. 'Constipated and pedestrian – oh, charming!'

'It needs additional work and polishing. And you need to relax. You're awfully tense, which is badly affecting your delivery. Try and put the speech across the way you put your ideas and views across to me at home.'

'Constipated, pedestrian – and now stilted! It gets better and better.'

'That's quite the wrong attitude to take. You should be positive. And there's no need to be so cross with me. I'm only trying to help.'

He made a disbelieving harumphing sound and stared blackly into the fire.

'I'll put the kettle on,' she said, and rose.

'Not for me.'

She sat down again.

'But don't let me stop you if you want a cuppa,' he said airily.

She silenty counted up to ten. 'Would you have preferred if I'd lied and told you it was bloody brilliant?'

'I don't think it's as bad as you're making out.'

'You said yourself it was lousy.'

He glared at her. 'I didn't mean that literally.'

'I should hope not, otherwise you'd have meant it was crawling with lice.'

'Don't be so damned pedantic!' he said, voice rising.

'That's exactly what you're being in your speech, pedantic,' she retorted.

He clenched his fists. 'Maybe I should get in touch with Tom Allen and tell him I won't be able to do it,' he said huffily.

'Don't be pathetic. The speech itself needs more work on it, that's all.'

'I don't know,' he mumbled, and poked the fire with the First World War bayonet they kept for that purpose.

'Do you want me to have a look at it for you?'

'No,' he replied emphatically.

'Oh, grow up!' she exploded, and strode from the room. He was being so unreasonable!

When she returned to the kitchen a little later, he was still staring into the fire but the speech had gone from the table. Nor would he discuss it further when she tried to broach the subject again. Silly bugger! she thought to herself.

Vicky and Tina were leaving the pictures when it happened. Tina suddenly stumbled and bent over groaning. 'Awful pain in my stomach,' she gasped. Tina tried in vain to straighten. 'It feels like I'm bleeding down there,' she whispered to Vicky.

'Is it your time of the month?'

'No,' came back the anguished reply.

'I'd better get you into the manager's office,' Vicky said. The pair of them had staggered only a couple of steps when out of the corner of her eye Vicky saw a taxi loom into view.

A couple flagged the taxi down first but quickly relinquished their right to it when Vicky explained that her friend had had an attack of some sort and she needed to take her to the hospital.

Providentially the journey was short. When they arrived, the driver ran to summon assistance while Vicky did her best to comfort the distraught Tina, who was still groaning. Two uniformed men appeared with a stretcher on a trolley and gently lifted Tina onto it. They wheeled her into the hospital, where she was immediately wheeled off to see a doctor.

Vicky gave Tina's details. Just over fifteen minutes later a young doctor came to inform her that Tina was being admitted.

'What's wrong with her?'

'She's on the verge of losing the baby,' the doctor replied.

Vicky looked blank. 'I didn't know she was pregnant!'

'Neither did Mrs Walker, it seems, but she is.'

She must be only just pregnant, Vicky thought. Otherwise she would have known. Two months gone at the most, with one missing period, or more likely a lighter period than usual which Tina hadn't twigged had been caused by pregnancy. If Tina was two months gone, she must have been sleeping with Sammy before the wedding. But that was none of her business.

'Is there anything I can do?'

'You can inform the husband.'

'I'll do that right away. How is Tina?'

'In pain. We don't want to give her anything for it until we know exactly what's what.'

'How about the bleeding? Has that stopped?'

'It has. Let's just hope it remains stopped. If it does, she has a chance of holding onto the baby.'

Please God it would! Vicky silently prayed.

'Right then, I'll be on my way. I'll take a taxi over to St Vincent Crescent, where she lives. The sooner her husband gets here the better.'

'Tell him to bring some personal things, nighties and such. She'll need those whatever happens,' the doctor advised.

Vicky thanked the doctor, then ran out into the night searching for a taxi. Her luck was in; she found one almost immediately.

'So that's it. I'm going to be here for quite some time if I'm to hold onto the little blighter. It's a case of feet up and stay that way.'

Vicky took hold of one of Tina's hands and squeezed it. 'You'll enjoy that, you always were a lazy bitch,' she teased.

Tina grinned. 'It's going to be dead boring in here, but if I win through and have the baby it'll be worth it. Sammy's besotted by the idea of having children. It would break his heart for us to lose this one.'

'Then you'll just have to lie there with your legs crossed,' Vicky replied, and they both laughed.

'But seriously, what about my job?' Tina went on.

'Don't you worry about that. I had already spoken to my mother about taking a full-time job, and she'd agreed to help, so I'll step in, if that's all right with you?'

'I was hoping you'd say that. It certainly takes a load off my mind.'

'Good. Worry is the last thing you need. Peace and tranquillity, that's the ticket, until the big event takes place.'

The next morning Vicky reported to the Kelvinhaugh Labour Hall, thoroughly delighted to be back doing the job she had come to enjoy so much.

Tom Allen was so pleased to see her that he actually made the eleven o'clock tea for the pair of them.

Vicky listened to the chime of church bells in the distance: midnight. When they stopped, it would be Friday morning. The meeting at which Neil was due to speak would start at half past seven that evening.

She put a thumb in her mouth and gnawed the nail.

Earlier, when Neil had thought her busy with Martha, she had overheard him rehearsing his speech. He had come over far more relaxed than previously, but the speech itself, though altered, was only fractionally less stodgy. The content was good, better than it had been, but the prose let it down.

'Neil?' she whispered very quietly. There was no reply. He was sleeping soundly.

She slipped from bed and put on her dressing gown and mules. Picking up his briefcase – he always left it in the same place beside his clothes, so she was able to lay a hand on it without switching on the light – she padded from the bedroom.

It was cold in the kitchen. Raking the remains of the fire, she uncovered some cherry-hot cinders, over which she laid some kindling, and a shovelful of coal on top of that. The crackling kindling told her that the newly set fire would soon take. She made herself a cup of coffee, then settled down at the table with his speech, which she had taken from his briefcase. Slowly she began reading it through.

Highs and lows, light and shade – that's what it lacked, she decided. And wit; there was nothing Glasgow folk loved and appreciated more than wit. She sipped her coffee, and re-read the opening paragraph. If he rephrased that, and maybe inserted a joke there . . . and if he simplified those three sentences, condensing them, and replaced the high-falutin words with ordinary workaday ones, the paragraph would not only come alive, it would be far easier to deliver.

She went over to the sideboard and took out pen and paper from the left-hand drawer. Sitting again at the table, she started to write.

She told Neil what she had done over breakfast, hoping that Martha's presence would stop him blowing his top. It did, but only just.

'All I ask is that you read my version and compare it with what you wrote. It's still the same speech. I haven't altered one jot of content, but I have, I hope, injected some life and excitement into it. The two speeches are in your briefcase. It's up to you which you use tonight.'

Neil, quivering with rage, wiped marg onto his toast, then spread it with some Victoria plum jam that Mary had made with a quantity of black-market sugar she'd come by.

'Up to you,' Vicky repeated.

Neil did not reply.

Vicky washed up, then got Martha ready to take over to Mary's. She always left before Neil. He had a later start at work than her.

'Bye, bye. See you at teatime then,' she called out to Neil after Martha had given him her usual parting kiss. She normally kissed him as well, but hadn't attempted to do so that morning because of his reaction to what she'd done.

There was no reply from behind the raised newspaper.

Vicky was about to slam the outside door, then stopped herself. She wouldn't give him the satisfaction of that.

The Cooperative Hall was packed with Cooperative workers and their families. It was a grand turnout, but then Tom Allen was a popular speaker.

There were three people on the platform: Tom Allen, Neil and a Cooperative official by the name of Beath.

Vicky was in the sixth row from the platform, sitting to one side. She had not wanted to be directly in front of Neil in case that put him off.

After tea, they had returned Martha to Mary, then come on to the hall. He had made no comment about her version of his speech, and she, although dying of curiosity, had not asked.

Mr Beath, a man so incredibly ordinary-looking that he seemed almost invisible, rose to appeal for quiet. He then made a short speech of welcome to those in attendance and to Tom Allen.

'And now I'd like you to give a generous hand to a new

speaker to us, but one whom Mr Allen assures me we're going to hear a great deal from and about in the future: Mr Neil Seton!' Mr Beath announced and led the politely enthusiastic clapping.

Neil stood up and approached the microphone.

Vicky, extremely nervous for him, closed her eyes and crossed her fingers.

It was her version of his speech! He hadn't allowed his wounded pride and feelings of masculine superiority to get the better of him after all!

She opened her eyes to see him standing quite relaxed, at ease with himself and audience. There wasn't even a trace of nerves! She knew then, without the shadow of a doubt, that the evening was going to be a success for him.

'You did fine, lad, just fine. But then I never doubted you would,' said Tom Allen, playfully punching Neil on the arm. The meeting was over, the people starting to disperse.

'I enjoyed it, just as Vicky predicted I would,' Neil replied, glancing sideways at Vicky and smiling at her.

'I have another meeting to address in Parkhead next week. How would you feel about speaking there?' Tom asked.

'I'd love to.'

'Consider it a date then,' Tom said, then turned to a knot of folk waiting to talk to him.

'You were terrific. I was real proud of you,' Vicky told Neil.

'I'd have gone down like a lead balloon if you hadn't rewritten my speech,' he confessed.

'The ideas were all yours. I just polished up your prose, that's all,' she protested.

'If I was successful tonight, it was because of you.'

She slipped an arm round one of his. 'Then let's agree to say that what was accomplished was accomplished together, as a team, the way a good marriage should be.'

He kissed her on the cheek. 'I love you,' he whispered.

'I know.' She smiled.
'Together,' he nodded.
'Together,' she echoed and kissed his cheek.

Ten

Vicky carried a bag of fruit, Neil several books about the Labour Party which he had found in a secondhand bookshop. It was June 1948 and they were in the Western Infirmary, en route to visit Tom Allen, who had suffered a heart attack three days previously.

That morning Mrs Allen had rung Vicky at her office in the Kelvinhaugh Labour Hall – since Tom's heart attack Vicky had been round to see Mrs Allen in her home, and had also rung twice inquiring about Tom's condition – to say that Tom was feeling a bit better and wanted urgently to speak to Neil.

The previous November Tina had given birth to a little boy, Ronald, and then decided, under strong pressure from Sammy, that she would not return to work. Consequently Vicky now had Tina's former job permanently.

Vicky and Neil found Tom's ward without difficulty but had to wait outside in the corridor for a few minutes for visiting time to begin. Then the handbell was rung and they went inside.

They found Tom at the top end of the ward. Vicky thought he looked absolutely dreadful. His face was dirty grey, his cheeks sunken. His hair hung limp and lifeless, while the whites of his eyes had a definite yellowy tinge. He smiled weakly and offered up his right hand, which Vicky grasped. Then Neil did the same.

Vicky sat on a wooden chair; Neil made do with the edge of the bed. They chatted for a wee while, then Tom dropped his bombshell.

'I'm going to have to stand down as MP for Glasgow Kelvinhaugh. The specialist has told me that, if I take it easy, I've probably got between five and ten years left. If I continue working, he doubts I'll be around for the Christmas after next.'

'Oh, Tom!' Vicky exclaimed softly, knowing how much politics and the Labour Party meant to him.

He gave them another weak smile. 'Mustn't grumble, I suppose. I've had a good run for my money, a damn good run. But that run's over now, and I've got to accept the fact.' He paused to catch his breath, then went on. 'Mind you, the attack wasn't totally unexpected. There's a history of heart attacks in my family. And I did have a warning a few years back. I should have paid it heed and slowed down then, retired even, but I didn't, and have now paid the penalty, though fortunately not the ultimate one.'

'I'm sorry,' said Neil.

'Well, look at it this way. One man's loss is another's gain. I want you to be the Labour Party candidate in the by-election.'

Neil's jaw dropped. 'You what!'

'You heard. I want you to be the Labour Party candidate in the by-election,' Tom repeated.

Neil shot a glance at Vicky.

'Why Neil?' Vicky asked.

'Let me explain. This isn't a sudden notion on my part. It's been in my mind that Neil would be my eventual successor ever since that first time he spoke at the Cooperative Hall, and if I had any lingering doubts these were dispelled when he spoke in the St Andrew's Halls alongside Stafford Cripps and myself. That performance was outstanding, and I knew then that I wanted Neil to replace me when the time came.' He went on ruefully, 'Though, to tell the truth, I hadn't expected that succession to be quite so soon . . . So what do you say, Neil. Will you do it?'

Neil bit his lip and glanced again at Vicky. 'You make my selection sound a certainty. What if the selection board reject me?' he asked, turning back to Tom.

Tom's lips twisted into a thin, cynical grin. 'That lot will do exactly as I tell them. If I say you're to be my successor, then my successor you'll be. You have my word on that.'

'Vicky?'

'All your life you've wanted to help the deprived and underprivileged. This is a chance to help them on a far grander scale than you could if you remained a solicitor. It will give you power and influence not only to have things changed on a local level but on a national one as well. If you're foolish enough to let this chance slip by, you'll regret it all the days of your life,' she told him.

'And you'll back me?'

'To the hilt.'

'I'm your man then,' Neil said to Tom Allen.

'I'll write out my resignation later on today, or have a nurse write it out for me, and I'll sign it. I'll have the selection board here in the next day or two and tell them what I've decided, and some time after that they'll be in touch with you. They'll have to appear to go through the proper procedures, of course, but when the candidate is finally chosen from the shortlist you'll be it, I promise you,' Tom replied.

All the way back to Parr Street Neil and Vicky talked excitedly about the forthcoming by-election and discussed in broad terms the many speeches Neil would have to make.

'Checkmate,' said Ken, voice swollen with emotion. It was the first time he had ever beaten Dov Berkoff, the South of Scotland chess champion.

The old Jew's eyes twinkled. It was rare for him to be beaten – an experience he enjoyed nonetheless, for it kept his interest in the game alive.

Berkoff brought his gaze to bear on Ken. 'You have developed an excellent endgame, a ruthless one even. That is most unusual for a British player.'

'Thank you,' Ken replied softly. A compliment from Berkoff was a compliment indeed.

Ken had joined the Nether Pollok Chess Club a little over two years previously. The top players in the city and that part of the country all belonged to it, and the best of them was the man now facing him; Dov Berkoff, a Russian Jew who had come to Glasgow shortly after the Red Revolution. Berkoff was a tailor by trade, chess master by calling.

'I knew you would beat me one day. I have seen it coming for some while now.' Berkoff waved a brown-spotted hand at the board between them. 'Your Zugzwang was particularly good.'

Zugzwang was from the German, *Zug* meaning move, *zwang* to force.

'I still have a great deal to learn, which I do every time I have the honour of playing you,' Ken replied.

'You learn quickly, far more quickly than most. And you have a natural aptitude for the game. You would have made a fine general.'

Ken laughed. The old Jew was closer to the mark than he realised. For, looking at it from his point of view, wasn't he a general already? A general with his own private army and war to fight and win.

'Do you know who your game reminds me of?' Berkoff said, and lit a cigarette. He was a chain smoker – except when involved in the process of playing.

Ken thought Berkoff was going to name another Scottish player but he was wrong.

'Alekhine, often called "the fighter",' Berkoff stated, and took a deep drag on his cigarette.

Ken flushed with pleasure. Alekhine was one of the greats, who had died a few years previously.

Berkoff went on, 'The strength of your game is the same as his – your ability to create and prepare a position long before you have conceived the form your winning combination or mating attack will take.

'And you have the same aggressiveness in your play. Oh yes, very much so. Like him, you don't just want to beat your opponent, but to annihilate the unfortunate.'

Ken could not deny it. He did prefer winning, as he would have put it, decisively.

'Now, as you've finally succeeded in beating me, I will first of all allow you to buy me a drink, then I shall hope to exact my revenge.'

'Wait!' Ken said, as Berkoff reached out to begin resetting the board. 'I'll order the drinks now, but before we start again there were several moves you made on which I'd like you to explain your thinking.'

Berkoff nodded. 'My pleasure.'

Ken beckoned to a steward and placed their order. Then he asked his first question of the old Jew, listening with brow furrowed in concentration as Berkoff replied.

Vicky glanced anxiously at the clock. She had thought Neil would have been home by now. He had gone to the Kelvinhaugh Labour Hall where, that night, the selection board was choosing the candidate from the shortlist. What if something had gone wrong? What if he hadn't got it? What if Tom Allen didn't have the sway over the board he thought he had?

Sitting here worrying like this was no good, she told herself. She must do something to help take her mind off things. She would polish the brasses, she decided. She always found that soothing. She started on the brass pole slung underneath the mantelpiece, and soon had it gleaming.

Yet another glance at the clock told her that a further twenty minutes had passed. Something must have gone wrong. Where was he! Going down on her knees, she attacked the fender. As she polished, she found herself listening to the tick-tick-ticking of the clock.

After the fender came the brass shellcase that stood on the hearth. The shell itself had been fired at Ypres – so the man who'd sold it to her father had told him when George had bought it as a present for her and Neil. She was just finishing the shellcase, and thinking that she would put the kettle on again, when she heard the sound of Neil's key in the outside door.

Instantly she was on her feet, wiping her hands on her pinny; then, using a clean area of her pinny, she cleaned away sweat that had gathered on her forehead and temples.

Neil came into the kitchen with a face so long that he was nearly tripping over it. With shoulders drooping he stopped and stared at her. Neither spoke. Then suddenly his gloom vanished and he gave a whoop!

'Oh, you beast for doing that to me!' she exclaimed, and ran at him, intending to pummel his chest.

Before she could do so, he grabbed her and held her fast. Then, lifting her right off her feet, he whirled her round and round, as she screeched with a combination of alarm and excitement.

Finally he set her down again and kissed her.

'Neil Seton MP: it has a ring about it, don't you think?' he said when the kiss was over.

'I think it sounds quite beautiful.'

They went over to the seats by the fireplace and there he told her all that had happened at his interview. Vicky eagerly drank in every word.

Vicky woke as dawn was breaking to discover she was alone in the bedroom. She lay for a while, thinking that Neil must have gone to the bathroom and would soon return, but when he didn't she got out of bed and put on her dressing gown and mules.

He was in the kitchen, huddled in darkness in his seat by the fireplace. He blinked when she switched on the light. His face was drawn, and there was a look of anguish in his eyes – anguish and terrible despair.

She went and knelt beside him. 'What is it, Neil?'

He ran a hand through her hair and grasped a fistful of curls, but not tightly enough to hurt her.

'Years pass, but the urge, the desire, never diminishes. I want you so badly I could scream with it. The mind wants but the body can't deliver. I'm just dead there, stone dead. Can you have any idea what that's like? To know, to have to live with the fact, that never ever in my life will I be able to do it?'

He took his head in his hands and his body shook.

She put an arm round his shoulders and tried to draw him close, intending to cuddle him. But he wouldn't let her. He shrugged himself free.

'If you don't mind I'd rather be alone right now. Please?' he said in a voice that was strangely grating.

With a lump in her throat and tears stinging her eyes, she left him and went back to bed.

Neil had spoken better than he had ever done before. His speech, which the pair of them had laboured at, had been an absolute cracker. It received a standing ovation from nearly the entire gathering.

This Tuesday night was the first time that all three candidates of the major parties had spoken under the same roof. The Tory and Unionist had spoken first, the Liberal second, and Neil last. His speech had been in a different class from his rivals'.

Both Vicky and Neil had wished that Tom Allen could have been there, but that had been impossible. He was home now, but bedbound. It would be weeks yet before he would be allowed out and about.

Tina had come though, having told Sammy that he had to babysit for wee Ronald. She had had Vicky in fits describing Sammy's horrified reaction.

'But I'm a man. Men don't look after weans!' he'd protested.

'Well, this man is going to have to, and that's all there is to it,' she'd informed him.

She had left him staring at the baby as though it was a bomb which might explode at any moment . . .

'Absolutely first rate!' said Mr Black, one of the Labour Party's selection board, coming up to Vicky and shaking her by the hand.

'Yes, it did go down very well, didn't it,' she answered with a smile.

'A right treat, hen, a right treat. By the way, have you met the wife?'

Vicky shook hands with Mrs Black and was again congratulated on Neil's speech. She glanced over to where Neil stood surrounded by admirers and well-wishers. He was deep in conversation. She was about to return her attention to the Blacks when she suddenly became aware of a woman studying her, a woman whose face was vaguely familiar. Their eyes locked for a brief second, then the woman broke contact and addressed herself to the Liberal candidate, a tall man called Brian Brown, who bent to listen. Vicky could see that the woman was speaking quickly and intensely.

'I understand Neil is speaking tomorrow night.' Mrs Black broke into Vicky's reverie.

She resumed her conversation with the Blacks, and before long had forgotten all about that vaguely familiar face across the hall.

The following afternoon Vicky was in the middle of typing a letter at work when, in a flash, the recognition came to her.

'Oh, my God!' she exclaimed, her hands dropping away from the typewriter.

Muriel Mitchell: the bitch who had nicked a new sweater from her, leaving an old threadbare one in its place, during her first days at Duncliffe. Muriel had been Miss Ganch's 'special friend' at the time.

So what had Muriel been saying to Brian Brown? Had she told him that she, the Labour candidate's wife, was a convicted thief and had served time in borstal and prison because of it? She went ice cold at the thought. She had to speak to Neil right away. Picking up the telephone, she hurriedly dialled the number of MacDonald, Lindsay and Hogg.

They met halfway between his place of work and hers. Already waiting impatiently when she arrived, he grasped her by the elbow.

'Now what is it that's so bloody important you had to see me so urgently?' he demanded, for it had not been easy for him to skive off from the office.

In a rush of words she told him.

When she was finished, he took a deep breath and swore. 'Are you one hundred per cent certain it was her?'

'Oh yes. I'm not mistaken. The hairstyle was different, and she's a lot older and thinner than she used to be, but it was Muriel Mitchell all right.'

'But Tina was also there last night. Why didn't she recognise her?'

Vicky shrugged. 'Maybe she didn't see Muriel. There was a large number present, after all.'

'And you say she was chummy with Brian Brown?'

'It appeared to me she was. There was something about the way she was speaking with him, a relaxed manner if you like, which suggested they were at least acquaintances, if indeed not friends.'

Neil's features creased into a scowl, while his eyes took on a worried, brooding look. 'Brown may come over as a bit of a softie and goody-goody, but nothing could be further from the truth. Underneath that carefully cultivated act he's as ruthless as they come and hard as tempered steel. If this Muriel has handed him a weapon he can use against me, then use it he will, without a moment's hesitation. He'll do his damnedest to discredit and destroy my candidacy.'

'We must go to Tom Allen for advice right away,' Vicky urged.

Neil thought about that and nodded.

'Hell's bells!' he cursed as they made for the tramstop.

Tom Allen, sitting up in bed, listened to their tale from behind hooded eyelids. He tried not to show it but he was shocked at the revelation that Vicky had been in borstal and prison. He never would have believed it if he hadn't heard it from the horse's mouth.

'You should have told me about Vicky's past before you agreed to be candidate,' he said angrily when they finished.

Neil blushed. 'I know. That was quite negligent on my part,' he admitted.

Vicky chipped in. 'The fault's mine. I should have made sure you were told. But I suppose like many skeletons in the cupboard you wish so hard they weren't there that you end up half believing that to be true.'

Neil shook his head. 'I should have said. It was stupid of me not to. I mean, most of Townhead knows about Vicky, so it was bound to come out some time. I suppose the idea of being an MP appealed so much that I played the ostrich.'

'We both did,' Vicky said.

There was a pause. 'Is there any way of salvaging this, or is that it for me?' Neil asked anxiously.

Tom stroked his chin. 'Muriel Mitchell or not, it's best this thing comes out now. If only we could somehow twist it to our advantage,' he mused.

'Would it help to know that, although I confessed to the thefts, in reality I was innocent of them. I was covering up for someone else,' Vicky said.

'Why on earth would you do that?' Tom queried.

Vicky glanced at Neil, then back at Tom. 'I was covering up for the man I loved at the time.'

'It's true. I know that for fact,' Neil added.

'There's no way you can prove this I suppose?' Tom said to Vicky.

She shook her head.

'Pity,' Tom muttered, and chewed a nail.

'Is that any help?' Neil asked.

'Possibly. I have to think it through first before I can say. But now I want you to tell me all about these thefts, and this boyfriend you were covering up for – in fact, the whole thing.'

And so Vicky did – everything, with one exception. She did not tell him that Neil had been made impotent as a result of the kicking Ken had given him.

Jim O'Donovan, a small, broad-shouldered man in his early fifties, was the general secretary of the Union of Longshoremen, which owned the ninth floor of a Jamaica Street building. He and the four members of his executive were gathered there in his office that Friday afternoon, as they were every Friday afternoon, to discuss and thrash through union business. He glanced at his watch. They had been talking solidly, without breaking for dinner, since mid-morning, and he was whacked. Thank God they were almost finished.

'What about Blacklaws? Have you heard any more from him?' Ritchie Allness asked.

Jim picked up a piece of paper he'd been doodling on and

noisily screwed it into a ball. 'Not a dickie bird since a fortnight ago when he sent us his latest offer for a merger – an offer we all agreed he could stick up his arse.'

'Do you think he's finally got the message that we've no intention of merging?' asked Bob Wyllie.

Jim had been clipping the end of his cigar. He now put the cigar in his mouth and lit it. 'To be frank, I doubt it. He's one of those bastards who thinks that, if he keeps coming at you, you'll eventually give in. But, no matter what offers, deals, inducements or whatever he comes up with, our answer is always going to be the same: our union stays independent, we remain in charge of it, and he can go fly a kite.'

A growl of approval ran round the room.

'We just have to remain solid and see that he doesn't get a hold on any of us as individuals. For, as we all know, it's been rumoured he's previously managed that amongst the upper echelons of other unions, unions he subsequently took over,' Jim went on.

Robbie Campbell thought of the mouthwatering temptation that had only recently been put his way. But he'd put two and two together, got Blacklaws as the answer and run a mile in the opposite direction. 'None of us can be too careful. That one's cunning and devious as a fox,' he said.

'And sly as one,' Tom Spicer added, which caused Ritchie Allness to nod in agreement.

'Anyway, enough about business and Blacklaws. We'll away over the road and have a bevy. I'm so dry I could spit cotton wool,' Jim said.

The five men in the office rose from their seats.

'As you've just become a grandfather for the first time, Bob, the first round is on you. Pints and large whiskies to wet the wean's head,' Jim said teasingly.

'Aye, all right then. I suppose I should,' Bob Wyllie replied reluctantly.

Jim chuckled. If Bob had a fault, he thought, it was that he hated parting with money. Bob would not have agreed with that at all. He wouldn't have described himself as mean, but as someone who was 'careful' with his bawbees.

Bob was an Aberdonian, though long resettled in Glasgow.

The five men were laughing and joking as they left Jim's office, bound for Carmichael's pub across the road, where, traditionally, they went every Friday after their weekly meetings. They walked down the corridor to the lift, to find the lift doors open and a workman tinkering inside.

'You fellows have timed it spot on. I've just finished,' the man said. Chucking a screwdriver into a bag of tools, he picked up the bag and got out of the lift, leaving it free for them.

'Thank goodness for that,' said the portly Ritchie Allness, thinking of the stairs to the ground floor. He loathed exercise of any kind.

Jim O'Donovan, exuding clouds of cigar smoke, pressed the button to descend.

'Sounded English, that workman chap,' Robbie Campbell commented to Bob Wyllie.

Tom Spicer, renowned for his dirty jokes, started to tell one about a cannibal and a missionary's wife with ginormous breasts, when the lift suddenly stopped dead.

'Christ, I hope it hasn't broken down again,' muttered Ritchie Allness, thinking again of the stairs.

Jim repeatedly pressed the descend button.

There was a creak, followed by the sound of a snap, and one side of the lift floor fell, to end up tilting downwards at about a twenty-degree angle. Bob Wyllie yelled as they were all thrown sideways.

'What the hell's going on!' Jim O'Donovan swore, groping for the cigar that had tumbled from his mouth. Robbie and Ritchie were still on their feet, the other three on their hands and knees.

Twang!

Someone screamed, but Jim O'Donovan didn't know who.

'Oh, Jean!' Jim whispered, thinking of his wife, as the lift plummeted downwards.

Then it smashed into the concrete bottom of the lift-shaft.

.

'Brown's over there. Do you see Muriel?' Neil muttered to Vicky and nodded in Brian Brown's direction.

Vicky glanced over and, sure enough, there was Muriel Mitchell in Brown's company.

'That's her in the blue dress and matching coloured hat,' she replied.

It was Friday night, and they were on the grassy area behind the museum and art gallery, where the second meeting featuring the candidates from the three major parties was due to take place. The museum and art gallery were situated in the north part of the Glasgow Kelvinhaugh constituency.

Vicky watched Muriel gazing about her, as if searching for someone. As before, their eyes met and locked. Muriel smiled, a vicious, razored smile that left Vicky in no doubt about two things: Muriel had told Brian Brown about her and, just as Tom Allen had said he would, Brown was going to denounce her that evening. Because the press attended these meetings in force, Brown would get maximum impact and coverage by choosing that occasion.

'How do you feel?' Neil asked Vicky.

'Sick as a pig with nerves.' She was not exaggerating.

'You can still back down, you know. You don't have to go through with it.'

She fixed him with a level stare. For some illogical reason, she could have slapped him for saying that. 'If I don't do as we planned, Brown will damn me and lose you God alone knows how many thousands of votes – if indeed you're not forced to resign your candidacy before polling day. This way there's the possibility we can defuse the situation and still get you elected,' she replied.

Twist the situation to your own advantage, was how Tom Allen had put it. Aye well, maybe. But Neil wasn't at all sure that this would work.

A camera flashed as a press photographer took a picture of Neil and Vicky. 'And another. How about a smile this time please, Mrs Seton?'

Vicky duly obliged, though the smile was so false that she felt it would crack her face.

Dickie Fleet, Neil's agent, came bustling up. His profuse perspiration had nothing to do with the August heat. 'It's fixed. The Tory and Unionist will speak first, then you, then Brown,' he said to Neil.

Neil grunted his satisfaction. It was imperative that he spoke before Brown. 'Good work.'

'The only problem was getting the Tory to agree to speak first. Brown was as keen to come after you as you were to go before him,' Dickie said.

'Give them laldy!' A Labour supporter cried out to Neil, who waved back that he'd heard.

'It's going to be a big turnout,' Dickie said, gesturing to the rear of the art gallery from where streams of people were continuing to appear.

So many people! Vicky thought. Her palms were oozing sweat, making the covers of the bible she was carrying glisten wet. She thought of the Black Room. What she had to do now would be a dawdle compared to what she'd endured in that hellhole.

The crackle of microphones filled the air. A man on the speakers' platform was making final adjustments.

'My seat in the front row has been reserved?' Vicky asked Dickie.

'Directly facing one end of the table. When Neil calls you, all you have to do is go up onto the platform and round the table.'

'Let's get to the platform,' Neil said, and the three of them moved in that direction, stopping, and being stopped, every few yards to talk to supporters and well-wishers. Vicky wondered cynically if the same people would still be wishing Neil luck after he and she had said their pieces.

Vicky became aware of swarms of midgies darting hither and yon, and even above the chatter she could hear the steady drone of flies. She blinked when several searchlights, relics of the war, sliced the gathering evening gloom. The searchlights began weaving patterns in the sky. More lights came on, round the platform itself. A cheer went up for the Tory and Unionist candidate, Alexander McGhie, a stockbroker on the Glasgow Exchange.

Finally the speakers were called onto the platform, and Vicky took her seat, Dickie Fleet sitting beside her. Then Alexander McGhie was introduced and the meeting began.

Vicky's insides were jumping and she had gone terribly dry. She stared enviously at the water jug and glass standing before each candidate. She felt that she could have drunk all three stone dry.

McGhie spoke well – from the Tory point of view, that is. He attacked the government's policy of nationalisation and the programme of 'austerity' instigated by Sir Stafford Cripps who held the combined post of Chancellor and Minister for Economic Affairs. Cripps had introduced heavy taxation on internal consumption and restrictions on overseas purchases and foreign travel to alleviate the country's foreign exchange crisis which had occurred the previous year.

McGhie received an enthusiastic hand from the small band of Tories present. Then it was Neil's turn. He glanced sideways at Vicky, who had gone white as a sheet.

'I had a speech prepared for this evening, a speech I've left at home. This is because last night my wife, whom many of you Labour supporters will know from her work at the Labour Hall, reminded me of what had happened to her a few years back, just before the war, and which, though serious it had been, even horrendous for her, I had so pushed to the back of my mind that I had more or less forgotten about it . . .'

Brian Brown suddenly sat up straight to stare with new interest at Neil. In the audience, six rows behind, and hidden from Vicky, Muriel Mitchell pursed her mouth and she stared at Neil through slitted eyes. Like Brown, she had guessed the drift of what was coming.

Neil went on, 'Vicky and I both come from Townhead, born and bred there, and the people of Townhead know about her past, though it's rarely if ever mentioned nowadays. Vicky says, and she's quite right, that the folk of Kelvinhaugh constituency should also know about that past, and you should know before voting takes place, not afterwards. And so, tonight, you're going to be told. But not by me – by my wife Vicky herself.'

Neil did not ask the permission of the two other candidates in case either refused. Instead he gestured to Vicky. 'Could you come up here please, Vicky?'

A buzz of puzzlement and general 'what's this all about?' ran through the audience. The press section were suddenly very animated and, as Vicky ascended the platform, at least a dozen camera bulbs popped.

She had been a bundle of nerves while waiting for this moment, but now a transformation came over her. Her apprehension and fear completely vanished, to be replaced by total calm and serenity. She feared no one, she was afraid of nothing. When she realised that her palms had stopped leaking, she gave a small, soft smile. Raising her bible, she held it just under her breasts.

In the front row Dickie Fleet put a hand over his face and closed his eyes. As far as he was concerned, the by-election was about to go down the plughole.

When Vicky spoke her voice was strong, vibrant and charismatically compelling.

'Thirteen years ago this month I was tried and convicted of theft. My sentence was three years, part of which I spent in Duncliffe borstal down the coast, the remainder in Duke Street prison.'

Pandemonium broke out. Camera bulbs started popping again. Alexander McGhie was so taken aback that he nearly fell off his seat. Brian Brown somehow managed to look both furious and pleased at the same time.

Despite the heat of the evening, Neil was icy from head to toe. He sat expressionless. There seemed to be a great gaping hole where his brain and mind had been.

Vicky held up a hand for silence and went on, 'I confessed to the thefts I was convicted of, but until tonight only a handful of people knew that I lied, that I wasn't the thief.'

Brian Brown spluttered in disbelief.

'And why would I do such a thing, you ask. The answer is, and I swear it on this bible I'm carrying' – she held the bible aloft for all to see – 'that I was in love with the man

311

doing the thieving, and lied to protect him because of that love, and because I mistakenly thought I might not be prosecuted, whereas he was bound to be.'

She paused for breath, fixing her audience with an unwavering stare.

'Only I was wrong. I *was* prosecuted and, as I've already said, sentenced to three years. And the chap I lied to protect? He ditched me during my time in borstal and married another.'

Still holding the bible aloft, she continued, 'I cannot prove what I have just told you, but may I stand damned in the sight of God for ever if it is not the Gospel truth. It is now up to you whether or not you believe me, and whether it will affect those amongst you, and those not here this evening, who intended voting for my husband. I sincerely hope it doesn't, for he's the man Kelvinhaugh needs, the right man for this constituency . . . Thank you.'

She lowered the hand holding aloft the bible and turned to Neil, who had been standing a little behind her. He took her into his arms and hugged her tight.

There was no reaction whatever from the audience. Vicky was surrounded by eerie silence as she returned to her seat.

A sixth sense warned Brian Brown not to attack Vicky over what she claimed was the truth of her past. Instead he ignored what she had said and made an impromptu speech attacking the Labour government as a whole and throwing in what he saw as some very cutting remarks and jibes about the Tory Party.

Not once did he mention either Neil or Vicky.

Tom Allen sipped a well-watered whisky. Vicky and Neil had gone directly to his house after the meeting and described in detail all that had taken place.

'No reaction at all?' Tom queried.

'None,' Vicky confirmed.

He lifted an eyebrow and shook his head. 'Well well,' he mused.

'So now it's just a case of sit back and wait to see what happens,' Neil said, biting a fingernail.

'That's it,' Tom agreed.

'It'll be all over the morning papers. I think every daily in Glasgow must have had a reporter and photographer there,' Vicky said.

Neil bit a thumbnail right down to the quick. What had possessed him to allow himself to be talked into standing as a candidate in the first place! Stupid stupid stupid! And now this, this unholy mess. An ostrich, that's what he'd been, a bloody ostrich! But what a golden opportunity to dangle before him – the temptation had just been too great.

Vicky was thinking how much she now regretted taking the blame for Ken Blacklaws. If there was one thing in her life that, by some miracle, she could have undone, it was that. But she had been young and in love, oh so desperately in love.

Tom Allen sipped more whisky. 'No reaction at all,' he repeated to himself in a bemused tone and shook his head.

The next morning Ken was humming when he appeared for breakfast. He always had a special breakfast on Saturdays and Sundays: fried egg, bacon, mushrooms, black pudding and fried bread. He referred to it as 'the works'.

'You're in a good humour today,' Lyn commented, thinking what a pleasant change it was to see him so bright and breezy. He had been terribly tense of late, given to dark moods and snapping at all and sundry.

Ken kissed her on the cheek, then ruffled Kenny's hair. At eight years old Kenny was a fine-looking, sturdy lad. Pity about the kid having to wear specs. Kenny's eyesight was even worse than his own.

'Slept like a log, first time in ages.' Ken beamed and sat at the table. Lyn rang the handbell to tell Craig, the butler, that Ken was down, then poured him some coffee while he shook out his napkin.

'Will you play a bit of footer with me today, Dad, please?' Kenny demanded eagerly. He was football and Rangers daft.

'Aye, sure I will. Wait till my breakfast has settled, then we'll have a wee game of kickabout out on the lawn.'

Ken and Lyn's house had once been Jack and Wendy Fyfer's. It had come to them on Wendy's death several years previously. Ken thoroughly enjoyed living in Balfron; though, like Jack before him, and despite the fact he had a chauffeur permanently at his disposal, he found the travelling something of a bind. Ken never drove any more. Shugs, a registered dockie, did that for him. Shugs had a reputation for being handy with his fists and feet when necessary.

There was a stack of papers beside Ken's sideplate. He picked up the top one and found what he was looking for on page two. His mood changed instantly when he read that Jim O'Donovan had survived what was described as a terrible accident. O'Donovan had two broken legs, a broken arm, broken collarbone and concussion. Amazingly he had no internal injuries. A few months and he'd be back at his desk, O'Donovan himself predicted. Ritchie Allness, on the critical list but expected to pull through, had also survived. Bob Wyllie, Robbie Campbell and Tom Spicer had all been killed.

Ken, face a thundercloud, tossed the paper aside and glared into his coffee cup. The team he had brought up from London had failed him. They had sworn that no one could survive that drop.

Rage seethed in Ken. He had thought that, at long last, Clydeside was his. For, with O'Donovan and the others dead, it would be a simple matter for him to bring about the merger of the Union of Longshoremen with the Clyde Dockworkers' Union, to give the Clyde Dockworkers' Union a monopoly on Clydeside.

Craig entered with Ken's breakfast. 'The egg was freshly laid this morning, sir,' he said. The plate was piled high with 'the works'. There might be food rationing in Britain but that didn't apply to Ken's household. He had long since arranged it otherwise.

Ken glowered at his breakfast. He had been looking forward to it since getting up; now he'd lost his appetite. God damn those English incompetents!

He pushed his plate away. 'Apologise to cook. Bit of a dicky tummy. I'll settle for the coffee,' he growled.

'What is it?' Lyn asked after Craig, and Ken's breakfast, had gone.

'Nothing,' he replied, lighting a cigarette.

If he wasn't going to tell her, then she wasn't going to persist; she knew better than that.

'If you're not having any breakfast, can we play right away?' Kenny demanded.

'Eh?' Ken answered, lost in thought.

'If I run up and get my ball, can we play footer right away?'

The last thing he wanted to do now was play football. He would get onto London right away. He hadn't paid the second half of the team's fee yet, nor would he until the bastards had rectified their mistake. He didn't care about Allness, but he wanted O'Donovan dead, as soon as possible.

'Can we?' Kenny asked again.

'You did promise,' Lyn softly reminded Ken.

It was on the tip of Ken's tongue to snap back that he wasn't in the mood any more, then he relented. What the hell! Half an hour and the kid's day, if not week, would be made. Kenny was his son, after all, and he did play with him so rarely.

'Get the ball,' he told Kenny.

Kenny whooped and ran from the room.

'Thank you.' Lyn smiled.

Ken was about to reply when his eye was caught by a picture in the paper he had tossed aside.

Picking up the paper again, he stared at the picture. Mrs Neil Seton, the caption proclaimed. The story was a long one, twice the size of the 'horrible accident'.

Slowly he began to read.

Later that morning Vicky was about to turn into her close, having done the weekend shopping at the Coop, when a monstrous car drew up at the kerb and a window hissed down.

'Hello, Vicky,' Ken Blacklaws said.

She stared at him, surprised at the little jolt that went

through her to see him again. 'What brings you to Parr Street?' she asked.

'I was coming up to chap your door. I want to speak to you,' he replied.

'Get knotted,' she said, and entered the close.

She had taken only a few steps when the man who had been driving the car ran round in front of her, blocking her way.

'The boss says he wants to talk to you.'

Then Ken was there. 'That's all right, Shugs. Get back in the car.'

'You've got fat,' she told him, a hint of relish in her voice.

He patted his stomach. 'Always did have a tendency that way,' he admitted.

'Pigs do.' She smiled.

He winced. 'I know I've treated you badly. I deserved that.'

'And you've got bald, I see.'

'Not bald, *balding*. I have a bit to go yet before I'm bald,' he replied testily.

She noted that he had shaved off his moustache. 'Well, I don't want to speak to you,' she said, and made for the stairs.

'It could harm Neil if you don't.'

She stopped and twisted to face Ken. 'In what way?'

'Let's go for a spin in the car while we chat,' he said, relieving her of her heavy shopping bag.

The upholstery was leather and smelled absolutely delicious, Vicky thought, as she sank into it.

'So what do you think of my Caddy?' Ken asked proudly.

'Your what?'

'Cadillac. It's an American car.'

Vicky had seen Yankee cars before, in South America. There they had seemed to fit. Here they screamed ostentation. Or, to put it another way, were dead vulgar. 'You always were a flash bugger.'

'The only Caddy in all of Scotland,' he said, still trying to impress.

'I'm not surprised,' she replied ambiguously.

Ken scowled and lit a cigarette. He now smoked Lucky Strikes, also American.

'Imagine you marrying Neil after all! Tell me, is he still troubled with spots?' Ken laughed unkindly.

Vicky's right hand curled into a talon. What a pompous, insensitive bastard! For two peas she would have raked his face the way she'd raked Miss Ganch's.

Coldly she replied, 'Neil isn't spotty any more. In fact he was the ugly duckling who turned into a swan. He's very handsome now, and . . .' Her eyes fastened on Ken's waist-line. 'He *kept* his figure.'

Why did she have to keep going on about his increased weight! Ken was as irritated as she had intended him to be. He hated being reminded that he had put on so much beef or that his hair was thinning.

'Are you still married to Lyn?'

He nodded.

'I feel sorry for her.'

She had the satisfaction of seeing his face colour.

'Now what's all this about harming Neil?' she demanded.

'I read the story in the morning papers.'

She should have guessed. 'And?'

'I was pleased, and relieved, that you didn't mention my name.'

'There was no need.'

'What happens if you're pressed to put a name to the boyfriend you took the blame for and who let you down?'

'Why should I be pressed?' she asked.

'It's a good story. The newspapers might well want to follow it up.'

She shrugged. 'If it'll help Neil's candidacy to name you, then I will. For I don't owe you anything, Ken, nothing at all.'

Ken leaned forward and pressed a concealed button at the back of the driver's seat. A panel slid open to reveal a miniature bar.

'Would you like a drink?' he asked.

'No, thank you.'

He poured himself a stiff whisky. He had tried to switch to rye and bourbon, but both had made him feel queasy and given him unbelievable hangovers.

In a voice devoid of all emotion, he said, 'If you do name me as the boyfriend, then I will release my version of what happened, which will be quite different to yours.

'I will insist you were the thief. I will say Neil mistakenly believed I was and, being besotted by you, made the phone call to Copland and Lye thinking it would result in my arrest and imprisonment, leaving the way clear for him to take over with you where I had been forced to leave off. Only, as it transpired, you, the real thief, were arrested and put away, while I, the innocent party, went free.

'You'll continue to be branded a thief, while Neil will be seen as someone who tried to hand his best pal over to the police. And we both know what the majority of Glaswegians think of people who do that sort of thing, don't we? Any chance Neil had left of winning this by-election would go right out the window.'

'You really are a first-class shit,' she said.

'Self-preservation. That's what this is all about, Vicky, self-preservation.'

Ken was right. Glaswegians loathed people who cliped, particularly when it involved the police. Even the fact Neil had done it for love wouldn't save him; his political career would be well and truly over before it had even begun.

Vicky felt tears edging into her eyes. She turned away from Ken so that he wouldn't see them.

'I've read about *you* from time to time. You've done well for yourself,' she said, voice rock steady.

'I always intended to get on, and have,' he boasted.

'No matter who you've had to stand on to get there.'

He didn't reply, knowing that she was referring mainly to herself.

'Have you any family?' he asked.

Panic flared in her. 'Why do you say that?' she replied sharply. Did he know something? Had he guessed?

'No reason other than curiosity.'

Her panic subsided. She believed him. Curiosity *was* the reason behind the question, nothing else.

'A girl called Martha. She's an adorable wee thing. And what about you and Lyn? Any additions to Kenny?'

He shook his head. He had insisted that Lyn have the operation which rendered her incapable of getting pregnant again. He couldn't have faced a second time what he'd gone through following Kenny's birth. It was only in the last few years that their sex life had regained a semblance of normality.

'We decided not to have any more. Kenny's eight now, shooting up like a weed.'

Vicky was about to say how old Martha was, then changed her mind when she realised it might, just might, give Ken cause to wonder.

'You can take me back to Parr Street now,' she said.

'So I can rest assured I'll never be named as the boyfriend you took the blame for and who let you down?'

'You can rest assured.'

The Cadillac stopped outside her close. She got out, and Ken handed her her shopping bag.

'It's been a pleasure seeing and talking to you again.' He smiled.

Vicky did not reply. She simply walked off into the close, leaving him staring after her.

The following Monday evening Neil came home from work looking pale and shocked. Vicky, back before him as she always was, had already given Martha tea and changed her into her pyjamas.

'What's wrong, love?' Vicky asked when she saw Neil's face.

He dropped his briefcase by the side of the fireplace and flopped into a chair. 'I've had the bullet from MacDonald, Lindsay and Hogg.'

Vicky bit her lip. 'Because of the press coverage about me?'

'Michael Lindsay argued on my behalf, but not very forcibly, I'm afraid. It was bad enough that I was standing as a Labour MP, but to have it revealed that my wife had done time, whether innocent or not – well, that was just too much! "Not consistent with the company image, don't you know",' Neil said, imitating old man Hogg's fruity upper-class tones.

'You were going to leave them anyway.'

'That was when I believed I was going to be elected. Now, who knows whether I'll be or not.'

'Then you'll just have to set up on your own, as you originally intended before the idea of you running for Parliament came up.'

He gave her a sickly grin. 'Two things against that, Vicky. Number one, I'm not really experienced enough yet. And number two, though I want to help the poor and underprivileged, on a practical level I'll need paying clients to make the business viable. If the voters turn against me, you can be sure potential paying clients will stay away for the same reasons.'

'Damn!' Vicky swore.

Martha, eyes wide, suddenly started to wail.

Vicky clutched Martha to her and began rocking the wee girl back and forth.

'At least I don't have to speak tonight, it would have been a right sod to do so in the circumstances,' Neil said.

'I don't want Mummy and Daddy to be unhappy,' Martha blubbered.

Vicky somehow forced a smile onto her face. 'There there, pet, it's just a little upset, that's all, nothing Mummy and Daddy can't cope with. So let's stop this crying, eh?' With that, Vicky kissed Martha on both wet cheeks and equally wet mouth.

'Come over here. Let's you and I have a big cuddle,' Neil said and held out his arms.

Neil lifted Martha onto his lap, where she noisily sucked her thumb while he hugged her tight.

'As Mummy says, it's just a little upset, nothing to warrant tears,' he murmured, consoling her, thinking to himself how marvellous children were.

After a while, Neil said, 'I'll take you through and read you a story. Which one would you like?'

'Goldilocks,' Martha replied instantly.

Vicky laughed. 'What else! Give her the choice and it's always Goldilocks.'

Once Martha was tucked in, and with Vicky cooking the adult tea ben the kitchen, Neil proceeded to spoil Martha by reading the story three times.

How Martha loved that! The third time, having long known it off by heart, she recited it with him, word for word.

Several hours later Vicky and Neil were sitting across from one another by the fireplace, she darning a pair of his socks, he sunk in gloomy thought, when there was a rat-tat-tat on the outside door.

Neil answered the knock and returned to the kitchen with Jock McLean, their local MP, who lived only a couple of streets away. They both knew him well.

Vicky put down her darning and jumped to her feet. 'Come away in, Jock. I'll stick the kettle on,' she said, and strode over to the stove.

'Were you really innocent of that Copland and Lye business?' Jock asked gruffly. Jock was a man who prided himself in always coming right to the point.

Vicky looked him straight in the eye. 'I was.'

Jock held her gaze for several seconds, then gave a slight nod of his head. 'Aye, well that settles that then,' he said and, sitting, produced a battered briar. 'Do you mind if I stink your house out?'

Vicky laughed. 'Go ahead. We both enjoy the smell of pipe smoke.'

'It would be Ken Blacklaws you were covering for then? I recall that you and he were going out together at the time, and he also worked at Copland and Lye,' Jock said.

Vicky glanced at Neil, then brought her attention back to Jock. 'I don't see any point in raking over those old coals. I have no intention of saying who the man was, not now or ever. It's unnecessary, and could only cause distress to the family the man now has.'

'Everyone round here will know who it was, of course, but no one will say to any outsider. The way they'll see it is: if Blacklaws is to be named, you're the one should do the naming. After doing a stretch in borstal and prison for him, that's your right.'

'Then he won't be named,' Vicky said firmly, and started putting some teacakes and slices of home-made cake onto plates. The cake was a walnut one, a gift from Mary.

Jock addressed himself to Neil. 'Now, how about the by-election in Kelvinhaugh. Do you think you can still win?'

Neil shrugged. 'You tell me. It isn't clear at all yet how Vicky's confession is going to affect the voting.'

'I spoke to Tom Allen earlier in the week. He confided in me why Vicky did as she did. I agreed with him. In the circumstances, it was the only thing to do.'

'Then Tom must have told you that Vicky was really innocent?'

· A thin smile stretched Jock's mouth. 'He did, but I wanted to hear her tell me that was so herself. I wanted to be absolutely certain.'

Neil was baffled. 'I don't wish to sound rude, but why should that be so important to you?'

'Tom tells me you'll make a first-class MP, given the chance. He says you've got tremendous talent and commitment. Personally I've only heard you speak once, but was most impressed. Aye, most impressed. And others, whose opinion in these matters I hold in high regard, have nothing but praise for you.'

'Well, thank you,' Neil replied, a trifle embarrassed.

'Which brings me to the purpose of my visit. After visiting Tom, I had consultations with the local powers that be, and it's been agreed, unanimously I might add, that, should you fail to be elected in the Kelvinhaugh constituency, we'd like you to stand for the Townhead seat come the next general election.'

Vicky gasped with delight and spilled some of the tea she was pouring.

'But what about you? You've been MP here for twenty-odd years?' Neil spluttered in reply.

'I'm well over sixty, Neil, and I've fought a hard battle all my life. First as a shop steward, then in local government, and as a Member of Parliament after that. It's high time I called it a day and retired, which is precisely what I'm going to do come the next general election.'

Neil was flabbergasted, quite stunned by this turn of events.

'So do you agree?'

'Agree? Of course I agree!' Neil exclaimed.

Vicky had a sudden thought, seeing how Neil could use this to current advantage. 'Would you, Jock, or the Townhead Labour Party mind if Neil told the newspapers about your offer?'

'You mean as a help to him in the by-election?' Jock replied shrewdly, not one to miss a trick.

'Exactly.'

Jock took a pull on his pipe. 'I don't think we'd have any objections. No. Go ahead, give it to the papers if you want. I'll happily corroborate the story if any of them want to get in touch with me.'

Then Vicky had another thought, a real bobby dazzler. Neil wouldn't like it, but she'd get round him.

Vicky arranged the press conference for the following afternoon. Neil took the afternoon off work, without a murmur of objection or protest from MacDonald, Lindsay and Hogg. As he said to Vicky, having already sacked him, the worst they could do now was dock him half a day's pay, which he was entirely agreeable to.

In preparation Vicky moved the kitchen table to one side and covered it with a snow-white linen cloth. Tom Allen had told her to lay on plenty of alcohol, and this she did with the help of the Kelvinhaugh Labour Club. There was enough whisky, gin and beer to sink a battleship, plus oodles of crisps, sausage rolls and fancy cakes.

But the most important item of all was Neil's Victoria Cross, which she displayed on the mantelpiece, its crimson ribbon showing up vividly and magnificently against the black satin interior of its presentation box.

'Now don't forget, when you talk to the journalists, you stand beside the medal so that they can't fail to see it. Not in front of it, beside it. And should they ask, it wasn't put on show especially, but is always kept there,' Vicky instructed Neil.

He pulled a face. 'I still hate the idea of it, Vicky. It's cheap and tricksie.'

'There's nothing cheap about a medal won for Conspicuous Bravery, the highest award a British serviceman can be given. You won it, and there's no harm in people being reminded that you did.'

Neil thought back to what had been tormenting him when he had stood up that day in December 1940 and all by himself walked into the murderous hail of machine-gun fire, while all around him the rest of his section lay dead or wounded.

Brave? Not him. The forces that had driven him to do what he'd done were fear, frustration, anger and self-pity. He had wanted to die and, because he had, death had perversely passed him by. There had been nothing conspicuously brave about his action. He was a fraud, a sham and, worst of all, in the final analysis, probably a coward.

'It just doesn't seem right,' he mumbled.

'Nonsense. Now pour us both a dram to get us in the mood for the invading hordes.' She smiled.

The press conference had been called for three o'clock. The first arrivals turned up at ten to. After that they came in quick succession.

As Tom Allen had told her to do, Vicky plied the booze and kept on plying it. A glass was no sooner empty than she refilled it. Tom had warned her that there was nothing nastier than a journalist who thought you were being tight-fisted with the bevy, and nasty journalists wrote nasty copy.

Finally Vicky judged it time to call the gathering to order. Neil took up a position in front of the fireplace, beside the VC. From there he told the gathering about Jock McLean's intention to retire at the next general election, and how Jock and the Townhead Labour Party had asked him to be their candidate then should he fail in his bid to win Glasgow Kelvinhaugh.

Pencils flew and flashbulbs popped. Questions were asked. Vicky eased herself round the room, refilling glasses as she went.

As she and Neil had expected, questions were asked about her conviction for theft and subsequent borstal and prison sentence. Vicky answered all these questions openly and truthfully. The only one she baulked at was the name of the man she alleged – in the journalists' words – she had taken the blame for.

She refused point blank to name Ken, giving the same reason she had given Jock McLean; that he now had a family and she had no wish to cause them any distress.

'Excuse me, Mr Seton, but what's that medal on the mantelpiece?' the journalist from the *Daily Record* asked.

Neil blushed. 'It's the Victoria Cross.'

An excited buzz ran round the room.

'Who does it belong to?' the same journalist went on.

Vicky piped up, knowing that Neil wouldn't blow his own trumpet. 'It belongs to my husband, and was presented to him by the King himself. He won it in Egypt, at Sidi Barrani.'

There was a new interest in the gathering. If no one asked what Neil had done to win the medal, Vicky intended volunteering the information.

'Here, I think I remember writing about that. Didn't you capture a whole bunch of Eyeties?' the man from the *Mail* queried.

'A number, yes,' Neil answered, still blushing, and swallowed a dollop of whisky.

Repeating almost word for word the article she had first read almost eight years previously, and which she still had in a bedroom drawer, Vicky said, 'Neil singlehand-edly attacked a machine-gun post, bayoneting seven men to reach the post, and shooting dead the two Italians manning it. Then, not bothering to wait for help, he made his way along a trench for a couple of hundred yards, attacked a dugout and forced thirty-seven enemy soldiers to surrender.'

The journalist from the *Express* whistled.

'By doing this, Neil turned the tide of the battle in favour of the British by allowing them to break through what until then had been an impenetrable wall of bullets. The British then went on to take their objective, the town of Sidi Barrani. General Wavell personally promoted Neil to the rank of captain after the battle was over.'

'So you were a war hero,' the man from the *Daily Record* said to Neil, who went a deep shade of crimson.

'That's maybe putting it a bit strong,' Neil mumbled.

'Everybody knows you have to do something very very special to win the Victoria Cross,' the *Guardian* chap said, admiration and awe in his voice.

'Would you give us a picture of you holding it up?' a photographer asked.

Neil shook his head. 'No, that I won't do. Sorry,' he said firmly.

'It would look terrific on page one,' the photographer cajoled.

'No,' Neil replied emphatically.

Vicky was about to intervene to try and make Neil do as the photographer wanted, then thought better of it. Perhaps Neil's instincts were right in this instance. It could be counterproductive if he was seen to come across as boasting about or capitalising on his vc.

She went back to refilling glasses.

Next morning, with the newspapers spread before her, Vicky rang Neil from her office in the Kelvinhaugh Labour Club.

'What do you think, eh? Haven't you got tremendous coverage?'

'There's certainly a lot of it,' he admitted.

'THE VC HERO OF SIDI BARRANI FOR TOWNHEAD IF HE FAILS AT KELVINHAUGH,' Vicky said, reading out one headline.

'There's a nice picture of us in the *Express*,' he told her.

She had already seen the picture but now had another look. It *was* a good picture, particularly of Neil. He came over as handsome, intelligent, relaxed and with a sense of humour. All in all, a winner. She didn't come over so badly either. They made a striking couple.

They talked about the various stories and photographs for several minutes. Then she said, 'Don't forget we're "on the knock" tonight.'

'I won't forget. I should get to your office about half past six.'

'There'll now be ten of us, and we've a thousand leaflets to distribute.'

He blew her a kiss down the phone. 'I love you rotten,' he whispered.

She returned the kiss. 'Till later, vc hero,' she replied, and laughing, hung up.

Vicky chapped her umpteenth door that night and waited. There was a strong smell of boiled cabbage in the close, that and whitewash, and the all-pervading odour from the half-landing wcs.

The door opened a crack and a suspicious eye peered out. 'Who is it?' an old female voice demanded.

'I'm here on behalf of the Labour Party candidate. Can I give you a leaflet?'

The door opened wider to reveal an ancient stooped crone with a tramlined parchment face. The pale blue eyes were lively and deep with intelligence. The crone might be ancient, but she most certainly wasn't senile. As the saying went, she still had all her marbles.

'Is that Seton you're talking about? Him that won the vc?'

'That's him.'

'See us a leaflet then.'

Vicky placed a leaflet in a gnarled and withered hand.

'He'll never replace Tom Allen, mind. Yon man's a gem,' the crone said.

'My husband also thinks very highly of Tom Allen. Mr Allen is an inspiration to him,' Vicky replied.

The blue eyes wrinkled. 'Your husband, eh? So you'll be the one cried Vicky Seton. I read about you. It was very interesting.'

Vicky had earlier decided not to disguise who she was when 'on the knock'. If people wanted to ask her questions, she was prepared to answer them, most of them.

'Is there anything about my husband you'd like to know? Or do you have any special problems or complaints you want looking into?'

The crone shook her head.

'Then can I ask you if my husband can count on your support?'

'You mean my vote?'

'That's right,' Vicky smiled.

'Aye, of course he can. Tom Allen personally recommends him, and that's good enough for me.'

'Thank you,' Vicky replied, and ticked off the house in the tally book she was keeping. 'And the rest of your household?'

'There's nobody else, only me. They all kicked the bucket years ago.'

'I'm sorry,' Vicky said.

'No' me. I prefer being on my own. My husband was a drunken slob, my two sons out the same mould. It was a relief to get rid of the buggers.' The pale blue eyes twinkled. 'Do you mind if I ask you something?'

'No. Go ahead.'

'Did you really do it for love?'

'You mean take the blame for those thefts?'

The crone nodded.

'Yes,' Vicky whispered.

The crone let out a long breathy sigh. 'That's ever so romantic,' she said wistfully.

With a faraway, dreamy expression on her face, the old woman started to shut the door. 'Goodnight then, hen.'

'Goodnight,' Vicky replied, a second before the door snicked shut.

Returning to the street, Vicky found Neil waiting for her. 'How's it going?' he asked.

'The feeling is good, very good.'

'Same for me and the others "on the knock" I've spoken to. I think, I really do think, I'm going to pull it off.'

Vicky held up a hand and crossed two fingers.

She went into the next close along, Neil the close after that.

Ken Blacklaws was checking through a new revised union contract form – the revisions made by him in the union's favour – when the door to his office flew open and Ina Finlayson burst in. A statuesque blonde, she was twenty-two years old and had a knockout figure. She had been Ken's secretary for the past nineteen months, his lover for fifteen of them.

'There's been a gas explosion at Camphill private nursing home, where Jim O'Donovan was being treated. He and fifteen others have been killed, and there are lots of casualties,' Ina said in a rush of words.

O'Donovan dead! Elation surged through Ken, but he strove to keep it from his face.

He placed the contract form on his desk. 'How did you hear this?' he asked quietly.

'Betty-in-records' boyfriend has just rung to say he won't be able to meet her early evening as they'd arranged. He's one of the firemen who've been called out to the explosion. He says it's likely he and his mates will be there for half the night.'

'And he mentioned O'Donovan specifically?'

'He did, thinking it would be of interest to Betty, she working for a dock union. According to Alan, the centre of the explosion was in the basement directly under Mr O'Donovan's room. Mr O'Donovan was blown to bits. Isn't that dreadful?'

'Dreadful,' Ken agreed, trying to sound as though he meant it.

So, the London team had succeeded in their second attempt. He would put a cheque for the balance of their fee in the post just as soon as O'Donovan's death had been officially confirmed.

He would move quickly. Within weeks, a couple of months at the most, the Union of Longshoremen would have merged with the Clyde Dockworkers' Union, leaving the Clyde Dockworkers' Union the last dock union on Clydeside. And with that he'd have achieved the Clydeside monopoly he'd schemed so long and hard to bring about.

His next target would be the Port of Leith on the east coast, and Dundee after that. One by one they would fall to him, till in the end there was only one union left, a national union, with him at its helm. The thought of that made his blood race and his ears pound.

'Choose a suitable condolence card for the wife – Jane, I think her name is, or it could be Jean. Better check on that. Anyway, choose a suitable card which I'll sign and you send directly O'Donovan's death is confirmed. And arrange a wreath or floral tribute for the funeral. The best the shop can provide.' Ken paused. 'By the way, did Betty's Alan say what caused the explosion?'

'They're not certain yet, but the theory is the main gas pipe coming into the Home cracked. A large amount of gas then swiftly built up, which was probably ignited by an electrical spark.'

Ken shook his head as if in sympathy. 'You never know, do you? You just never know.'

'How terribly unlucky for him after surviving that appalling lift accident.'

'Terribly unlucky,' Ken agreed.

'When the evening papers go on the streets, I'll pop out and buy copies. They should be carrying the story.'

'Excellent idea,' he said.

She started to turn away.

'Oh, Ina?'

She turned back again.

'I've had some really good news today and thought we might go out this evening for a celebratory meal? We could go on to your flat for an hour or two afterwards.'

Her face lit up. 'I've nothing planned, so that would be terrific.'

'Pick a restaurant, one you fancy, and then go ahead and book a table.'

'How about Ferrari's? I've always fancied going there.'

Ken went ice cold inside. Pictures jumped into his mind of the last time he'd been there, with Vicky. He had bumped into the gorilla whose house he'd twice burgled. If it hadn't been for Vicky crowning the sod with an ashtray, he would have ended up in the nick that night, to be sent down for God knows how long. He had never been back to Ferrari's since, nor did he ever intend to. As far as he was concerned, Ferrari's was a bad-luck place.

He shook his head. 'Any restaurant but that one. I don't like it.'

Ina had been Ken's secretary, and lover, long enough to know that when he used that tone of voice there was no arguing with him. 'How about Sans Souci then?' she suggested.

'Fabulous.'

'Do you wish to pick me up later? Or would you prefer to come home with me after work and wait while I bath and change?'

Before the meal and after: that would be very nice indeed, he thought. Her flat was owned and maintained by the union: it didn't cost her a penny to stay there.

'I'll be in the mood for a bath then myself.' He smiled.

She matched his smile, knowing full well what that meant. They would bathe together and make love in the bath.

Still smiling, Ina left Ken's office.

Ken took a deep breath. O'Donovan dead! He could have shouted for joy.

The union was going to need new premises, he decided, something far larger and grander than they now had. He would begin making inquiries directly after the merger.

Picking up the phone, he dialled Balfron and told Lyn about the gas explosion and Jim O'Donovan. He then explained his plans for the merger, using that as his excuse for having to work late. It was doubtful that he would be home before the wee hours, he said. She shouldn't bother to wait up.

Ritchie Allness, now off the critical list, and the only remaining member of the UOL upper echelons, was the key to the merger. For appearances' sake, he'd wait until after O'Donovan's funeral before paying Allness a visit. He would take Sawyers, his tame KC with him. And Paddy Troy, a Dublin-born dockie of terrifying strength, who was now his shadow and general right hand. Between the three of them, they would persuade Allness to see things their way.

Vicky felt sick with a combination of fatigue and nerves. It was a quarter to one in the morning. She had been on the go for over twenty hours. The polls were long since closed, counting nearing an end. The declaration would take place at any minute.

Neil sat worrying a nail. He was white as a sheet and – Vicky wasn't sure whether or not it was her imagination – every so often he seemed to twitch.

The three candidates and respective entourages were in a room off the hall where the counting was proceeding. Brian Brown, the Liberal candidate, was deep in conversation with his wife Fiona, a mousy thing with about as much personality as a limp teatowel. There was no sign of Muriel Mitchell, nor had there been all night. Vicky had been keeping an eye out for her.

Alexander McGhie, the Tory and Unionist candidate, his wife Charlotte, and a gaggle of his party workers, stood grouped in a corner. Their mood was buoyant, though everyone knew McGhie hadn't a hope of winning. If Neil lost, it would be to Brown.

Dickie Fleet lit yet another cigarette. The fingers of his right hand, which he used to hold his cigarettes, were stained saffron. 'This is murder,' he complained, thinking that, with Tom Allen, the result had always been a foregone conclusion; whereas, with Neil, who knew what was going to happen!

'I was sure up until this morning and then, suddenly, I wasn't so sure any more. The confidence seemed to drain out of me,' Neil confided quietly to Vicky.

She took one of his hands and squeezed it reassuringly. 'Not long now.'

'Jailbird.'

The word stood out clearly and distinctly above the hum of conversation. Vicky didn't know who had spoken it, but it had definitely come from the Brown contingent.

Neil started to rise, but she pulled him back down again. 'Leave it, it isn't worth it,' she told him.

Neil glared at the Brown lot. 'Ignorant bunch of sods,' he muttered angrily.

Alexander McGhie had also been angered by what had occurred. He crossed to where Vicky and Neil were sitting and produced a silver flask from an inside pocket. 'I'd be honoured if you'd take a drink with me, Mr and Mrs Seton. I want you to know that, despite our political differences, I think highly of the pair of you,' he said, not particularly loudly, but loud enough for everyone in the room to hear.

Neil stood, as did Vicky. 'We'd be pleased to have a dram with you, Mr McGhie,' Neil replied.

McGhie filled the top of his flask and handed it to Vicky. She drank it off, and gave it back.

When Neil had drunk his tot, Vicky said, 'You're a gentleman, Mr McGhie. Head and shoulders above some I can think of.'

The returning officer entered the room. 'I can declare now,' he announced.

Throat dry, and with what seemed like a dozen or more butterflies fluttering around inside her tummy, Vicky went side by side with Neil out into the hall, where counters and supporters milled. The three candidates and their wives mounted the rostrum at the head of the hall.

The returning officer asked for silence and launched into

a short speech. Then he said, 'I shall now announce the results.'

Vicky glanced at Neil. His eyes had gone glazed and, almost impossible to believe, he was even whiter than before.

The results were to be announced in alphabetical order. The returning officer cleared his throat and Vicky took a deep breath. A cold and clammy hand crept into hers.

'Brown, Brian Robert Scott: ten thousand, four hundred and seventy-two.'

The Liberal supporters erupted; they obviously thought that good enough to send their man to the Palace of Westminster. Brown acknowledged the applause by punching the air.

'McGhie, Alexander Ogilvie Maitland: six thousand, three hundred and seventy-four.'

Vicky's hopes were rekindled. That was a rotten result for the Tory, well below what she'd expected him to get. It meant that Neil still had a chance.

Brian Brown was no longer jubilant. He shifted nervously from foot to foot.

Neil stood rigidly still, staring out over the crowd, seeing nothing. His brain and senses had gone completely numb. He might have been a statue carved from stone.

'Seton, Neil Malcolm: twelve thousand and eighty-eight. Mr Neil Malcolm Seton is duly elected as the Member of Parliament for Glasgow Kelvinhaugh.'

Vicky shrieked with delight. They had done it, they had bloody well done it. Neil was an MP!

Neil pulled her into his arms. She could feel his heart thudding nineteen to the dozen. Tears dribbled down her cheeks, but that didn't worry her. They were tears of happiness and joy.

After a few seconds she pushed Neil away from her, and straightened his tie, which had become skewwiff. 'I think the Honourable Member is expected to make a speech.'

He smiled at her, and ran a thumb across one of her wet

cheeks. Then, squaring his shoulders, he stepped forward to the microphone.

I am so proud of him, Vicky thought to herself. So proud.

Eleven

'My God, it was a close-run thing. Only an overall Commons majority of six. Not a lot of room there for manoeuvre,' Tom Allen said from the back seat of Neil's car.

It was 25 February 1950, two days after the general election which had returned Neil as Member for Glasgow Kelvinhaugh. He had increased his personal majority over the Liberals, and Brian Brown again, by three thousand and twenty-nine, a personal triumph.

'But it *is* an overall majority, thereby allowing the government to remain in power, that's the main thing,' Vicky retorted. She was sitting beside Neil, who was driving.

'An overall majority *just*,' Neil said.

Vicky and Neil had picked up Tom from his home and were taking him to the site in Glasgow's south side where building had just started under the great new housing scheme. Tom had never really recovered from his heart attack and now rarely left the house. This outing, at his suggestion, was one of the exceptions.

The car was a wee Singer that Neil had bought the previous year. He found it tremendously helpful in getting round his constituency and Glasgow in general. It would allow him to get more done in the day, was the argument he had used to persuade himself to buy it, and so it had proved. Now both he and Vicky had licences.

Neil went on, 'It's a worrying situation right enough, with the PM not in the best of health, and Bevin and Cripps in the same boat.'

'Aye, it's very dicey,' Tom Allen agreed.

This part of Glasgow was new to Vicky. Once they were clear of the Gorbals, conditions had rapidly improved; there was a lot more space than in Townhead and the streets were noticeably cleaner.

'Do you think you'll be able to stay in power long enough to get iron and steel nationalised?' Tom queried. It was always a treat for him to see Neil and have a good old chunter about politics.

Neil shrugged. 'I certainly hope so, but with such a slender majority, and with some of the bigwigs poorly, who can tell?'

'He's going to be a bigwig himself one day, you mark my words,' Vicky said over her shoulder to Tom.

'I've no doubt about that,' Tom replied. He knew from correspondence with old friends in the House that Neil was marked for higher things. He was potential ministerial material; no less a personage than Attlee had said so.

They made their way up through Croftfoot, arriving eventually at a street bordering what had been Campbell's Farm, the site of the new housing scheme. Neil parked the car on the verge of the road, then helped Tom get out. The three of them stood staring over the rich farmland now being dug up by earth excavators.

Vicky looked at a vast pile of drainage pipes and, adjacent to that, an enormous stack of water tanks. Besides the excavators there were dozens of tractors and lorries going this way and that.

Tom Allen's eyes shone with pride and pleasure. 'This is the beginning of the realisation of a dream. When those houses are finished, a working-class family will be able to live here in comfort and, above all, dignity.'

'Above all, hygienically,' Vicky chipped in, causing Neil to smile at her practicality.

Tom gave a small mock-bow. 'I stand corrected.' He went on enthusiastically, 'Inside toilets, running hot and cold water, electricity in every room, lots of glass to let in the light and green grass front and back: a veritable paradise.'

'And smell that air, fresh as can be. It'll do the children who come to live here a power of good,' Vicky said.

'It's taken the Corporation long enough to get round to it, but now, at long last, the scheme's under way. And the great thing is there isn't going to be just one scheme, but many,' Tom breathed.

'A whole new Glasgow, a far better Glasgow than the dirt-encrusted, vermin-infested slums existing today,' Vicky said, and gave a soft smile; it *was* a dream come true.

Tom gazed out over the acres rolling off into the far distance, visualising in his mind's eyes the rank upon rank of houses that were going to be built there, and was gratified to think that he had played no small part in bringing all this about. For years he had carried the banner for new housing, a banner Neil had picked up when he had been forced to drop it.

'I can't tell you how glad I am I was able to come out here and see the beginning of the birth before – well, before I go,' Tom said in a quiet, emotionally charged voice.

'Och, don't haver. Take life easy and you've got years left in you,' Vicky admonished.

A secretive smile crept onto Tom's face, as though he were enjoying some private joke. 'When the folks are settled in the new schemes, the old slums must be razed to the ground, wiped from the face of the earth. It must be as though they'd never existed. Promise me you'll see that happens,' he said to Neil.

Neil shared his wish: the slums were an abomination, a running sore that had to be cauterised to extinction. If they remained standing, they would be refilled with newcomers to the city, and that must never happen. 'I promise. If it can be done, I'll do it,' he answered.

Tom grunted. That was good enough for him. Neil would find a way.

He turned to gaze one last time over the fields of tomorrow. If there was a climax to his life's work, all that he'd striven for, it was here and now. 'Let's go back,' he said quietly.

Less than a month later Tom Allen was dead.

Early the following morning Vicky was wakened by Neil tossing and turning beside her. She touched him and her

338

brow knitted in concern. His skin was feverishly hot and slick with sweat.

She switched on the bedside light. 'Neil? Neil, are you all right?'

He groaned, then coughed. A wet rattly cough that sounded ominous.

'Neil?' This time she shook him.

His eyes slowly blinked open. 'Feel . . . terrible,' he mumbled, and coughed again.

This was a case for the doctor, Vicky decided.

Getting out of bed, she put on her dressing gown and mules, then got a towel, with which she wiped his face. She had hardly started on his chest when his face was awash again.

'Thirsty,' he croaked.

She gave him some water to drink, then went through to rouse Martha. 'Your daddy's ill, so I want you to get dressed and run over the road and get grandpa. Understand?'

Eyes large, Martha nodded.

Vicky hurriedly helped Martha into her clothes, then saw her out the door. Returning to their bedroom, she began setting a fire, which she soon had lit. With a temperature like Neil had, it couldn't be good for him, even though well covered with bedclothes, to be in an icy-cold room.

Martha arrived back with not only George but Mary. In a few terse sentences Vicky explained the situation.

'So could you go to the public phone box for me and telephone the doctor?' she asked George.

'On my way,' George replied and disappeared from the room.

Mary went over to Neil and had a good look at him. His upper lip was beaded with pearls of sweat, the whites of his eyes had gone dull and yellowy. He told her that his pyjamas were soaked through.

'You air a clean pair of pyjamas in front of that fire while I put the kettle on. We'll sponge him down and dry him, then slip him into the clean pyjamas. At the very least that'll make him feel a bit better,' Mary said.

Vicky crossed to the chest of drawers where Neil's clean

pyjamas were kept, and was about to come away from there again when Mary caught her eye in the mirror hanging above the drawers. She made a sideways motion of her head, signalling that she wanted to speak to Vicky in the kitchen.

Vicky laid the clean pyjamas on the bed. 'I'll get that big Turkish towel from the kitchen press,' she said to Neil and followed Mary out of the bedroom. Martha, now alone with her dad, did her best to comfort him.

'It could be pleurisy or pneumonia,' Mary said in a quiet voice, once she and Vicky were in the kitchen.

'Exactly what I thought, which is why I was so quick to send for the doctor.'

The two women stared at one another, each well aware how dangerous, indeed potentially fatal, pleurisy and pneumonia could be.

'He's got a very strong constitution, and there are many new drugs out nowadays,' Vicky said.

'I'll put the kettle on,' Mary replied.

Vicky bit her lip, then took the Turkish towel from the bottom of the press and hurried back to Neil.

The clean pyjamas had been nicely warmed by the time Mary appeared with a basin of hot water and a couple of flannels. As Neil was to be stripped, Vicky sent Martha from the room. It was an indication of how ill Neil was that he didn't protest about Mary helping Vicky to take off his sodden pyjamas, sponge him down and dry him. In the middle of this, George returned to say the doctor wouldn't be long. Roughly ten minutes later a chap on the front door announced his arrival.

Vicky remained with Dr Sharp while he made his examination; the others closeted themselves in the kitchen. Vicky hovered anxiously while he took Neil's temperature.

'Flu, a very bad dose of it,' Dr Sharp pronounced.

Vicky gave a sigh of relief. 'My mother and I feared he might have pleurisy or pneumonia.'

'Aye, well in this case the symptoms, to the layman that is, would appear similar. But it's flu, no doubt about it.'

Vicky smoothed Neil's bedclothes. 'So what do we do?'

'The most important thing is that he stays in bed. Do you have a po'?'

Vicky nodded.

'He's to use that. I'll give him some tablets now, then I'll write out a prescription which you've to get from the chemist as soon as it opens. I'll come back this evening round about six o'clock to see if there's any improvement.'

Neil, who had been listening to this, attempted in vain to struggle onto an elbow. 'Can't stay in bed, have an important engagement to attend, and speech to make, tonight,' he gasped.

'You can forget all about that. You're going to remain in bed for the rest of the week, *at least*,' Dr Sharp replied sternly.

'It's an awfully important engagement and speech for me,' Neil persisted.

'Don't be bloody stupid. You're in no fit condition to go anywhere and speak,' Vicky said firmly.

Neil coughed, the same wet rattly sound as before.

Dr Sharp took a box of tablets from his bag and handed Neil two. Vicky held a glass of water to his lips and he washed them down.

'I want to remind you that, even with modern medical advances, people can still die of flu. I strongly advise you not to forget that,' the doctor said to Neil.

Tears brought on by his fever burst from Neil's eyes. When he started to splutter, Vicky quickly found him a handkerchief.

'You did the right thing in putting the fire on. Keep it on twenty-four hours a day for now,' Dr Sharp told Vicky.

'And sponging and changing him?'

'Use your own judgement about that. Hopefully the tablets will begin to reduce his temperature by this evening, and when that's nearer normal sponging and changing won't be quite so necessary.'

'I understand,' Vicky replied.

The doctor wrote out Neil's prescription, then took his leave. He paused at the front door to remind Vicky yet again that it was imperative Neil stay in his bed; she mustn't be swayed by him pleading or any argument he might come up with. Vicky assured him that Neil would be staying put, even if she had to tie him down.

When the doctor had gone, Vicky went into the kitchen to announce the verdict. George and Mary were just as relieved as she had been – though, as Mary pointed out, corroborating what the doctor had said, flu might not now be in the same category as pleurisy or pneumonia, but nor was it to be lightly dismissed.

George and Mary left after it had been arranged that Mary would come back over at eight o'clock so that Vicky could take Martha to school and go from there to the chemist's to get Neil's tablets.

Vicky then had a little chat with Martha, telling her that she had been a big help, and not to worry about her daddy, he would soon be well again. As they talked, Vicky helped Martha change back into her nightie. Within minutes of crawling underneath the covers of her bed, Martha was once more fast asleep.

Returning to their bedroom, Vicky banked up the fire, then went over to sit with Neil.

'Thanks to those tablets the doctor gave me, I'm feeling a lot better. Things aren't so hazy,' Neil said.

'Could you manage a cup of tea?'

'In a minute or two maybe. With only an overall majority of six, Vicky . . .'

She placed a finger across his lips. 'For the meantime it's going to have to be an overall majority of five, and that's all there is to it. You'll catch the train for London when you're over this, and not before. Is that clear?'

He pulled a face. 'You can be a gey stubborn woman, Vicky.'

'I've told the doctor I'll tie you down if needs be and, so help me, I will.'

Picking up the Turkish towel, she wiped down his face, neck and the top of his chest. As she did this, he regarded her with an expression of deep frustration.

'The speech is such a good one too, and it's a tremendous

honour to be asked to speak on the same platform as McIntyre,' he said when she was refolding the towel.

Hector McIntyre was the Secretary of State for Scotland. That night he would be present at the famous Kelvin Hall, where a Labour victory rally was to be held.

Also, Jock McLean was to give his farewell speech there. True to what he had told Vicky and Neil eighteen months previously, Jock had not run again for the Townhead seat at the general election, that having been successfully fought on behalf of the Labour Party by a chap called Jimmy Downie.

'It's a shame, right enough,' Vicky replied. A crowd of about ten thousand was expected.

'There's no way I can cajole you into letting me go?'

Smiling, she shook her head.

'Bugger!' he swore, and coughed.

'I'll get you that tea now,' she said, and left him.

When she returned with two steaming cups, she found him looking thoughtful. 'I've had an idea,' he said.

'Oh aye?'

'If I can't deliver the speech, why don't you?'

She stared at him, aghast. 'Me!'

'Why not?'

'Because . . . Well, because I've never spoken in public before – with the exception of when I made my confession, that is.'

'You did that all right. In fact, you were damned good.'

'Maybe so, but that was a special circumstance.'

'Special circumstance or not, you spoke damned well, which shows you have that capability. What you can do once you can do again, particularly when you have the material to back you, as you have in this speech.'

Vicky did not know what to think. The thought of delivering Neil's speech scared her stiff. Then she had been scared stiff prior to speaking at the museum and art gallery, but once she had started to speak, her nervousness and fear had vanished.

Neil went on, 'It's not as if you don't know the speech. You've been over it a dozen times with me, and even wrote large chunks of it yourself. So, come on, what do you say?'

'They might not want me to speak in your place.'

'You'll merely be delivering my speech because of my illness. No one is going to object to that.'

She sipped her tea, her mind racing. 'And you definitely think I'd be all right?'

'Vicky, the last thing I'd do would be put you in a situation where you're likely to make a fool of yourself. On the contrary, you'll be first class. I know it.'

She hurriedly thought over her wardrobe. What could she wear?

'I'm sure Mary won't mind looking after you and Martha,' she said hesitantly, not yet entirely convinced.

Neil opened his mouth to reply, but instead broke into a prolonged bout of coughing, during which he brought up a great deal of horrible slimy phlegm. At the end of the coughing, he was so exhausted that he closed his eyes and almost instantly fell asleep.

Vicky went to Neil's briefcase, where she knew his speech, typewritten by herself, to be.

Neil would sleep for a while, she decided. Probably an hour or two. She went through to the kitchen and there began quietly reading the speech aloud.

They had expected ten thousand; they got twelve, with many more turned away at the doors. Inside the Kelvin Hall the Labour supporters were packed like sardines. The atmosphere was euphoric, carnival almost. VICTORY 1950, huge banners in red and yellow proclaimed. Behind the speakers' platform hung a huge picture of Clement Attlee, Labour leader and Prime Minister.

Vicky regretted having agreed to speak in Neil's place. One glance at that enormous crowd had been enough to make her want to bolt, to get out of there and as far away as possible.

Dickie Fleet entered the ante-room where the speakers and various others connected with the event were congregating. He crossed over to Vicky. 'How are you feeling?'

'Terrible.'

'Just try and . . .'

She held up a hand to silence him. 'Please, Dickie. I appreciate you're doing it with the best of intentions, but right now the last thing I need is advice.'

'Suit yourself,' Dickie replied, looking none too pleased, and slouched off again.

She knew that she had upset him, which she hadn't wanted to do at all. It was just that she was in such a state!

A smiling Jock McLean came over. 'I feel like a horse about to have its last race before being taken to the knacker's yard and melted down into glue,' he said.

His joke helped ease the tension for her, and she laughed. She had a mental picture of Jock in a large pot or cauldron being boiled down, the top half of him as he stood before her, the bottom half a gooey mess.

'It's time to go and face them,' Jock went on, still smiling.

Her laughter died. The dreaded moment had arrived. 'Let's get it over with then,' she replied, and stood up.

Clutching the speech in her right hand, she walked alongside Jock, making for the door that led to the platform from where they would speak. Hector McIntyre was in the lead.

There were six speakers in all. McIntyre, Jock McLean, Leonard Carter, MP for Renfrewshire North, Danny Rose, an official with the Boilermakers' Union, Peter Strathern, representing the Corporation, and Vicky. She was scheduled to speak third, after Leonard Carter and Peter Strathern.

She sat beside Jock McLean, laid her speech in front of her, then looked out over the gathering. Her heart leaped into her mouth; there were so many of them! And all of them seemed to be staring directly, and critically, at her.

Jock leaned close to Vicky. 'This is a victory rally. All of these here will be members of the faithful, come to celebrate and generally have a good time. They'll be on your side, and very sympathetic because they know you're filling in for Neil on account of his illness. You've nothing to fear, lassie, I promise you,' he whispered.

345

She could have given him a big smacker for putting it all into perspective. 'Thank you,' she whispered back.

Leonard Carter, a portly jovial man in his late fifties, got up and led off. Within seconds he had the audience roaring and clapping in appreciation.

Peter Strathern was a dry stick of a man with a biting, incisive wit. Most of his speech consisted of tearing into the Tory Party, which he did extremely effectively. Four times he called Winston Churchill a warmonger, and four times got a round of applause for it. He wound up by extolling the government for recognising the Communist government of China, which it had done the previous month.

Then it was Vicky's turn.

As she rose, she underwent the same transformation as had occurred behind the museum and art gallery. Her nervousness completely vanished, replaced by total calm and serenity. When she spoke, her voice was strong, vibrant and compelling, the voice of a natural orator. She soon had her audience spellbound, hanging on her every word.

'. . . There is a continuing need to nationalise, to give the nation's wealth back to its rightful owners, the people. This will lead to greater efficiency, pride in job, and greater sense of work responsibility. The time of the bloated, parasitical capitalist is over. This is the beginning of the time of the people, the ordinary working keelie and his family . . .'

The audience lapped it up, and cheered her to the echo when, finally, she sat down again.

'Marvellous. Best female speaker I've ever heard,' Jock McLean whispered.

She had enjoyed that! she thought in wonder. She had thoroughly *enjoyed* that. In fact, she only wished it could have gone on for longer. She saw Hector McIntyre looking at her with a surprised, yet appreciative, expression. He smiled and nodded acknowledgement of her success. She flushed with pride and a tremendous sense of gratification.

She had to force herself to concentrate on the next speaker, Danny Rose of the Boilermakers' Union.

•

Tina squealed with delight and threw her arms round Vicky. 'You were absolutely amazing, absolutely! Wasn't she, Sammy?'

'T'rific,' Sammy agreed.

'I was helped a lot by having a good speech to deliver,' Vicky said modestly.

'Speech be blowed. It was you yourself that was magic. I couldn't take my eyes off you, and neither could anyone else. You had us all, each and every one, in the palm of your hand.'

'. . . Palm of your hand,' Sammy echoed.

'You were outstanding,' the man with Tina and Sammy said.

'Vicky, I'd like you to meet Chris Walker, Sammy's brother. Be careful what you say in front of him. He's a policeman.'

Vicky shook Chris's extended hand. He seemed a personable chap – a few years older than herself, she judged, which would make him about thirty-five.

A pipe band that had been playing earlier started up again. Vicky saw Jock McLean wave to her, and waved back. He was talking to Hector McIntyre.

'Listen. What do you say we get out of here and find a pub?' Tina suggested.

'I'd love to but, as you know, Neil's at home with the flu. I really should get back right away.'

'Och, after the triumph you've just had, a wee celebration is in order. Come on, don't be miserable, Neil won't mind. I'm sure if you could ask him he'd tell you to go right ahead. And we won't stay long, I promise,' Tina argued.

Vicky knew Tina was right, that Neil wouldn't object to her having a dram with her old pal and Sammy. And she could certainly use a whisky, if not two.

'Only ten or fifteen minutes then,' she said.

Sammy and Chris went first, carving a passage through the crowd towards the nearest exit. Vicky and Tina followed close behind the two men, Tina with an arm hooked round one of Vicky's. As they progressed towards the exit, Vicky was tapped again and again on the shoulder and told how good her speech had been.

As the pubs round the Kelvin Hall were bound to be choc-a-bloc from the people who had attended the rally, Vicky had everyone pile into the Singer and drove them to the Byres Road, where the pubs would be quieter.

Once inside the pub they'd selected, Sammy made a beeline for the bar, while Tina excused herself to go to the ladies' room.

Vicky and Chris sat down. When Chris glanced at her, his look was of admiration tinged with awe.

'I didn't know Sammy had a brother. Neither he or Tina have ever mentioned it,' she said.

'Probably because I was in Hong Kong for twelve years. I only came back to Glasgow in November,' he explained.

'Were you in the police out there?'

'I was a superintendent when I resigned. I originally started with the Glasgow police, who've taken me on again, but at a reduced rank to what I was in HK. I'm a sergeant now.'

'Why did you come back? Homesick?'

Chris looked over at Sammy, who was still waiting to be served. There was still no sign of Tina.

'My wife and little boy died in a street accident. They were crushed when a lorry shed its load of steel girders. I couldn't stomach staying on in HK after that, so I came home,' he said, voice tight and an expression of indescribable sadness on his face.

'I am sorry,' Vicky whispered.

'She was a lot younger than me, only twenty-four. The lad was three and a half.'

'What was her name?'

'Wei Wei, my boy's name was Keng Meng.'

He saw Vicky's look of surprise. 'Yes, she was Chinese, and we gave our son a Chinese name because that was what she wanted.'

Chris offered Vicky a cigarette, which she refused, explaining she didn't smoke. He lit up.

'Would you like to see a picture of them? If it wouldn't bore you, that is?'

'I'd like to very much, and it won't bore me, I assure you,' she replied.

He produced a picture from his wallet and handed it to her. Wei Wei was petite with long black lustrous hair that had a brace of bone combs in it. She was very beautiful in a delicate, sculptured way. Keng Meng was plump and smiling, with black spiky hair. The only non-Oriental feature about him was his eyes; they were western and just like Chris's.

'It must have been dreadful for you to lose them, and in such a horrible way,' Vicky said sympathetically, returning the picture.

Chris shrugged, but did not reply. For the moment he did not trust himself to speak.

He was putting the picture away when Tina reappeared. With that, the subject was changed and the conversation brightened. Before long the four of them were laughing and joking – having, as the Glasgow saying went, a 'rer old ter' together.

It was during March that Tom Allen passed away in his sleep, and several days later he was cremated at Craigton crematorium. Neil came north for the ceremony, as did Hugh Gaitskell, representing Mr Attlee. The opposition had allowed Neil and Gaitskell to be paired for the visit. Tom had been well liked and respected on both sides of the House.

When the ceremony was over, Vicky and Neil had a few words with the widow, who was distraught with grief. Hugh Gaitskell also spoke to her, giving her a personal message of condolence from the Prime Minister.

While Vicky and Neil were talking to another mourner, Gaitskell came over. Neil introduced Gaitskell to Vicky and the mourner, then Gaitskell asked Neil if they could have a chat outside.

'Private?' queried Neil, meaning should he include Vicky or not? Gaitskell shook his head.

Outside, a flurry of snow was blowing and the wind was sharp as a razor's edge. Vicky shivered when a gust swirled up her dress.

'Missed you on the train up, Neil. What train are you taking back?' Gaitskell asked.

'I thought I'd catch the late sleeper, that gives me a chance to do a little constituency work,' Neil replied. What he didn't say was it also gave him a few extra hours to be with Vicky, whom he was missing like mad in London.

Gaitskell nodded his understanding. 'This tiny majority is playing havoc with constituency work. Those outside the Home Counties are finding it nigh on impossible to get any in at all, so you're right to maximise the chance when you have it. I shall be returning on the three o'clock and will be lunching at the Central Station hotel before that. I would like you and Mrs Seton to join me. I have something to discuss with you that you might consider to be in your interest.'

Neil glanced quickly at Vicky, then brought his attention back to Gaitskell. 'What time would you like us to be there?'

'One thirty in the restaurant?'

'One thirty it is,' Neil agreed.

'Cheerio for now then,' Gaitskell said, and left them, heading for the car and driver that had been laid on for him.

Neil turned to Vicky, and raised an eyebrow. 'In my interest?' he echoed.

Vicky stared thoughtfully after the rapidly receding car. She was just as intrigued as Neil.

The wine, Chateau Lascombes, was the best Vicky had ever tasted. It was like smooth, warm, red velvet.

'Tom Allen was a great man, and in his day a tremendous influence within the Labour Party. That's why I was honoured when the PM asked me to represent him at the funeral,' Hugh Gaitskell said.

'I've always had an interest in politics, but it was Tom who activated me. It was his idea I run for his seat when he stood down,' Neil explained.

'We thought the world of him. I still can't believe he's gone,' Vicky said.

The waiter appeared with their main course, which was then duly served up. Vicky was having veal and spaghetti, her first experience of a dish which she had only read about. Used to simple Glasgow cooking, it seemed quite exotic to her.

Gaitskell waited till the waiter had left them, then said, 'I have some news.'

Vicky tried to keep excitement from her face. Neil, without realising it, leaned fractionally forward.

'I've been offered the post of Minister of State for Economic Affairs. When I see the PM tomorrow, I shall be telling him I accept.'

'Congratulations!' Neil exclaimed, genuinely pleased. He was a great admirer of Gaitskell, a rising star if ever there was one, though somewhat left of him in his beliefs.

'Congratulations also,' Vicky smiled, thinking there had to be more to this than that news. Gaitskell hadn't invited them out to lunch just to tell Neil, a backbencher, that he was going to be Minister of State for Economic Affairs.

'Val Tester, my PPS, is excellent, but with my new responsibilities he's going to need help. I've had my eye on you for some time, Neil, and was wondering if you'd be interested in the job?' Gaitskell went on.

Neil, a tinge of red staining his neck, slowly laid down his knife and fork. What little appetite he'd had had just vanished. 'You're asking me to be your second PPS?' To become a Personal Private Secretary was often a stepping stone to higher things.

'I am.'

Neil swallowed. 'Then of course I accept, and am delighted to do so.'

'Marvellous. See Val tomorrow and he'll brief you on your new duties. I'm very pleased to have you on the team,' Gaitskell said and raised his glass in salute.

PPS to Hugh Gaitskell, a man being more and more spoken of within Labour circles as a future Prime Minister! Now Neil really was on his way, Vicky thought jubilantly.

•

'Neil, how are you love?' Vicky was ringing Neil at his office in the House of Commons from her own office in the Kelvinhaugh Labour Hall.

'Whacked out. We were sitting till two a.m., and then went back hard at it first thing today. None of us dares miss an important division in case the government suffers a premature defeat, and this pressure is beginning to tell, particularly amongst the older Members. Then there's the bill for the nationalisation of iron and steel on the stocks. We're having to absorb a tremendous amount of flak and pressure over that. The Tories are dead set against the bill going through, but go through it will – we're all determined about that!'

'Two a.m! No wonder I didn't get a reply when I rang you at the flat last night. I tried several times, then finally gave up just after eleven,' Vicky said. Neil shared a flat with three other Labour MPs in Petty France, a short walk from the House of Commons.

He sounded dead beat, she thought. But that was hardly surprising with so many late and all-night sittings to contend with. The last time he had managed to come north, in a lightning twenty-four-hour visit, she'd discovered that he had lost nearly a stone in weight and looked quite haggard.

'I'm ringing to tell you I've received an invitation to speak at the Hamilton Miners' annual gala,' she said.

'You mean, speak on my behalf?' he queried. She had now done that on a number of occasions since the Kelvin Hall, acting as substitute because of his general unavailability to speak personally.

She laughed. 'That's the thing. The invitation is for me, not you. I've been asked to speak in my own right. I wanted to know what you thought before I answered the invitation.'

'I don't see why you shouldn't speak, if you want to, that is.'

'I do, very much so. But I didn't want you getting jealous or taking the hump.'

This time it was Neil who laughed. 'You should know me

better than that. If you want to speak, go ahead, and with my blessing.'

He was a real sweetie, she thought. There were many husbands wouldn't have liked her striking out on her own. Glasgow men in particular could be very possessive and restrictive where their wives were concerned. But not Neil. He was bigger, and more understanding than that.

'Any chance of you getting up here soon?' she asked.

'Not a hope. Johnny Gaskin, Houghton-Le-Spring, was taken into hospital this morning with appendicitis, which means our majority is down to four, because another Labour Member is also in hospital with meningitis. It has to be virtually life or death for any of us to get away at the present moment.'

'Your summer break isn't all that far away. We'll just have to look forward to that,' she said.

'I love you, Vicky,' he whispered.

She blew him a kiss down the receiver. 'Speak to you soon, darling,' she replied, and hung up.

She studied the invitation from the Hamilton Miners that lay in front of her. She was thrilled at the prospect of speaking as herself and not on behalf of Neil. She would get working on her speech that night, she decided. It would be the first speech she had ever written totally on her own, and she was looking forward to it.

She had just typed out and signed her acceptance when there was a tap on the door.

'Come in!' she called out.

Chris Walker entered. It was the first time she'd seen him since the night they'd met.

'Why, hello. How are you?' she greeted him. He was wearing fawn trousers and a matching windcheater, which she guessed from their cut and quality had come from Hong Kong.

'I'm fine,' he replied, and gazed around. 'So this is where you hide away.'

She indicated a chair. 'Take a pew. And to what do I owe the honour?'

He had a very easy physical way about him, she thought, as he sat. He moved effortlessly, like a cat.

'Tina tells me you're always on the lookout for helpers, and I was wondering if you'd have me?'

'But how about your job? I thought policemen work all sorts of long hours.'

'Well, for a start, it's shift work, which means I often have free mornings, afternoons and even entire days. And, as I don't seem to require a great deal of sleep, I end up having time on my hands, time I'd like to fill doing something constructive,' he answered.

Time other men his age devoted to their families, she told herself grimly. His story of losing his wife and boy had touched her deeply. She had thought about it, and him, more than once.

'Right then. Are you free now?' she asked.

He nodded.

'Then get that windcheater off. I've a whole stack of envelopes for you to address.'

During their coffee break, he regaled her with tales of Hong Kong. She found him a natural storyteller, fascinating to listen to.

Ken lay staring at Ina Finlayson's gently rising and falling naked breasts. He found them wondrously beautiful, erotic works of art.

He and Ina were lying on her bed, having just made love. Her eyes were closed and there was a small smile of contentment and satisfaction playing round her lips.

Reaching out, he laid a hand on the breast nearest him. It was so smooth, warm and perfect. He never tired of touching and caressing her breasts, enjoying that almost as much as the act of sex itself. He flicked a nipple and flicked it again. It deepened in colour and stiffened slightly. He rolled it between thumb and forefinger.

Ina opened her eyes. 'Again?' she queried throatily.

'Not yet,' he whispered in reply, and kissed the nipple he had been manipulating.

'Hmmh!' Ina murmured, and a shudder ran through her, causing her buttocks to wriggle.

'I'll get us a drink,' Ken said and, rising from the bed, crossed to the occasional table on which stood the bottle and glasses. He poured himself a hefty one, Ina only a dribble, which he topped up well with lemonade.

Returning to the bed, he gave her hers, then went over to the window and stared out. She regarded him through slitted eyes. His mood had suddenly changed.

'What's wrong?'

He shrugged.

Laying her glass by the side of the bed, she padded over to him. She squashed her breasts against his back, knowing he loved that, and placed her hands on his hips.

'Is it me? Have I done something, or not done something?'

'It isn't you, Ina. It's those damned new premises I want for the union, and which I can't find. It depresses me every time I think about it.'

She remembered then that she had made an appointment for him to see a building earlier on that afternoon, a building that had only come on the market at the beginning of the week.

'No luck at the Broomielaw then?' she asked.

'Awful. The place was awful. Besides needing gutting from top to bottom, it was the ugliest building I've seen in a long time.'

Ken took a pull of his whisky. 'As you know, I've looked at everything that's been on the market since I decided the union needed new premises, and there just hasn't been anything suitable. It's either too big or too small or too ugly, or something else is wrong with it,' he said miserably.

'Sooner or later the right place is bound to come up,' she replied, trying to console him.

He snorted his impatience and exasperation. Beyond the window, the hundreds of thousands of white and yellow lights reminded him of those he had recently seen in a magazine photograph, lights that had formed the backdrop to a spectacular building.

'There's a building in Chicago designed by a chap called

Frank Lloyd-Wright which is so stunning to look at it actually took my breath away. The outside is made entirely of glass and steel, and with night lights playing on it the whole thing gleams like a highly polished, sparkly diamond.'

He paused, then went on. 'Now that's what I would give my eye teeth to have for my future national union headquarters. A building that would be the best, the most modern, in all Scotland.'

Ina thought of central Glasgow, old and antiquated, a place of mausoleums. 'If you want a building like that, you're going to have to have it built yourself,' she said.

He stared at her in astonishment. 'Why didn't I think of that! Of course, that's the answer,' he exclaimed.

'Could you . . . I mean, could the CDU as it stands afford that?' she asked.

'Oh aye, no bother. You'd be surprised at the financial depth the CDU has behind it. From Picassos to Argentinian beef, our money is well invested, and growing with the vigour of an adolescent all the time.'

Then Ken had an idea that was an extension of hers. 'I know what I'll do, I'll buy that monstrosity in the Broomielaw and have it torn down. The site is ideal for my new building.'

He took another pull at his drink, excitement and pleasure racing through him. Turning, he took her head in his free hand and kissed her lightly on the mouth. 'Not only gorgeous, but a genius with it.' He smiled.

She felt him stir against her thigh. 'Again?' she asked, repeating her earlier query.

He placed his glass on the window ledge and swung her up into his arms.

'Again,' he confirmed, and crossed to the bed.

Later he would telephone Sawyers, his lawyer, and give him instructions to find out the best architects in Glasgow and to set up an appointment for him to see their top man. After he'd spoken to Sawyers, he would draw a rough sketch of what he had in mind. Dammit to hell, he was so excited!

Ina gave a small groan of appreciation as he sank into her.

•

Vicky glanced up from her typewriter and over at Chris, who was engrossed at an adjacent desk. He had been helping for six weeks now, and a more willing or industrious helper she could not have hoped for – nor one who made her laugh so much; he had a tremendous sense of humour. She suddenly realised that she knew nothing about him other than that he was Sammy's brother, that he'd lived in Hong Kong and had lost his wife and boy.

'Chris?'

He stopped writing and looked at her.

'You've never said. Where do you stay?'

He sat back in his chair. 'I've got police accommodation just off the Dumbarton Road.'

'What sort of accommodation, a house?'

A rueful smile twisted his mouth. 'Aye, a section house, which isn't the sort of house you mean. It consists of individual bedrooms plus communal areas. There's also a canteen where we eat.'

'Like a barracks?'

His mouth twisted even more. 'If there's a difference, I couldn't say what it is.'

'And what about the food?'

'I've tasted worse. It's not exactly home cooking, but it keeps you going and your strength up.'

'The whole thing comes across as being pretty grim,' she said.

'Och, the section house leaves a lot to be desired, but it's not that bad. It is convenient for someone on his own.' He tried to inject a cheery note into his voice, which didn't sound at all convincing. 'I'm the daddy, being the eldest and only sergeant there. The rest are all young constables, a good bunch, but I don't mix too much with them because of the age and rank difference.'

She could just imagine how lonely it must be for him in this section house, and her heart went out to him.

'Do you go to Tina and Sammy's quite a lot?' she asked.

'They've got their own life to lead so, although I'm always made welcome, I try not to intrude too often. I'm sure you understand?'

She did not inquire about his parents, knowing from a conversation she had once had with Sammy that they were both dead. Nor were there any other brothers or sisters.

'I was wondering, would you like to come over to my place for tea one night?' she said.

He hesitated. Was this invitation out of pity for him? If so, he wouldn't accept.

'I'm not that great a cook, but I'm sure I can manage something better than your canteen,' she went on.

He gave a dry laugh, but still did not answer.

Vicky guessed why he was holding back. She could see it in his face and eyes. 'It would be company for Martha and myself. Neil being away so much, we get quite lonely at times,' she said, which wasn't true at all. With Mary, George and various neighbours in and out the house like a fiddler's elbow, they were never that. But she wanted him to think he was doing her a favour, rather than the other way round.

'How about Saturday evening?' she suggested.

'That's out. I'm on late duty.'

'Friday then?'

'You're on,' he said.

She wrote out her address. 'About seven?'

'I'll be there,' he grinned.

She returned to her typing, pleased he was coming. In fact, she was more than pleased; she was really looking forward to it.

That Friday, a little after three in the afternoon, Ken left his architects' offices with a rolled-up set of preliminary sketches under his arm.

The architects Sawyers had recommended had jumped at the chance of designing a new building for him, seeing it as a very prestigious contract and, because this ultra-modern building was to be erected in the central city area, one of the most important ever to come their way. They had said that they understood perfectly what he was after, and the preliminary sketches now under his arm, which he'd given the go-ahead to be expanded into proper drawings, proved them right.

The other good news was that the monstrosity in the Broomielaw had become CDU property that morning. The demolition would be starting first thing Monday.

A satisfactory set of sketches, procurement of the ideal site: this called for a celebration, he decided. He would pick up Ina and together they'd paint the town red. Red! They'd paint it bloody tartan, the way he felt!

Ken was not the only one to decide on a celebration that Friday. George Devine had won five pounds seventeen and six on the dogs, having placed his bet with the bookie's runner who came round the tram depot every day the dogs and horses were running. Bonnie Mary, his dog had been called, and, although it was a rank outsider, he'd chosen it because of the name. And by God, rank outsider or not, the beauty had won, beating the favourite by a head at the last moment.

George finished his pint and gazed about. There had been a few other tram depot staff in but, despite its being pay day, they had now left. He glanced up at the wall clock and saw that it was time he was heading for home himself. In fact it was well past time he was heading for home.

Och, Mary wouldn't mind him being late, he thought. It was a rare enough occurrence, just as it was a gey rare occurrence for him to have one of his occasional flutters come up, and so handsomely at that.

Raising a hand, he signalled to a bartender. 'Another pint and large whisky,' he said, his fifth such since coming into the pub.

Ken and Ina were in the back of Ken's Cadillac, having just left the private club where they had been drinking since the latter part of the afternoon. Shugs was driving, Paddy Troy beside him. They were en route to Ina's flat, where Ken intended spending an hour or two before being driven back to Balfron.

Ken pressed the concealed button at the back of the driver's seat and the panel slid open to reveal the miniature bar. 'Another *g* and *t*?' he asked.

Ina shook her head.

He contemplated the whisky decanter, wondering whether he really wanted one or not. He switched his gaze to the mixers. His throat was so parched that he would have had one of those if they'd been cold instead of warm. And then he had it. What he needed to wash away the desert in his throat was a dirty big pint of thirst-quenching heavy.

'Pull up outside the first boozer you come to,' he instructed Shugs.

He explained to Ina why he wanted to stop at a pub, and she agreed that a beer was the very dab. She was dry too.

George was well away with the fairies and thoroughly enjoying himself. He would take a taxi home, he thought. And he'd pick up a bunch of flowers on the way. He would get the cabbie to go via the main entrance to Union Street station; a flowerseller had a pitch on the pavement there.

Five pounds seventeen and six! he thought jubilantly, and congratulated himself for the umpteenth time. Besides the flowers, he'd slip Mary a couple of nicker to buy herself a wee something. She'd like that. And he'd take home a carry-out as well, some screwtops and a half-bottle.

A last one for the road, he thought, and raised a hand to signal a barman. He suddenly found himself swaying and had to grab hold of the bar to stop himself from pitching over. Enough, he thought. He'd had enough for now. He'd leave it till he got home and could get stuck into the carry-out. He burped, and beer and whisky fumes filled his mouth, mixed with the sour taste of vomit. He'd go out into the street and wait there for a passing cab. Being a Friday night, it shouldn't be too long before one happened along – he hoped.

The fresh air hit him like a slap in the face. His stomach heaved and the taste of vomit was back in his mouth. Then it wasn't just the taste of vomit but the actual stuff itself. He noticed an alley leading off. Best be sick there, he told himself, less embarrassing.

It was only a few gobfuls of vomit, not the gush he'd expected. As he was wiping his lips with his hanky, a big foreign car drew alongside the street kerb and parked in a spot visible from where he was standing.

He ran a hand through his hair, then over his eyes. Bile churned in his gut. Was he going to throw up again? George leaned against a wall, and in that position heard two voices talking, a woman's and a man's. The man's was strangely familiar.

'Oh, Ken, that was ever so funny,' the female said, and laughed.

George twisted round and peered at the chap the woman had been addressing. The chap was plump and balding and wore glasses. He did know him, he was sure of it.

'Do you want me to come in with you or remain here?' a second man asked the first, this one speaking with a pronounced southern Irish accent.

George could now see there were three men, including a driver, who was still behind the wheel of the big foreign car.

'Come in with us. You never know,' the chap with glasses replied to the Mick.

Then George had it. The years flew back and he saw that face as it had used to be: slimmer, with more hair on top, and glasses that had been nowhere as fancy as those Blacklaws now wore.

Ken Blacklaws: the stinking rat who had let Vicky take the blame for his thieving, then abandoned her while she was still in borstal to go off with another – maybe even this blonde piece he was now staring at.

Anger blossomed in George. Fuelled by alcohol, the anger was almost instantly transformed into blind raging hatred. Heedless of his churning stomach, stumbling and lurching, George went after Ken.

'You, Blacklaws!' he yelled.

Paddy Troy whirled round. Ken and Ina turned more slowly, Ken frowning.

George came to a halt several feet away from Ken and glared at him. 'Remember me?' he demanded in a harsh voice.

'Mr Devine from Parr Street. How are you?' Ken smiled.

'For years I've been hoping to bump into you again. I'm claiming you, son,' George snarled, and launched himself at Ken, to grab him by the jacket lapels.

A split second after George moved, Paddy Troy did likewise. Paddy hit George twice, very hard, in the kidneys. The breath whoofed out of George. Groaning, he released Ken and doubled over. Paddy grabbed hold of George and threw him backwards away from Ken and Ina.

Arms flailing, George smashed into the side of the Cadillac. He went over the fin nearest the pavement, from where he fell head-first to the ground. He landed awkwardly, to lie in an untidy tangle of limbs.

'What was that all about?' Ina asked. She had been rooted to the spot with surprise while the brief rumpus had taken place.

Ken ignored her question and took a deep breath. He had found that quite distressing. Stupid drunken old fart! he thought, for it had been obvious that George was guttered.

'You all right?' Paddy Troy demanded.

Ken nodded.

Shugs, worried about damage to his beloved Caddy, had come out the car like a shot when George had hit it and was now hurriedly inspecting that side panel and fin. He sighed with relief to find there was neither mark nor dent. He was about to walk round George when something about the way he was lying stopped him. The angle of George's head was wrong, unnatural. Kneeling beside George, he turned him over. George's eyes were open and glazed, his expression one of total amazement.

'Shit!' Shugs muttered and placed an ear against George's chest to confirm what he already knew to be so.

'Boss, this man's dead,' Shugs said quietly to Ken.

'Eh!' Ken exclaimed, completely taken aback.

Shugs looked at the disbelieving Paddy Troy. 'He must have broken his neck when he hit the deck,' Shugs said.

Panic surged through Ken, but he quickly brought it under control. Mind racing, he gazed about. They were alone on the pavement. Two young boys had appeared on the other side of the street, but they seemed interested in the car more than anything else. He was almost certain they hadn't been there when the rumpus had taken place. A tram clanked by but it was nearly empty. Only one woman on it stared curiously at them.

Paddy Troy had knelt beside Shugs. There was no mistake. George was dead as mutton.

Ken made a decision. He must not be associated with George's death. No matter that it had been a genuine accident. He could just imagine what the police would think. He had been known to George; therefore there had to be a reason for George attacking him – an assumption which would be entirely correct.

Then it would emerge – and how the newspapers would love it! – that he was the boyfriend who had let Vicky down, and whom she had taken the blame for. He would then have to counter with his version of events and, although certain he could wriggle out of her accusations, vindicate himself, it would all be messy messy messy! The last thing he wanted was the public eye focused on him and his union. The last thing!

No. There was only one thing he could do, and that was dissociate himself from this, and fast. Brain working at lightning speed, he began speaking very quickly, the words machine-gunning from his mouth.

Half a minute later Ken and Shugs were en route up the alley and Paddy Troy was heading for the pub to ask if he could use their phone to report an accident to the police.

It had been a huge stroke of luck that, apart from the two young lads and the tram that had gone by, the street had been deserted, Ken thought to himself as he strode along.

As for him and Shugs? They had been a couple of passers-by who had paused briefly, having seen nothing of the incident, then continued on their way, refusing to get involved. So Paddy and Ina would tell the police as their presence was bound to be mentioned when the two young lads were questioned. It would also square with the woman on the tram's testimony, should she either be located or come forward of her own volition.

Ken and Shugs emerged from the alley at its far entrance, where they split up. Going in opposite directions, they both disappeared into the night.

Chris Walker arrived with a bottle of Chinese wine which he presented to Vicky at the door.

'How lovely, and unusual. Thank you,' she said, ushering him through to the kitchen, where Martha was waiting.

Martha solemnly shook hands with Chris. 'Pleased to meet you,' she said, very formally.

'And I'm pleased to meet you,' Chris replied.

Vicky told Chris to sit. Then, getting out a corkscrew, proceeded to open the bottle of wine he'd brought. Chris offered to do it for her, but she replied that she was quite capable.

'I can mend fuses and change plugs too,' she added, which made him laugh.

While she was fetching glasses from the sideboard, he had a quick shufti round. He liked the room, he decided. Like Vicky herself, it was warm and friendly.

'How on earth did you manage to find Chinese wine in Glasgow?' Vicky asked.

He tapped his nose.

'Oh well, stick then,' she retorted, making him laugh again.

'There's a Chinese importer lives in my manor. When he found out I'd developed a taste for Chinese wine while living in Hong Kong, he arranged for me to buy some through his firm whenever I want to. I buy a case at a time.'

She handed him a brimming glass and raised hers in salute. 'Slainthe!'

'Slainthe!' he responded.

It was awful, sweet and nasty, she thought. She wouldn't be able to stomach much of this.

'What do you think?' he asked eagerly.

'It's absolutely delicious,' she lied, not wanting to hurt his feelings.

He beamed at her. 'I always get this particular label, it was Wei Wei's favourite. I'm pleased you like it also.'

Vicky had gone to town on the meal, for points rationing had ended the previous month after being in force for eight years. It was still difficult to believe that you could go into the butcher's or grocer's and purchase whatever you wanted, in whatever quantity you desired.

She served up plump gigot chops, two each for Chris and her, one for Martha, cauliflower drenched in cheese sauce, diced baby carrots smothered in butter, and haricot beans. For sweet it was a milky rice pudding she'd made from an Australian recipe, and prunes. It was a veritable feast compared to what had been available during the war years and after.

All through the meal Chris kept up a steady banter. One of his jokes convulsed Vicky so much that she had to be thumped on the back to stop her choking. Chris and Martha both thumped. He was so easy, Vicky thought. And, like this, so full of joy. Yes, that was the right word, joy. He fairly bubbled with it.

When the meal was finished, Chris said that he would help wash and dry, but Vicky wouldn't hear of that. Martha then piped up to ask coyly if he would read her a story.

Vicky had just begun drying, and Chris was nearing the end of the story – thankfully, Goldilocks was now long in the past – when there was a knock on the outside door.

'Probably my mother,' Vicky said to Chris.

But it was a uniformed constable. Immediately Vicky presumed that he had come for Chris on police business.

'He's in the kitchen. Follow me,' Vicky said and returned to the kitchen, leaving a perplexed constable staring after her.

'I said, he's in here!' Vicky called out. Then to Chris, 'It's one of your lot, looking for you.'

A puzzled Chris rose from his seat. He hadn't mentioned to anyone either at the station or section house where he was going that night. How the dickens had they known where to find him!

The constable, holding his hat, entered the kitchen.

'I'm Sergeant Walker. Mrs Seton says you're looking for me,' Chris said to the constable.

'Sorry, sergeant, there's been a misunderstanding. It's Mrs Seton herself I've come to see,' the constable replied.

Vicky became uneasy. 'Yes?' she asked, frowning.

'I've just been over to your mother's, where I've left a female colleague. It was Mrs Devine who requested I call on you. I'm afraid I bring bad news. There was a street accident, and your father was killed,' the constable said.

Vicky, totally stricken, stared in horror at the constable. 'Killed?' she echoed.

'I'm sorry.'

'How?' she choked.

The constable glanced at Chris, then back at Vicky. 'He died as the result of a broken neck.'

As if she'd been physically hit, Vicky staggered where she stood. She clasped a bewildered Martha tightly to her.

'Oh, Dad!' Vicky whispered, tears sparkling in her eyes, and slipping down her face.

Chris took charge of the situation.

'Death was due to misadventure. The defendant is hereby dismissed,' Lord Smellie-Cameron pronounced.

Vicky bowed her head. It was the verdict she, and everyone else, had expected. Drink, or the excess of it, the curse of the Glasgow working man, she thought bitterly. It had been rare for George to get belligerently drunk, but not unknown. Jekyll had become Hyde, and he'd died as a result.

She glanced over to where the defendant Patrick Troy was being congratulated by his girlfriend, Ina Finlayson. The story was that George, lurching drunk, had bumped into Ina. Troy had told him to mind where he was going. George had thrown a punch at Troy, who, defending himself, had pushed George away. George had then fallen over the rear of Troy's car and broken his neck on impact with the pavement. Such a silly way to die, but fatal nonetheless. She bore no enmity towards Troy. How could she? The fault had been George's.

'You go on out to the car. I'll secure release of the body, and ring the undertaker's to confirm he can now come and collect it,' Chris Walker said softly. He was sitting beside Vicky.

It was six weeks since George's death, but his body had been impounded until the trial was over.

'Thank you,' Vicky replied and, standing up, made her way from the High Court to the Singer.

Anticipating the verdict, Chris had suggested that they have the funeral that coming Saturday, so Neil could manage up from London for it.

She thought of Chris. How marvellous he had been in Neil's absence. He had taken over and organised everything. Neither she nor Mary had had to do anything.

She would never forget this help and support he'd given them. Never.

Twelve

One bitter cold day in October Vicky's office telephone rang. It was Neil. She had been expecting the call.

'Wait a mo',' she said and glanced over to where two helpers were sorting through piles of jumble donated for the Kelvinhaugh Labour Hall's forthcoming jumble sale. Edna Galloway and Mr Porteous were both old-age pensioners.

'Do you think you could go for an early teabreak? It's my husband in London ringing. We've something personal to discuss,' Vicky said.

'We'll away over to the café across the road then. They've some fresh custard creams in,' replied Edna and giggled. She was a great giggler.

'All right, love,' Vicky said to Neil once the two were out of the room.

'It's happened. Sir Stafford Cripps has resigned. It'll be announced in about an hour that Gaitskell is to be the new Chancellor.'

Vicky knew from previous telephone conversations with Neil that Cripps's resignation, in consequence of continuing and worsening ill health, had been expected daily. What neither Neil nor anyone else, with the possible exception of the PM, had known before now was who the new Chancellor would be. Gaitskell had been heavily tipped, but there had been several other strong contenders. Chancellor at forty-four! There would be no stopping Gaitskell now, Vicky thought.

'And what about you?' she asked excitedly.

'Gaitskell has already spoken to me. I'm to soldier on as one of his PPSS,' Neil replied, disappointment in his voice, for he had been hoping for promotion.

Prior to the phone call, Vicky had already worked out

something comforting and consoling to say to him should the hoped-for promotion fail to materialise.

'Well, you know this government can't continue on for much longer with its slender majority. Again and again you've told me yourself that its demise is only a matter of time, and a short time at that. And when the next general election takes place Labour are bound to be returned with a far larger majority. That's when Mr Attlee will make big changes, and when your opportunity will come. If you stop and think about it coldly and rationally, you know I'm right,' she said.

'I suppose that's so.'

'You know it is. So don't start getting depressed. Your opportunity is just round the corner, perhaps only a few months away.'

She *was* right. It was daft of him to be downhearted. The election, and the new Labour government which would be formed afterwards, would sort things out for him.

'You've cheered me up, so thanks. But I'm going to have to run now. There's a division in just a few minutes, and it would be worth my life, and prospects, to miss that,' he replied.

'Remember to keep eating properly. I don't want you getting thin again,' she said. It had taken her the entire summer recess, and lots of mince and tats, to put weight back on him.

'Don't worry. I've learned my lesson. I'm taking care of myself,' he reassured her. 'Now I really must dash.'

She blew a kiss into the receiver. 'Ring again soon,' she said and hung up.

She stared thoughtfully at the telephone. She was not surprised that he had not been promoted. If she had been PM she would have done just as Mr Attlee was doing; rock the boat as little as possible, to minimise the chances of it sinking. If she was surprised it was that Neil hadn't also realised the importance of that. Then again, removed from the hustle and bustle of the House, perhaps she could be more objective about this than him, especially as his objectivity would have been clouded by personal ambition.

She realised that she needed to go to the ladies' room. Then she'd away over to the café and join Edna and Mr Porteous; she liked the sound of those fresh custard creams. But she never made it to the café. On entering the toilet, she heard someone crying. It was Mrs Malarkey, the cleaner.

'Oh, I'm sorry, Mrs Seton. Whatever must you think of me?' Mrs Malarkey said when she looked up and saw Vicky staring at her. She wiped her face with her sleeve and reached for her mop.

Vicky took Mrs Malarkey, a woman in her late forties, by the elbow. 'What's wrong? Can I help?' she asked gently.

Mrs Malarkey shook her head, then burst into a fresh bout of tears.

'There there,' said Vicky and fumbled for her hanky, only to discover that she'd left it behind in the office.

'Now what is all this about?' Vicky persisted.

There was no reply.

'Are you in some sort of trouble? Is that it?'

Mrs Malarkey took off her pinny, scrunched it up and used it to dab at her tear-streaked face.

Vicky stared at Mrs Malarkey in consternation. She was genuinely fond of the woman, a right good soul, and most upset to see her this way.

She saw that her eyes were haunted with worry, while the crows' feet round her eyes had deepened considerably so that they now showed up starkly against her greyish pallor.

'Have you got a fag for yourself? If not I'll run and get you some,' Vicky suggested.

'My handbag's in the cleaning cupboard. I've got a five packet of Pasha in it,' Mrs Malarkey choked.

'I'll get them for you. I'll only be a minute,' Vicky replied, and hurried from the toilet.

She was soon back with the cigarettes and a box of matches. In the meantime Mrs Malarkey had managed to pull herself together a bit. She had stopped crying, but her chest was heaving, and her hands shaking. They shook like billy-o as she lit up.

Mrs Malarkey took a deep draw on her cigarette, then

slowly exhaled. 'That's better,' she muttered, and pushed a stray wisp of straggly hair away from her face. 'I'm sorry I broke down like that. It must have been embarrassing for you.'

'Och, don't be silly. But I still want to know what your problem is. I can't have one of the Hall's employees in such a state. Apart from the fact I want to know as your friend, I have to know because of my position here. Has it to do with your work? Has someone upset you?'

Mrs Malarkey gave a quick shake of the head. 'It's nothing to do with this place. It's . . . something at home.' She took another draw on her cigarette. 'I shouldn't really be smoking when we can't afford it,' she said, as though telling herself off.

Vicky recalled how George had been forced to stop after Agnew's had closed down, and what a trial that had been for him.

'Are you saying you're short of money? Have you got yourself into debt?'

Mrs Malarkey's expression crumpled into one of total wretchedness. 'We're not in debt yet, I've been able to avoid that by paying the rent and penny in the slot out of my wages. We only had a few pounds put by, living week to week as we do, like, and Mr Malarkey was never one to save when he could spend, and that soon went on food . . .' She trailed off, biting her lip.

'Are you saying Mr Malarkey has lost his job?'

'Not . . . not yet. But he will, this Friday.'

Vicky was baffled. Mrs Malarkey wasn't making sense. 'If Mr Malarkey is still in work, why are you having to use your wages to pay the rent?'

'He's in work, but not in work. He's not earning,' Mrs Malarkey mumbled.

Vicky was further confused. 'How can he be in work but not earning?' she persevered.

'I can't say. He told me not to tell anyone.'

Vicky took a deep breath. This was like trying to solve a puzzle where you were denied half the clues. 'Is Mr Malarkey at work now?' she asked.

'No, he's at home.'

'Right then. You're going to take me to him and he can explain all this to me himself.'

'I can't do that!' Mrs Malarkey exclaimed in alarm.

'Yes, you can, and will. I intend to get the pair of you out, if I possibly can, of whatever mess it is you've got yourselves into.' Vicky paused, then switched to a brighter tone. 'Now, if you've gone through your savings, when did you last have a square meal? And the truth mind!'

Mrs Malarkey dropped her gaze. 'Twelve days ago. We've been living off bread and dripping since,' she said quietly.

'Twelve days ago!'

When Mrs Malarkey glanced up again, her expression tore at Vicky's heartstrings. 'The rent was more important than food, you see. If we hadn't paid that, then the factor would soon have had us out in the street. He's a terrible hard man our factor. Fall behind and before you know where you are you're evicted.'

'But what about the neighbours. Haven't they helped?'

'They don't know we haven't been eating properly. We've kept that to ourselves. Mr Malarkey is an awfy proud man, you must understand, no' the sort to go cap in hand to anyone.'

'And that includes relatives I suppose?' Vicky said drily.

'Aye,' Mrs Malarkey whispered.

Vicky hadn't made any inquiries about children because she knew that the couple were childless. 'We'll get your coat, then mine,' Vicky said, steering Mrs Malarkey towards the door.

Vicky's curiosity was well aroused. In work but not in work, and not earning. It was a real teaser.

En route to the Malarkeys' she stopped off at the chippie and bought fish suppers for them. Mrs Malarkey tried to stop her, but she was insistent. Mrs Malarkey devoured hers in the street with a ferocity Vicky hadn't seen since the bad old days of the Depression.

'I won't take charity!' Mr Malarkey thundered, glowering at Vicky and the fish supper she was holding out to him.

Vicky was shocked by Mr Malarkey's appearance. Both his eyes had been blacked – each now a riot of colour, thanks to the healing process which was under way – and his nose was broken. Swathes of bandages were visible beneath his open shirt neck.

'It's not charity. It's . . . well, I've been starving hungry myself and know what it's like,' Vicky replied gently.

Mr Malarkey softened a little on hearing that.

'Oh, come on man, get stuck in. If you feel you have to, then you can pay me back some time,' Vicky urged.

Still Mr Malarkey hesitated, clinging to his pride.

'I'll put it on a plate for you,' Mrs Malarkey said to her husband, and took the succulent-smelling newspaper-wrapped bundle from Vicky.

Mr Malarkey stared at the steaming meal that his wife placed on his lap. Slowly, and with tremendous dignity, in complete contrast to the way Mrs Malarkey had wolfed hers down, he began to eat.

When he was finished, Mrs Malarkey offered him one of the two remaining cigarettes in her packet. 'There's nothing like a good bit of cod,' he said gruffly, and lit up.

'I found Mrs Malarkey in the Hall toilet. She was in floods of tears,' Vicky said to him.

Mr Malarkey looked at his wife, his expression grim.

'She won't tell me why you're apparently employed, yet not at work, and not earning. Are you in difficulty with your work because of an accident? Don't think me rude, but you look in a right old state,' Vicky said.

Mr Malarkey gave a wry, bitter, laugh. The laugh changed to a grimace of pain, causing him to clutch at his chest.

'Cracked ribs?' Vicky queried.

'Broken. Four of them,' he replied.

'How did that happen?'

Mr Malarkey glanced again at his wife, but did not reply.

The silence in the room lengthened and lengthened. 'I've heard Mrs Malarkey speak about you many times. I'd have never believed you to be a coward,' Vicky said eventually.

'I'm no' that!'

'You're *scared* to tell me what this is all about, aren't you? What's that if not being cowardly?'

Mr Malarkey opened his mouth. Unable to think of a suitable reply he snapped it shut again. He stared hard into the empty grate.

'I could arrange a loan for you until you start earning again,' Vicky suggested.

'Lex?' Mrs Malarkey said, hope creeping into her face.

Mr Malarkey turned to Vicky. 'I've already tried to get a loan, but nobody would gie me one. They all wanted what they cry collateral, which I don't have.'

'Being an MP's wife has its advantages; there are ways and means.' Vicky smiled.

Mr Malarkey studied her. 'I need two hundred pounds,' he stated bluntly.

'Two hundred pounds!' Vicky exclaimed, shocked a second time since entering the Malarkey home. No wonder he had been asked for collateral.

'Two hundred pounds, by Friday. After that it's too late. After that I'm out of work with no hope whatever of finding another job, for at fifty-three I'm too damned old for anyone else to take me on.' Mr Malarkey's voice was tight and crackling with emotion.

Vicky looked straight into his tortured eyes. 'You tell me your story from beginning to end and then I'll tell you whether or not I can get you a loan of this two hundred pounds you appear to so desperately need.'

'Lex. Please?' Mrs Malarkey said.

Several seconds ticked by. The woman started to cry again, the hot tears spilling down her cheeks.

'If I do tell you what this is all about, will it be in the strictest confidence? For if it gets out that I've yapped, I'll pay for it,' Mr Malarkey said to Vicky.

'You have my word.'

He ground out the remains of his cigarette in an ashtray on the hearth. 'I'm a dockie, Mrs Seton, have been man and boy. It's all I know. Well, over the past few years, I've been getting more and more disturbed by the way my union keeps putting in higher and higher demands to the employers. I mean, it's getting ridiculous. Loading and unloading fees have gone right through the roof. And although it's marvellous to earn a bloody good wage, the whole thing could be in the long run, as I see it, a case of cutting off your nose to spite your face.'

A dockie! Vicky hadn't known that. For some reason she had thought him to be a labourer. She listened intently as Mr Malarkey continued.

'I've said my piece at a number of union meetings, explained how I was worried that, if we continued to make such high demands, it could get to the stage where the employers would say, sod you!, and move their business to another port where they'd get a far better deal. And if that happened, Clydeside dockies would go from being excellently paid, to on the 'Broo, unemployed.

'Although some of the men were interested, the shop stewards and other officials weren't. Then at the meeting before last I was told not to bring the subject up again, to put a sock in it.

'Well, I didn't. I did argue the point yet again at the last meeting – and paid the penalty for not heeding their warning.

'I was walking home with several pals, like, when suddenly Paddy Troy and some shop stewards appeared beside us . . .'

'Who?' Vicky broke in, frowning.

'Paddy Troy. He's a right brute of an Irishman who's Blacklaws's bodyguard. Blacklaws is the president of the union,' Mr Malarkey explained.

Paddy Troy . . . Patrick Troy? A Patrick Troy had been involved in her father's death. Troy, like Malarkey, was an uncommon name in Glasgow, even though the city did boast a large population of Irish and Irish descent. As Irish Patricks were often called Paddy, could it be that they were one and the same man? A man who worked for Ken? She went cold at that thought.

'Go on, please,' she said to Mr Malarkey, feeling both

electrified and confused at the possibilities opened up by this new dimension.

Mr Malarkey shrugged. 'I'd heard whispers, rumours, but I'd always taken them with a pinch of salt. That night I learned otherwise.

'My pals were told to hop it. Troy and the shop stewards wanted a confidential word with me. Reluctantly my pals went, for you don't argue with Troy. When they were gone, Troy told me I was a trouble-maker and that the union had no time for those. He then, all by himself, proceeded to beat the living daylights out of me. When he'd finished he bent over me – I think he'd left me conscious deliberately – and said that, if I ever mentioned this to anybody, he'd look me up again and break both my legs in several places.'

Mr Malarkey paused for breath.

'That's not the worst of it, not by a long chalk,' his wife said shrilly.

Mr Malarkey continued, 'I got myself home here, and the doctor had been sent for but not yet arrived, when there was a knock on the door. It was my own shop steward with a hand-delivered letter from the union. The letter said I had been fined two hundred pounds for dangerous work practices – a completely trumped-up charge, I assure you – which had to be paid four weeks from that Friday. In the meantime I was temporarily suspended from work, and if the fine wasn't paid by the expiry date I'd lose my union membership, and with that of course my job, as the docks are a closed shop.'

Vicky was appalled by the terrible tale. The two hundred pounds' fine was clearly a device to get rid of Mr Malarkey, for what ordinary working man, even a well-paid one, could lay his hands on that sum in such a relatively short time?

'Does this sort of thing go on a lot in the union?' Vicky asked.

'Well, let me put it this way. I knew the union was rotten, but I never dreamed it was so rotten. These are out and out Nazi tactics,' Mr Malarkey replied.

He was dead right, Vicky thought. Ken must know this

was going on in his union, and it had to be going on with his blessing. What had he become!

'It's the ones coming after us that I worry about most. If the Clydeside docks do eventually close because of greed, what happens to them? Families who for generations have worked these docks will have to go elsewhere, if their menfolk are lucky enough to find employment, that is. As for the area itself, if people move out in large numbers, and those that are left are idle, it won't take long for the place to run down, become a partially inhabited ghost town . . . But the shop stewards and other union officials I've been telling you about won't have that; they think the goose will go on laying bigger and bigger golden eggs for ever.'

Today was Wednesday. Forty-eight hours in which to raise the money, Vicky thought.

'You'll have your two hundred pounds, I promise you,' she said.

'Oh, lass!' exclaimed Mrs Malarkey softly, and bit into a thumb.

Mr Malarkey had gone very still. He stared at Vicky, his gaze penetrating. 'You really mean that?'

'I really mean that. I'll have it here on time, you can rely on it,' she answered levelly.

Mr Malarkey bowed his head, not wanting Vicky to see the look on his face. 'Thank you, Mrs Seton.'

'Now tell me all you know about this Paddy Troy. I have personal reasons for asking,' she said.

Before Vicky left it was agreed that, on resuming work, Mr Malarkey would repay the loan which Vicky would arrange on a weekly basis. He gave her his unsolicited word of honour that he would never default by so much as a single week.

Vicky was so dog tired that she had asked Chris to drive. They were returning from Camlachie, where she had given a speech to the local Women's Guild. The speech had gone down well and had been enthusiastically applauded. Within a few minutes of standing up she'd had them eating out the palm of her hand.

She brought her mind back to the story Mr Malarkey had told her the previous day. She had been waiting for the right moment to speak to Chris about it.

'Will you do me a favour?' she asked.

Chris changed gear. 'If I can,' he replied, and gave her a quick sideways smile.

He was a godsend, she thought. More and more he was acting as a sort of personal manager to her: taking her here and there, organising this and that, generally making life easier for her.

'What I'm about to tell you was told to me in strictest confidence, so that strict confidence now applies to you. This stays between the pair of us, all right?'

Chris nodded.

She repeated Mr Malarkey's story while Chris listened in brooding silence.

'So what I'd like you to do is find out if this Paddy Troy and our Patrick Troy are one and the same. And if they are, I'd like you to discover his police history. For, if they are the same man, that just might put a different complexion on what supposedly happened to my dad.'

'You think he might have lied in court?' Chris asked.

'Well, you see, there's more to it than I've so far explained. Paddy Troy's boss, whom he's bodyguard to, according to Mr Malarkey, is an old friend of mine and Neil's . . . Did you know I'd been in borstal and prison?'

Chris gave Vicky another sideways glance, but this time he was not smiling. 'Tina mentioned once that you and she had been in borstal together. That was all though, she didn't elaborate.'

'Didn't that make you curious?' she asked, curious herself that he apparently hadn't been so.

'If Tina had wanted to tell me about her being in borstal, the full facts and details, that is, she would have done. She never has, nor has Sammy. So as far as I'm concerned, that remains their business and it would be rude of me to probe. Same applies to you. If you want to tell me the whys and wherefores, fine. But I'd never ask.'

She understood now. To take such a line was not only

thoughtful and considerate, it showed sensitivity, a quality she already associated with him.

'I was convicted of theft and sent down for three years. But I wasn't the thief. I was covering for the real thief, whom I was in love with at the time. He was my boyfriend, Ken Blacklaws, who's now president of the Clyde Dockworkers' Union, and Paddy Troy's boss.'

Digesting that, Chris took a handful of seconds before replying. 'You must have loved him very much to do that?'

'I was head over heels. The sun rose and set on him.'

'And now?'

'Now I'm a happily married woman,' she answered.

He let it go at that. 'So what you're wondering is: if Paddy and Patrick Troy are one and the same, was this Blacklaws somehow involved? I take it your dad wouldn't have known Troy, or the Finlayson female?'

'That's exactly what's going through my mind. For if Paddy and Patrick are the same person, the whole thing becomes far too coincidental don't you agree?'

'I do,' Chris replied grimly.

Vicky was suddenly aware of Chris's maleness and potency. She had been vaguely aware of it on previous occasions, but nowhere near as strongly as she was now. She experienced a slithering sensation in her stomach, while her muscles there began to quiver. There was a warmness and a tingle where there hadn't been for years. She looked at Chris. He was an attractive man, very attractive. A shiver ran down her spine.

'Are you cold?'

'No, just someone walking over my grave, that's all.'

His eyes flicked sideways, then returned to the road again. 'You asked me to do something for you. Now will you do something for me?'

'Of course.'

'I think you're overdoing it, doing far too much. You've got your full-time job as Neil and Sandy Millar's secretary, plus the work you do for the Kelvinhaugh Labour Hall and Bridgeton Labour Hall. And, with Neil away nearly all the time, you've been taking his surgeries and fulfilling his speaking engagements, on top of which there are your own speaking engagements, whose number are far greater than those you do for Neil. As if all this wasn't enough, you have a home and daughter to look after. My own opinion is that you should ease off somewhere before you collapse from total exhaustion or, worse still, have a nervous breakdown.'

She was touched by his concern and amused by the rather schoolmasterish way in which he had delivered his wigging. She could just imagine him talking to erring constables like that.

'It's not quite as bad as you think, Chris. I hardly do a hand's turn round the house any more. My mother Mary does virtually everything for me, shopping, cleaning, etc. Nor do I mind her doing it, for with my father gone it helps fill the time for her. It's the same with her looking after Martha, which she does so often; it's another filler for her, and one which she loves, as she absolutely dotes on Martha, and Martha on her.'

'Be that as it may, you're still doing far too much. Why don't you cut back on the speaking engagements a bit? That would be a help.'

She had an almost overwhelming desire to reach out and touch him. His personal odour was heavy and pungent in her nostrils and made that tingle even stronger.

'I'll see,' she replied, having no intention of cutting back at all. She decided to change the subject. 'I want to call in at the Malarkeys' before I go home. I have his money on me.'

Chris reacted in alarm. 'You mean you've been carrying that amount on you all evening!'

She had to laugh at his outraged expression. 'It was perfectly safe.' Then teasingly, and tauntingly, 'After all, I had a big strong polisman to guard me.'

Chris coloured in the darkness.

Vicky laughed again. It was a good-humoured laugh, but there was a trace of mockery in it. Or perhaps it wasn't mockery. Perhaps it was something else.

As the Singer continued to sigh through the night, Vicky fell asleep to dream about her and Chris, about what Chris could do which Neil couldn't.

•

The skeleton of the new building was now complete. Ken stood on one of its topmost girders staring out over the Broomielaw and Glasgow's south side, the latter a legion of tenements belching black smoke into a grey, lowering sky.

It was a terrific feeling being so high up and in such precarious surroundings, Ken thought. The ground and river below seemed a terrifying distance away. Another eight to ten months and the building would be ready for the CDU to move in. What a red-letter day that would be!

Ken had had Ina choose the carpets, furniture and decorations. For his own office he had indulged himself by buying two American pictures of Western scenes in the nineteenth century, one by an artist called Lou Megaree, the other by E. Irving Couse. The subject of the former was of a group of cowboys, of the latter several plains Indians stalking game.

A gust of wind caused him to clutch at the upright girder at the junction where he was standing.

'All right?' inquired the foreman who had brought him up.

Nodding, he gazed out over Clydeside, seeing all the way down to Yorkhill Quay where the river bent and was lost to view. His kingdom, *his*!

His thoughts turned to the port of Leith, making him frown, and a thundercloud settle on his face. Of the two dock unions there had been in Leith, the larger had now fallen and was merged with the CDU. The smaller was being far more resistant, and that resistance was now proving damned annoying. There was nothing else for it; he would have to dispatch Paddy through there. If the union had a weakness, it was its limited financial reserves. That was the Achilles heel he'd work on, through Paddy Troy.

First of all there must be a series of disruptions, all designed to slow down work and invoke the time-penalty clauses inbuilt in the contracts that union still worked under. (Honest to God, if nothing else, that showed how much they needed him and the CDU. Still accepting time-penalty clauses, it was unbelievable! Not to mention downright stupid.)

These disruptions would consist of 'accidents', both to personnel and machinery, acts of sabotage such as fires, and of course the old favourite, strikes, which Paddy Troy would organise within the union ranks by employing 'friendly persuasion'. As the disruptions got under way, he would think of other means and ploys to bleed the union of its cash until, in the end, the union would be forced either to merge or expire.

Vicky was on the point of finishing Neil's bi-weekly surgery when Chris turned up. 'Let's go for a drink, I've got some information for you,' he said to her when the last constituent had left.

They found a quiet pub and settled themselves with their drinks in a secluded corner.

'Your Patrick Troy and Blacklaws's Paddy Troy are the same man,' Chris announced.

It was as if a sharp knife had been thrust into Vicky's chest and twisted. 'I see,' she said quietly. The words came out as a hiss.

'I ran a check on him and drew a blank. Although he was in our records because of your father's death, he has no "previous" in this country. So I asked our Irish colleagues what they knew of him, and that turned out to be quite a history. They've done him for larceny, assault, assault causing GBH, and finally, but not least, several times for procuring. In Dublin he's known as what we would call a hard man, a dyed-in-the-wool villain.'

Vicky's eyes narrowed to slits. 'Ken had to be somehow involved in my father's death. It just doesn't make sense otherwise.'

'I also spoke to the officers who attended the scene of your father's death. According to them, there was absolutely nothing to arouse their suspicions that Troy was telling anything other than the truth. The drawback was of course there were no witnesses, but then you know that from the trial.'

'So basically it boils down to us taking Troy and the Finlayson woman's word that what they say happened actually did.'

Chris nodded. 'Just as it was at the trial.'

'But then we didn't know that Troy worked for Ken, or that he was a villain.'

Vicky brooded on this information for a few moments. As far as she was concerned the whole thing stank to high heaven. 'And the police officers who attended the scene of my father's death say that, in the circumstances, there was nothing unusual? Nothing at all?'

Chris shook his head. 'Nothing other than the car Troy was driving, which they all remembered. A huge American job, the size of a tank, one of them described it as.'

The knifelike pain was back, stabbing and twisting in Vicky's chest. 'Was it a Cadillac by any chance?' she asked slowly.

Chris's whisky stopped halfway to his mouth. 'Yes, it was. Why, is that significant?'

'Just that Ken owns a Cadillac – the only one in Scotland, he once boasted to me.'

Seconds ticked by during which Vicky and Chris thought about that.

'But Troy works for Blacklaws, so there are all sorts of reasons why he might have been driving it at the time,' Chris said.

'Maybe so. But in court, by assumption I now realise, we were led to believe that the car belonged to Troy. Ken's name was never mentioned, neither as car owner, or Troy's employer.'

'I can certainly find out who the car *does* belong to; that'll be a matter of record,' Chris suggested.

'You're thinking Ken might have sold or even given the Cadillac to Troy?'

Chris shrugged. 'It's possible.'

More seconds ticked by. 'If Ken is still the owner, then he was there that day, and Troy is covering for him, just as I covered for him all those years ago,' Vicky said.

They stared hard at one another, each trying to imagine what had really happened on that fateful day.

Chris rang Vicky at her office next morning just after coffee break. 'The Cadillac doesn't belong personally to Blacklaws, or to Troy; it belongs to the Clyde Dockworkers' Union. Therefore, technically, it can be argued that the car belongs to both of them, just as it belongs to every member of the union. I also checked the insurance policy, but that was no use, as the union have a blanket policy covering all their cars, of which there are a number. Troy is a named driver on that policy, as is Blacklaws, and others,' Chris told her.

They chatted for a few minutes, then said goodbye.

Vicky stared thoughtfully at the phone. It didn't matter that Troy was off the hook over the ownership of the car; she knew damned well that he had lied in court.

An ashen Ina Finlayson knocked, and entered Ken's office. 'It's Mrs Seton, the daughter of that Devine man who died, here to see you,' she blurted out. She hadn't been aware that Ken and Vicky knew one another. Ken had kept stum about that.

A heavy lunch had made Ken feel drowsy. When he heard of Vicky's arrival, the drowsiness abruptly left him. 'You'd better let her in.'

'Why can she be here?' Ina whispered, as though Vicky might have been able to overhear, although there were two doors and a passageway separating her from them.

'Maybe she's paying us a visit for old times' sake. She used to work here once.' Ken smiled.

Ina gave him a strange look and waited for him to elaborate. When he didn't, she left the room to fetch Vicky.

Ken stood in front of his desk and straightened his tie. It might have nothing whatever to do with George Devine's death, he told himself. Then he realised that Vicky now knew Ina was a CDU employee – and Ina had been in court as Paddy Troy's supposed girlfriend, and she had been there when George died.

'Fuck!' he swore.

He was smiling again when Ina ushered Vicky in. 'It's good to see you again,' he said, approaching Vicky with an extended hand.

Vicky ignored the hand. 'So Miss Finlayson is your secretary. How extremely interesting.'

Ken flinched.

'And Troy works for you as well.'

Ken regained his composure. 'Right on both counts,' he replied casually, and headed for the drinks cabinet. 'Dram?' he asked.

'No, thank you,' she replied coldly.

He poured himself a hefty one, noting as he did so that his palms were sweating.

'A very pretty female Miss Finlayson. I never really took that in while we were in court. But I can see now she is; quite a stunner in fact.'

'I suppose she is,' Ken replied vaguely, and added some bottled spring water to his whisky.

Vicky glanced over at the door beyond which was the small apartment where she and Ken had so often made love. Martha had been conceived in there. Their daughter, whom Ken didn't know was his, nor would he ever know.

'What do you think of this?' Ken said, going over to a table adjacent to his desk and indicating a scale model of his new building.

'I'm having it built down at the Broomielaw. It's the new union premises to replace this dump. Something eh?' His voice oozed pride.

'How often has Miss Finlayson been through there?' Vicky asked, pointing at the apartment door. There was a flicker in Ken's eyes, which was quickly gone. But it was enough; it told her that she was right.

'Miss Finlayson is Paddy Troy's girl,' Ken answered levelly.

'Come off it! Are you seriously asking me to believe that you could have such a gorgeous female as a secretary and not have her as your mistress, that you'd let one of your minions have the privilege? No, no. She's yours, not Troy's.'

Ken sipped his dram, studying Vicky over the rim of his glass.

'What's all this in aid of? Why are you here?' he demanded, a vein of harshness creeping into his voice.

Vicky went over to stare at the model. It was an attractive building, she thought, vibrant, somehow full of energy.

'Do you know what I think really happened the day my father died?' she said softly.

Ken gave no response.

'I accept he could have been lurching drunk – the post mortem proved he had an extremely high level of alcohol in his blood when he died. But if that's true, it's about the only truth in Troy and Miss Finlayson's story.'

Ken, lips thinned, stayed silent.

Vicky turned to fix him with her gaze. Holding his eyes, she continued, 'My father came out that pub and bumped into you, you with *your* ladyfriend, I now realise. I've no idea why you were in that area, probably on union business, but it doesn't really matter. All that does matter is that you were there.

'My father recognised you, approached you and, from a combination of alcohol and emotion, began abusing you. A fight then developed, during which either Troy or yourself killed my father.'

She paused, noting that he had gone pale just as the Finlayson female had done a few minutes earlier when they had come face to face. 'Never slow off the mark, you realised there weren't any witnesses, quickly concocted the story Troy and Miss Finlayson gave to the police, and fled, leaving Troy and Miss Finlayson to report as an accident what in reality had been murder.'

There was now a jagged bitterness in her voice and a shrill note of potential hysteria.

'So which one of you killed my dad, you or your hired thug?' she demanded.

Ken was much more shaken by her accusation than he appeared. 'Neither Paddy nor I killed him. Nor Shugs my chauffeur, who was also present,' he replied, having decided that the best thing he could do now was tell her the truth in the hope that that would calm things down again and stop her going to the police. Then a horrible thought hit him. 'You haven't already been to the police with this, have you?' he queried, his composure slipping.

'And if I have?'

He ran a hand over his damp forehead. The small of his back had also begun to sweat. 'It's as I say, I swear. We didn't kill him. He broke his neck, just as Paddy Troy described in court.'

In her mind Vicky was seeing her father, remembering him from all sorts of occasions during her childhood, and later. 'Liar!' she spat.

'I ran because I had to. I knew your dad. Once the police had established that, which they were bound to have done, they would have suspected that he had a motive for attacking me as he did . . . When I say I had to run, let me rephrase that. It was prudent of me to do so, for your and Neil's sake as well as my own.'

'How do you make that out?'

'Do you remember that day I took you for a run in my Caddy? I explained to you then what I would do if you named me as a thief, and it's what I'll do still if you have gone to the police now. Any shit you throw will boomerang back to you and Neil, I promise.

'As for me? I can well do without any such publicity, even when I will be vindicated.'

Ken stared at Vicky. Now he'd had time to think it through, he was certain that she hadn't been to the police yet. She wouldn't be here like this if she had; the police would have been with her or – more probably, here without her – if she had.

'Now this is what actually happened that day,' he said, and related in detail all that had occurred.

Vicky listed in stony silence. When he finished, she crossed to the window and stared out. She believed him. His account of the tragic affair had the distinctive ring of truth about it.

She thought of Ken and all the misery and pain he'd brought into her life: Duncliffe, Miss Ganch, the Black Room, Duke Street prison, and now, because of her past association with him, the death of her father. On the one hand, it was true to say that he hadn't killed George, that George had died as the result of an accident. But, on the other, was it not also fair to say that he had killed George by what he'd done to her, just as surely as if he'd broken George's neck himself? If Ken hadn't treated her the way he had, George would never have gone for him, and George would still be alive. So the fault was his, if not by direct action, then by past deed.

It is said that there is a fine dividing line between love and hate. Having reached the conclusion she had, Vicky passed over that divide. The great love and passion she'd once felt for Ken was now transformed into a hatred of equal intensity.

'You haven't been to the police yet have you?' Ken said.

'No,' she answered, her voice cold and distant.

He came to her and would have touched her, but she shrank away from him. 'It's best to let sleeping dogs lie, Vicky, for all concerned.'

'I'll have that drink now,' she replied.

She watched him as he poured the whisky and added spring water.

'I really am sorry for what happened,' he said, handing her the dram.

She threw the whisky and water straight into his face.

Eyes brimming with tears, she marched from his office, past a startled Ina Finlayson, and on out of the building.

Thirteen

One night during the following April, 1951, Vicky had said goodnight to Martha and was filling the kettle with the intention of making herself a cup of coffee, when the phone rang. They had had the phone, the only one in Parr Street, installed nearly a year now. It was Neil telephoning from his flat in Petty France.

'Have you heard the news?' he asked.

'What news?'

'Bevan, Harold Wilson and John Freeman have all resigned because Gaitskell put charges upon the supply of spectacles and dentures in his budget.'

Aneurin Bevan was Minister of Labour, Harold Wilson President of the Board of Trade, and John Freeman Parliamentary Secretary to the Ministry of Supply.

'That's a big loss to the government,' Vicky replied, thinking that Bevan was a particular loss. She was a great admirer of his.

As for the spectacles and dentures charges, Vicky knew that it was the heavy costs of the rearmament programme necessitated by the Korean War which had forced Gaitskell to levy them. Or, to put it another way, depending upon your point of view, the war was his excuse for doing so.

'There's something else,' Neil went on. He paused, then added, 'I agree with the stance these men have taken, and because of that have resigned my post as Gaitskell's PPS.'

Vicky was immediately alarmed. 'I'm not certain that was the right step to take,' she said slowly.

'I am. A man has to stand by his beliefs and principles. He isn't a man if he doesn't.'

Vicky sighed. 'It's all very well for established, and major figures within the party to make these gestures, but you're neither yet. So don't you think it was somewhat precipitate of you?'

'No, I don't. If anything, it could be the making of me.'

'What you mean is, it sets you clearly within the left's camp.'

'But I *am* of the left,' he replied tartly.

'Maybe so, but that doesn't mean you have to let yourself be so clearly identified with them. For, you mustn't forget, the moderates are the majority within the party.'

On the other end of the telephone Neil was scowling. There were times when Vicky's arguments irritated him, and this was one of them. As far as he was concerned, the issue was clear cut and, by his lights, he had done the right thing.

'Well, I tendered my resignation and Gaitskell accepted it. Even if I wanted to, which I don't, I can't undo that now,' he said.

'You might have talked it over with me first,' she chided.

'I don't have to ask your permission. I wear the trousers in our family,' he retorted. Then, realising what he had said, and his own sexual inadequacies, his face flamed scarlet. 'You know what I mean,' he added lamely.

It was a political error on his part, Vicky was convinced of that. A luxury which a man of ambition who was still in a lowly position couldn't afford. 'I didn't say you had to ask my permission. I just said you might have talked it over with me first.'

There was silence between them. The line crackled with static.

'You think I've made a mistake, don't you?' he said quietly.

'Yes, I do.'

They spoke no further on the subject.

'The results for Bury St Edmunds are . . .' the announcer intoned.

Vicky, Neil, Chris Walker and Mona Bryce, Chris's girlfriend, leaned closer to the wireless set. It was the early morning of 26 October 1951, the day after the general election.

Neil had been re-elected as Member for Glasgow Kelvinhaugh a little before one a.m., again with an increased majority, mainly at the expense of the Liberals. There had been drinks at the Labour Hall after his re-election had been confirmed, then it had been back to Parr Street to await the rest of the results.

So far, those results had not been good for the Labour Party; vital seats had been slipping away to the Conservatives. But all was not yet lost, not by a long chalk.

'W. T. Aitken, Conservative: twenty-four thousand, six hundred and seventy-nine. N. Stanley, Labour: twenty thousand, six hundred and ninety. There is no Liberal candidate . . .'

The rest of what the announcer had to say was drowned out by groans and a loud expletive from Mona Bryce.

'Another Tory win,' Neil said despondently.

'But the last two were Labour,' Chris reminded him.

'True, except that they were safe seats. It would have been unthinkable for us to have lost either.'

Mona yawned and glanced at her watch. It was 3.52 a.m., and there were still quite a number of results to come through. 'I could murder a cup of tea,' she said.

It annoyed Vicky that Mona had felt that she had to ask. She had been just about to stick the kettle on anyway.

'Perhaps you'd care to make a pot if I show you where everything is?' she smiled at Mona. She didn't care for Mona, thinking her a bumptious little bitch. She could not think what Chris saw in her.

'Certainly,' Mona replied, returning Vicky's smile, and rose to smooth down the shantung-silk dress she was wearing. She had a beautiful figure and was well aware of the fact. She always tried to show it off to best advantage.

It might be a beautiful figure, Vicky thought, but the face left a lot to be desired. It was the sort of face that would have gone down well with a bag of chips.

Mona, still smiling, contrived to touch Chris's shoulder as she passed him. She was always touching him, Vicky thought. In fact she couldn't keep her hands off him. Not for the first time she wondered if Chris and Mona were sleeping together; it always made her angry to think they might be. Not that it was any of her business.

'And now the results for Aberdeen East . . .' the announcer said.

Vicky stopped and turned, as did Mona. In unison, Neil and Chris leaned closer to the set.

'Ronald Arthur Abercrombie Hughes, Conservative: twenty thousand eight hundred and twenty. Hector McQuarrie, Labour: twenty thousand and thirty nine. Philip Alan Watson, Liberal: four thousand nine hundred and sixty-three. Thomas Troon Gallacher, Independent: one thousand five hundred and forty-four. Ronald Arthur Abercrombie Hughes is therefore . . .'

'Buggeration!' Neil exclaimed, and smashed a fist into an open palm. It was another Tory win, and *gain*.

Neil glanced over at Vicky and their eyes locked. 'If we do hang on, it's not going to be with the larger mandate that's so essential,' he said.

For the first time Vicky started to consider the dismaying prospect of Labour losing the election. 'I've got some Battenberg; we'll have that with the tea,' she told Mona, and led Mona over to the cupboard where the cake and caddy were kept.

Neil sat staring gloomily into the fireplace where, in complete contrast to his mood and expression, a cheery fire was blazing. He and Vicky had recently returned from a restaurant where he'd taken her for a celebratory meal. It was 24 March 1953, Vicky's thirty-fourth birthday. Neil had managed to get paired and come north to spend a few days with her. He had arrived in late that afternoon.

Since the October 1951 election, which the Conservatives had won with an overall majority of seventeen, it had been possible for him to come home more often than previously. Not that there was a tremendous amount for him to do when he did get up; Vicky had the constituency business well under control. The only important thing he had to do was put his face about and shake a number of hands. The rest had become Vicky's domain.

Vicky came into the kitchen, having been through to their bedroom to change. She was wearing a cotton, floral, Japanese wrap that was his birthday present to her. The label on the inside said it came from Harrod's.

'All right, you can forget it's my birthday now. Out with whatever's been bothering you since you arrived,' she said.

Neil roused himself and sniffed. 'Since we went into opposition, I feel I've become bogged down, that I'm failing to make headway. If only . . . Well, if only I could find some way of distinguishing myself, of making myself stand out from the herd, most of whom are also trying to make a name for themselves, their eyes fixed firmly on the next Labour government, which surely must be formed after the next election.'

'What about your articles for the *New Statesman*? Aren't they helping?'

'I thought that appearing in print alongside such luminaries as Foot, Driberg, Crossman, etc., would do the trick. But, sadly, it hasn't. It's a firecracker where I need a stick of dynamite.'

Vicky laughed. 'Well put. A stick of dynamite indeed!' She refrained from saying that his position would have been a lot better if he'd remained as Gaitskell's PPS. It would only have annoyed him for her to have done so.

Neil made a fist and shook it in front of him. 'There's so much I could do in, and for, Glasgow if only I had access to power. Power to use and trade,' he declared.

'The housing schemes are going ahead.'

'They're a start, but only that.' He gave a weary sigh and sank back into his chair.

'You look dead beat,' she said sympathetically.

'I've had a lot on of late, and that train journey always takes it out of me. Especially when the train's jam-packed, as it was this time.'

She went over to kneel beside him. 'Away through and get your head down. I'll be in shortly.'

'Do you want me to . . .'

She shook her head, knowing that he was referring to the one-sided lovemaking they indulged in. 'No. Tomorrow night maybe,' she whispered.

He caressed her cheek. 'I don't know what I'd do without you and Martha. The pair of you are the sun and moon to me.'

'She loves you too. And is very proud of you and your work.'

'And what about you, Vicky?'

'I'm proud of you too.'

He smiled inwardly. She had answered only half of his question. She had never told him she loved him, never had, not once. But still he was content. He might not have her love, but he did have her, and that was the next best thing. Taking her face in his hands, he bent down and kissed her, lingering over the kiss, savouring the sweetness of her mouth and her delicious smell.

'Now, away ben, I won't be long,' she said, rising to her feet and drawing him to his. 'Start on my side, warm it up for me.' She smiled.

He pecked her on the cheek.

When he was gone, she sat where he'd been sitting and gazed into the fire's flickering, dancing depths. If only Neil *could* find a way of distinguishing himself from the other Labour backbench hopefuls! she thought. Something that would draw attention, praise and respect. He was right about the stick of dynamite.

Lost in thought, Vicky remained transfixed by the fire.

As the mantelpiece clock chimed midnight the idea came to her. It made her go cold all over and imagine that she could see her father's face in the glowing embers of the now dying fire.

Next morning during breakfast Vicky bided her patience while Neil chatted to Martha about her forthcoming qualifying exam, or 'quali' as it was generally called. The results of this exam would determine whether she went to junior or secondary school, and in the case of the latter which grade of class she would be assigned to. They were all hoping that she would achieve an S1 pass, the highest. That would put her into senior secondary and class 1A, the top class.

Vicky waited till Neil returned to the kitchen from seeing Martha off to school at the outside door, as he always did when at home, then said. 'I think I might have the answer, that stick of dynamite you were talking about last night.'

Neil, about to pick up the newspaper, stopped, turned to her and raised an eyebrow.

'Do you remember that business with the Malarkeys, and the loan I raised for Mr Malarkey to enable him pay off his union fine?'

'I mind it fine.'

'And that Chris Walker helped me establish that Patrick Troy and Paddy Troy were one and the same – Troy being Ken Blacklaws's bodyguard, who'd given poor Mr Malarkey such a beating?'

'Aye,' said Neil, nodding. Vicky had written to him about that, spoken about it on the telephone and, as he recalled, brought it up again the next time he'd come home.

'Well, I believe Ken could be your stick of dynamite.'

Neil frowned. 'I don't understand?'

'What I've never told you is, because of Troy's involvement in my father's death, and also, I suppose, because I was curious about Ken and the sort of person it appeared he'd become, I made several inquiries into CDU matters. Oh, nothing extensive, but enough to be a real eye-opener. The union is rotten through and through and, as Mr Malarkey claimed, employing Nazi tactics to achieve its ends. And when I say union I mean Ken, for he is the union.'

'I still don't understand what you're driving at? How could Ken be my stick of dynamite?'

'We know for fact that the union uses intimidation and violence, Mr Malarkey proved that. I also heard of sabotage, arson, blackmail, and murder even.'

Neil gazed at her in amazement. 'Are you serious?'

'The people I talked to were. Couldn't have been more so.'

Neil's brow clouded in thought. 'Ken certainly has

become very powerful over the past few years. That union of his just keeps on growing and growing, and at a remarkable pace too.'

'I'm suggesting that we have Ken and his union investigated properly – we'll get Chris Walker to help us there; and then, when we have enough to hang Ken and his union, bring a case against them and smash them,' Vicky said.

Neil blanched. 'Are you mad! I'm a Labour MP. Labour MPs don't go round trying to smash unions. Without unions the party couldn't financially exist. We're dependent on them.'

Vicky gave a razored smile. 'That weakness is also your strength. A union like the CDU can only harm and dishonour the entire trade union movement. Smash the present Nazi hierarchy of the CDU, give it back to its members, and you would be a Labour hero, a champion of the people, and bound to be offered a position, and who's to say not a senior one, in the next Labour government.'

Neil's eyes gleamed. 'Labour hero, eh?'

'And champion of the people. A man who found corruption on his own doorstep and wasn't afraid to purge that corruption. To scour the evil clean, and banish it from the shores of Clydeside.'

Neil's mind flew back to that night in the downstairs dunny when Ken had claimed him, giving him the kicking that had rendered him impotent. How he hated Ken for that. Ken had deprived him of so much; now here was a chance to pay him back a little, and do himself a lot of good at the same time.

'Murder even?' he queried.

'So the rumours and stories say.'

'What about proof?'

'That's what we'll have to get: witnesses and proof for all that we eventually come to accuse Ken and his union of in court.'

Neil licked his lips. 'It could be dangerous?'

'So can crossing the street. Last night you said there was so much you could do for Glasgow if you only had access to power. Well, this could give you that access. And, if we pull it off, is almost surely likely to.'

A senior position in the next Labour government, he thought excitedly. 'Who knows, maybe the PM might even make me . . .' Neil took a deep breath, then exhaled slowly. 'Secretary of State for Scotland?' Oh, that would be a dream come true indeed!

'Why not?' Vicky smiled in reply.

'If there's a post in a Labour government I covet, it's that one,' he admitted.

'There would be a certain irony, not to mention justice, should you achieve that ambition at Ken's expense,' she replied.

'Yes . . . exactly,' he breathed. Then he was frowning again. 'The only trouble is that all this is going to take a great deal of hard work, work that has to be done on the spot, and my time in Glasgow and Scotland is limited, as you know.'

'Leave all that to me, and Chris Walker, I hope.'

'How is Chris? You haven't mentioned him much of late.'

'He hasn't been in touch, or around the Labour Hall for a while.' Her brow creased as she totted up the weeks. 'In fact, it's nearly four months since I last saw him.'

'Perhaps something's wrong. He might have been ill, say? You should have contacted him.'

'I did ring the section house several times and leave messages but he never replied to any of them.' She turned away from Neil so that he couldn't see her face. 'He's probably been busy with that Mona Bryce. The pair of them out gallivanting together during most of his spare time.'

'In which case he might not want to help you?' Neil said.

'If not, he can at least give me some advice on how to go about things. I'm sure he won't refuse me that.'

'I'm sure not.'

She would try and contact Chris directly after she had done the dishes, Vicky decided. She would telephone his section house, and if he wasn't there try him at his station.

The street was just off Anniesland Cross. The close bearing the number she'd been given had a metal gate at its mouth and smelled of fresh whitewash inside. It was a good close, proclaiming that the folk who lived in and up it were respectable people who took a pride in where they lived.

Going up the stairs, Vicky had a peep in the first stairhead toilet she came to. It was neat and clean, well looked after. She found Chris's name on the middle door of the third landing. She tugged the brass handle pull and the bell gave a series of dull clangs.

'Hello, stranger.' Vicky smiled to Chris when he opened the door.

Surprise and pleasure flashed across his face. 'Hello, yourself. It's good to see you.'

They stared at one another.

'I was hoping you might offer me a cup of tea?' she suggested, breaking the pregnant silence that had fallen between them.

'Oh, aye, sure. Come away in,' he said, and stood aside to let her pass. 'How did you find me?'

'The section house told me you'd moved out, so I went to your station and got your address from them. That and the information it was your day off.'

She saw a kitchen and another room. Through an open doorway she glimpsed an unmade bed, then Chris was ushering her into the kitchen. It sparkled like a new pin, everything tidy and in its place. The linoleum had been polished so hard that the effect was positively dazzling. Mona? Vicky wondered. She gazed about, looking for female signs.

'It's very nice. Did you decorate it yourself?'

'I did,' he answered, chuffed that she liked his taste.

'I know the station shouldn't have given me your address, but I wangled it out of them by telling a wee lie or two. Of course, being an MP's wife they never dreamed I was lying. I hope you don't mind?' she said, and smiled sweetly.

'No. I really should have notified you of my change of address,' he replied somewhat lamely.

No tang of perfume or smell of powder other than her

own. No female garments, or female accoutrements that she could see. Yet the place smacked of a female hand.

'I have tried to reach you on the phone several times and did leave messages,' she said, and stared at him, waiting for an explanation.

He shrugged. 'I've been doing an awful lot of night shifts, sleeping all day and working all night. I just haven't had the time recently to come round and help,' he lied.

And Vicky knew it was a lie. There was that in his voice told her so.

'How's Mona?' she asked.

'We, eh . . . broke up six weeks ago. It didn't work out, I'm afraid.'

'I'm sorry to hear that,' she lied.

He shrugged again. 'Just one of those things. Not the right woman for me.'

And who do you think is? Vicky nearly found herself saying, but bit it back. 'I'm sure you'll find another right woman for yourself one day,' she said instead.

'I'll make that tea then.'

Vicky watched him as he filled an electric kettle and switched it on.

'I must say you're an excellent housekeeper,' she said.

He laughed. 'Not a bit of it. There's a wifey in the next close comes in and does for me. The place would be a shambles if it wasn't for her.'

Though it was really none of her business, Vicky was pleased that it wasn't a girlfriend who'd replaced Mona.

Chris put Penguin and Blue Riband biscuits on a plate. 'Mrs Bone, that's the wifey, also does my shopping. That's useful as well.'

'And what about cooking?'

'Och, I can scrape by at that. Stews, casseroles, chops and suchlike. Occasionally I do a Chinese dish. Quite a few of those are fairly simple.'

They chatted till the tea was ready and poured. Vicky accepted her cup, but refused the biscuits.

'I've come here to ask your help, on a personal matter,' she announced.

Instantly a change came over Chris. Gone was the easy-going civilian; he was now all policeman. 'Are you in some sort of trouble?'

She shook her head. 'Remember the story I told you about Mr Malarkey?'

'Aye.'

He listened intently while she spoke about what she intended to do and her and Neil's reasons for doing so. She didn't mention Neil's impotence or how that had come about.

When she finished, Chris took her cup from her and refilled it. He could understand the political reasons behind it; it was Vicky's personal motivation that made him uneasy.

'Vengeance is a bad thing, Vicky, often just as damaging to the person who wreaks it as to the person it is wreaked upon,' he said slowly.

'My dad would be *still alive* if it wasn't for Ken Blacklaws!' She paused, then continued, 'And there's something he did to Neil which I can't tell you about other than it was terrible, and Neil has suffered agonies because of it. Now his exposure and downfall can, and will if I have anything to with it, be the making of Neil's career.'

Chris sipped his tea. 'And you want me to help bring all this about, is that it?'

'Will you?' she replied quietly, voice brittle with intensity.

He thought how marvellous it was to see her again, to be in her presence. He had missed her dreadfully. 'Tell me about those inquiries you made yourself, and who you spoke to and what they said.'

When she left his house an hour later, a plan of campaign had been mapped out between them.

Ken's intercom, a relatively new toy, buzzed. He depressed the lever that allowed him to talk to his secretary, and she to him. 'Yes, Ina?'

'There's a Mr Heggie here insisting to see you personally. He's a union member, and says it's important.'

'Send him in,' Ken replied and let go the lever.

Heggie was a small, wiry man of about thirty. He was wearing his Sunday suit and a neat collar and tie.

Ken stood and shook Heggie by the hand. These little courtesies were always winners. 'Not working today?' he asked.

'I didn't go in because I wanted to come and speak to you,' Heggie answered.

Ken gestured Heggie to a chair, then sat himself. 'So what's your problem?'

Heggie shook his head. 'It's not a problem, at least not for me, that is. It's more what you might call a matter of information, information I think you might be interested in.'

Ken studied Heggie. The eyes were bright and had depth. They also had a certain animal craftiness about them. 'I'm listening,' he said.

'I won't beat about the bush. I'm after something you're capable of giving me. If my information is as important as I think it might be, will we have a trade?'

Ken smiled. 'Depends on the information and what you want.' He liked the man's directness and lack of apology.

'I want to be a gaffer,' Heggie stated.

Ken nodded. 'Now I know what you want. What's the information?'

'There's a copper called Walker whom I had a run-in with some time back, a sergeant at Tobago Street, and a real hard-nosed bastard. Well, suddenly I start noticing him round the docks, always chaffing to dockies in corners and out-of-the-way spots, and somehow being furtive like.

'Then, just yesterday, he saw me, only instead of facing me down as coppers would normally do in that sort of situation, he backed off and did a disappearing act.

'After he'd gone, I tried to have a word with the bloke he'd been talking to. Honest to God, I thought the bloke was going to shit himself when I asked him what he and Walker had been speaking about. He said Walker had only stopped him to inquire the time, and with that scarpered, walking away from me so fast it was almost a run.'

Ken tapped a pencil on his desk. 'Is this Walker CID?'

'No, he's not. And that's another point. On each occasion I've seen him sniffing round the docks he's been in plain clothes.'

'He might have been transferred to CID,' Ken mused.

'Uniformed copper or CID, whichever, he's up to something and I thought you would be interested in that,' Heggie replied.

Ken swivelled round his chair so he could gaze out of the window. It was a marvellous view of the Clyde and southside. He could not have been more pleased with his new building; it was a jewel among dross, a stotter.

Heggie was right. He was interested to learn about this. If the police were poking their noses into the docks, he wanted to know what they were after.

'Well?' Heggie demanded anxiously.

'You did the right thing in coming to me,' Ken replied, swivelling his chair back again.

'And the job as gaffer?'

'Let's just wait until we find out what this is all about first. For the moment, go and sit outside again, will you?' Ken answered.

Heggie left the office. As the door clicked shut, Ken depressed the intercom lever.

'Find Paddy Troy and send him to me,' he instructed Ina.

Paddy Troy appeared a few minutes later and Ken related what Heggie had told him.

'So what do you want me to do?' Paddy asked.

'Take Heggie to Tobago Street nick. He may be able to do it today, or you may have to go back tomorrow or the next day even, but hang around there until Walker appears and he can identify him to you. From there on in I want Walker watched round the clock – you'll need a team for that which you can organise yourself – until we know what he, and anyone else he might be working with, are up to.'

'I understand.'

'On no account are you or any of the others to lay so much as a finger on him. He's a policeman, don't forget. If you rough up one of their lot, it's just like pulling the pin out of a hand grenade. Before you know where you are, there's a very loud and damaging explosion.'

Paddy Troy grinned. 'I won't so much as breathe on him,' he said. This was a private joke between him and Ken, who the previous week had chided him for smelly breath.

He would soon find out what this was all about, Ken thought after Paddy Troy had gone. Probably, from his and the union point of view, nothing to worry about. But better to be safe than sorry. His thoughts then turned to Aberdeen, the last bastion that would soon be falling to him. When that happened, and his union reigned supreme in Scotland, he would change its name to the Scottish Union of Dock-workers.

'Scottish Union of Dockworkers,' he said, speaking the name aloud, lovingly.

Weeks, that's all it was now. A matter of weeks and all his long schemes and plans would come to fruition.

Three days later, mid-afternoon, Ken's office telephone rang.

'You'll never guess who Walker has met up with,' Paddy Troy said.

'Who?'

'Remember Mrs Seton, the MP's wife whose father broke his neck?'

Alarm bells went off in Ken's head. Walker and Vicky! 'Is he still with her?'

'They're in a teashop in Rottenrow. Walker met up with Mrs Seton, then the two of them went to a school in Townhead, where they picked up a lassie, and from there they drove to this teashop which they've just gone into. I'm in a phone box across the way.'

A lassie from a school in Townhead; that would be Vicky's daughter. What was her name again? Vicky had told him, if only he could mind. Martha, that was it. And Vicky and Walker had taken her to a teashop; that could only mean that Vicky and Walker were friends. He didn't like the sound of that, not one little bit. He decided that he wanted to have a look at this Walker himself.

'Where exactly in Rottenrow are you?'

Paddy told him.

'I'm coming there to join you. But should they leave before I get there, go with them, otherwise I'll see you shortly,' Ken said, and hung up.

Vicky friendly with a bluebottle who was nosing round the docks. He didn't like the sound of that at all!

Martha laid her third cake, this one a meringue, on her plate. It was a scrumptious-looking meringue, thick in the middle with cream. 'It's just as well I don't get the opportunity to do this very often or I'd be fat as a pig,' she said.

Chris laughed.

'Let's just hope it's going to be an S1 pass,' Vicky replied, for Martha had sat her 'quali' that day, and this was the treat she had promised her for afterwards.

'It wasn't that difficult, but difficult enough.'

'Did you get stuck on anything?' Vicky asked anxiously.

'My old bogey spelling was hard, at least for me.' To Chris she explained, 'Spelling's given orally, you see. The teacher calls out the word and you write it down.' Bringing her attention back to Vicky, she went on, 'The first word was "leopard", which stumped me. Then I got it later on.'

'How did you spell it then?' Vicky queried.

'L-e-p-p-a-r-d,' Martha replied, straight-faced.

'Oh!' Vicky exclaimed, and bit her lower lip.

'Got you! I spelled it l-e-o-p-a-r-d.' Martha laughed, and sank her teeth into the meringue.

'Minx!' Vicky said, wagging an admonishing finger at her. To Chris she added, 'She really had me believing that.'

Chris, thoroughly enjoying himself, indicated to a passing waitress that they wanted a fresh pot of tea.

Ken had Shugs drop him off round the corner from where Paddy Troy had said his Zephyr was parked. He told Shugs to wait for a few minutes and if he didn't return in that time to drive back to the Broomielaw. He then walked away from the shining black Lincoln Continental that had replaced the Cadillac and turned into Rottenrow.

The Zephyr was still there, with Paddy Troy slumped in the driver's seat. Opening the passenger door, Ken slid in beside him.

'Just in time. They're about to leave. That's Walker at the cash desk,' Paddy said.

Chris Walker was plainly visible through the teashop's plateglass front window. Ken saw a man roughly his own age whose face had a pleasant but determined stamp about it. The door to the teashop tinged open, and Vicky and the lassie came out to stand on the pavement, waiting for Walker.

It was nearly three years since he had last seen Vicky, and she had aged, but not drastically so. Her face was thinner and more taut somehow. The figure was still trim, the hair that cap of curls he remembered so well. If he'd been closer, he would have seen that the curls were now streaked with grey.

He turned his attention to the lassie. She had chestnut-coloured hair cut at neck length, a rather podgy adolescent figure and glasses. The face . . . the face held him. Had he seen Martha before? No, of course he hadn't, he was certain of that. And yet her face was strangely familiar.

Chris joined Vicky and Martha, and the three of them exchanged a few words.

Powerfully built, and intelligent, very much so. Intelligent, determined and exuding authority – that was how Ken would have described Chris Walker. He knew from long experience of dealing with men that this was one to be reckoned with.

Then the threesome were making off up the street, Martha between the two adults.

'Their car's about a hundred yards up on the opposite side,' Paddy said, switching on the Zephyr's engine.

'I've seen all I wanted to. Drop me off at the first set of lights you have to stop at.'

As the Singer joined the traffic, Paddy did a quick U-turn and set off in pursuit, eventually tucking the Zephyr into a position several cars behind the Singer.

'Has Walker been down at the docks today?' Ken asked,

knowing from the reports given him by Paddy and his team
that Walker hadn't been near the docks since being put
under surveillance. The last report had been that morning
from Chic Henderson, whom Paddy had taken over from.

'Nope.'

'Well, maintain the round-the-clock watch all the same.
It's even more important now we've discovered he knows
Mrs Seton.'

For the rest of that day Ken was plagued with the memory
of Martha Seton's face and the feeling of déjà vu he'd
experienced when looking at it.

The pub was in Maryhill, an area as rough as any to be
found in Glasgow. The very air was menacing.

The outside of the pub was covered with graffiti and the
yellow-tiled façade beneath the graffiti was chipped and
scarred in a thousand places. Both front windows were
protected by thick iron bars.

'Very salubrious,' Vicky said sarcastically as they went
inside.

Chris gave a dry chuckle. He didn't mind places like this.
In fact, perversely, he rather enjoyed them.

The pub was busy, the three barmen working flat out. A
brace of females smiled brazenly at Chris. Then, realising
that he was with a woman, dropped the smiles and went
back to their drinks.

Vicky glanced about. The man they'd come to meet had
not given them a physical description of himself. He had
said that he would know who they were when they came
in and make contact. Chris was about to pay for the drinks
he'd ordered when a man standing beside him suddenly
turned and said, 'You'd better get another pint in if we're
to talk.' Chris did as he was bid.

The man led them through the throng to the rear, where,
miraculously there was a free table. He told them to sit.

'The name's Norrie Telfer,' he said, and stuck out a hand
to Chris, who shook it. He then greeted Vicky.

'I've heard what you're trying to do, which is why I rang.
I want that bastard Blacklaws and his cronies to get their

comeuppance, and I'm prepared to do my bit to help. And I *can* help in a big way,' Telfer announced.

'Are you a dockie?' Chris asked.

Telfer shook his head. 'But my brother Andy is – or was, rather. He lives in Leith, having married a lass from there. He has three children, and no legs now,' Telfer replied grimly.

'Accident?' Chris queried.

Telfer, eyes flashing with anger, supped from his pint. 'That's what it was called, but Andy and I have another name for it. I presume you know of Paddy Troy?'

Chris nodded.

'Just before the CDU took over Andy's union, the old Leith Dock Workers' Union, Troy put in an appearance, and from that moment all hell broke loose. There was a spate of so-called "accidents", one of which was when a conveyor belt Andy was working on suddenly went berserk; part of the belt snapped and neatly severed Andy's legs just below their knees. Troy had been noticed hanging round the belt's motor only minutes before it went daft.'

Telfer paused, then continued. 'And my brother wasn't the only one to suffer. Quite a few of his pals also came to grief, one of them actually drowning in another so-called "accident".'

'So how can you help us bring Blacklaws and his thugs to book?' Vicky asked.

Telfer lit a cigarette, then had another pull at his pint. 'Did you know Blacklaws owns a yacht?' he said quietly.

Vicky looked at Chris. This was new. She shook her head.

'Or that he owns a villa over in Spain, at a place called Marbella?'

Vicky shook her head a second time.

'I was at sea for a number of years, working as a steward. The last job I had was on the *Seven Seas*, Blacklaws's yacht. A yacht he paid for out of union funds, but which is registered in his name.'

Excitement gripped Vicky. 'Are you sure about that?'

'Oh, aye, just as I'm sure the villa was paid for the same way, and that it is also in Blacklaws's own name.'

'This is it, what we're looking for,' Vicky said to Chris.

'Embezzlement of funds, that should put Blacklaws away for quite some while,' Chris answered softly.

Vicky made a tight fist and shook it in triumph. Until now there had been nothing they could use personally against Ken. This was the breakthrough she'd been praying for.

'How do you know the yacht and villa are in Blacklaws's name, and that he paid for them out of union funds?' Chris queried.

'The *Seven Seas* might seem a fair-sized yacht but, relatively speaking, it's actually quite small inside. A person in the position I held was bound to hear many things he shouldn't. What I've told you about the yacht and villa were two of the things I inadvertently overheard,' Telfer replied.

'How do we prove this though?' Vicky asked Chris.

'There are ways and means. You leave all that to me. In the meantime though we should tell Kingsland about this development when we meet with him tomorrow morning,' Chris said. Sir Oliver Kingsland would be acting for them when they brought their case against the CDU.

Chris rose. 'I'll get another round in,' he said and headed for the bar.

At the bar, and partially screened by a pillar, Jim Robertson, a member of Paddy Troy's team, had been watching Telfer, Vicky and Chris. He had already placed Telfer as an ex-steward on the *Seven Seas*, Telfer having served him a number of times on the one occasion he'd sailed with the boss and others to Spain on the yacht.

Seeing Chris approaching, Robertson left the spot where he was standing and slipped outside.

Vicky parked the Singer outside Chris's close. She was still filled with excitement and elation after their meeting with Telfer.

'I'll pick you up at nine tomorrow morning, and we'll go

straight to the central station,' Vicky said. Neil was coming from London; they'd collect him, then the three of them would go to see Sir Oliver Kingsland.

Chris glanced at his watch. 'It's early yet. Do you fancy coming up for a nightcap before going home?'

'There's nothing I'd like more,' she replied, knowing that it was going to be hours before she calmed down sufficiently even to consider going to bed.

As they went up the stairs, they both fell silent. His hand brushed against her when he reached for his key, causing a sudden ripple of gooseflesh across her back.

Chris clicked on the lights and opened a window, for it was a hot and sultry June night. He then closed the curtains. He turned to her and smiled. The smile turned rigid as electricity flashed between them.

'Just a small dram, as I'm driving,' Vicky croaked, her throat feeling constricted.

His hand trembled a little as he poured their whiskies. She asked for water with hers. He gave her lemonade. Neither noticed.

They spoke, but their conversation was unnatural, stilted. She refrained from looking him directly in the eyes in case he read what was in her own.

She finished her drink, not having tasted any of it. 'I'd better go now,' she mumbled.

She didn't know how it happened, but she was in his arms, their mouths joined, his tongue darting and flicking against her tongue. One of his hands dropped to her bottom, to cup and caress it. His other hand sought out a breast. Her heart was thumping, and she was filled with a roaring liquid fire. Laying her head on his shoulder, she moaned.

'I've been in love with you right from the beginning, you must have known,' he whispered.

How she wanted him! Wanted what Neil had never been able to give her: joining and total satisfaction – not just the partial satisfaction that had been her lot since marrying Neil. Then, with a shock, she realised that it wasn't merely the sex she craved but Chris himself. She *loved* him, the first man she'd fallen in love with since Ken.

But why hadn't she realised that before now? Maybe she had subconsciously, but been afraid, unwilling, to admit it to herself. And the reason? Because she was a married woman with a husband who not only loved her but worshipped the very ground she walked on. A husband who needed her and was dependent on her. A husband whom she would destroy if she ever left him.

'Oh, Vicky!' Chris whispered and sought out her lips again.

She could feel his manhood against her thigh. How she longed, ached, to touch it, to have it inside her.

She forced Chris from her and took several steps backwards. 'No,' she stated emphatically.

He gazed at her, stricken.

'It's not that I don't . . . feel for you, Chris. I do, a great deal. But I have Neil to think about. I can't let him down. I won't cheat on him, nor will I leave him.'

Chris could see she meant what she said, that no amount of argument on his part would change her mind. He bowed his head.

'I think I've known that all along, why I never made a move before now. And I didn't mean this to happen either; it just sort of did.'

He looked up at her. 'Do you forgive me?'

'There's nothing to forgive. If things were different, if I wasn't married, then I'd jump at the chance to be yours. But things are the way they are, and that's that.'

He ran a hand through his hair. 'I don't seem to be very lucky in love.'

'No.'

'I stopped seeing you, coming round to the Labour Hall to help, because of what I feel for you. I tried to make the break and then you came back into my life.'

'I'm sorry,' she said softly.

'To tell the truth, I don't know what's worse. Not seeing you at all, or seeing you and not being able to do anything about my feelings.'

'The devil and the deep blue sea.' She smiled.

He nodded.

'Can we just be good friends? I appreciate it'll be difficult, for both of us. But if it's possible, I don't want to lose you again.'

He stared at the floor, as if studying it.

'Should you meet someone else, I'd understand. But I don't want to lose your friendship.'

He glanced up again, having forced a smile onto his face to match hers. 'All right, friends it is. Now and always,' he replied.

She held out her glass. 'I've changed my mind. I'll have another drink before I leave. And blow the driving, make it a biggy.'

On leaving Chris's, she drove till she came to some waste ground, where she pulled the car off the road. She slumped over the wheel.

'Oh, Chris!' she sobbed, filled with agony, despair and thwarted love.

But she could not let Neil down.

Ken woke with a start and sat bolt upright in bed. Now he knew where he'd seen Martha Seton's face before. It was a younger, female version of his own! No wonder it had taken him so long to place it, for who, straight off anyway, recognises himself! It had been like looking into a mirror, the image gazing back distorted by time and a change of gender.

Could he possibly be wrong? No, he wasn't. That face was out of the same mould as his own. There was no doubt whatever about it.

Martha Seton was *his* daughter.

Ken laid down the phone. It was later on that morning and Jim Robertson had just delivered his report.

A copper nosing round the docks, a copper who turned out to know Vicky, and now the pair of them having a comfy little chat with a steward who had worked on the *Seven Seas*. The whole thing was beginning to stink to high heaven.

Picking up the telephone again, he dialled Paddy Troy's

number. When Paddy answered, he said, 'Now listen carefully, Paddy. This is what I want you to do . . .'

Chic Henderson rang through his report on Chris that afternoon. Ken listened intently. When it was over, he cradled the telephone and went to his window to gaze out over the Clyde and the southside.

Sir Oliver Kingsland was a legend, the most famous and successful prosecuting counsel, Judge Advocate, in all Scotland. The man was number one in his field. If he'd ever lost a case, Ken had certainly never heard of it.

Of course it could still be that all this had nothing whatever to do with him and the CDU. But he would know for certain, one way or the other, before long. Paddy Troy would make sure of that.

Norrie Telfer was getting ready for the evening shift at the posh West End hotel bar where he worked when there was a knock on the outside door.

'I'll get it,' said Agnes, his common-law wife. Drawing her pink candlewick dressing gown around herself – she and Norrie had just made love, as they often did in the afternoon, Norrie having a liking for it at that time – she left Norrie whistling tunelessly while knotting his black bow tie.

'Some friends to see you,' Agnes announced, returning with three men.

Norrie's whistling died when he saw that one of the three was Paddy Troy.

'I've come to have a word, Telfer,' Paddy said with a chilling smile.

Norrie Telfer was stock still, as though rooted to the spot, his expression one of stark terror.

'Aren't they friends then?' Agnes queried, forehead creasing into a deep frown.

Paddy Troy unzipped the leather message bag he was carrying and took out a dockie's hook. Two feet long and an inch in diameter, it curved into a needle-sharp point. Dockies used these steel hooks to shift and manipulate cargo.

'Oh, my God!' Norrie croaked.

Agnes opened her mouth to scream, but before she could make a noise she was backhanded across the face and sent sprawling. Her attacker was one of Paddy Troy's two companions.

'Not a squeak or you'll get this after Telfer,' Paddy said and waggled the hook at her.

With three of them between him and the door, Norrie Telfer knew that he hadn't a hope of escape. There was the window, but they were on the fourth floor.

Paddy Troy advanced on Telfer, who retreated until he could go no further, eyes bulging, back pressed hard against a wall. Paddy slipped the hook between Telfer's legs, bringing its tip up and forward till it was lodged behind his scrotum.

'Now I want to hear all about your conversation with Walker and Mrs Seton,' Paddy Troy said.

Shugs turned the Lincoln into Parr Street and pulled up behind Jim Robertson's car. Ken was about to get out when Martha emerged from her close to walk past the Lincoln. He waited in the Lincoln till she was out of sight, then got out, allowing Jim to assist him.

'Are they both still in?' he asked Jim, who nodded.

Ken glanced up at Neil and Vicky's window. He had taken Paddy Troy's team off Walker to follow them. He had wanted to speak to them as soon as they were home together. It was a bonus that the lassie had gone out.

He looked along at his old close. So many memories, so long ago. It seemed a different lifetime.

Taking a cigar from the case he always carried with him, he lit it with a silver-coloured Ronson which had the initials K.B. engraved on one side in fancy script. Old now, and with several bashes in it, but still in good working order, it was the lighter Vicky had given him for his seventeenth birthday, nineteen years before. He'd had other lighters since, but had always gone back to the Ronson because he liked it, and for sentimental reasons.

He instructed Jim Robertson and Shugs to wait. Then,

entering Neil and Vicky's close, he began to mount the stairs.

Vicky was washing up – they'd just had tea – when there was a chap on the front door.

'Will you get it? My hands are wet. It's probably Martha back for something she's forgotten,' Vicky said to Neil, who was leafing through a batch of parliamentary papers that he'd brought north with him.

Ken stood on the landing thinking that Parr Street hadn't improved any; it was still as mean and squalid as ever. It amazed him that Neil and Vicky continued to stay in it. Then again, knowing Neil, maybe he wasn't so amazed.

Vicky was scraping at a Pyrex dish that had a hard crust rim on its inside when Neil returned to the kitchen. She looked up and, when she saw who was with him, the knife she was using froze in mid-action.

'I'm sure you can guess why I'm here,' Ken said.

Vicky laid the dish and knife aside and dried her hands on a teatowel. 'You always did have a brass-neck cheek,' she replied.

Ken had a puff of his cigar. 'I could bring up the business of Copland and Lye, and tell how it was Neil who cliped on his best pal. That would sink him,' he said to Vicky.

'We'd deny that accusation, say it was a crude attempt on your part to discredit Neil. Crude and completely unfounded. There would be no question of people believing you, not after what's going to come out about you and your union during the case. So this time, that club won't work.'

Ken had another puff of his cigar. The atmosphere in the room was electric. It reminded him of a card game he'd once played when the stakes had been exceptionally high.

'You've got me then,' he said, as though conceding defeat.

'That's right,' Vicky replied, flushing with triumph.

Casually, Ken strolled over to the mantelpiece. Standing on it was a silver-framed photograph of Martha, which he had noticed on coming into the room.

Staring at the photograph, he said over his shoulder to Vicky, 'I won't ask why. I've given you reasons enough over the years to want to destroy me.'

He turned his head sideways to look at Neil. 'As for you getting in on the act, is it purely being supportive of her? Or is there a political motivation?'

Neil's lips thinned.

'Well, it's one or the other, no matter which.' Ken smiled and brought his attention back to Martha's photograph.

Ken picked up the photograph and turned again to Neil. 'By the way, did Vicky ever tell you Martha is my daughter?' he asked lazily.

Neil's mouth fell open.

'That's a lie!' Vicky said, taken so completely by surprise that there was no conviction in her voice.

Ken went over to Neil and held the photograph up in front of Neil's face. Neil's expression told him that he hadn't known until that moment.

'So Vicky *didn't* tell you. Well, well, well. Mind you, I'm surprised you never noticed the resemblance. It really is quite startling. Two peas in a pod, that's us.'

Vicky dashed across and snatched the photograph from Ken's grasp.

'She's even more like me than Kenny is.' Ken smiled.

Vicky hit him as hard as she could, the flat of her hand cracking against his cheek. He reeled back but never stopped smiling.

Neil was in a daze. Martha, Ken's daughter! Ken was right: the resemblance *was* startling. Why had he never seen that before now?

Ken took another puff of his cigar, thinking that the look on Neil's face was priceless. He noted that there were tears in Vicky's eyes.

'I'm not sure how to play this yet. On the one hand I can say she hoisted another man's child on you, *mine*. Or on the other I can say she cuckolded you with me, and passed off my child as yours.'

Ken paused for emphasis, then went on, 'Whatever way, coming as it will during the trial the newspapers will have a field day. From John o' Groats to Land's End you'll be a laughing stock. And your public career? That'll be finished. For how would you ever again be able to face your colleagues, opponents or an audience knowing what was going through their minds?'

Ken paused to let that sink in, then continued, 'So, the pair of you have it within your power to drag me down, but if I go so do you, Neil, all the way. I want that clearly understood.'

Ken threw his cigar into the empty grate and walked to the door. There he stopped and turned.

Neil stood in a slumped position, a man devastated. Vicky was clutching Martha's picture to her bosom while hot tears spilled down her face.

'The choice is up to you,' Ken stated. Then he smiled again and left the house.

Neil stared out of the train window, seeing nothing of the passing scenery. He was writhing inside, grappling with a combination of humiliation, hurt and profound sense of loss.

Ken Blacklaws. The name burned in his brain, writ there in letters of searing fire. All his life he had played second fiddle to Ken, been second best. Ken the high and mighty, the perpetual winner, and spoiler. It was Ken who'd robbed him of his manhood, kicking it out of him that night in the back-close dunny, robbed him of the ability to make love properly to the woman he loved – a woman whom, he'd now learned, Ken had cast aside not only once but twice. A woman who had never loved him, but had loved Ken.

How Ken must have laughed to learn that he'd married Vicky and accepted Ken's child as his own. He must have laughed himself sick! Ken had not only made it impossible for him to father a child, but had stolen back the one he'd fallen heir to, and whom he loved next only to Vicky herself.

As for Vicky, how could she have let him marry her without telling him the child she was carrying was Ken's? How could she do that!

Self-pity welled in Neil. What had he ever done to deserve all that had happened to him! What had he ever done to deserve Ken Blacklaws!

Last night, in bed – if only he could have taken Vicky,

everything might still have been salvaged between them and he might not have felt as he now did; a fool, second-rate, used and useless.

Black, black despair rose up to engulf him, and in that pit of despair a face, beckoning. The face of his father.

Vicky was on the telephone when Dickie Fleet, Neil's agent, appeared in her office. She waved him to a chair but he remained standing.

She hung up and laughed. 'What's wrong with you, Dickie? You look like you've lost a pound and found six-pence.'

He twisted the flat cap, or hooker doon, he was holding. 'I'm afraid I've got some terrible news about Neil . . .'

After a while, Dickie took her home.

She had expected the ashes to be similar to the ashes from the fireplace, but they weren't at all. They were pure white and in crystalline lumps that were jagged at the edges. She scattered them over the grave where his mum and dad were buried, certain that that was what he would have wanted.

She had gone south for the cremation and brought the ashes back with her. Originally she had intended to bring back the body, but on learning how drawn out and complex a business it was to take a corpse from England into Scotland she had opted instead for cremation.

A ticket inspector had forced the toilet door at Crewe to discover Neil hanging from a metal fixture on the roof. Neil had torn the towel into strips and used that.

Everyone, and most of all Chris, had been marvellous. The story she had given the newspapers, which they had accepted without question, was that Neil had been working so hard that he had suffered a nervous breakdown and killed himself as a result.

She turned to where Martha and Chris were standing by the graveside, Martha holding a floral display. Others had wanted to come, but she had refused them all, with the exception of Chris. He helped Martha forward to lay the flowers on the grave.

Vicky closed her eyes and offered up a silent prayer for Neil's soul.

'He was so young still,' Martha said, clinging onto Chris.

'Yes,' he agreed, grim-faced.

As they were leaving the cemetery, Vicky asked Chris if he would first of all drop Martha off at Parr Street, then drive her into town. She intended speaking to Sir Oliver Kingsland.

Neil's death had placed him beyond further pain, hurt and humiliation. It was a death that had to be paid for, and Ken Blacklaws was going to do the paying.

As God was her judge, she swore it.

Three nights later Dickie Fleet came to see Vicky. 'The selection board have discussed it and their decision was unanimous. There's no one more fit, or better qualified in their book, to replace Neil as MP for Glasgow Kelvinhaugh than you. Will you stand for us in the by-election?' he asked.

Vicky took a deep breath, then exhaled slowly. 'I have Martha to consider. If I was elected, it would mean being in London a great deal. That wouldn't be fair on her.'

Dickie turned to Martha. 'What do you say, lass?'

'I say, if it's what Mummy wants, then it's what she should do. Granny and I would manage when she wasn't here, and although I'd miss her, I'd understand she was doing something worthwhile.'

Martha went over to Vicky and took her by the hand. 'I think you should continue Daddy's work. Do all the things for Glasgow that he wanted to.'

Vicky pulled Martha down and kissed her on the cheek. 'I knew you were grown up but, until now, hadn't realised how much. Thank you, darling.'

She looked at Dickie Fleet. 'I'll run,' she announced.

Postscript

Chris met her off the Euston train. It was almost seven months to the day since Ken had been arrested, to be held without bail.

'Well?' Vicky demanded, knowing that Ken was due to have been sentenced that afternoon.

'Life, for being an accessory before the fact,' Chris replied.

Vicky let out a soft sigh of satisfaction. The original charges of embezzlement against Ken had proved to be only the start. Once the can had successfully been opened, the worms had come pouring out.

'And Troy?'

'The death penalty for the murder of John Elder.' Elder had been a Leith dockie, and friend to Norrie Telfer's brother. He had been murdered by drowning – a crime to which, as it had transpired, there had been witnesses.

Tears blossomed in Vicky's eyes. Tears for Neil, tears for her dad. And tears for herself.

'I said I'd give you my answer when this was all over, and now I will. I'd be honoured, and very happy, to marry you,' she told Chris.

He didn't give a damn who might see them. He kissed her passionately but gently, a kiss full of love.

When it was over, she wiped her eyes with a hanky and blew her nose.

Linking arms, they made their way along the platform.

WHEN DREAMS COME TRUE

Emma Blair

Norma McKenzie's bubbly, irrepressible Glaswegian spirit ensured that she would never remain downtrodden. When her family are forced to move into a Glasgow tenement, it is not long before she meets popular, handsome, blue-eyed Midge Henderson. Captivated by each other, their lives seem blissfully entwined as they embark upon a glamorous ballroom-dancing career. But then, out of the blue, Norma's life is shattered by bitter betrayal . . .

It is many years before love re-enters Norma's life – a daring aristocratic Scots officer rekindles the flames of passion amidst the devastation of war. But returning to Glasgow as man and wife in 1945 imposes new strains on their relationship. And when Midge reappears, Norma feels her love for him returning and she is faced with the most agonising choice of her life . . .

STREET SONG

Emma Blair

Susan's parents had wanted a son . . . and they did little to hide their disappointment with her. As soon as was decently possibly they packed her off to boarding school.

If only they could have known . . .

Because of the tradition-bound Scotland of the 1920's there was no place for a woman like Susan. But she was determined to find one – even if it meant beating her wealthy parents at their own game . . .

STREET SONG – Emma Blair at her best . . . a passionate saga

A MOST DETERMINED WOMAN

Emma Blair

For Sarah Hawke, daugher of an impoverished minder, life offered little beyond the grime of Glasgow in the 1890s and the eternal drudgery of back-breaking work. Until a mysterious stranger entered her life. A stranger who turned out to be her real father – and the owner of a vast and prosperous shipping empire . . .

Catapulted into a world of luxury, of servants and stately homes, Sarah begins a new and glittering life. As sole heiress to a fortune, she has much to gain – and everything to lose. For she takes over the business, and with it the risks and rivalry, deceit and intrigue – and the prospect of undying love . . .

THE BLACKBIRD'S TALE

Emma Blair

From Glasgow on the brink of the Great War to the cut-throat world of London publishing – the spellbinding saga of three remarkable generations:

Cathy: A Glasgow factory-girl who experiences love, its loss and a kind of victory in the space of two turbulent wartime years . . .

Hannah: The daughter whose marriage enjoys the fruits of undreamt prosperity. But her love must learn to endure the turmoil of a very personal hurt . . .

Robyn: The product of her generation. Modern, extrovert and vivacious, her heart is broken by the only man she'll ever love. Yet she finally comes to control her destiny – and that of the lover she never really lost . . .

This is the unforgettable story of three women united in their love for books, for life, and for their men. A story which began with the little bookshop that Cathy fell in love with thirty years before. The Blackbird . . .

SCARLET RIBBONS

Emma Blair

Sadie Smith, born with a degenerative hip, is unable to walk. Sent to a Dr Barnardo's home for treatment, she is so excited that she fails to realise she will never see her beloved family again.

In 1927, once fully cured, Sadie is offered the opportunity of a lifetime: to start a new life in Canada. But when she arrives at the Trikhardts' farm in the heart of Ontario, her new life seems far from perfect. Worked from dawn to dusk, she treasures the scarlet ribbons her mother gave her and seeks solace in her friendship with fellow orphan, cheeky-faced Robbie.

A freak hurricane finally provides Sadie with a lucky escape. From Canadian parlourmaid to pilot in Britain's Air Transport Auxiliary, from office clerk to managing director, Sadie has to draw on her courage and strength in a determined struggle to find the lasting happiness that had eluded her as a child.

Other bestselling titles available by mail:

☐	Flower of Scotland	Emma Blair	£6.99
☐	A Most Determined Woman	Emma Blair	£6.99
☐	Street Song	Emma Blair	£6.99
☐	When Dreams Come True	Emma Blair	£6.99
☐	Nellie Wildchild	Emma Blair	£6.99
☐	Where No Man Cries	Emma Blair	£6.99
☐	Moonlit Eyes	Emma Blair	£6.99
☐	Finding Happiness	Emma Blair	£6.99
☐	Twilight Time	Emma Blair	£6.99
☐	Little White Lies	Emma Blair	£6.99
☐	Three Bites of the Cherry	Emma Blair	£6.99
☐	Sweethearts	Emma Blair	£18.99

The prices shown above are correct at time of going to press. However, the publishers reserve the right to increase prices on covers from those previously advertised without prior notice.

———————————— sphere ————————————

SPHERE
PO Box 121, Kettering, Northants NN14 4ZQ
Tel: 01832 737525, Fax: 01832 733076
Email: aspenhouse@FSBDial.co.uk

POST AND PACKING:
Payments can be made as follows: cheque, postal order (payable to Sphere), credit card or Maestro. Do not send cash or currency.

All UK Orders   **FREE OF CHARGE**
EU & Overseas   25% of order value

Name (BLOCK LETTERS) . . . .

Address . . . .

. . . .

Post/zip code: . . . .

☐ Please keep me in touch with future Sphere publications

☐ I enclose my remittance £ . . . .

☐ I wish to pay by Visa/Mastercard/Eurocard/Maestro

Card Expiry Date ☐☐☐☐   Maestro Issue No. ☐☐

FINDING HAPPINESS

Emma Blair

In 1920s Glasgow, happiness can be hard to find . . .

Sandy McLean's life changes the moment he meets Sophie. French, sophisticated and beautiful, she is a model at the local art school – a glamorous world away from Sandy's training to become a surgeon. So when Sandy rescues her from the unwelcome advances of a drunk, he hopes it is the start of something special.

But the more Sandy gets to know Sophie, the more complicated his life becomes. Sandy dreams of becoming an artist in Paris – against the wishes of his father – and when Sophie agrees to pose for him, it sets him on a direct collision course with his family. And though Sandy wants Sophie to be more than just his muse, her past makes a normal relationship all but impossible . . .